DAY OF THE DEAD

MARK ROBERTS was born and raised in Liverpool. He was a teacher for twenty years and now works with children with severe learning difficulties. He is the author of *What She Saw*, which was longlisted for a CWA Gold Dagger.

Also by Mark Roberts

The Sixth Soul

What She Saw

The Eve Clay Thrillers

Blood Mist

Dead Silent

DAY OF THE DEAD

MARK ROBERTS

HEAD
of ZEUS

First published in the UK in 2017 by Head of Zeus, Ltd.

9 7 5 3 1 2 4 6 8

A catalogue record for this book is available from
the British Library.

ISBN (HB): 9781784082963
ISBN (XTPB): 9781784082970
ISBN (E): 9781784082956

Typeset by Adrian McLaughlin

Printed and bound in Great Britain by
CPI Group (UK) Ltd, Croydon CR0 4YY

Head of Zeus Ltd
First Floor East
5–8 Hardwick Street
London EC1R 4RG

WWW.HEADOFZEUS.COM

For Linda and Eleanor

Love alters not with his brief hours and weeks,
But bears it out even to the edge of doom.
If this be error and upon me proved,
I never writ, nor no man ever loved.

—SHAKESPEARE

Prologue

29th September 1986

'Do not move a muscle, Eve! Stay exactly where you are!' commanded Mrs Tripp, head of St Michael's Catholic Care Home for Children. 'And if anyone comes into my office and attempts to talk to you, do not speak a word!'

Eve Clay noticed a sheen of sweat and anxiety on the fat woman's face as she hurried from her office, slamming the door shut after herself.

In silence, she counted to ten, listened hard and heard no one moving in the corridor outside.

Eve moved to the filing cabinet, recalling her first day in St Michael's two years earlier, when she was six years old, and the fat card file on Mrs Tripp's desk marked with her name: EVETTE CLAY.

She eyed the top door labelled 'A–E'. She opened it, flicked through the slender card files. TOM ADAMS, JENNIFER BRADY, TONIA BREEN.

The bulging collection of papers marked EVETTE CLAY was at the tips of her fingers and she lifted it out with her heart beating fast and her mouth suddenly bone dry. She looked at the thickness of the file and didn't know whether her memory was playing a trick on her but, fat as the file still was, it looked it as if it had thinned down.

'Yes, something's definitely missing,' she said to herself.

She opened the file and, with her free hand, flicked through the papers in search of one specific document.

If other pages have gone missing, she reasoned, *why not my birth certificate?*

'Jesus Christ,' she whispered, finding the red-and-cream-coloured sheet of paper a third of the way into the file.

Approaching noise erupted in the corridor outside. Eve picked up Mrs Tripp's voice coming closer to the door along with her footsteps and those of another adult who *Hmm-hmmed* in the beats between Mrs Tripp's hurried speech.

Eve shoved her file back in place, shut the A–E drawer and felt sick to the core as she made her way to the exact spot where she had been when Mrs Tripp hurried from her office. Looking out of the window at the ambulance parked next to the police car with its back doors wide open, she folded her birth certificate and hid it in the pocket of her jeans.

As the office door opened behind her, Eve watched a pair of paramedics carrying a man in his twenties on a stretcher. He was covered from the neck down by a blue blanket, a mop of blond curls framing his bloodstained face.

'Eve, what are you doing at the window?' Mrs Tripp sounded confused and panic-stricken but disguised it by filling her voice with bogus compassion.

'I'm doing exactly what you told me, Mrs Tripp. I haven't moved a muscle. I've stayed exactly where I was.' She remained there, looking out of the window as the paramedics loaded the unconscious man into the back of the ambulance. 'Will they be taking Christopher Hawkins to hospital?' asked Eve as the last of his body disappeared.

'Eve, it's rude to speak to grown-ups when your back is turned to them!' Mrs Tripp advanced.

And it's rude to speak to anybody's back whatever age they are, thought Eve, turning.

A tall policewoman in a neat blue uniform stood in the doorway. Eve looked beyond Mrs Tripp and directly at the policewoman.

She smiled at Eve and closed the door. 'I've come to have a little chat with you, Eve. My name's Gwen Jones and I'm a woman police constable.'

'Admiral Street?' asked Eve.

'That's right. That's where I'm based.'

'There's no need to be scared of the police officer,' said Mrs Tripp.

As Eve walked towards WPC Jones, Eve wondered if Mrs Tripp was talking to herself.

'I'm not scared of you.' Eve tried to smile but she felt a sad expression in the muscles of her face.

The policewoman stooped to Eve's eye level and, although she looked very tough, there was a kindness in her eyes that calmed the bottled-up storm inside the little girl. Her eyes danced across Eve's features as if she was reading a book.

Then WPC Jones glanced behind her. 'You can go now, Mrs Tripp.'

Relief poured through Eve's whole being.

Silence.

The policewoman stood to her full height and pointed at the door. Mrs Tripp, her face now almost scarlet, closed the door on her way out with a meekness Eve had never seen in her before.

WPC Jones gave Eve a gentle push in the back, pointing at the seat across from the desk. As Eve sat down, she felt a pulse of pleasure when the policewoman sat on the edge of Mrs Tripp's desk.

'When I ask you to start at the beginning, Eve, I could well be talking about events that happened before you got up this morning. In your own words, Eve, and in your own time – and we've got as much as you want – tell me what happened.'

'We're not allowed pets. Some of the kids who live here haven't been very nice to animals. You know what I mean?'

WPC Jones nodded, her whole attention focused on Eve.

'But there's this wild cat called Rufus who kind of lives in the garden at the back of the house. I – I'm not supposed to but I feed

Rufus. He's wild but he's OK with me because I'm OK with him. Well...' Eve felt a rush of tears. She dug down and, taking a deep breath, stemmed them. 'Three weeks ago, Rufus disappeared – just stopped appearing in the garden. Some of the kids said he'd moved on because other cats were in the neighbourhood. Some said Rufus had been run over. I did the sensible thing. I accepted the loss and started to move on. When I was in Botanic Gardens, Chris...'

'Christopher Hawkins?'

'Yes. He works here. He's always looking at me but he never talks to me, but this morning he did. He said he'd seen Rufus back at St Michael's, in the garden.'

'Who was in Botanic Gardens, Eve?'

'Everyone. Every kid. Every adult. Mrs Tripp even.'

'How come?'

'It's St Michael's Day. Chris said, *Why don't you go back to the home and see if Rufus is there? If anyone asks where you are, I'll tell them I've just seen you over there. So don't you worry no more.* So I ran off and when I got back here I had to climb over the back wall to get into the garden. I looked all over the garden but Rufus just wasn't there. Then I heard Chris's voice. *Any luck, Eve?* I nearly jumped out of my skin. It was like he'd appeared out of thin air. I said, *How did you get here?* He had this big smile on his face but a strange look in his eyes. He said, *I think Rufus might be in the shed.* And he hands me the shed key and he said, *Go on, undo the padlock, Eve.* So I did and I opened the door and it was dead dark inside. He said, *I reckon he's in there. Why don't you go inside and see if you can find him. It's not like Rufus doesn't need you no more. Go on, Eve...* He gave me a little push, right here, between the shoulders and I went inside the shed. He followed me in and I heard the door creak as he closed it and it went even darker. He said, *You look like you could do with a cuddle.* I said, *No I don't. Rufus isn't in here at all.* He said, *Yeah, but we are.* And I could hear him breathing, all heavy and it was horrible. Then...I can't remember what was said or happened next because it went all quiet in my head, like. It. A blackout. Then. Then, all of a sudden, like, the shed door gets yanked open and I'm back and I heard, *Get away from her yer effing perv!* It was Jimmy, Jimmy Peace's voice.'

'Jimmy Peace lives here, right?'

Eve nodded proudly, a smile lighting up her eyes briefly. 'Jimmy's my best friend in the whole world. He says he's always going to look after me.'

'That's great, Eve.' The policewoman smiled too. 'Tell me about Chris?'

Eve fell silent and felt as if she was falling into a hole inside herself. 'Chris tried to turn and push past him and it was all dead quick but Jimmy had him in a headlock outside of the shed.

'Jimmy looked dead angry but when he looked at me he smiled and said, dead gentle, *Go back to Botanic Gardens. You're not going to get in any trouble. I'm going to have a little chat with Chris.* Christopher was saying, *Honest to God, mate, on my mother's life, I was only trying to help her find her bloody cat. I wasn't going to hurt her no more.*

'And I don't remember much more. I don't remember getting back to Botanic Gardens and coming back here to the home...'

'Eve!' A voice came from outside the home.

Eve danced closer to the window and called, 'Jimmy?'

Jimmy, the tallest, strongest fifteen-year-old boy in the world, was being dragged backwards by two fat police constables. He looked up and made eye contact with Eve as they dragged him to the back door of the police car. 'I'm not going to let anyone hurt you, Eve!' he shouted as he disappeared into the police car.

'Eve.' WPC Jones spoke softly behind Eve, her hands settling on her shoulders. 'I'm going to have to go. I need to let them know what you've told me. It'll make a huge difference to the way Jimmy is treated. Do you understand?'

'Yeah, I do. I had this really bad feeling Chris was going to do something horrible to me. He tracked me to the shed. Jimmy stopped him. Jimmy saved me.'

'That's right, love. That's exactly right.'

As WPC Jones left the office, Eve watched Jimmy's face as he turned at the back window of the police car and she was filled with sorrow. He spoke his final words to her and, although she couldn't hear him, she saw tenderness in him.

'I'm sorry I got you into this mess, Jimmy.'

The police car pulled away.

'Thank you, Jimmy.'

For the first time since her guardian Sister Philomena had died, the woman who'd cared for her for the first six years of her life, she uttered the words to the big brother she never had. 'I love you, Jimmy Peace.'

She tried to picture his face, to remember what he looked like but, as soon as he was gone, her memory of his looks deserted her.

And, as soon as the police car was out of sight, she was filled with a dark certainty.

Jimmy Peace would never return to St Michael's.

Part One
Los Llorones –
Weeping Children

Day One
Wednesday,
23rd October 2019

1

6.30 pm

'Actions have consequences. His sins found him out and he died because of the things that he did to me.'

Detective Chief Inspector Eve Clay gripped the receiver of her landline telephone and felt Samantha Wilson's voice drift inside her head like a bitter wind.

She looked at the pictures of David Wilson's dead body spread across the surface of her desk in the incident room at Trinity Road police station and felt a strong echo of the shiver she had experienced nine days earlier when she had walked into his bedroom and saw, for the first time, what had happened to him.

'Are you there, Eve?' asked Samantha Wilson.

'Yes,' replied Clay. 'I was just thinking about what you said, about your father.'

'He systematically raped me when I turned thirteen and it went on for two miserable years.'

At her core, Clay felt the onset of a nausea that knew no end.

She focused on a single photograph of David Wilson's body, face down on his bed, a pool of blood on the mattress either side of his hips, his back blistered where seven incense cones had burned down into his flesh and the word 'Vindici' carved in elegant cursive on his left shoulder.

'It's the funeral tonight, Sammy,' said Clay, focusing on the next picture of David Wilson, turned over on to his back, his penis and testicles hacked off, leaving a small bloody puddle between his legs.

'Good!'

'Are you still not attending?'

Clay picked up the statuette that had been left at the murder scene, a three-dimensional Weeping Child from the Mexican festival of the Day of the Dead.

'No, I will *not* be going to his funeral.'

Clay thought she heard the catch of buried tears in Samantha Wilson's voice as she looked at the statuette of the child's face, the black curly hair, the singlet that dropped to its naked knees and the tag tied around its neck with one word: 'Samantha'.

'If you change your mind, Sammy, I'll instruct Detective Sergeant Karl Stone to accompany you, to support you.'

'Mmmm.'

In that sound Clay detected a softening in Samantha's demeanour and waved Stone over to her. 'Do you want to speak to Karl Stone?'

Without hesitation, Samantha said, 'Yes.'

Stone was grey-haired and forty with the beginning of a hunch. The nickname Clay had given him on first sight but had never uttered out loud crossed her mind: the human vulture.

'Karl, it's Sammy Wilson.' Clay covered up the receiver's mouthpiece. 'She's still refusing to go to her father's funeral.'

'What do you want me to do?'

'I want her at the funeral. I want to see if anything significant gets said when she's with her mother.'

'Leave it with me, Eve.'

Clay handed the receiver to Stone.

'Hello, Sammy. How are you doing?'

Prompted by the photographs on her desk to her memories of the night David Wilson was murdered, Clay walked to the window, took out her iPhone and opened Voice Memos. 'New Recording 15/10/2019'.

She looked over her shoulder at her desk where Stone was listening intensely to Samantha Wilson and recalled the moment her landline had rung as soon as she'd walked into the incident room from the David Wilson murder scene and how it had stopped ringing as soon as she reached it.

When her landline had rung again almost immediately, she had pressed record on Voice Memos as she lifted the receiver.

Now she pressed 'New Recording 15/10/2019' and listened to her own voice.

'DCI Eve Clay speaking.'

The display on her landline had registered 'Caller Withheld'.

'Hello, Eve...' By the sound of his voice he was smiling, as though he was pleased to be talking to her.

'Who is this?'

'Who am I?' he replied, his voice now verging on gentle laughter. *'I know who you are, Eve, and it's good to know you.'*

'I'll tell you what I am. I'm dead tired and I haven't got time to play games or untangle meaningless riddles when I've got so many real problems to solve. So, please tell me who you are or I'll have to hang up.'

After a brief silence, he said, *'I don't mean to vex you or waste your time, Eve. I'll send you a picture via a third party. It should iron out one idea that's running around your brain as we speak. Would you like that?'*

'Yes I would. But who are you?'

'I'll tell you who I am. Are you ready? I am Vindici.' His voice was a whisker away from the sing-song cadence of a nursery rhyme, and she felt the deepest pull of childhood memory.

'Did you murder David Wilson?'

'Come and find me...'

'Did you murder David Wilson?'

'...and all this will stop.'

'Did you murder David Wilson?'

'Or shall I find you first?'

A dead tone after Vindici hung up.

'Eve?' She heard Detective Sergeant Bill Hendricks's voice behind her and she turned to him.

'I'm still reeling, Bill. I was convinced it was a hoax call.'

'Well, it wasn't a hoax, Eve. The sound techie's analysis proved it.'

She remembered the way her skin had puckered when she saw the identical spikes thrown up by the Met's recordings of their interviews with Vindici and her recording of the person who called her.

'He's back in business, Eve. I'm convinced Vindici's our man, that he killed David Wilson. The timing of his call to you was immaculate.'

'I don't get it, Bill.'

'What don't you get? The MO is almost identical to the killings he perpetrated in London and Brighton eleven to twelve years ago.'

'But he's been on the run for five years. Why come out of retirement now? And why switch his territory to Liverpool?'

'Let me think about it,' said Hendricks.

She glanced at her iPhone and a train of thought pulled away in her mind.

We've never met...

The second coming of serial killer Justin Truman, aka Vindici, scourge of paedophiles, had begun under her nose.

She looked at the window, saw her own reflection on the surface of the glass and felt something pull away from the centre of her foundation.

...but you spoke to me as if you knew me...

2

6.45 pm

Since the night of David Wilson's murder, the most satisfying task that Detective Constable Barney Cole had engaged in at DCI Clay's request was putting together a beginning, a middle and an end in Justin Truman's life story.

After days of hard slogging, in the early hours of the morning, he'd arrived at the promised land through a combination of conversations with officers from the Met, documents supplied by them and a critical trawl through the Vindici fan sites on the internet.

'Hey, Eve,' called Cole. 'I've got the lowdown on Vindici.'

Clay looked up and saw four sections of A4 paper on Stone's desk: a one-centimetre pile, and three stacks at twelve centimetres, fourteen centimetres and sixteen centimetres, dwarfing the baby of the bunch.

As she walked across to his desk, Stone pointed at the one-centimetre pile and said, 'Justin Truman, early pre-criminal life.' He patted the twelve-centimetre pile. 'Manhunt by the Metropolitan Police, before his arrest and while still operating.'

Clay read the yellow Post-it on the fourteen-centimetre pile: 'Justin Truman, interviews with the Met after his arrest and pre-trial'. She touched the unlabelled sixteen-centimetre pile. 'What's this?' she asked.

'Justin Truman aka Vindici's trials, imprisonment and escape from custody.'

Cole dropped a Berocca into a polystyrene cup and poured a bottle of mineral water over the orange energy tablet.

'I worked like a dog to get a beginning, a middle and an end.'

'Thank you, Barney, you're a Trojan and I really appreciate it.'

'There are so many Vindici fan sites out there, the internet's crawling with him.' Cole swiped the mouse on his laptop and the iconic mugshot of Vindici, taken after his arrest by the Met, filled the screen. Above his head the word *Vindici* appeared and below his neck, moving left to right, the words *Destroy All Paedos*. 'Like this one.'

Clay focused on Vindici's face. Olive-skinned and handsome with black hair in a quiff, he had the look of a seasoned rock star. Although his face was set into neutral for the purpose of the photograph, his brown eyes shone with happiness.

'This one's kind of typical but it's got something about it that's really of interest to us,' said Cole. 'It's one of two websites based in Liverpool.'

'Really?' said Clay, a light going on inside her. 'Where in Liverpool?'

'I'm working with Poppy Waters on that. Look at this, Eve.'

Cole clicked a tab marked 'Method' and his laptop screen was filled with an image of items set out on a table.

Clay read the words at the top of the image. *What you will need to commit a Vindici-style execution.*

She focused on a lethal-looking carving knife and thought, *Castration*. She counted seven incense cones. *To burn them*. And one sharpened bicycle spoke. *To slash their brains*. And her mind connected with the pictures of David Wilson that she had just looked at as she spoke to Samantha.

The image on screen dissolved and a picture of a pair of skeletons dressed up as a bride and groom appeared. Beneath the bones of their feet, the words *mid-October to early November* appeared and were replaced by *the time window, the Day of the Dead*.

'The things he left at the murder scenes were all items related to the festival, the Day of the Dead.'

'I've got a big why,' said Clay. 'Why is the Day of the Dead festival so important to him?'

'I hate to disappoint you, Eve, but I don't know why. What I do know is that he murdered ten men between October 2007 and November 2008. He only operated between the months of October and very early November, the window of time for the Mexican celebration of departed loved ones. The rest of the time he hibernated.'

'So this time round he's giving himself about a fortnight to top other paedos,' observed Clay.

'Each man he took out was a convicted paedophile,' said Cole. 'Each man was tortured and murdered in his own home. Burn marks from the incense. Castration. A spike into the brain. His arrest was a complete fluke. Vindici burned incense at the scenes and when he was pulled over by a young traffic cop, the constable smelt it on his clothes. He was driving away from his tenth and final kill when he was pulled in. Truman offered no resistance to the rookie. He came in like a lamb. He didn't deny anything but he refused to explain any of the symbolism found at his kills. The incense? The food?'

'The food?' Clay thought out loud.

'Yeah, food. Vindici used to leave sweets at his murder scenes, Day-of-the-Dead-related sugary treats. We're talking candy skulls, sugar skeletons, macabre but sweet for sure.'

'Hang on, Barney.' In her mind, Clay moved on fast forward through each and every room in David Wilson's house. 'He didn't leave any food at the Wilson murder scene. That was one detail that didn't emerge during his trial, or make it into the media,' she said.

'Maybe he's changed his MO.'

'Maybe. Or maybe it's not him. No, I spoke to him on the phone. It's not a copycat. It's him.' Clay heard a note of scepticism in her own voice and, pushed by intuition, found her attention drilling into the Vindici website on Cole's laptop. 'Keep on the path of those websites, Barney.'

'It's complex, finding the geographical locale of a website. But, sure, will keep trying.'

'What happened at the trial?' asked Clay.

'The trial was a media circus. All he kept repeating was, *I celebrate innocence and I mourn the death of innocence.* The shrinks were unanimous. Truman was one hundred per cent sane. After one mistrial – one of the female jurors confessed to have fallen in love with Truman – he was found guilty at the second go on ten counts of murder and sentenced to life.

'During the trial at the Old Bailey, he became a cottage industry, his mugshot sold on thousands and thousands of T-shirts and as many posters and mugs again. It's still a highly popular screen saver and the subject of an iconic work by Banksy on Camden Lock. Vindici's an all-round public hero.

'Off to Category A nick he goes. He was a model prisoner, liked by the screws and Jesus on a plinth to other prisoners, who showered him with gifts and respect because of the nature of his crimes. Things around him became a little slapdash and in the January of 2014, he barricaded himself in his cell with a screw called Vincent Reagan. He had Reagan in there for twelve hours, torturing him and informing the authorities that Reagan was a paedo. Reagan had no track record for this at all and the hostage negotiators told Truman that he had taken the wrong man. But he told them to fuck off, that he knew what he was talking about and that they should go and check his house.

'Reagan lived at home with his elderly mother. The other screws had him marked down as a loner. Turns out his place was crawling with child pornography and a forensic investigation of his laptop showed that Reagan was a kingpin in a very large paedophile ring. Five continents, thirty-three arrests and convictions, seven related suicides followed, with countless suspects running for the hills never to be seen or heard of again. It was Vindici's finest hour. He tortured and killed Reagan, broadcasting images on the internet from a mobile phone he'd been given by the nick's top dog Manc gangster Eddie Christian.

The pictures went viral, worldwide. After twelve hours, he pushed the sharpened point of the handle of a spoon through Reagan's ear and into his brain. Goodnight, Mr Reagan. Then he calmly opened the door and held his arms out to be cuffed and taken away. Reagan was removed from the cell in several bags – fingers, ears, nose missing – and Vindici went on to become an even bigger global superstar.'

'How about the escape?' asked Clay.

'He was being transferred from Strangeways to permanent solitary in the basement of Wakefield, when the convoy was involved in a multiple pile-up. In the ensuing chaos, Truman did a runner and was never seen again.'

'Well done, Barney. You've just lit the blue touch paper in my head.'

'Well, I'll go back to the hunt for those Liverpool Vindici websites.'

Clay didn't answer, silenced by a notion about the two websites.

'Go on, Eve,' said Cole. 'I can hear the cogs of your mind turning.'

'I'm thinking domino effect. If we pin down one Liverpool-based Vindici website – I'll bet my house on this – the other one will follow, maybe on the same day but shortly after.'

'How do you figure that out?'

'Geographical location; shared passion. They know each other. They'll cover each other's back. They could shed light on the murder.'

'Well, I hope you're right, Eve.'

She could tell he didn't share her point of view and she wondered to herself if she was engaging in wishful thinking.

'So do I,' said Clay. 'We'll see. Show me Vindici's mugshot again, please.'

Clay looked at the screen of Cole's laptop and was drawn to Vindici's eyes, the happiness radiating from a newly arrested man in spite of facing the certainty of life behind bars.

'We'll see,' Clay repeated, 'We'll see.' She turned away to

watch Karl Stone bringing his telephone conversation with Samantha Wilson to a close. She noticed the body language of a man speaking to someone very close to him; the edge of his face had been softened by what she couldn't hear him say.

He replaced the receiver and, smiling, looked across at Clay. 'She's going to Springwood Crematorium tonight. Myrtle Chapel. On condition I escort her. I told her she needed closure.'

'Well done, ladykiller!' said Clay, wondering what would slip through the cracks when Samantha Wilson and her mother collided.

3

7.58 pm

DCI Eve Clay stood at the door of Springwood Crematorium and watched Samantha Wilson and her mother, Sandra.

A cloud drifted from the moon and the ethereal light sharpened their toxic body language, picking out the anger in the daughter's face and the distress in the mother's.

The slow progress of a pair of funeral cars towards the crematorium drew Samantha's attention and made her shift further away from her mother.

Actions have consequences! Clay rolled the words around her mind as she gave the nod to DS Gina Riley and DS Karl Stone.

'Mrs Wilson?' said Detective Sergeant Gina Riley, advancing towards her.

Stone walked towards Samantha. She smiled at him and offered him her cheek. As he kissed her, his eyes found out Clay's.

'I'd like to sit with you if I may, Mrs Wilson, during the service,' said Riley. 'Is that all right with you?'

Clay checked her watch. Two minutes to eight.

Mrs Wilson looked towards her daughter, who was now locked in an inaudible dialogue with DS Stone.

The crunch of the hearse's tyres ground into silence. The undertakers in the second car prepared to carry David Wilson's coffin into the chapel.

The head undertaker approached Clay.

'Thank you for agreeing to this extraordinary request,' said Clay. 'And for working outside your regular hours.'

The undertaker, a tall man with an indelible stamp of gravity in his face, nodded. 'Twenty-five years I've been doing this. I think this is the most...' He looked for the right word. '...sensitive funeral I've overseen.'

Clay took in Samantha's expression as the six undertakers shouldered the coffin. She mouthed something only Stone could hear.

'That's completely understandable, Sammy,' he replied.

Samantha walked sideways and, sheltering behind Stone, peered over his shoulder at the funeral procession.

The head undertaker took his place in front of his colleagues carrying the plain coffin in which David Wilson's mutilated remains were laid out.

As the men walked towards the chapel, Mrs Wilson reached out a hand and touched the side of the coffin, silent tears rolling down her face. Riley walked alongside the widow.

'I see you still believe him,' said Samantha. 'Delusional to the bitter end, Mother!'

Clay's iPhone vibrated inside her coat pocket.

'Do me a favour,' said Stone, turning to Samantha. 'I'll help you. Just get through the service. OK?'

Samantha nodded.

The vibration of Clay's iPhone seemed to pick up energy with each purr, urging her to pay attention to it. She folded her hand around it in her coat pocket as she caught Samantha's eye. 'Why the change of heart over attending your father's funeral?' she asked.

Without hesitation, Samantha said, 'I wanted to see the coffin slide through the curtains on its way to the oven. Two thousand degrees Fahrenheit. I had to be absolutely certain he's gone.'

'Are you coming in with us, Eve?' asked Stone.

'I'll join you inside in a minute,' said Clay.

As Detective Sergeant Bill Hendricks advanced towards her,

Clay watched Stone's back. Samantha hooked both hands around his right elbow as they stepped through the main door of the chapel.

Clay plucked her phone from her pocket, saw the call was from 'Central Switchboard', connected and held DS Bill Hendricks back with a light touch to his arm.

'Clay speaking. What's up?'

'This has just come in, Eve. I'll play it back to you.'

She pressed speakerphone.

Above the silence on the phone, a TV set played out in the background.

'Hello, police, where are you calling from?' asked the operator.

Someone was crying, either in the place the call was made from or from the TV set, Clay couldn't decide

'I can see from my display that you're calling from landline number 496 7370.'

A door closed and the sound of the TV died.

'I'm calling from 699 Mather Avenue.'

A mannered androgynous voice with no trace of an accent, thought Clay. Someone somewhere in their thirties, she speculated; male or female she just couldn't tell, but definitely not the voice she'd heard on the call from Vindici.

'What's the nature of your problem?'

'A man has been murdered and his wife has been tortured. Tell Eve Clay to get over here as fast as she can – 699 Mather Avenue.'

The recorded call went to the dead tone. Clay hurried towards her car.

'Operator, I want all available officers to block off Mather Avenue, Garston and Allerton Road ends. I want the roads leading off Mather Avenue swamped. Bill. 699 Mather Avenue. Call Barney Cole and see what he can find on the residents, a man and his wife.'

She got into her car. 'And, Bill, I'll meet you at the scene – 699 Mather Avenue. The real Vindici never tortured a woman in his previous outings. This is a copycat, right?'

'Maybe he's changed his MO *again*. He didn't leave food last time, this time he tortures a woman. Who knows how he's changed over the years?' replied Hendricks.

'His MO has definitely changed. He used to work alone, now it looks like he's got an accomplice.'

Within seven seconds, Clay was driving at seventy miles per hour towards the entrance of Springwood Crematorium with the caller's cool words spinning inside her skull.

'Murdered, tortured... Tell Eve Clay... murdered, tortured... Tell Eve Clay... murdered, tortured.... Tell... Eve... Clay...'

Her heart pounded as she hit eighty miles per hour on Springwood Avenue.

'I am Vindici. Come and find me and all this will stop. Or shall I find you first?'

'So you're back, Vindici,' said Clay. 'But why here? Why now?'

4

8.03 pm

Ninety miles per hour was DCI Eve Clay's top speed as she hurtled from Springwood Crematorium to a detached house on Mather Avenue, not far from Merseyside Police Training Academy.

As she pulled up outside the house, Clay saw a pair of uniformed constables making their way up the path to the front door of 699 Mather Avenue.

'Stop!' called Clay, heading for the wrought-iron gate. 'The killer could still be inside!' She passed them as she made her way up the path, showed her warrant card and drank in their silent relief. Clay threw torchlight along the edges of the front door. There were no apparent bloodstains and Clay's instincts screamed that a neat but brutal scene lay inside the house, just as it had in David Wilson's home.

Clay pushed the door but it was locked. She recognised Hendricks's footsteps as he made his way quickly towards her back. 'Got the ram, Bill?'

He stepped next to her and with one blow of the ram had the door open.

The lights in the hall were all on and she sensed the presence of life and death in the same space.

'Police!' shouted Clay. 'Call out if you can hear me!'

No reply.

Clay listened. She could hear crying, but it was not the sound of a woman in extreme pain. *A child crying*, thought Clay and there was something in the sound that made her sick and hot in the same moment.

She smelt burned incense and looked at Hendricks. 'Same smell as in the Wilson house.'

'Same smell. Same perpetrator,' replied Hendricks. 'I'm waiting to hear back from Barney Cole on what he's found about the owners.'

Clay looked around the hall and saw a small table with a shelf underneath. On the shelf beneath was a Yellow Pages and Thomson's Directory. On the table was a notebook, a pen and an empty space rimmed with a square of dust where the landline phone had been.

'The person who made the call has gone!' said Clay, stepping towards the closed door of the front room. 'And taken the phone they called from. You look upstairs, Bill, I'll stick down here.'

The front-room curtains were drawn, the main light was on and nothing seemed to be out of place. She listened, and heard the sound of tears leaking through the wall of the adjoining room and Hendricks's footsteps as he raced around the space above her head.

Clay made her way to the next room, and the crying grew louder, drawing her to the door.

She paused, making a mental journey based on the call to the switchboard.

The caller stood in the hall, made the call to switch, walked across the hall to close the door, to kill the sound of the TV...

Outside, many sirens gathered volume, descending fast along the wide and tree-lined avenue.

'All the lights are on up here!' called Hendricks. 'The bathroom and bedroom doors are all wide open except the back bedroom. The door's locked!'

Clay raised her arm and with her bunched fingers and thumb pressed the top right-hand corner of the door.

The door opened slowly to a dark room. The only source of light came from a television set against the wall. Eve could not make out the picture on the screen but it was emitting a pitiful sound of someone in extreme pain and distress.

Between the door and the television set, a naked woman was seated and bound to a hard-backed wooden chair.

Clay switched on the light and called out, 'Bill! Bill! Call the paramedics! She's still alive!' The woman moved sharply, startled by the sudden influx of light, her voice strangled by the black cloth that gagged her.

Behind her, Clay heard Hendricks hurry down the stairs, on his phone. 'Thanks for that, Barney. That's really helpful!' Hendricks stopped at her back. 'Eve…' He spoke quietly. 'This is the home of Steven and Frances Jamieson. Barney looked them up on the NPC.' His face told the story.

'And Steven Jamieson has a similar track record to David Wilson?' asked Clay softly.

'Yes.'

'Thank you.' She took a deep breath and stepped into the room.

5

8.05 pm

As she approached Frances Jamieson, Clay spoke as evenly as she could, and kept her eyes on the victim. There was a bloodstain on her left shoulder, running down the side of her back. A pattern of blood covered the visible side of her face, leaking into the gag on her mouth.

'Frances? Frances Jamieson? It's all right, Frances, please don't be scared...' Slowly, she moved towards her, in front of her. 'My name's Eve Clay, I'm a police officer.'

The pitiful crying from the TV set behind her crawled under Clay's skin, but she resisted the urge to turn and look, focusing instead on the woman in front of her as she held up her warrant card and looked her up and down. Her arms were stretched behind her back, her hands and feet bound to the chair with thin blue rope. Clay placed her in her fifties.

She felt her stomach turn as she looked at the woman's eyes, wild and rolling. It looked as though she had been weeping blood, and Clay saw with horror that her eyelids had been removed.

She was glad when she heard Bill Hendricks moving deeper into the room.

'The paramedics are outside,' said Hendricks.

'Go get them immediately, please. Tell them to hurry!'

Check her airway's clear, thought Clay, untying the gag's knot at the base of her skull. 'Open your mouth, Frances. I need to check…' She turned her face away. Her mouth appeared to be full but she kept her lips tight and snorted air through her nostrils.

Clay looked around for a weapon, thinking *Stanley knife*, but knowing in her heart that if the perpetrator had taken the landline telephone used to call the central switchboard, then they'd have also taken the tool used to inflict damage to the victim's face.

Clay looked at the woman's eyes, saw wild disbelief and was reminded of a pair of tiny rafts on a stormy sea. 'Your husband? Do you know where he is?'

She didn't move her head, appeared not to hear or understand.

As she stooped in front of the woman, Clay inspected the neat knot that sealed her hands together. The crying from the TV dug into the top of her head like razor-sharp knives, but still she refused to look at the screen, aware that every second counted if she was to persuade this traumatised woman to talk.

Moving behind her, Clay took a series of photos on her phone of the band of blood that had flowed from the wound on her left shoulder. As with David Wilson, the killer had carved the word 'Vindici' in elegant script on the victim. But unlike David Wilson, this victim had been left alive.

Clay looked up as Hendricks entered the room, followed by a tough-looking brunette in a green NHS uniform.

The paramedic froze and shielded her eyes with her hand. 'Jesus!' she said, clearly shocked to the core. 'Oh my God!'

Squeamish? puzzled Clay. *With all the things you must have seen?*

Panic filled Frances Jamieson's face at the sound of another woman's voice at her back, and Clay kept her voice calm. 'It's all right. She's a paramedic. She's come to help you. And there's another police officer in the room.'

Something dark passed through Hendricks's features as he picked up a remote from the floor and turned the television off. When the crying from the TV stopped, Clay heard Frances taking deeper and deeper ragged breaths through her nose.

Crouching, Hendricks spoke softly to Frances Jamieson. 'Can you hear me?'

She nodded.

'It's finished.' He motioned the paramedic over.

The paramedic looked at Clay but indicated the woman's hands. 'Can I...?'

'Yes, please do.' Clay pulled a pair of evidence bags from her pocket, dropped the gag into one. 'Wait a minute please,' she said.

Clay looked at the neatly tied bows of the knots on Frances's wrists and whispered to Hendricks, 'Unless he's changed radically since he's escaped, Vindici would never have done this to a woman. Even if she did stand by her paedophile man.'

'But we can't rule out his involvement,' said Hendricks. 'The phone call to you directly after Wilson's murder was definitely him. How do we know he hasn't changed his MO? Or decided to work with an accomplice?'

'There was no food at the Wilson scene, and we won't find any here. Vindici was a stickler for detail – and that was the one detail withheld from the media during his trial.'

Clay turned to the paramedic. 'Untie her hands now, please.'

Hendricks opened an evidence bag and, as the paramedic dropped the thin ropes into it, he said, 'Whoa, what's that?'

Clinging to the rope was a long blond hair. Clay checked Frances's short dark hair and the paramedic's brown hair.

She looked towards the sound of turning wheels and saw a short, wiry male paramedic pushing a wheelchair into the room. With a nod of the head, Clay urged him to hurry as she squatted down so she was in Frances' eyeline. A line of thick mucus rolled from the right corner of the woman's mouth.

'What's in your mouth, Frances?' asked Clay.

Frances turned her face towards the ceiling. 'Look at me,' said Clay. 'Bill?' It was all she needed to say. She felt him press an evidence bag into her hand. 'Look down, Frances.' Slowly, her head sank. 'Frances, when you're looking down, I'm going to open an evidence bag under your mouth. I want you to spit out whatever's in your mouth.'

Clay placed the evidence bag just beneath Frances's lips. She opened her mouth and Clay felt the weight of something soft and wet drop into the bag. And a moment later, another similar weight.

Clay stood up and, looking into the transparent bag, felt her stomach lurch.

'What is it?' asked Hendricks.

Clay glanced at the paramedics. 'I don't know what you did or didn't see then but keep your mouths tight shut. It's a detail we're going to withhold from the media to weed out crank confessions.'

As the female paramedic untied Frances' feet from the legs of the chair, her colleague pushed the wheelchair closer.

'Neat and tidy knots around her ankles?' said Clay.

'Same style of neat bows,' replied the paramedic.

'Our mystery caller took their time then.' Clay turned to Hendricks. 'Steven Jamieson's body will be upstairs behind that locked door. Please open it for me.'

6

8.09 pm

As Hendricks left the room, the paramedics wrapped a blanket around Frances Jamieson and supported her to her feet.

'We're going to sit you down in the wheelchair and take you to A & E.'

Clay watched as the male paramedic wheeled Frances, eyes rolling and mouth clamped shut, out of the room.

Clay caught the eye of the female paramedic, checked her ID badge and spoke quietly. 'One minute please, Cara. I'll send a Scientific Support officer to the Royal to meet you there. We'll need to look at her body for any potential evidence from the perpetrator.'

She dialled Detective Sergeant Gina Riley, who picked up after two rings. In the background, she heard a woman crying and assumed it was David Wilson's widow at Springwood Crematorium. 'Gina, you need to get to the Royal. A & E. You're going to be meeting a Mrs Frances Jamieson.'

'Is she a paedophile?'

'Her husband was. She's been tortured. She must have seen the killer. I got the call as you were going into the chapel.'

'I wondered where you'd got to.'

'The killer tipped us off to the scene of their own crime through central switchboard.'

'Male or female?'

'I really couldn't tell. It was a put-on androgynous voice. It didn't sound like Vindici though. I've got to go.'

Above her head, a loose floorboard creaked under the weight of Hendricks's feet. He stopped.

'Cara?' Clay looked around. They were alone.

'Yes?' replied the paramedic.

'You did this, Cara, when you entered the room.' Clay copied the paramedic's actions, turning her head away from the TV set and holding her hand in the air as a screen. 'What did the perpetrator force Frances to watch on television?'

'An adult male forcing a female to have sex with him,' whispered the paramedic. 'I guess she was about six years of age.'

'Thank you,' said Clay. 'I'm sorry you were exposed to that.'

The paramedic shivered. 'Horrible, just horrible...'

As the paramedic left the room, DS Terry Mason, lead Scientific Support officer, arrived. Clay handed him three evidence bags. 'The ropes used to bind Frances Jamieson and the cloth that gagged her.'

'Jeez,' he said, looking at the third bag.

'I believe these are David Wilson's testicles taken from Frances Parker's mouth cavity. Terry, you've got a female available?'

'Sergeant Cindy O'Brien.'

'Send her to the Royal, A & E. She's to meet a Frances Jamieson there. Tell her to get a move on. Jamieson's on her way there now. Thank you.'

From upstairs, Clay heard a loud bang and caught the edge of something aromatic and smoky.

As Clay made her way quickly up the stairs, the smell of incense intensified and from behind the door that Hendricks had just kicked open came the unmistakable aroma of fresh blood.

7

8.13 pm

At the top of the stairs, Clay drew in the incense-perfumed air.

The same kind of ash, she said to herself. *It's only what we found beside David Wilson's corpse. The same smell from jasmine-scented incense cones.*

'Eve, I'm in here!' called Hendricks from a bedroom at the end of the corridor.

Walking towards Hendricks's voice, the smell intensified.

'It's a lot like last time,' said Hendricks.

In the doorway, Clay's eyes were drawn to the bedside table on which sat a commercially produced twelve-inch pottery statue of an androgynous child, face deadpan but given a sinister cast by the closed eyes and the elongated eyelashes painted in black lines on the top and bottom of both eyes. The figure was dressed in a simple ceramic singlet that reached the knees and left the feet bare and the shins exposed.

'Same statue as at the Wilson scene,' said Clay. '"Fabricado en Puebla" on the base. From the same ceramics factory. Made in Puebla. Mexico.'

Clay noticed how the left hand, index finger extended, pointed down and the right hand made a fist, close to the child's face, knuckles exposed to the viewer as if ready to knock on a door.

Taking in the position of the child and its relationship to

Steven Jamieson's face, Clay said, 'This was probably the last thing that Jamieson saw before he died.'

She turned over the small white tag hanging down the child's back from a thread tied around its neck and read out loud, 'Sally'. Jamieson's victim must have been called Sally. The statue that was left at David Wilson's bedside had had a tag marked 'Samantha'. A Vindici-styled calling card.

Clay made her way to the bottom of the bed and turned her whole attention on to Steven Jamieson's corpse. Stomach down, his face was turned to the wall, his arm and legs stretched out at angles and his hands and feet bound by silk neckties to the bed posts. On his back were seven small mounds of burned incense and beneath the ash were scorch marks where the perfumed cones had burned down from the smoking red tip to the flat circular base, just as they had done with David Wilson.

The puddle of blood on the mattress leaked from the space between his open legs.

Clay watched Hendricks stoop below the window ledge to get a closer look at his face and noticed that something made the usually poker-faced Hendricks wince. Her eyes followed the path of Jamieson's back up to his neck and head.

'There's bruising around his throat and neck,' said Hendricks. 'He's been strangled but, if it's the same as methodology as in the Wilson case, that won't be the cause of death.'

'We'll confirm that when we get him down to Dr Lamb's autopsy suite.'

Clay recognised DS Terry Mason's footsteps rising upstairs before she heard the lead Scientific Support officer call, 'Eve?'

'We're in here, Terry,' called Clay.

As DS Mason paused in the doorway, she listened to the rapid clicking of his camera and took a closer look at the back of Steven Jamieson's body. The large bloodstain at the base of his back, just above his left buttock, had partially dried out and, on his left shoulder, she could see a single continuous line, the signature 'Vindici' written in elegant cursive.

'Seven burn marks on this man's back just like on David Wilson's. Why?' asked DS Mason, stepping inside the room. Clay recalled the seven red burn marks on Wilson and something Vindici had said at his trial – she'd seen it in a headline, a response to the Crown Prosecution Service barrister when she had asked him why he always burned seven incense cones on his victims' backs.

'First of all, I would like to make one thing clear. I never explain anything. Me, I'm a modern-day Mary Poppins.'

The CPS barrister had cross-examined Vindici for hours on the significance of *seven* but all she got was nothing.

Seven incense cones. Clay pointed at the statue of the Weeping Child. 'But who is Sally? One name amongst so very many. Her name counts for something.'

The whiff of cooked human flesh crept through the dominant smell of blood and perfumed smoke.

The back of his legs were covered in thin, red lines and, to Clay's eyes, it looked as though he'd been whipped with a thin piece of wood or metal.

'This is new, Terry.' DS Mason stepped beside Clay, paused in taking pictures. Clay pointed at his lower half. 'The perpetrator didn't whip David Wilson.'

'Hang on a second!' Hendricks sounded surprised, assaulted by a fresh thought. 'I remember. Vindici – I say we drop this tabloid talk, the guy had a real name. Justin Truman used to whip any victim who used their position or authority in society to shield themselves or gain access to children. It was a case of you're going to die but I'm going to really humiliate you before I finish you off.'

'You've got a great memory, Bill.'

'I analysed it in my thesis for my PhD.'

Clay looked at the side of Steven Jamieson's face that was exposed to the air and the bruising where he'd been punched. The skin was purple and blue and his cheeks were swollen; blood had dried in his ear. She imagined the kind of anger that could power the killer's fists into doing a job Mike Tyson would have been proud of.

'Justin Truman's got no connections with Merseyside that I can think of. The paedophiles he murdered were all in Greater London with one exception. Brighton.'

'Oh, he has got a connection to Merseyside,' said Hendricks.

'What is that?'

'It's not a what. It's a who. It's you, Eve. He phoned you up. You had a cordial, brief and significant conversation with him. It was definitely him on the line, we know that.' Hendricks's phone rang. 'It's Barney,' he said, walking out of the room.

As Mason took multiple photographs of Steven Jamieson's corpse, Clay surveyed the seven scorches on his back and the mounds of ash that littered his flesh.

Seven, she thought, *What is the significance of seven?* A strange and unfamiliar sickness overwhelmed her as the smell of the burned human flesh on the bed seemed to crawl inside her through her pores and nostrils, sinking to the pit of her stomach and turning to hot jelly.

'Hey, Eve.' Hendricks returned, sounding anxious to talk.

'What else has Barney come up with?'

Hendricks walked to the bottom of the bed, looked Steven Jamieson up and down and then at Clay. 'Get ready for this.'

8

8.18 pm

She lay down in the hot bubble bath, her head the only visible part of her body. From the neck down she was completely covered with a layer of thick bubbles from the quarter-bottle of lavender-scented bubble bath from Avon.

The bathroom light was off but the room was infused with amber light from the streetlights outside the frosted window. Alone in the house, the only thing she could hear was the wind outside, shaking the branches of the trees and scattering dead and fallen leaves.

She scooped a handful of bubbles and massaged them into her short, smoke-scented hair and scalp and felt the onset of immense inner peace.

Looking at the surface of the bubbles, she squeezed the muscles of her feet, her toes, her calves, her thighs, her buttocks and made a mental picture of a mermaid, floating on a warm green sea, the scales on her tail glittering in the overhead sun and the perfect sky, her mane of human hair shimmering in the water as it reached down to where her tail met her human half.

The mermaid turned in the water, her breasts small and firm, nipples the colour of coral, waist tight and arms long and slender.

She hung on to the picture, and was excited by the sensual details that she imagined.

She couldn't see in the half-light, but on the surface of her bubble bath, a red cast had risen from her skin and coated the soapy bubbles like scum on a pond.

'I wish I was a mermaid,' she said to the shadows who absorbed her wish and sealed it with their silence. 'Half-woman, half-fish. She's just like me,' she confided to the darkness. 'Neither one thing nor another, yet both fish and woman.'

She opened her eyes to gaze into the amber-infused darkness. 'Just like you, half-light around me, neither darkness nor light, yet both darkness and light. Neither one thing nor another, like me, just like me.'

She sank beneath the bubbles and fully submerged, imagined herself transformed into a mermaid by the power of wishful thinking and, in her mind, she was deep beneath the warm current, looking up through green ripples at the silhouette of the mermaid of her dreams as her dark tail swished and her arms, hands and fingers danced gracefully and her hair fanned out under the tender caress of her lover, the sea.

Neither one thing nor another, she thought, *like me, just like me.*

9

8.18 pm

'Barney says he's only just scratched the surface on this one but Steven Jamieson served five years of a nine-year sentence in Strangeways for abusing an eight-year-old girl. In prison, he turned to Jesus and made all the right noises, attended all the courses. It was the tip of the iceberg but South Yorkshire Police couldn't make anything stick apart from the one girl. Jamieson had serious money and connections. People were either bought off or intimidated into silence. He didn't move back to Sheffield. He came to Merseyside when he was released from nick, where he had no connections whatsoever, so he could hide anonymously. He registered as a sex offender at Belle Vale and hasn't been the subject of any police investigation since then.'

At her sides, Clay's hands turned into fists. She unclenched her hands and stuck them in her coat pockets. 'Anything else, Bill?'

'Barney's been in touch with DCI Lesley Reid, the Senior Investigating Officer who put Jamieson away.' Hendricks turned to Mason. 'Terry, you're going to have to empty the contents of Jamieson's mouth.'

'What's in it?' said Mason.

'I don't know. I didn't touch his face. But there's something in there.'

'Wait a minute, wait a minute, no,' said Clay. She recalled the advice of the pathologist to who she had delivered David Wilson's remains, if there was a *next time*. 'Dr Mary Lamb wanted the body delivered to the mortuary as it was discovered at the scene. We need Doc Lamb's Anatomical Pathology Technicians down here with a body bag as soon as possible. We'll leave it to them to bag him.'

'Anything else?' asked Mason.

'After you've gathered all the forensic evidence you can I want you to order a furniture van. I want the house stripped bare. I want the floorboards up.'

She left the room and headed downstairs towards the front door. She needed to call her husband Thomas with a request but had no intention of making a call home from inside *that* building.

10

8.29 pm

DS Gina Riley stood on the pavement of the ambulance loading bay, clutching her coat at the throat and shivering as a cold wind blew in from the River Mersey. Only one ambulance had arrived in the five minutes that she had been there, and a check with reception confirmed that Frances Jamieson was still on her way.

Slowing down from forty miles per hour, an ambulance turned the corner and headed to the front entrance, its siren off but its blue light flashing. The paramedic driving pulled up so that the rear of the vehicle was close to the entrance to A & E.

As the paramedic jumped from the driver's door and ran towards the back of the ambulance, Riley became aware of voices and people coming towards her from the hospital.

The driver opened the back door and a pair of doctors and three nurses streamed past Riley.

Riley moved forward and looked at the blonde paramedic who had been riding in the back with Frances Jamieson as she checked the time on her watch.

'She passed out in the back of the ambulance,' said the paramedic. 'At the junction of Mather and Booker Avenue.'

'Is she still breathing?' asked a young doctor.

'Yes,' replied the paramedic.

'Excuse me,' said Riley. The doctors, nurses and paramedics

all turned to her and she guessed from the looks on their faces that they had her down as a voyeuristic ghoul.

She showed her warrant card to the doctor nearest to her and then spoke to the paramedic. 'Is she critical?'

'She's not going to die, if that's what you mean!'

'When she comes round and you're done with her, I need to speak with her.' Riley looked at the paramedic. 'In the meantime, can we talk?'

The paramedic nodded and said, 'Sure.'

Riley addressed the nurses, making eye contact with all as she spoke. 'I'm going to need a private room to speak with your colleague. Can you please fix that for me as soon as possible?'

'Follow me,' said the oldest nurse of the three.

The paramedic manoeuvred Frances Jamieson on a wheeled stretcher on to the pavement and Riley said, 'Just a moment.'

Riley looked at Frances Jamieson's face, the wind blowing her short dark hair. She turned her lidless eyes to the sky and looked stunned by the stars.

'Finished?' asked the male paramedic.

'Thank you,' replied Riley.

A sudden strong wind whipped in singing and laughter from a distance.

'Come with me,' said the nurse. 'I'll take you to the family room.'

11

8.35 pm

In the family room in the Royal Liverpool Hospital, Riley faced the brown-haired female paramedic who had been with Frances Jamieson in the ambulance, and pressed record on her iPhone.

'Did you speak to her...' Riley took in the woman's ID badge. '...Cara?'

'I asked her if she wanted pain relief. I was setting up a spray to keep her eyes moist and I explained to her that her eyelids could be rebuilt and would grow back from a small graft taken from the roof of her mouth – reassuring her, like.'

'Did she say anything to that?' asked Riley.

The paramedic shook her head. 'I set up the spray and called to Kevin, my colleague, to drive away. She was lying on the wheeled stretcher at this point, looking away from me. I put two and two together. I realised she was either a paedophile herself or was married to one, and tolerated all that nastiness. As we turned right to get into the lane leading towards town, I asked her who'd done this. She made this noise, like an animal caught in a metal trap, and she said, *It!* Kind of horrified, like.'

'She definitely said, *It*?'

'Definitely. Absolutely. *It.*'

The paramedic drew a deep breath.

'OK, take a minute. What happened after that?'

'Nothing.'

'Are you sure that's everything?'

'That's everything.'

Riley pressed stop and said, 'Thanks for that, Cara. If you think of anything else, anything you've missed, here's my card. I'm based at Trinity Road. I'd be very grateful if you can keep everything you've seen tonight to yourself. Don't even tell your nearest and dearest.'

'Definitely, Brownie's honour. I wouldn't want to infect anyone with what I've seen and heard tonight.' The paramedic shuddered. 'What she was watching on TV... Sick...' She shut her eyes and, Riley guessed, was trying to block out the memory.

When the paramedic opened her eyes, she asked, 'Is Justin Truman involved, like everyone's saying he was involved in that paedo getting topped in Aigburth last week?'

'It's an ongoing murder investigation,' explained Riley. 'I'm not at liberty to reveal any details, or to speculate openly about the identity of the perpetrator.'

'Oh, OK...'

'I'm sorry to disappoint you, Cara.'

'It's not that. I understand the need for confidentiality. It's just I've got a six-year-old girl and an eight-year-old boy. That's how old the girl was in the DVD she was watching. It got me. And yeah, I am disappointed it's not him personally. Send every paedophile in Liverpool running for the hills and keep all our kids safe.'

Riley held the door open and allowed the paramedic out. She followed her down the corridor, spoke to her back.

'*It*? That was all she said?' asked Riley, wondering if the paramedic knew more and was holding back information.

'That was all. *It*.'

Riley called Clay and when they connected, Clay asked, 'Have you caught up with Frances Jamieson, Gina?'

'I'm sorry, Eve. She was passed out in the ambulance en route and they're working on her right now in A & E.'

Clay swallowed the expletive that sprang to her lips. 'Did the doctors give you any idea of when she'll be able to talk to us?'

'*We haven't assessed her yet*, they said. *We couldn't possibly estimate*. Wouldn't even give me a ball park.'

'Did she say *anything* in the back of the ambulance?'

'She said, *It*. When the paramedic asked who'd done this to her. Want me to stick around here?'

'I'll send Maggie Bruce over. When Frances Jamieson comes round she can talk to Big Maggie.'

'What do you want me to do?'

'Get back here – 699 Mather Avenue – and see if you can work out who the Jamiesons' associates are. Let's see who they know and who knows them. We'll start in Liverpool and work out. The killer could be known to them.'

'I'm sorry to be the bearer of inconclusive news, Eve.'

'I guess it could be worse,' said Clay. 'I could be a Catholic.'

12

8.35 pm

In the car park facing Myrtle Chapel, DS Karl Stone looked in the direction that the funeral cars had taken as they left the crematorium and its darkened grounds, and wished in that moment that he was one of the undertakers.

Instead, he was in the passenger seat of Sandra Wilson's car, in the middle of a stand-off between mother and daughter. Samantha stood in front of the vehicle staring in accusation at her mother who sat motionless, in the driver's seat. And Stone felt like one corner of a septic triangle.

The silence inside the car was deep and the five minutes it had lasted felt like five hours.

'Look at me!' said Samantha. Mrs Wilson continued staring down at the steering wheel. 'Or have you opted for deafness as well as selective blindness?' Arms tightly folded across her chest, Samantha repeated, 'Look at me!' The pain in her face made Stone want to reach through the windscreen, to touch her, to reassure her. Compassion softened his bones and flooded his whole being.

Silence followed, and then Sandra Wilson spoke, but in a voice so small and lost that Stone had no idea what she had said.

'Can you repeat that, please, Sandra?' asked Stone.

'I... I didn't know...' she sobbed and her head sank down on to the steering wheel. 'I swear to God I didn't know what was going on.'

Right under your nose, thought Stone, staring ahead at Samantha.

'I've said I was sorry, over and over again, but she won't accept it.'

Mrs Wilson lifted her head now and looked at Stone. 'What do you think, Detective Sergeant Stone? *Why* won't she forgive me?'

Stone was astonished by the self-pitying tone in her voice and told himself to disguise his incredulity when he replied. 'I've spoken at length with Sammy over the past week and a half. She told you what her father, your husband, did to her.' He waited and saw *And?* behind the tears in Mrs Wilson's eyes. 'You didn't believe her. Stone wall. Not even a crumb of doubt. How come?'

'She was always at odds with her father from being knee-high. She never got on with him and she was always telling lies about all kinds of things. She got in trouble in school for lying. He had to go up to the school because of her lies.'

'What kind of lies, Mrs Wilson?'

Stone looked at Samantha and the total compassion he just felt gave way to hopelessness. There was nothing he could do or say to repair the damage done to her and he chided himself for thinking he could make a difference even if it was only for a few moments.

'That she was signed up for a deal with CBS Records...'

'How old was she when she said this?'

'Twelve. Thirteen maybe...'

'Given her age that's hardly lying, Mrs Wilson. It's fantasising out loud.' *And hiding from the stark horror of her home life,* thought Stone.

'She told terrible lies about her father in school. That he took photographs of the children in the school playground opposite our home with a telescopic lens. That's when he first had to go up to her school, to clear his name. Do *you* think he'd do such a thing?'

We found those pictures on his laptop, thought Stone, *along with a whole load of other things.*

'Then she told a teacher in school... her father... was crawling into her bed at night and... forcing her to do all manner of... disgusting things.'

He felt the weight of her eyes on the side of his face, turned to meet the woman's gaze. *How could she?*

'That's a pretty devastating lie, Mrs Wilson, for a daughter to tell about her father. You know' – Stone drilled into her eyes – 'Samantha told me... She told me you were angry with her when she told you your husband was systematically molesting her. Then she went and told the teacher in school.'

'I thought she was being malicious because her father had refused to pay for her to go on a school skiing holiday. I thought she was getting her own back. I thought she didn't fully understand what she was saying and was just repeaing something she'd heard in the playground about that kind of thing. I thought, *If you only knew how serious this is?* And when she ran away from home...'

Aged fourteen, thought Stone, *three weeks on the streets of London.*

Silence descended.

'You didn't report her to her police as missing, Mrs Wilson. Why?'

'I thought it had been reported. My husband told me he'd reported it to the police and that he'd deal with the school because my nerves were shattered.' She blew her nose into the crumpled handkerchief in her fist.

'You didn't think it was odd that the police didn't contact you once and ask if there'd been any communication between you, your husband and your missing daughter?'

'I thought there had been. The police rang when I was out. That's what he told me. And that the police had advised us not to tell any family, friends or neighbours because it may harm the chances of Samantha returning...'

'Your daughter wasn't a liar, Mrs Wilson. But your husband was.'

'You shouldn't speak ill of the dead.'

'I'm not. You asked me why I thought your daughter can't forgive you. Listen to what you're telling me. Answer the question *why?* for yourself.

'What do you mean?'

Stone looked at Samantha and the story of her life that she'd told him flashed through his mind. The relationships that didn't work out, the jobs she couldn't hold down, her inability to set patterns in life that could lead to happiness, in and out of Broad Oak and other psychiatric units.

'When he was accused of grooming another child you stayed with him.'

'It came out in court. No physical harm came to *that* child or any child!'

'Because Samantha *was* that child. Online, she pretended to be a twelve-year-old girl. And your husband took her out of the chat room for a *private* conversation of a very inappropriate nature.'

'It was entrapment.'

'But Samantha handed the evidence over to the police and you.'

'I don't like your tone.'

'You say you're sorry to her but you still make excuses for your husband. You still apportion blame to Samantha.'

'That's quite enough—'

'You buried your head in the sand—'

'My husband's been murdered!'

'—and you stayed with him. *Sorry* is just a word.'

'Stop picking on me! You should be supporting me.'

'I'm trying to, Mrs Wilson. You asked me *why?*' Stone drew a deep breath, feeling as though he was going to be sick. He opened the passenger door and was anointed by the cold air that poured over him and into the car. 'I'll be honest, Mrs Wilson. It's all too late for forgiveness.'

He stepped out of the car, closed the door and smiled as he approached Samantha.

'I know what she'll have been saying to you, Karl,' said Samantha. 'But what did you say to her?'

He stepped into the tight space between Samantha and her mother's car, blocking Mrs Wilson's view of her daughter with his body.

'That she'd let you down. In no uncertain terms.' He looked at her and saw raw relief pass over her features. 'You've got my contact details. If you ever need to talk, ever think there's anything at all I can do for you, you can call me twenty-four/seven. I have so much respect for you. *I'm* here for *you*.'

'You believe me?' said Samantha. 'Not her?'

'I categorically believe you.'

Stone saw a weight lifting from her shoulders and tears filling her eyes. 'I'd like to make a suggestion if I may,' he said.

'Go ahead,' said Samantha.

'I want you to walk away from her car. I want you to keep away from her at all costs. I'd do my best to forget her if I were you. She'll never change.'

Slowly, Stone moved out of the way.

Samantha looked directly at her mother and turned her back on the windscreen.

'Karl,' said Samantha. 'Do you mind if…? Will you hold my hand?'

He folded his hand around her hand and said, 'Let's walk away. Heads high.'

They walked.

'I'll drop you off at your flat,' said Stone. 'Don't look back. Look forward. Keep looking forward, Sammy.'

13

8.41 pm

On the central embankment on Mather Avenue, Clay listened to her husband Thomas read back the list of clothing and toiletries that she required.

On her iPhone, the sound of his voice in her ear was reassuring, reminding her that filth she was currently wading through was not the sum of her whole life.

'Thomas, I've got to go. Listen, don't bring the bag here to Mather Avenue, take it to Trinity Road and leave it with the custody sergeant, Sergeant Harris. I love you, Thomas. Tell Philip I love him.'

'I will do and you know what he'll say back to me. *I know she does, and I love her.* I'm sorry you're going through this, love. It won't last forever.'

As soon as she ended the call, her iPhone rang with a number on display that she didn't recognise but an area code that she did: 0114. She connected and said, 'DCI Lesley Reid, thank you for contacting me.'

Reid laughed. 'You *are* as good as people make out, Eve. How did you know it was me?' Her voice had the husky undertone of a heavy smoker and Clay, in her mind, saw DCI Lesley Reid, stone-faced at a tense press conference after she had charged Steven Jamieson with abusing a minor.

'I recognised the area code for Sheffield which is where you're based. How's work?'

'I retired a year ago.'

'Enjoying it?'

'Loving it. Working cold cases three days a week and sleeping well at night. Your colleague Barney Cole gave me your number, said it was to do with Steven Jamieson but wouldn't say what. Has he been up to his old tricks again?'

'He's been murdered, Lesley.'

'No way?'

'Way. It's the second act, following on from the David Wilson case.'

'Do you think Vindici's back? Or is it a copycat?'

'We think he's back but this time he's not alone.'

'Let me just…' Clay heard the metallic click of a cigarette lighter. '…celebrate Jamieson's untimely demise with a cigarette.'

Clay looked at the open door of 699 Mather Avenue, lights on in every room and pouring from the hallway, and drank in Reid's throaty chuckling. 'So, Lesley, dish the dirt on Prince Charming, Steven Jamieson.'

Reid coughed and pulled the ring on a can of drink. 'With a cigarette and a can of Stella Artois. So Jamieson ended up in Liverpool, the slimy little bastard. OK, Eve. I'll give you the rundown on Jamieson. I had him right on the ropes for one eight-year-old girl called Sally Davies. We found a picture of her on the internet engaging in forced sexual activity with a man. Do you need the details?'

'No. No thank you.'

'The so-called man's face wasn't on the picture and there were no identifying features on the trunk of his body but we knew it was Jamieson.'

'How?'

'Because Sally Davies told us it was him. She told us it happened twice a week at least and it had started when she was six years old and finished when she was eight.'

'Logistically, how did he manage to do this to her?'

'Jamieson used to pay the girl's mother, a hundred and fifty pounds a session. She was a heroin addict and so I guess in her eyes it beat peddling her own worn-out carcass on the streets and telephone booths of Sheffield. When Sally became a looked-after child, she dished the dirt on Jamieson to her carers. Round about this time, the kid's mother made a bloody big mistake.'

Clay pictured the forlorn statue of the Weeping Child on the bedside next to Jamieson's corpse. Sally.

'When the mother was initially pulled into our custody on a totally separate matter – she knifed a dealer, stole his cash and stash of drugs – she cracked on to a cellmate, on remand, about how she'd squeezed cash from the rich and powerful Steven Jamieson, he of much fame in South Yorkshire as the founder of Steven Jamieson Property Management. I believe he still owns huge chunks of Sheffield and thereabouts. Well – owned. Ha!' She drew in a lungful of smoke, exhaled with what Clay detected as quiet satisfaction and a deeply buried laugh of vindication. 'It was his wealth and power that enabled him to get away with it for so long.'

Clay pictured the whip marks on Jamieson's legs and made a mental note to congratulate Hendricks on his eye for detail. 'Tell me about this jail-cell confession.'

'Mary Davies, that was the mother's name. Mary's cellmate was disgusted but pretended to be impressed to squeeze as much of the lemon as she could. First opportunity she gets, the good thief comes singing like a canary to us. Mary Davies was the one to put that picture she'd secretly taken on the internet. After Jamieson binned Sally off because she was getting too old for his tastes, Mary tried to blackmail him but he calmly responded that he could have her killed for fifty quid and it would just look like a heroin overdose... You all right, Eve? That was a bloody big sigh.'

'You're paralysing what little faith I have left in human nature but go on, you're doing a great job letting me know what I'm dealing with here.'

'We dug Sally out of the care home she was in and the child

protection officer managed to get a much more detailed story from her point of view. Sally identified the man in the picture as Steven Jamieson. Turns out she's a feisty little lady, and even though Jamieson scares and disgusts her she identified him on a computerised line-up. Absolutely no shadow of a doubt.'

'But I guess there was no forensic evidence?'

'No forensic evidence. But Jamieson had a three-inch scar upper-left thigh. It was visible on the photograph. Sally knew his body inside out and spilled the intimate details in court via a video-link.'

'I can't imagine she was his only victim.'

'We identified at least fourteen other children from the rumour mill with offences going back over twenty years. All girls. All from geographical locations in and around Sheffield. He was a two-tier pervert. He liked them six to eight years old, and twelve to fourteen. God knows what he got up to when he was away on business. It was the worst-kept secret in South Yorkshire. We had another paedophile on remand who stepped forward and tried to do a plea bargain in exchange for more names of Jamieson's historical victims.'

Reid laughed and, taking a slurp of lager, reminded Clay that she could have done with a drink in that moment. 'He gave us the names but got two years more than he thought he'd negotiated. We approached all fourteen. Seven denied all knowledge of Jamieson. One was severely mentally ill. Three couldn't speak highly enough and three had recently left the area. Jamieson was rich and powerful enough to either buy silence or scare witnesses into it. Which leads to another complication with the case against him. He always seemed to be one step ahead and fully prepared for what we were coming at him with. You know where this is leading, don't you?'

'Jamieson had a bent copper on the inside acting as his eyes and ears,' said Clay.

'It was a detective constable. John Weston.'

'That name rings a bell.'

'Hillsborough-denier. *My father was there on duty and it was all the fault of drunken Scousers.* The little bastard. I could never categorically prove it but Weston was the rotten apple. The case against Jamieson went to court and Sally was a little star. She identified Jamieson as the man in the photograph, described every nook and cranny of his body. Her mother went up in the dock as the remorseful reformed junkie, confirmed she'd sold her daughter's body for up to two years. The cash machine withdrawals record showed him pulling out a hundred and fifty quid twice a week, three times during sunny weather. He got an abysmally short nine-year sentence down to the crack legal team he employed. I suffered chronic insomnia for years afterwards. I hate to say this, Eve, but part of me hopes you don't catch whoever's topped Jamieson.'

'I understand.'

'Saying that, if there's anything I can do just call me straight away. I can even come to Liverpool if it would be a help.'

'Thank you,' said Clay. 'I get the feeling I may well be calling on your advice.'

'Listen, Eve. I'm sure I don't have to tell you but cases like this can really get under your skin and from the public's point of view you're in a no-win situation. I was the SIO on the Jamieson case and in the eyes of the general public I wasn't seen as the copper who put Jamieson away, I was seen as the copper who put him away for what he did to one child when there were so, so many more. The key should've been thrown away and it wasn't.' The tone of her voice was suddenly laden with a heavy sadness.

'If it's any consolation,' said Clay, 'he'd have been better off in jail. Chances are he'd still be alive now if he was behind bars. He paid with his life for what he did tonight.'

'Have you met his wife, Frances?'

'Briefly. She was tortured by the perpetrator.'

'The evening just goes from good to great. Bring on the champers.'

Clay laughed. 'It must be wonderful being retired. Drinking

mid-week and speaking your mind. What was Frances Jamieson like?'

'An out-and-out bitch. She blamed Sally for leading him on and her mother for putting them together. Eve, I know you're busy so I'm going to leave you there. Call me if you need me, OK!'

'Thank you, you've been really helpful.'

'Nice to talk to you. Keep me in the loop.'

The line went dead.

As Clay stored Reid's number in her phone, she looked at Jamieson's house. The thought of a bent copper and liar being involved in the case turned a key in her head.

The murder of one paedophile in their home could easily have been perpetrated by one of the victims, who knew their tormentor's address. But with the murder of a second convicted paedophile came the disconcerting probability that someone with access to the National Police Computer and the Sex Offenders Register was passing out secret information.

Clay crossed the road towards Jamieson's lair, with a weight on her shoulders that she knew would only get heavier.

14

8.59 pm

After a journey largely travelled in silence from Springwood Crematorium to Percy Street on the edge of Liverpool city centre, Detective Sergeant Karl Stone pulled his car up to the kerb and turned off the ignition. Bathed in orange streetlights, the tall Victorian terraced houses looked like a location from one of the many Hammer Horror films he had loved since his teenage years.

For several moments, neither Stone nor Samantha Wilson moved or spoke but the silence was not uncomfortable. Stone, who would have happily remained there, felt the pricking of his conscience and the need to get back to work.

'Sammy,' he said. 'I'm going to have to go now.'

'What's happened?'

'There's been a murder. On Mather Avenue.' He recalled the text he'd received from Barney Cole and opened as he followed Samantha and her mother from Myrtle Chapel at the end of the service. 'I don't know the finer details, but I do know I'm needed. Quickly.' He turned to her and saw she was looking at him.

'You've been very kind to me, Karl, and I know you're a busy man, but I'm a bit scared of going back into the flat by myself.' Something glittered in her eyes and Stone felt as if he was floating, watching the scene as a spectator.

'You want me to go in first? Put on the lights and check there's nothing for you to be frightened of?'

'Would you mind?' She smiled sadly. He took the keys from the ignition and, as he double-checked that the gearstick was in neutral, he felt the weight of her hand on the back of his. 'This is really very kind of you, Karl.'

Her touch sparked off a shiver of pleasure through his body. Stone looked at her hand on his, and then at her face, and smiled. This once-ordinary woman had transformed in the twinkling of an eye into the most beautiful being in the history of time.

Stone dragged his eyes away from her lips. 'Yes, I'll see you inside safely. Come on, Sammy.'

15

8.59 pm

Clay stood in the doorway of 699 Mather Avenue and tried to cleanse herself with fresh air. The wind sounded a bass note and fallen leaves scraped along the tarmac of the strangely deserted dual carriageway.

She heard the rumble of advancing vehicles and, walking down to the gate to get a closer look, noticed the damage to the black Citroën parked in the driveway. A single line had been carved on the driver's door and the back door, a childlike drawing of a rolling set of hills, and Clay reckoned that it had been put there by the killer with the same blade that had been used to cut off Frances Jamieson's eyelids and carve the name Vindici on both targets.

Clay watched the Anatomical Pathological Technicians pull up in their black mortuary van outside the house. At the same time a removals lorry stopped outside the house next door and two plainclothes officers climbed down swiftly from the cab. Clay waved to them and they joined her at the gate.

'DS Terry Mason is gathering forensics,' said Clay. 'As soon as we've removed the body and Terry's satisfied that he's got everything we need, you're to strip the house of everything and take it to the warehouse.'

The officers, one in his twenties and the other in his fifties, looked cold and their breaths mingled in the chilly air as white mist. The younger officer looked at Clay with a mixture of what looked like awe and disbelief. She smiled at him and said, 'Close your mouth, please, it's rude to stare.'

'I – I'm sorry, I've heard such a lot about you...'

'It's not just the two of you surely,' said Clay.

'We've got a team following,' said the older officer. As he spoke, his name and context came into place.

'Colin. You ran the log for me on the Baptist's final murder scene.'

'You've got a good memory, DCI Clay.' He sounded flattered.

'It wasn't a good memory but you did a good job, Colin. I'm sorry, guys, but you're going to have to wait outside until Terry's ready.'

The younger officer had his phone out and he looked at Clay eagerly. 'Can I get a selfie with you?'

'Not here, not now. Sorry.' She pointed to the removals lorry and, as they headed off, she chuckled as the older man said, 'You're a fucking A-one lemon, Tony.'

'Eve?' said Michael Harper, the head APT, limping towards the gate of 699 Mather Avenue.

'What's up with you, Harper?' asked Clay.

'Sciatica. My back's killing me. We heard it's the same killer as David Wilson's. Is the victim a paedophile?'

'Yes.'

'Got what was coming to him,' said Harper's colleague.

'We're here to sort out a murder,' said Clay, leading them to the front door. 'I'll take you to the body. We're not here to judge,' she added to Harper's new assistant as she took them upstairs, regretting the hollowness of her tone, and hoping they didn't notice.

16

9.02 pm

As Detective Sergeant Karl Stone walked up to Samantha Wilson's second-floor flat, he noticed her perfume as she followed behind him. It had a fragrance that put him in mind of summer flowers, sunshine and aromatic spices.

Stepping on to the second floor, he turned the key to Flat 5 in his hand and noticed that, in spite of the cold night air, his palms were moist and his throat and mouth were dry.

At the door of Flat 5, he said, 'Wait out here, Sammy. I'll turn on all the lights and check the rooms.' He turned the key in her lock.

'I'm sorry to put you to all this trouble,' she said.

'It's the first and most important part of my job, to protect members of the public.'

He opened the door and stepped inside the well-maintained and tidy flat. He'd visited twice before when he'd called to speak to Samantha about her father and the past and he knew the layout well. In the narrow hallway, he turned on the wall switch and light fell into the doorway of the galley kitchen and the wide living room overlooking Percy Street.

Kitchen, light on. Living room, light on. No one and nothing to fear in either space.

He opened the bathroom door wide, flicked on the switch and winced at his reflection in the mirror. Prematurely grey hair slicked back, his face a map of lines, *Mr Car Crash*, as he often mocked himself. Each time he caught his reflection, he was shocked and disappointed, which was why he only had one mirror – for shaving – in his flat.

He turned his eyes away and headed off to the bedroom at the back of the flat, the one room he hadn't been in.

When he turned the bedroom light on, he saw a simple but feminine space with a large bed in the left-hand corner and a modern white dressing table, matching the bed, at the window to catch the light. The wardrobe against the opposite wall coordinated with the other two pieces of furniture.

He thought of his own untidy though clean flat, around the corner and five minutes away on Princes Avenue. *I could do with her coming around and sorting my place out.* A thought he dismissed as soon as it formed in his mind.

It was in her bedroom that the smell of summer flowers was at its strongest and Stone realised, as he gazed at the bed, that it wasn't a manufactured scent, it was a body odour that was personal to her.

Stone imagined her asleep in the bed on a warm's summer's night, naked beneath the thin sheet draped over the curves of her body, and he heard himself give the deepest sigh.

'Sammy!' He stepped away from the bedroom and called to the landing outside her front door.

'Yes, Karl?'

'I've checked all the rooms: there's absolutely nothing for you to be frightened of.'

'Thank you.' He could hear the smile in her voice, and the relief behind that smile.

'Want me to turn the lights off?'

'I can't afford to waste electricity. Yes, please.'

Within moments, the only light on in the flat was the hall light. At the door of the front room, Stone noticed the way that the bay window in the living room was flooded with yellow streetlight and found himself walking deeper into the front room, drawn towards the ghostly illumination.

'You can come in, Sammy. You're safe!'

He looked across the street at the tall off-white Victorian terrace that mirrored the building he was in and heard the front door close softly. A floorboard creaked as Samantha stepped inside her home. Stone sensed her moving closer, entering the front room. She didn't turn on the light or speak as she made her way towards him.

Her natural perfume hit his senses and he felt something turn tightly in his core.

Her arm brushed his as she stood beside him in the bay. 'It's magnetic, isn't it?' She looked not at him but out of the window.

'What's magnetic, Sammy?'

'This window, amongst other things. When the woman from the Housing Trust showed me the flat, the thing that really attracted me was this window. It was daytime, obviously, but I did exactly what you did. I walked over to the window and stood right where you are, looking out at the street and the houses over the road. Isn't it strange how we both did the same thing?'

'No, it's beautiful.'

'Beautiful, Karl?'

'This feature.'

'Yes.'

He turned his head to look at her and she was facing him.

'It's not the only thing of beauty, Karl.'

'What else is beautiful?'

'You are.'

He recalled his recent encounter with his reflection and waited for her to laugh. Instead, in the amber light that engulfed them, she pleaded with her eyes. *Believe me.* He looked directly into her eyes and felt the foundations of his whole self crumbling into dust. He pushed back with all his willpower but his weight seemed to vanish into nothing. Then another picture flashed through his mind.

It's a warning, he thought, *an instinctive warning.*

'What are you thinking, Karl?'

He turned. Her breath caressed his face and the sweetness intensified.

'I think you've been through a great trauma,' he heard himself say. 'And I don't think you're quite seeing straight.'

She pressed her hands against his neck, her lips against his and the numbing effect of three years of loneliness disappeared and was replaced by something vivid and painful.

The tip of her tongue pressed into the small but yielding gap between his lips and an image from the recurring nightmare Stone had suffered since he'd met Samantha as part of his work on the Wilson murder filled his head and made him pull away from her.

'Don't you like me, Karl?' Hurt and loneliness marbled each word.

At their first meeting, the day after he had seen her father's naked corpse, Samantha had shown him a picture of herself aged thirteen.

'Yes, I like you very much, Sammy.'

That night, as he slept, he had dreamed he was paralysed, standing in the corner of Wilson's bedroom.

'If you like me very much, Karl, why won't you kiss me? Hold me? I'm desperately lonely and you're so nice to me.'

In the dream, on the bed, Wilson had grunted as he raped thirteen-year-old Samantha, then laughed as he turned his head and looked directly at Stone, frozen and screaming silently. *'You can go next, Stone!'*

'Sammy, listen to me, please. I'm on my own too. I have been for a long time and I do like you very much. But I'm a senior officer in a team investigating your father's murder. Two things. I can't get involved with witnesses...' He could hear blood pounding in his ears. 'And there's been a development tonight that's just made your father's killing a lot more complex and serious.'

Tears rolled down her face. He placed his arms around her. Her whole body stiffened and he felt her withdrawing from him.

'When we sort out this mess, maybe we could go out to dinner. Can you wait a while? Can you give me a chance when the time is right?'

'Can you let me go!'

He dropped his arms and she walked towards the door.

'You're a very kind man. You're saying that to be kind to me but you don't want me...'

He followed her as she drifted towards the front door of her flat. 'Sammy, please...'

She shook her head and opened the front door wide. 'You're also a very busy man. That's obvious. You must go back to work now.' She pointed to the space beyond the door. 'Thank you.'

He looked at her as he left but she turned her head away. The door closed and he waited. Silence.

As Stone walked to the stairs, he heard a muffled noise from behind her door.

He hurried down the stairs and the sound that followed him grew louder with each step.

Alone in her flat, Samantha Wilson wept.

17

9.04 pm

From the doorway of the bedroom, Clay watched what looked like a deathbed scene from a bizarre dream.

On the right-hand side of the bed, Harper, senior APT, unzipped a silver-grey body bag. The rasp of its unclenching teeth was the only sound in the room. At the foot of the bed, Hendricks looked down on Steven Jamieson's body and prepared his iPhone to film the transfer of the body from the mattress into the body bag. On the left-hand side of the bed, Harper's colleague cast a cold eye over the corpse, working out the best way to move it.

Behind Clay, on the landing, DS Terry Mason asked, 'Hey, Harper, do you want me and Paul Price to help?'

'Yes.' His voice was little more than a whisper. 'If you'll hold the bag open, top and bottom, so we can get the body in cleanly.'

Clay moved aside and, within moments, DS Mason and Sergeant Price were crouched, keeping the interlocking teeth of the zip wide apart down the centre of the bag.

'Turn him over!' said Harper.

The junior APT dug his latex-gloved hands under the shoulder and hip and carefully lifted the weight of Steven Jamieson's corpse. As the chest and front thigh came into view, Harper said, 'Get ready for it! Carefully, carefully...'

'Oh my giddy God,' said Mason, who had a close-up view of the turning corpse.

Clay took a deep breath and hummed three random notes at the base of her throat.

The source of the bloodstain on the mattress came clearly into view. Between his legs, and rising to his pubic bone, was a bloody cave the size of a large orange.

Clay looked at Mason's face as Jamieson's head flopped towards him. His eyes were covered with a black blindfold. His cheeks bulged and his mouth was sealed by silver masking tape.

Harper held the weight of Jamieson's body as it came to rest on its back.

'You did what you did, sure enough, Mr Jamieson,' said Harper. 'And sure enough you paid for it.' He looked at Clay. 'The killer's removed the victim's genitalia with the same or a similar surgical scalpel as was used last time.'

'Twenty-four-carat Vindici,' said Harper's assistant with restrained admiration.

That recurring detail of Vindici's murders was common knowledge. The removal of the victim's genitalia was plastered all over the media during his killing spree back in 2007 and 2008.

'Harper?' She drew the attention of both APTs. 'Let's get the body bagged and off to Dr Lamb at the mortuary.'

Hendricks moved aside as Harper made his way towards Jamieson's head and shoulders. His assistant stuck his hands around the victim's ankles. 'Still warm, said Harper placing his hands under the shoulders

Harper winced, his face full of pain.

'I'll lift him into the body bag for you, Harper,' said Clay.

'Well, if you don't mind.'

'Do you want me to do that?' said Hendricks.

Yes please, thought Clay. 'It's OK, Bill,' she replied. 'Keep filming.'

Loathing mounted up inside Clay and the thought of touching Stephen Jamieson made her nauseous. She looked from his mutilated groin to his bulging cheeks.

She dug down to the deepest layer of grit in her being and, taking a stiff breath, said, 'OK, let's just get on with this.'

As she stooped next to Stephen Jamieson's head, Clay placed the backs of her hands between the mattress and his shoulders and was deeply grateful that she was wearing latex gloves. She cupped her fingers into his armpits and, feeling the coarse texture of hair, felt as if her scalp was suddenly overrun with lice.

'On the count of three, lift! Ready?'

She nodded and counted with Harper's assistant, 'One, two, three.'

Hendricks's iPhone rang out, Yazz's 1980s number-one hit 'The Only Way Is Up'. 'Can you picture me on the dance floor in the Cabin with a bunch of rather uninhibited student nurses?' A ripple of laughter ran round the room and, as the music stopped, Clay was grateful for the brief distraction.

Lifting the dead man from the mattress, Clay looked at his gagged mouth, blindfolded eyes and then at the curve of his forehead, imagining what kind of darkness, what decadence had filled his brain when he was alive. *In life you were a predator and a menace, but in death you're just a dead weight,* she said to herself, trying hard to concentrate on getting him into the body bag.

The smell of his burned flesh clashed with his sour body odour.

'Stop!' said Clay, her head swimming. She looked down at DS Terry Mason at the head of the body bag, holding it wide open.

A bead of perspiration rolled down Clay's forehead.

'Ready to lower him in?' asked Harper's assistant.

'Let's just do it!' said Clay, hating the touch of his head against the tops of her thighs.

'One two three, lower!'

She bent her knees and as she came closer to the ground the weight of his body seemed to double.

'I really appreciate this, DCI Clay,' said Harper, touching the base of his back.

As Clay slowly sank the shoulders between the open zip, his head flopped back, giving him a momentary semblance of life.

Shoulders in the bag, Clay pulled her hands away as quickly as she could, feeling the teeth of the zip comb the backs of her hands.

As she stood to her full height, Clay looked at her hands in the light and wanted to sink them in boiling water laced with industrial-strength bleach.

Harper's assistant pulled the zip of the body bag up from the base towards the top, sealing in Steven Jamieson's remains. Clay looked again at his blindfolded eyes and gagged mouth as the closing zip folded over them and wondered what his eyes had seen, what he'd said to his victims, what weeping and begging for mercy he'd heard, and how the pain and terror must have elevated his senses and made him buzz with illicit pleasure.

'I'll stop filming now,' said Hendricks.

She felt the weight of a hand on her left shoulder and was reassured by Hendricks's touch.

'You did well, Eve. Not the easiest thing to do.'

'Thanks, Bill...' A thought struck her and she paused.

'What?' asked Hendricks.

'We're going to have to dig out the sex offenders' register, contact every paedophile in Merseyside area and warn them to be vigilant. We can use constables for the little fish, but we may well have to bring in the sharks.'

She clenched and unclenched her hands, the texture of Stephen Jamieson's hair still alive on her fingertips.

'You want me to call Barney Cole and get him to organise that?' asked Hendricks.

Clay nodded. 'Please.'

'I'll call him.' He looked at the display on his phone. 'That was a missed call from Carol White.'

Clay pictured Sergeant White, child protection officer, and was sorry for her. 'How is she?'

'She's wading through the filth from David Wilson's laptop. I spent a lot of time with her last Friday. A lot of tears. A lot of silence. She's getting through.'

'How on earth does she do it?'

'I don't know – but what's wrong, Eve?' asked Hendricks. 'You look like you've just lost your engagement ring.'

Clay took a moment to straighten out her thoughts. 'We've got a leak and they're in league with the perpetrator.'

'How are you going to address this, Eve?'

'Head on. Before the team meeting in the morning. I've got no choice.'

18

9.46 pm

In the cool and brightly lit air of Autopsy Room 1, Clay tied the belt at the back of a green plastic apron and watched the elderly-looking pathologist washing her hands at the aluminium sink, her name etched in indelible ink around the tops of both rubber boots: 'DR MARY LAMB'.

Clay turned on the hot tap, the sensation of Steven Jamieson's dead body still alive on her fingers and hands. As the stream of water turned quickly from warm to hot, she sank both hands into the liquid, turning them over, spreading her fingers to allow the water to cover every last piece of the skin from the base of her wrists to the tips of her fingers. The water burned as it ran down the lines on her palms and, slowly, she withdrew her hands from the flood.

From the pocket of the blue theatre tunic that she had dressed in to watch the post-mortem, Clay's iPhone rang out.

'Domestic or private?' Dr Lamb smiled.

Clay looked at the display – 'Home' – and said, 'Private.'

'Better go get it, Eve. I'll wait for you before I begin.'

As Clay slipped back into the privacy of the dressing room and connected the call, something sharp and deadly cut through the centre of her being. 'Thomas, what's the matter?' She tried to filter out panic from her voice.

'Look, I'm sorry to call and I know you're up to your eyes

in it, but it's Philip. He wants to have a word with you.' He dropped his voice. 'He's had a nightmare.'

'Put him on, please.'

'Mum?' Four years old now and raring to go to school next September, on the telephone his voice sounded younger and the terror of his nightmare took away from his usual joyfulness. Clay felt the pieces of her heart falling apart.

'Hi, Philip. You OK?'

'I had a bad dream and I woke up screaming.'

'Philip, I'm very sorry to hear that.' Clay sat on the bench. She felt tempted to tell him she would be home in twenty minutes to get him back to sleep but knew there was as much chance of flying to the moon. 'It was just a dream. Dreams aren't real. Whatever bad thing happened in the dream, it's like a cartoon on TV. Can cartoons on TV hurt you?'

'No. But it was a horrible cartoon dream.'

'Have you told Dad what it was about?'

'No. I wanted to tell you because *the bad man* was talking about you in the dream.'

The smell of the mortuary's chemicals hit the back of her throat and the sound of running tap water striking the aluminium sinks beyond the door sounded like a cacophony.

The door of the dressing room opened and Hendricks entered. 'Want me to stay or go?' he asked.

Stay, she mouthed, grateful for the arrival of a friendly face. 'What happened, sweetheart?'

'A man dressed in black, with pointy face and a... and a big black hat. On a cart, holding the reins of a horse. He came to ours, calling, *Philip, come here, I've got sweets for you*. He had this cage. I said, *Go away. I'm with my mum*. He laughed and shook his head and I was all alone and I turned to run in the house but I, I was like a, like a, like a statue!'

On the brink of tears, Philip fell silent.

'Philip, do you remember last summer when we watched that old movie *Chitty Chitty Bang Bang*?'

'Yes?'

'You watched it three times in three days after we'd watched it together twice in one afternoon and evening because you loved it so much. Remember?'

'I do.'

'The bad man you've been dreaming about was from the film *Chitty Chitty Bang Bang*. Remember the Child Catcher?'

'Yes. Yes… it *was* the Child Catcher.'

'You know that films, like cartoons, aren't real. But everything you see and hear, love, sinks into your head and even if you think you've forgotten it, it's still there and it very often comes out when you're dreaming.'

In silence, he worked through the information.

'Do you feel a little bit better, Philip?'

'Sort of. Do you know what happened next in my dream?'

'No,' she replied evenly, with a mounting sense of dread.

'He got down from his cart. I was a statue still. He came towards me. He laughed. He picked me up with one hand, threw me in the cage. I said, *My mum's a policewoman*. He said, *Your mum's on my side*. That's when I woke up. Screaming.'

'Philip, I'll always be on your side, no matter what.' She felt her stomach turning and the colour in her face rising. 'It was a dream. That was all. A dream. I love you with all my heart and I won't let anyone hurt you or take you away from me and your dad.'

'Will you come home in the morning before I go to nursery?'

'Yes I will. I promise I'll be there in the morning, Philip.'

He gave out a long, slow yawn.

'I'll be there after you wake up in the morning. Go to sleep now knowing that.'

'I love you, Mum.'

'I love you, Philip.'

She waited for a moment and, as the line went dead, a deeply buried memory surfaced from her childhood at St Michael's Catholic Care Home for Children.

In her dream, Sister Philomena was still alive. A faceless stranger dragged Eve's surrogate mother to a storm-lashed sea and cast her into the waves. Eve, aged eight, had stood on the shore, frozen, helpless and screaming, 'Bring her back, Death!'

When she woke up, she recalled, James Peace was sitting on the edge of her bed.

'It's OK, Eve, it's just another one of your bad dreams. You're safe. You're with me now. Close your eyes. I'll watch over you until you sleep. Always loved you. Always will.'

She looked at Hendricks and explained, 'Philip had a nightmare.'

'What time does he get up?'

'Half seven.'

'You're going to have to be there come what may, Eve. Whatever shit crops up, I'll cover you in the morning. He's fine. He's with his dad. But go see him. Put your mind to rest.'

She didn't move or speak.

'I caught up with Carol White. She was in floods of tears on the phone.'

'The woman with arguably the worst job in the whole wide world.'

'Those reports she writes on the child pornography she watches are clinical and detached but it's really getting to her. I'm quite worried about her.'

Clay weighed everything up. She looked at her watch, painfully aware that she was keeping people waiting. 'As soon as we're through here, Bill, arrange to see her as soon as possible.' She pictured Carol White, dead-eyed but forcing herself to smile in the dining room of Trinity Road police station, and was full of sympathy for a good woman with a vile workload. 'You're a kind man, Bill. I think that's just what she needs right now.'

Clay dug deep and walked into Autopsy Suite 1 where Dr Lamb and Harper waited next to the rubber board on which Steven Jamieson's hairy body was waiting to be taken apart.

19

9.46 pm

Somewhere deep in Trinity Road Police Station, a cleaner was listening to a radio and the strains of Barry Manilow's 'Mandy' seeped into the incident room. Alone in the room, DC Barney Cole looked at the screen of his laptop, saw the last page of a long list of known paedophiles on Merseyside and clicked print. 'I don't know what's worse. Looking at this? Or hearing that?' he said to the shadows around him.

As paper was sucked into the communal printer on Karl Stone's desk, Cole stood to his full height and stretched, the tiredness and stress of the past week making his forty-year-old gym-trained body feel like that of an eighty-year-old couch potato.

He reached towards the receiver of his landline phone to ring Gina Riley when the phone rang on Clay's desk.

Picking up Clay's receiver, there was a muddy silence and Cole guessed the caller at the other end was far away. 'Good evening, Detective Constable Barney Cole, Merseyside Constabulary, speaking. How can I help you?'

'You are not Eve Clay?'

Cole recognised the accent straight away, from the last major holiday he had taken in Mexico with his wife Veronica before the kids, David and Gary, came along.

'Are you phoning from the Puebla City Police, Puebla State?' asked Cole.

'Can I speak with Eve Clay?'

'I'm afraid she's not here at the moment. Who am I speaking to please?'

'Sergeant Eduardo García, Puebla City Police.'

'Thank you very much for getting back to us,' said Cole. 'At last.' *Though we've been emailing and phoning you every day for the past week and a half and we've had absolutely nothing back from you,* he thought with frustration.

'I am just back from leave. Your request ended up on my computer with a note from my colleague. Pushed from this desk to that and back and in the end, I was not here, so the request sits on my desk when I can no deal with it. But, hey, I am here now.'

'Well, it's great to have you on board. You are aware that this request we have made to you is a part of a murder investigation?'

'Yes I heard. Very serious business. It's the holiday season here. We are very, very at short work, at the moment. It is the big festival here in Puebla and the rest of Mexico. The Day of the Dead.'

'So you're aware that the photograph and email that I sent your department relates to an item definitely a part of those festivities?'

'No, Mr Cole, I wasn't here when the email and picture arrived.'

'Well, do you have your computer with you, Eduardo?'

'I do.'

'Well, go to your inbox—'

'Your email and picture are missing. While I was away, the computer system crashed and a lot of data was wiped away, your email included. Detective Clay's landline number was written on the note on my desk. I call her.'

'I'll send it again, along with an attached picture. Your direct email address please, your landline, and your mobile.'

Cole clicked his pen into action and wrote the details into Clay's notebook. He said, 'I'm going to send this email and attachment to you right now, Eduardo. When you receive it, let me know straight away please that both have arrived safely. Are you going to be the named person dealing with our request?'

'Uh-huh.'

'If you could wait at your computer please, Eduardo. Thank you for getting back to us.'

Cole hung up, hurried to his laptop and, getting on to his emails, opened 'Sent items'. After scrolling through two weeks' worth of emails sent, he came to the one headed 'Puebla City Police'.

He opened the attachment and looked at the pottery figurine left in David Wilson's bedroom murder scene, then he double-checked the contents of the email:

Dear Sir or Madam

I am writing to you on behalf of my boss Detective Chief Inspector Eve Clay. The item pictured in the enclosed attachment was discovered at the scene of a murder last night in Liverpool, England, United Kingdom. Our initial investigation shows us, from the inscription on the base of the ornament, that the figure of the Weeping Child was manufactured in Puebla City. Our belief is that the figure of the Weeping Child is an ornament used during your festival for loved ones who have passed from life to death. Looking at the object, we do not believe it is hand-made but rather mass-produced. We would be grateful if you could track down the factory that manufactures this ornament and check to see if this has been exported to England in general and Liverpool in particular.

We currently believe that an escaped murderer, Justin Truman, aka Vindici, is responsible for the murders we are currently investigating. His previous murders were committed in the time window of your Day of the Dead festivities and we are working on the premise that he will continue to kill until the festival is finished. (Photograph attached.)

DCI Clay's landline number is 44 151 496 0950.

Clay's mobile number is 44 7700 900956.

Please do not hesitate to contact her or me if you have any

questions or need any clarification. Thank you in anticipation of your cooperation.

Yours faithfully
DC Barney Cole
pp DCI Eve Clay, Merseyside Constabulary

He attached Justin Truman's mug shot, clicked forward, typed in García's email address and pressed send.

As the printer on Stone's desk stopped spewing out pages of names and contact details of known paedophiles, Cole picked up his iPhone and got through to Gina Riley after a few rings.

'Hi, Barney, what's up?'

'I've got the contact details for the Society of Punchable Arseholes. I'll send it to your phone and leave a hard copy on your desk.'

'You're a star. Many people to deal with?'

Cole looked at the wad on the printer. 'Enough to keep an awful lot of people busy tomorrow.' Across the connection and in her silence, he sensed his colleague's burden and filled his voice with as much kindness as he could. 'Gina, I'll let you go.'

'Thanks, Barney.'

Hanging up, he heard the ping of an incoming email on to his laptop. He went to the inbox and opened the email from Sergeant García.

Barney,

Email and attachment received. It is a *Llorón* (Weeping Child), correct. Will visit all factories but most shut for holiday. If shut will visit owners or managers and get information for you. Open office even if holiday.

Good wishes
Ed

'You, Eddie, are my brand-new best friend!'

Outside, 'Mandy' ended. Silence. Cole sighed with relief. Then the opening bars of 'Copacabana' infiltrated the walls of the incident room.

'Ah, Jesus wept, *Manilow*!'

20

9.53 pm

In the family room of the Royal Liverpool University Hospital, Detective Constable Maggie Bruce looked at the screen of her iPhone in the palm of her large hand and watched footage from the third round of her last amateur boxing match; she smiled at the moment when she'd decked and knocked out her arch-rival. As the referee counted to ten, and the number *seven* left his lips, she heard someone at the door and turned the clip off.

The door of the family room opened and a tall, gaunt male nurse who looked as though he'd stepped from the set of a low-budget horror movie stood in the frame.

Maggie stood up. 'Great, take me to Mrs Jamieson.'

He shook his head and DC Bruce wondered if the man had the power of speech.

'No?' asked Bruce, the buzz of euphoria she had just experienced watching her most recent success in the ring fading fast.

'Mrs Jamieson's dead.'

'Dead?' DC Bruce heard disbelief in her own voice.

'Just now. She had a massive cardiac arrest,' confirmed the nurse.

'Did she speak before she died?'

'She did. I asked her who had attacked her.'

He fell silent and DC Bruce was filled with the aggravating

sensation that the bogeyman in green was playing games with her. She looked into his eyes but couldn't find any hint of emotion.

The nurse stepped into the room and closed the door.

'What did she tell you about the perpetrator?' asked DC Bruce.

'It shocked me, I'll tell you that...'

21

9.55 pm

On the rubber board in the mortuary, the air of unreality around Stephen Jamieson's corpse in the bedroom at 699 Mather Avenue solidified and, for a series of moments, it appeared to Clay that he was made of wax.

'I guess this is going to be pretty much a repeat of what happened to David Wilson's body,' said Dr Mary Lamb, her eyes alive with intelligence as she looked up and down the corpse. 'Take the blindfold off please, Harper.' The pathologist pointed at Jamieson's corpse. 'From the neck down, once he's been opened up, he'll look just like any other person I've ever seen in this place.' She slid latex gloves over her hands. 'Last week, when you brought David Wilson's body to me, Eve...?'

'Yes, it's another paedophile,' Clay anticipated.

As Clay spoke her iPhone buzzed and, stepping away from the rubber board, she answered the incoming call from DC Maggie Bruce.

Dr Lamb leaned in closer to Jamieson's face as Harper raised his skull from the board with one hand and pulled at the knot at the back of his head. 'Have you found David Wilson's penis and testicles yet, DS Hendricks?' she asked.

'We're pretty sure where they are and have been tonight. Secreted in the bodies of the victims. Wilson's testicles were in Frances Jamieson's mouth and I'd put a lot of money on his penis being behind the tape in Jamieson's mouth.'

Clay returned to the rubber board.

'So he took Jamieson's penis and testicles, just as he took David Wilson's genitalia?' Dr Lamb addressed Clay, looking directly at her.

'It's not a *he*,' said Eve Clay. 'The killer's female, Dr Lamb. Genital removal was one of Justin Truman's signature details, but the killer in 699 Mather Avenue was a female.'

'How do we know that?' asked Hendricks, his words laced with hope and doubt.

'Frances Jamieson lived long enough to answer the question, *Who did this to you and your husband?* Jamieson categorically said, over and over, *It was a woman, just one woman.* There was more than one witness to this and they're all stone-cold certain. Then she had a massive cardiac arrest.'

Beneath her skin, Clay felt an intense cold that spread from the crown of her scalp to the nerves beneath her toenails. All eyes were on her, faces wreathed in disbelief and shock, their silence demanding more.

'And, sadly for us, that's all she said,' responded Clay. 'Shall we continue, Dr Lamb?'

The pathologist nodded at Harper. He pinched the corner of the tape covering Jamieson's mouth and carefully pulled the tape away. For a moment it appeared Jamieson had no mouth, just a white, horizontal scar beneath his nose.

Harper placed the tips of his thumb and index finger at the centre of Jamieson's lips, welded together by white crusts. He opened the mouth as wide as it would part, revealing clenched teeth.

'Gently with the scalpel,' said Dr Lamb to herself as she placed the sharp tip between his clenched front teeth. When there was enough space between his teeth for her finger, Dr Lamb lifted his top teeth and pushed down at the bottom set. His jaw cracked. She turned his head to the left and there was a sound of something soft shifting within his mouth cavity.

A trail of blood-laced saliva oozed from the left corner of

his lips and gravity came into play inside Jamieson's mouth. Flesh hung out of his mouth, seemed caught between the light of the autopsy suite and the darkness inside his mouth. Dr Lamb pressed her fingers against his right cheek and pushed.

A limp piece of flesh protruded from his lips.

'A disembodied penis,' observed Harper. Reaching inside Jamieson's mouth with one hooked finger, he scooped out the dead flesh and placed the penis next to the dead man's face. As he turned Jamieson's head back, so that he directly faced the ceiling, there was a look of open-mouthed shock on the dead man's face.

Clay looked at Dr Lamb's kind, elderly face and caught the pathologist watching her. 'Penny for them?' asked Dr Lamb. 'I've known you a long time, Eve. You have that look about you. Like a very nasty penny has just dropped...'

'It's David Wilson's penis,' replied Clay. She looked at the pathetic scrap of flesh. In death, she thought, it looked like the corpse of a small, defenceless animal. But in life, she reminded herself, it had been a lethal weapon that corrupted and abused Samantha Wilson, the daughter he was supposed to protect and cherish. 'The killer, she's harvested Steven Jamieson's genitalia for her next outing.'

Footsteps echoed on a set of stairs outside the autopsy suite. Clay looked towards the source of the noise. Dr Lamb indicated the corpse.

'That's his spirit trying to escape before we cut him open,' she said.

Clay smiled and wished she could escape as easily and, as the futile desire bloomed, the disturbing knowledge that the female killer was convinced of her own rectitude slammed into her. With two successful hits, the murderer's appetite for blood would be massive and her craving for revenge would send her out on the hunt as soon as the first chill settled on her latest kill.

'Harper!' said Dr Lamb. 'Please turn him onto his front. I need to look at the back of his neck.'

'Eve?' said Dr Lamb. 'Can I have a word with you?' The pathologist drew Clay out of the APTs' earshot. 'You've attended over a hundred autopsies that I've conducted. I have to say, you don't look yourself.'

'I'm OK.' Clay smiled at the pathologist. The kindness in Lamb's eyes had sparked a sensation she used to experience all the time when she was a little girl in the care of Sister Philomena. As though something large and warm and invisible was wrapping itself all around her.

'Your phone call from home? Is everything all right?'

'There's a huge part of me that's a mother and the mother in me doesn't like working this case.'

'I'd advise you to ask to be pulled from it, but I know what your response would be. You'd say, *Another huge part of me is a police officer. I won't ask to be pulled. It makes me look weak and unprofessional.*' Dr Lamb smiled at Clay. 'It doesn't matter what awful things these people have done. We cannot tolerate a vigilante roaming round Liverpool doling out the death sentence. It doesn't matter what people think or say. To live in a civilised society we must make difficult choices and do things that sometimes go against our human nature.'

'It's as if you've read my mind. That's what I've been telling myself from the moment I knew about Wilson's past.' Clay looked at Jamieson's body on the rubber board. 'And now this.'

Dr Lamb placed her hand on Clay's right forearm, curling her fingers around her wrist. In the bright overhead lights of the mortuary, for a moment, the sight of her thin-skinned hand and the tender gesture sent Clay back in time to Sister Philomena and her gentle touch.

'I know you've got your husband to talk to about this at home. But if you need an extra pair of ears, call me any time, Eve,' said the pathologist.

Clay watched Dr Lamb return to her work and felt a weight lifting from her whole being. As the pathologist spoke to Harper, for a brief moment she even looked like Sister Philomena dressed in a pathologist's theatre clothes. The moment passed, and she whispered to Hendricks, 'I'm seeing things.'

'What was that, Eve?'

Clay pressed down on her feelings and commanded herself with a silent rebuke: *Work!*

'I can see the bruising on his neck and throat in keeping with strangulation as in the last case. Let's shave the hairline at the back of his head, see if the cause of death is the same as with the oh-so-charming Mr Wilson,' said Dr Lamb.

'The bookies won't be taking bets on it,' said Harper.

Harper rubbed water into the hair at the centre of Jamieson's neck and massaged shaving foam into it. Then, without looking, he took a cut-throat razor from the aluminium trolley behind him.

'Anything for the weekend, sir?' he said as he drew the edge of the razor across Jamieson's skin and hair.

Beneath the buzz of an overhead fluorescent light, Clay heard the rasping sound of Harper's razor on Jamieson's flesh and the hairs on her arms rose.

'Took us ages to find on the last one. Such a tiny yet lethal entry wound,' observed Dr Lamb.

Harper placed the razor back on the trolley and took a torch from it. He directed a beam of light where he had shaved Jamieson's neck and Dr Lamb crouched behind the corpse to take a close look.

'Yes, yes,' said Dr Lamb. 'It took us such a long time to work it out last time. But the cause of death is the same as Wilson's. Someone's pierced his brain with a two-millimetre-wide spoke, probably from a bicycle wheel. The spoke's been sharpened at the tip and down each side. The spoke went into the brain, and when it was inserted as far it could go, the killer used the spoke like a windscreen wiper, over and over and over. They... she certainly knew what they were doing. Harper, take some pictures of the entry wound, please.'

The pathologist looked at Clay and Hendricks. 'Same methodology as last time. Same methodology as Justin Truman aka

Vindici back in the day. She took Wilson to the point of passing out with strangulation. Then she entered his brain while he was conscious. Vindici was a creative killer. As copycats go, she's very good. This man died in agony. Then she took his genitals.'

As Harper and his assistant turned Jamieson's body on to its front, Clay felt the buzz of an incoming text on her iPhone; she ignored it to home in on the rectangular bald patch at the base of his neck.

Jamieson's skin tone was lighter than Wilson's and so the bloody dot inside the shaved skin was clearer to see.

As Harper's assistant took picture after picture of Jamieson's back, he said, 'Look at that! She's carved Vindici on his shoulder, almost like she's branded him as an animal on a farm.'

'No sign of any penetration to his anus,' said Dr Lamb. 'Count the whip wounds to the back of his legs. Judging by the narrow width of the cuts, she used the bicycle spoke to do this, I think.'

Clay looked at Jamieson under the harsh overhead fluorescent lights, at the dark hair that obscured his buttocks and legs, and was put in mind not of a farm animal but of an ape that by some freak malfunction of nature had morphed into the approximation of a man.

22

10.13 pm

Alone in the dark of a small bathroom, warmth flooded her heart, and a satisfaction that was even deeper than the glowing pride she'd experienced on the first outing to Aigburth Vale to visit David Wilson, a week and a half ago. She recalled how she'd hidden on the corner of Lugard Road, in the shadows of the school railings, and watched Sandra Wilson walk out of her house in Dundonald Road, get into her car and drive away, leaving her husband David all alone in the house.

With each passing day, the warmth that she'd gained from torturing and killing Wilson had slowly diminished until she was as cold as ice once more, cold enough to completely focus, cold enough to kill. And just as the warmth had faded, the peace in her mind which accompanied that warmth had crumbled and her night-dreams were once more filled with chaos.

She looked into the mirror over the sink, her eyes growing accustomed to the solid darkness of bathroom, the sodium street-light outside seeping through frosted glass into the bathroom just bright enough to make out the outline of her face and head in the glass.

Points of light shone in her eyes and reflected in the mirror; around her eyes, she saw white circles.

Pipes rattled, the faulty bath tap stuttered and leaked drips of water. With each drip she spoke into the mirror. 'He loves me, he loves me not, he loves me, he loves me not, he loves me!'

The dripping stopped and she fell silent but other words echoed inside her head.

'Of course he does? Of course he does...'

She felt a smile filling her face and could make out the patterns of black and white paint that covered her features.

Dead and alive. Alive and dead. Skeleton and shadow. Shadow and skeleton. Neither one thing nor another.

With warmth back in her heart and peace in her mind, she went back in time as she'd walked along Mather Avenue in the bitterly cold evening air, the wind lifting dry autumn leaves in random patterns on the pavement as she made her way to the second destination.

She remembered the feeling and the thoughts inside her as she took step after step.

Colder than the night that cloaks me.

More chaotic than the wind that scatters the leaves.

Passing the Merseyside Police Training Academy, on the other side of the dual carriageway, she pulled the hood of her blood-red coat over her head and watched a police car speed past her in the direction of Garston, while across the central island, an 86 bus, alive with light but with not a single passenger, rumbled towards the city centre.

She reached into the pocket of her coat, felt the solid handle of her Stanley knife and the first crumbs of returning warmth, the first drops of precious peace. In her backpack, she felt the weight of the tools that she would need, and, tucked neatly in the lining of her coat, her spoke.

Perfect. Perfect. Perfect.

She walked and walked. Time collapsed as she reached the lower 600s of Mather Avenue. The odd side of the road. Out of the teens and into the big houses of the 650s and 660s.

She tripped a security light at 671 and at 689 she looked at an empty driveway, saw the blinking red eye of a CCTV camera pointing out at the closed gate of the darkened, empty house.

Cameras held no terror for her, for how could a lens tell what she was, neither one thing nor another? How could they read what was and wasn't her?

As she approached 699 she could almost smell the interior of the house, even though she was yet to step inside that particular lair with its smell of air fresheners that did nothing to mask the foul stench of corrupted flesh.

A police car travelled at eighty miles per hour on the other side of the dual carriageway, siren wailing, as she walked into the shadow of a tree and became the tree and became the shadow, neither one thing nor another.

Through the cold and chaos, she carried on in silence, and went about her business: 695. 697. 699.

The drive. Nice car. Citreon. Shiny and new.

As she passed the rear door, she dug the lethally sharp tip of her Stanley knife into the car's paintwork and, carrying on slowly up the path, drew a continuous curving pattern, up and down, across the driver's side, past the door, along the body to the headlights. Up and down. Down and up. Not one thing nor another.

The security light came on as she reached the open porch at the front door.

She looked down. Flat black shoes from Clarks. White socks pulled up to the knees. Red duffel coat a size too big for her body.

Now, in the mirror in her bathroom, she could see her face because a band of cloud that concealed the moon had passed by, and she laughed at the memory of the way he'd looked when he saw her painted face.

She laughed and it echoed in the confined space of the bathroom.

Jamieson had opened the door.

She had sprayed deodorant into his wide-open eyes, the hiss of the spray drowned by the cry of fear and pain from the bottom of his being.

She laughed and the noise travelled in a circle around the walls of the bathroom, rippling from her heart at the memory of

Jamieson, the Human Abomination, falling back as she delivered five massive punches to his right ear, destroying his balance and turning him into human putty.

His Slut Wife, astonished and terrorised, gasped as she fell back under his weight, the crack of her skull as it connected with the post at the bottom of the stairs like music.

She kicked him on his face, and the Human Abomination butted the Slut Wife with the back of his head.

She read their faces and knew they understood. This was their worst nightmare come true and they had no hope of escape.

The Slut Wife's head was bleeding and, as the Human Abomination ground the heels of his fists into his eyes, she reached a hand to the wet spot on her scalp. The Slut Wife opened her mouth to speak, to beg for mercy, but closed her mouth when she hissed at her for silence.

There could be no mercy for those who have had no mercy.

The Slut Wife looked up at her, her body heaving with sobs as he wept and made noises like an animal with its leg trapped between the jaws of a metal trap.

She took the My Little Pony backpack from her shoulders and, taking out two rags, stuffed one in his mouth and showed the other to the Slut Wife.

The Human Abomination rolled right on to the floor and passed out. She kicked him in his back but he didn't react. She gripped the Slut Wife's face and squeezed the cheeks hard, stared into her terrified eyes.

She laughed deep inside the redness of her hood and the Slut-Wife let out a feeble *ha ha*.

She laughed again, longer, louder, harder this time, poked the Slut Wife in between the breasts and she responded by laughing as best she could.

Ha ha ha ha ha ha ha ha.

The Slut Wife laughed as if she didn't have a care in the wicked world.

The Slut Wife laughed, even though her husband was coming

round now and weeping at the bottom of the stairs in the hall behind them.

Ha ha ha ha ha, laughed the Slut Wife. Mechanical and alone now because she had stopped laughing in the depths of her blood-red hood.

Ha ha ha ha ha...

She swung her arm back and slammed the palm of her hand at full force into the Slut Wife's laughing face, silencing her as she dropped to the floor. She stuffed the rag into the woman's mouth and watched terror rising in her eyes at the sight of a Stanley knife coming closer to her face.

The Slut Wife's words were buried in the dense rag, but she pointed at the Human Abomination, and pleaded with her eyes. She plucked the rag from the Slut Wife's mouth as the Human Abomination crawled three steps towards the door.

Exhausted, he stopped, looked at the Slut Wife, silently pleading with her to help him.

'*Do it to him! Don't do it to me*,' said the Slut Wife. '*Kill him if you want to but spare me.*'

23

11.01 pm

In the shadows at the entrance of the Yewtree Road car park in Calderstones Park, DS Bill Hendricks stood outside his car and watched Carol White's headlights swoop between the stone gateposts. Painfully aware of the time, Hendricks followed at speed towards her vehicle as she parked it under the skeletal braches of an oak tree.

Carol turned off her headlights and flicked on the little light above her head.

To Hendricks she looked as though she had just been hit with considerable force. She stared straight ahead, mouth open, eyes fixed and wide.

Stepping from the darkness, Hendricks jangled his car keys and called her name, firmly but kindly, 'Carol, it's me, Bill.'

When she looked at him, Hendricks had a fleeting insight into what it was like to be a ghost. She leaned across the empty passenger seat and unlocked the door.

As he sat and closed the door, he asked, 'Are you all right?'

Carol looked directly at him, pushing her blond hair behind her ears, the blue of her eyes accentuated by the dark rings beneath them. For a moment, Hendricks thought the power of speech had deserted her.

'I had to get out, Bill, I just had to.'

He read her face. The last time he had seen her, as she took a break from trawling through the pornographic films found on David Wilson's laptop, she had seemed calm and tearful in equal measure. Now she looked lost.

She dropped her window with one hand and produced a packet of cigarettes with the other.

'Do you mind?' she asked, lighting up.

'I thought you gave up?'

'I did. When I got pregnant after all that IVF. Damien's three now.'

'So what made you go back to it?' he asked, knowing the answer and looking at the time on her dashboard.

'When I began trawling through the laptop and pen drives discovered at Wilson's den.' She blew a stream of smoke into the darkness.

'But, Carol, you've seen so much…' He left the semi-concluded question in the tight space between them.

'Yes, I've seen so much filth, so much violent oppression and heartless perversion, you'd think I'd be bomb-proof.'

'That's true but you're only human.'

'So are the children who I watch on film being abused. So are the adults abusing them. Suddenly I've gone from being numb and professional to this feeling like my entire skin's crawling and the blood in my veins is toxic.'

'Do you feel you *need* to come off the job? Get reassigned—?'

'I can't!' she interrupted. 'I've got the biggest overview of what Wilson and so many others used to watch for pleasure and I'm trying to work out if there was a connection between what he watched and what killed him.' She drew in a lungful of smoke.

Hendricks knew she had a point.

'If someone else takes over they'll have to either rely on my reports or go back to square one. It's a time-waster and we simply have no time to lose.' A cold breeze blew through the open window and silent tears rolled down Carol's face.

'I've read all your reports. You've seen some grim stuff.'

'Yeah.'

Her small, forlorn voice made Hendricks want to help her as quickly as he could. 'Have you seen something tonight that's upped the ante on what you've already seen?' he asked, wondering if that was humanly possible.

'No,' she replied immediately. 'It wasn't good. How could it be? It was awful. But was it the worst? No.' As she flicked the cigarette butt out of the car, Hendricks realised she'd smoked it in four or five drags. 'But I sat there watching my laptop and suddenly my head felt like it was made of glass and about to explode into thousands of splinters. I could feel the tears rolling down my face and I wondered why? Why has this section of film affected me like this? I rolled it back to the point where I was aware I'd started crying. At first I couldn't see. I couldn't connect the action on screen to me snapping inside. It was a boy who I knew by sight. I've watched him grow older online. What Wilson had on his computer was new to me but it was a boy I'd seen from some other fucker's treasure trove of misery.'

Hendricks placed a hand on her shoulder and encouraged, 'Keep going!'

'After five reruns it clicked. It was the little boy's face. It was his eyes in particular but his face... He looked... bored, like it was so normal and such a regular part of his life that he was tiring of it but it had no end in sight. Like his whole spirit had been broken and sucked out of him, leaving just a physical shell for the gratification of others. Their pleasure was the only point of his existence. I saw brokenness in a way I'd never seen it before. I saw the thousands of victims condensed into one little boy. As the woman he was masturbating climaxed, she made this noise in her throat like a wild animal. He yawned.' What colour there was drained from her face and she opened the driver's door wide.

'How old was the boy?' asked Hendricks.

'About four.' She leaned closer to Hendricks. 'Every time I close my eyes, I see his face as if he was right in front of me.'

'I know how much you're hurting,' said Hendricks. 'And that pain isn't pleasant but it's a good thing that you can still be affected by the things you see. I've seen others doing your job turn to stone.'

In the silence that followed, Hendricks nursed a bleak notion and asked her, 'How do you feel towards paedophiles?'

'I hate them, every last one of them. And I'm glad Wilson and Jamieson have been murdered. If they're dead they can't harm any child.'

'Are you talking to your husband about this, Carol?'

'My husband?'

'He knows you inside out. He can help you in ways I can't.'

'My husband? My husband walked out on me three weeks ago.'

Carol turned her body away and leaned over the ground. She vomited on to the tarmac. Hendricks placed a hand on the centre of her back, felt the beginning of convulsive sobbing.

'Take a deep breath, Carol, hold it, take control.' Hendricks stroked her back until the rising storm subsided and she sat up, wiping her mouth with the back of her right hand. 'You're a human being first and a police officer second. You can call me anytime.' He dabbed the tears from her face and then gave her the tissue.

'Thanks, Bill. You'd better get back to Mather Avenue but before you do...' She handed him a brown envelope.

'What's this?'

'It's a picture of the little boy who's breaking my heart. With the filthy cow who's abusing him.'

Hendricks resisted the urge to decline and put the envelope in his coat pocket. 'I've got to go, Carol.'

With an overwhelming weight of sadness, Hendricks waited at the wheel of his car until Carol White was gone. He took out his phone and texted Clay.

24

11.05 pm

Riley stood near the bottom of the stairs of 699 Mather Avenue, concluding that the killer had not only taken the landline telephone but had taken the address book that probably sat beside it. She figured the logic of such a theft. It took away a set of investigative shortcuts for the police and it gave the killer a potential treasure trove of future hits.

Show me your company, Riley remembered her grandmother's favourite axiom, *and I'll show you who you are.*

'Gina!' called Terry Mason from upstairs. 'I'm in the study. I've got the roll-top desk and its drawers open, just as you asked.'

She ran quickly up the stairs and found herself in a room bare except for an open roll-top desk with four drawers, a desk seat, a pair of grey metal filing cabinets and an empty bin. Mason took a series of pictures of the empty surface of the desk and before she could ask why he was photographing it, she saw on the clean surface a laptop-sized rectangle at the centre hemmed in by dust.

Riley looked down at the skirting board near the bottom of the roll-top desk and saw a black plug in the electrical socket, a cable, a transformer and another length of cable leading to a jack plug.

'The laptop,' said Riley, thinking aloud. 'I think the killer's taken it, depriving us of another vital piece of evidence.'

'You sound depressed, Gina. Let me cheer you up a little. Come and have a look see at this.' Mason opened the top-left hand drawer to reveal a mini-junkyard of stationery, small coins, a ball of string, junk.

'Looks like a load of old shite but you never know,' said Riley.

'I'll sort through it, don't you worry.'

Riley turned her attention to the top right-hand drawer and felt disappointed when she saw a smartly produced portfolio marked 'Home Sweet Home Property Development and Management'. 'Must've changed the name and taken the words Steven and Jamieson off any of his company's stuff when it came out he's an evil little fucker,' she said. She took the document and placed it in the evidence bag that Mason handed her. 'What's in the bottom drawers, Terry?'

'Bottom left's empty. Wait for it, Gina.' He closed the top right-hand drawer and opened the bottom right-hand drawer.

She smiled. 'If I wasn't married and you weren't so ugly, I'd kiss you.' She reached into the drawer and took out a green leather-bound address book.

Riley opened it, flicked through the pages and saw it was crammed with handwritten names and addresses.

Sergeant Paul Price, Mason's assistant, entered the room.

'When we're done here, we'll take the filing cabinets to Trinity Road and sort them out there, Pricey.'

'Thanks, Terry,' said Riley, holding up Steven Jamieson's address book.

'Happy hunting, Medusa!' replied Mason.

25

11.13 pm

The only light on in the incident room of Trinity Road police station was the lamp on DC Barney Cole's desk. Eyes pulverised by days and nights of trawling the internet to pin down Vindici websites, and reading document after document about the story of Justin Truman's criminal life, Cole drifted into a light slumber. But as soon as he drifted from consciousness, he was jarred back into it.

Bam bam bam.

He sat up suddenly and, before he could react, the door opened wide and Poppy Waters, mid-twenties but looking years younger and with eyes that brimmed with intelligence behind her black-rimmed spectacles, almost skipped into the room with her open laptop in her arms.

'I'm going to blow your mind, Barney!' Usually calm and reserved, Poppy looked set to do a cartwheel.

'What's happening?'

'Oh my God!'

'Poppy!' he said. 'Have a seat.' He rolled a seat from Hendricks's desk and placed it beside him.

'I think our luck's turning,' said Poppy. She placed her laptop on Cole's desk and ran an index finger along the trackpad to bring the dark screen back to life. As Poppy typed in her password, she said, 'So we've currently got two Vindici websites being run within the Liverpool area. We used geolocation software to establish that.'

'Have you found out *where* in Liverpool?'

'No. So I went to the Regional Internet Registry for Europe, the Réseaux IP Européens Network. I've given them all that we have and I've just had a phone call back from a Françoise Flamini. I told her it was within the context of a murder investigation and she stayed behind in her own time to work on it. She says she can mine for a closer match by using other data to narrow it down further, to a neighbourhood or an address even. She'll pick it up again in the morning.'

'You know, Poppy, I always liked the French. Is there anything else?'

'Oh yeah, I've got to show you this. I've been monitoring both Liverpool Vindici sites on an hourly basis to see if I can register any new or unusual activity. Look at this.'

Justin Truman's mugshot, the one taken when he was arrested, came up on the home page with the name 'VINDICI' in bold red letters above his head. She rolled the cursor to the gallery tab.

'Look what's come up in the last hour.'

She clicked the gallery and an image appeared that Cole had never seen before came on screen. It was a man in a white suit who looked nothing like Justin Truman in the Metropolitan Police's mugshot.

'This is him,' said Poppy. 'Justin Truman. Vindici. One of the Liverpool websites posted it; the other hasn't.'

Cole wondered how he could throw cold water over her without making her wet.

'It's the only photograph of him since he escaped from the prison convoy,' said Poppy.

'Justin Truman had thick dark hair. This man has short platinum-white hair—'

Poppy grabbed Cole's wrist, the first time she had touched him. 'Look at the buildings in the background. It's a Mexican town. Look at the people around him. All dressed as skeletons and corpses. He's the only one who isn't, Barney. Look at his eyes.'

She zoomed in on his face and his eyes shone with kindness and light, smiling, always smiling.

A shiver ran through Cole's core. 'Show me the mugshot, Poppy.'

She returned to the home page and Cole examined Truman's eyes.

'The gallery picture please.'

He looked at the eyes of the man in the white suit, the man in the sunshine walking in the procession for the Day of the Dead.

'Mugshot, Pop.' He looked at the image and felt fire rip through his head. He examined the bone structure of Truman's face following his arrest. 'Gallery, please.'

The cheekbones, chin and nose on both pictures now seemed almost identical to Cole but the closest similarity was in the eyes. Cole's body turned to stone. 'My God, Poppy Waters, you have just blown my mind. That looks like it *is* Justin Truman. In Mexico.'

'Look at what he's holding in his hand, Barney, and look what he's pointing to.'

Cole focused on the newspaper Vindici was holding. *Mexico Star*. He was indicating the date: *14 Octubre 2019*. 'The day David Wilson was murdered. And he was in Mexico at the time.' He reached for his iPhone.

'The person who runs this website absolutely adores Vindici. Quote: *The greatest human being to have ever walked the face of the earth.* Quote: *Angel in human shape and true champion of children everywhere.*'

'You did better than well. You did brilliantly. Get a copy of this picture to Clay, Stone, Hendricks, Riley, me and the rest of the team.' He dialled Clay's number.

'I already have done,' said Poppy.

'Keep bugging the service providers for any data whatsoever about these two websites and feed it to your contact in France. Great work, Poppy!'

Clay connected. 'Barney, I just got the picture and an email from Poppy. Just double-checking. It was posted on a Liverpool-based website, right?'

'Yes and I believe it's definitely Justin Truman. Looks like he's in Mexico.'

He heard her opening her car door.

'I've just come out of the post-mortem. I'm heading back to Mather Avenue now. With the European RIR on our side, it looks like we're closing in on someone who's in direct touch with Justin Truman, someone who maybe knows who our girl is, someone who may even be our girl.'

As her car door shut, Cole asked, 'Anything you want me to do, Eve?'

'Yes.' Her engine sparked into life and she pulled away. 'I want to know more about Justin Truman. He wasn't always a serial killer. Who was he before he became Vindici?'

26

11.23 pm

As she drove on to Edge Lane, Clay remembered that buildings in the neighbourhood had changed. St Michael's was no longer a Catholic care home for children but was now student accommodation.

Gripping the wheel, Clay shivered as she saw the disused Littlewoods Building and the big news of twelve months standing: Money from the Americas had been attracted to the huge disused Art Deco building and in recent weeks work had started on making it safe and redeveloping the interior.

Clay looked at the entrance to Botanic Gardens and wished in vain that James Peace would walk out of the park on to Edge Lane to greet her.

She gave in to a momentary but impossible fantasy, that the grown-up version of Jimmy would leave the park and flag her car down as he crossed the dual carriageway. She pictured herself pulling up and walking to meet him halfway. As they embraced, she would ask, '*What did you say to me that last time, Jimmy, when I was at Mrs Tripp's window and you were in the back of the police car?*'

Clay pulled over, half on the pavement, half on the road, and looked across the broad expanse of Edge Lane and whispered, 'Rufus? Rufus!'

Clay stepped out of her car and, even though Botanic Gardens was illuminated by the bright lights overhead, she pictured it as it had been many years earlier, drowned in natural autumn sunlight.

Deep in her brain, a door opened and the still image of that day turned into a slow-motion film. Even though her mind was full of a day years ago when the weather had been hot, the sun shining and the entire population of St Michael's Catholic Care Home for Children was out playing in the green fields of Botanic Gardens, the memory felt full of shadows and silent secrets.

Clay looked at the time on the dashboard – 11.25 in red LED lines – and recalled a moment from her childhood when she had been out walking on Mason Street with her protector Sister Philomena. She remembered laughing at an old lady as a bead of sweat dripped from the end of her nose like a dewdrop.

'You'll be old yourself one day,' said Clay, out loud, recalling Sister Philomena's words. It had been the closest to a telling-off that she had ever had from Sister Philomena.

'*I'm sorry.*'

Philomena squeezed her hand. It was OK.

'*The only ones you should laugh at, Evette*' – her full name, used when Philomena wanted to make a point stick – '*are the Devil and his followers. It's the last thing they'll expect you to do and the thing they'll like least.*'

Eve switched back to the day out in Botanic Gardens.

With her back turned momentarily to the fun and games on the grass, Eve had looked with awe at the huge Littlewoods Building on the other side of the park.

She gazed at the enormous white body and the tower that rose from the centre of the building. *A submarine*, she thought, *not curved but all straight lines and sharp corners*. She imagined it coming down from the skyline, sinking under Edge Lane into an imaginary arm of the River Mersey and setting off for the Pier Head and beyond to the Irish Sea.

'Here you are, Eve…' His voice came from behind her. Male, gentle, a voice that seemed to float up to the blue sky. She turned. He loomed over her and the sun was behind his head, obscuring his face. She knew his name. Christopher. But he had only been working at St Michael's for a few weeks and he had never spoken to her. Just watched her. On a few occasions she'd turned suddenly and seen him. Watching. Unsmiling.

His arm reached out and he offered her a double-coned Mr Whippy ice cream smothered in sweet raspberry sauce.

She took the ice cream from him and felt the warmth of his palm on the biscuit of the cone. 'Thank you, Christopher.'

She looked around. None of the other kids were holding ice creams. The music of the ice-cream van cruising the busy child-dense neighbourhood sounded ghostly.

'What's that music?' she asked aloud. 'From the ice-cream van?'

'It's "Für Elise" by Beethoven,' replied Chris. 'Do you like it?'

'I don't know. It's kind of sad.'

'You look awfully hot, Eve,' he said. 'Hot enough to buy an ice cream for.'

A cloud got in the way of the sun and his face became clear, his pale blue eyes and his stony smile.

'Lick it before it melts and drips into the grass.'

She half turned away – she didn't know why but she did – and dug her tongue into the fruity surface and the sweet body of the soft white ice cream. Eve drew a cocktail of ice cream and sauce into her mouth.

'You look like you're enjoying that, Eve.'

She swallowed the ice cream.

'Für Elise' stopped.

'Thank you,' she said, walking away towards the fun and games.

'Eve, we need to talk about Rufus!'

'Rufus?' She stopped, turned. 'But he's either run away or been run over on Edge Lane.'

To her left, traffic zoomed in two directions down both carriageways of Edge Lane, and its roar echoed from the walls of the Littlewoods Building. The notion of Rufus being flattened on the unforgiving highway brought a pricking of tears to the backs of her eyes.

The jingle-jangle music of the ice-cream van started up again and Beethoven's melody floated towards her.

'Or...' she said and hoped and prayed, 'he's still in the neighbourhood but has had to move on a few streets because of a scrap with some other stray cat.'

'Well, Rufus has definitely, definitely done neither of those two things what you said no more, Eve Clay.'

'How do you know that, Christopher?'

She felt melted ice cream, warm and sticky, crawling down the back and heel of her hand.

'It's all over your hand, Eve. You need to lick it off.'

'Rufus? Just what do you mean by that?'

'I mean I was, like, one of the last people to leave the house when we were all walking over here. Yeah? Yeah. Like, all the doors and windows were open because it was so hot like. So Mrs Tripp says to me, *Chris, here are the keys. Go round and lock all the doors, shut the windows and follow the rest of us to Botanic Gardens.*'

Within a slither of a moment, she said, 'Why would Mrs Tripp give you such an important job when you've only been working there for a few weeks?'

He was silent for a moment, made a noise, *mmmn*, and then said, 'Good question, good question, Eve.' Silence. 'I said exactly what you said to Maggie Anderson who's been there, like, years. She said to me, *It's an initiation, she throws big jobs at new people to test them out, see if they're any good.* Anyway, do you want to know about Rufus or what no more?'

'I want to know about Rufus.'

She looked at the fun and games and made out Jimmy Peace, the nicest but the toughest boy in the home, motionless in the middle of it all, watching her, and she wished he'd stop standing and come running over.

With her free hand, Eve waved to him and, for the first time in the years she had known him, he turned away. Christopher's eyes twitched towards the bustling crowd. She looked in the direction Christopher was exploring and saw nothing but children playing.

'Rufus?' she urged him, unaware she had just dropped the melting ice-cream cone into the grass.

'The last but one door I locked was the back door, the kitchen door leading out into the garden – but guess what, Eve, guess what?'

The door in Eve's memory slowly started closing and the pictures in her head started fading yet the words *but guess what, Eve, guess what?* played out, over and over, as though there was a needle inside her stuck in scratched vinyl.

But guess what, Eve, guess what? But guess what, Eve, guess what? But guess what, Eve, guess what? echoed over music from that day: the music of the ice-cream van, the melody of Beethoven's 'Für Elise'.

'Guess what I heard, Eve, when I was locking the door? Guess what I heard, Eve, coming from the bushes at the bottom of the garden?'

Mechanically, Clay got back into her car and began driving at speed down the deserted southbound carriageway of Edge Lane.

As the door of her memory slammed shut, she accelerated to eighty miles per hour and when the slamming door echoed, she heard herself say one word.

'Rufus?'

27

11.33 pm

Cole looked at the image on his laptop of Justin Truman in the Day of the Dead procession, and felt the twinkling of a connection with a man who he furtively admired.

He settled at his desk to email Sergeant Eduardo García of the Puebla City Police.

Dear Eduardo,

Please find attached a photograph that has just come to our attention. We firmly believe it is a picture of Justin Truman aka Vindici, a fugitive from the law in the UK. I would be grateful if you could circulate it to your colleagues locally and nationally with a view to looking out for Justin Truman and bringing him in to custody. Also, would it be possible to identify the location where this picture was taken? Thank you for your help and cooperation.

Yours sincerely
Detective Constable Barney Cole
Merseyside Police Constabulary

Cole copied in Clay, Stone, Hendricks and Riley and fired off the email. Then he picked up the receiver of his landline phone and called Clay. 'Where are you, Eve?'

'I've just turned off Edge Lane and I'm on Queens Drive heading for Mather Avenue.'

'You want to hear Justin Truman's back story?'

'Most certainly. Thank you, Barney.'

'It's dull but patchy, an unremarkable childhood and adolescence in Tamworth, growing up with a doting mum with mobility problems and visual impairment, not blind exactly but she wouldn't get a driver's licence.'

'He was a child carer then?' asked Clay.

'Yes, in an era when child carers truly were an invisible army.'

The word *invisible* resonated in Clay's head as she pulled up at the traffic lights at the junction of Queens Drive and Thingwall Road.

'Then there's a great big grey patch in his late teens. He went to London aged nineteen and more or less vanished from the face of the earth. Came back to Tamworth and his dying mother aged twenty-one. Vanishes off the face of the earth again and crops up seventeen years later as a serial killer using a Day of the Dead timetable and fully blown symbolic system.'

'I've got a big *why*,' said Clay. 'Any fresh daylight on why the Day of the Dead festival is so important to him?'

'The only person who could tell you that is Vindici himself. He really dished up information in interview and at trial but he clammed up on that one.'

She massaged her disappointment with a little mental maths. 'So that gives our girl about a fortnight to top other paedos.'

'Basically, yeah.'

'She's going to go out again, Barney.'

'For sure.'

In her mind, Clay saw Vindici's eyes in the Met's mugshot and the picture of him in the Day of the Dead procession, and understood how a woman could fall hopelessly in love with an iconic stranger, so much in love that she would kill for the object of her flawed passion.

'For sure, Barney. For sure she will.'

28

11.53 pm

As Clay stepped out of her car at 699 Mather Avenue, she saw Detective Sergeant Terry Mason carrying a large plastic stacker box to a white transit van parked in front of the furniture removal lorry she had ordered. Behind him, his assistant Sergeant Paul Parker wheeled a metal filing cabinet on a trolley.

Steven Jamieson's Citreon was loaded on to a Merseyside Constabulary car-carrier trailer.

'We're almost done now,' said Mason to a group of five non-uniformed officers standing near the gate of the house. He hung on to the stacker box as if it was a small child. 'Eve wants the house stripped and the floorboards up. If you come up with anything, anything that stands out, call me back immediately!'

Dressed in protective white suits, the quintet of officers walked in silence against the cold wind that blew down Mather Avenue.

Parker pushed the filing cabinet up a ramp on to the Scientific Support transit van, as Detective Sergeant Gina Riley came towards Clay clutching a book.

'How's it going, Gina?'

'I've been busy,' said Riley. 'I've worked through his address book and I've looked at some documents from his filing cabinets related to his business. According to what I've seen, there are no personal links to anyone on Merseyside. His address book's full of details of contractors, a lawyer called Daniel Campbell and estate agents in Sheffield and the South Yorkshire area. As soon as he got in the shit with our brothers and sisters across the Pennines, he transferred all his assets into his wife's name, closed his company down and reopened it trading under a new name. His wife took over the reins while he was inside and as soon as he got out and moved here, he took it back over and ran the business in Yorkshire from Merseyside.'

'Good work, Gina. Did you speak to anyone?'

The wind whipped the trees on the central embankment and it sounded like the sky was shushing the earth into silence.

'His solicitor, Daniel Campbell.' Riley paused and laughed.

'Go on.'

'I got him on his home landline. He tried to deny all knowledge at first, dismissed me as a crank caller, threatened me with the police. I said, *Cut out the middleman, I'll have a word with me.* I gave him two minutes to drop the bullshit and call me back. Which he did. He pretty much confirmed everything I'd worked out. Gave me a nice little lecture on the law being impartial and fair to all.'

Sweating in spite of the bitter cold, Mason and Parker came to Eve's side and waited for her, their breath heavy and white on the night air.

'What do you want me to do now?' asked Riley.

'Hand over all Steven Jamieson's contact details to South Yorkshire Police and get your head round the task of organising the uniformed officers for their joyous day ahead, warning child sex offenders on Merseyside to watch their backs. Anything comes up from their dealings with the paedos, you're the first point of contact.'

Clay turned to Mason.

'Go on, Terry. Show me what you've got on the transit.'

Clay and Riley followed Mason and Parker. Mason opened the back doors and Parker shone bright torchlight inside the vehicle.

'The brass bed and mattress that Jamieson died on. We didn't get single print from it.'

Parker illuminated the details.

'That's no surprise, Terry,' said Clay, thinking back to Vindici's heyday. 'She'll have been wearing white gloves. Justin Truman always did.'

'We've got the chair his wife was tied to, the TV set, DVD player and Sky box. We cut out a bloody section of carpet from the hall and the bottom of the stairs – that's in the bubble wrap. The killer must've battered the shit out of him as soon as she was over the threshold.'

'She's a hard-knock, for sure,' said Parker.

'That's right, Paul,' said Clay. 'Dr Lamb said she used her fists on Jamieson's head, not a blunt instrument. An up-close-and-personal revenge killing.'

Parker's torch lit up the filing cabinets.

'What's in them?' asked Clay.

'Initially, it looks totally related to his property business in South Yorkshire,' said Riley.

'We'll fine-tooth-comb through the filing cabinets once we've fired off the other evidence to the relevant people.' Mason tapped the list out as he spoke, right index finger on left-hand palm. 'We've got both sets of clothes they were wearing when their unannounced visitor called and the bags you gave us, including the one with a blond hair on the ropes, they're at the lab already.'

Clay heard two sets of footsteps and recognised them as Hendricks and Stone approaching.

'When the guys have emptied the house,' said Mason, 'we're coming back to strip out all the carpets. You can't see it because all their other belongings are in the way but we've got their marital bed, bedding and mattress at the front of the space.'

As Hendricks and Stone flanked Clay, Mason glanced at the small stacker box in his hands.

'What's in there?' asked Clay.

'The goose that laid the golden egg, I think,' said Mason. 'When we were picking up the mattress, I felt something heavy and solid inside the fabric. OK, we know the killer's pulled the laptop from his study but she didn't hang around long enough to go truly rooting. I found a cut-out in a section of mattress on his side of the bed, thirty-six centimetres long by three centimetres high. I stuck my hand inside and guess what he's been sleeping on?'

He lifted the lid of the stacker and Clay felt a smile light up her entire face.

'His really *special* laptop,' said Hendricks.

Clay looked at the black Lenovo laptop, the cable, plug and transformer, and saw an infinity of opportunities for the darkest truth.

'It's locked, but fully operational,' said Mason.

'Well done, Terry. Take it to Trinity Road right now. Get Poppy Waters to crack it open.'

Parker closed the back doors of the transit van.

'We'll have one last walk through the house, Paul,' said Mason to his assistant. 'Double-double-check everywhere.'

'I'm coming with you,' said Riley as she followed Mason and Parker back to 699 Mather Avenue.

Clay looked at Hendricks and Stone, read the question on their minds and answered it.

'I'd like you to pool all the information we have, comparing and contrasting the Wilson and Jamieson murders, compose an email, let me check it out and edit it, and then we'll copy the whole team in with the message *Read, read, read.* Team meeting, seven am, incident room, Trinity Street. But I want everyone there for six forty-five.'

Clay turned at the sound of the door of 697 Mather Avenue opening and saw a bewildered-looking man in the doorway.

'Is it true, what they're saying about him on the radio?' he asked. 'But he looked so normal. And he lived so close. Next door. My God.'

'I'm sorry this has distressed you,' said Clay, wishing for arrival of the arrival of daylight. 'Did you hear or see anything?'

He thought about it.

'Not a thing.'

Part Two
The Souls of Returning Children

Day Two
Thursday,
24th October 2019

29

3.15 am

Pale moonlight poured into the darkened room though a skylight directly above her head and she felt connected to every distant piece of the universe. Lying on the floor, she interlocked her fingers, placed her hands on the wall of muscle at her core and felt a throb of pleasure at the physical memory of squeezing Steven Jamieson's throat until his eyes bulged.

In the ethereal light, a picture of Vindici formed in the air, an imaginary hologram projected from her mind. Vindici, eyes smiling not at just anything, but directly at her. Justin Truman, photographed by the police, freshly arrested for murdering ten so-called men. Vindici Justin Truman looking calm, happy and satisfied with himself for a series of jobs well done.

Vindici Justin Truman, being neither one thing nor the other, like me, just like me…

The projection of Vindici's face descended towards her; his eyes, shining with loving kindness, locked on hers and, although his lips were sealed, she heard his voice falling from the stars.

Neither one thing nor the other, like us, just like us…

And his features dissolved into another face.

How different he looked now from the picture the Metropolitan Police took of him on the day he was arrested. His eyes hovered inches above hers and, as she drew in the sweetness of his breath through her nostrils, desire rose up inside her like a trapped moth beating its feathery wings within the walls of her iron pelvis, sending wave after warm wave to the space between her legs.

Vindici Justin Truman tilted his head, placed his lips close to her ear and she felt the soft curve of his lips on her earlobe as he whispered something hot and inviting.

'Come with me to the carnival. Come with me to the Day of the Dead, when we welcome back the spirits of dear departed loved ones.'

The picture of him flashed through her, caught the corner of her soul and came alive. He smiled at her and he turned back to follow the human skeletons, and the white sleeve of his arm descended on her shoulders as she processed with him through the heat-baked and noisy street. The moving pictures faded and she sighed as he slowly pulled away from her ear and his face drifted over hers.

His lips settled against hers and she drank in his breath, and with his breath she absorbed his essence, his goodness and strength, his thirst for natural justice and the sheer weight of his righteous anger, and she was transformed from female to male, from male to female and two became one and one was neither one thing nor the other.

'Like us, just like us,' she whispered as his face faded and re-formed as their face, his and hers, yet not his or hers.

Within the mind, a picture formed of a small girl on a hot day, walking alone and calling, 'Rufus?' It was a story someone had published on a Vindici website. Hovering above, the mind's eye saw someone was following the girl, someone very, very bad. But the bad someone was followed by the infinitely good someone.

She had gone on to read everything she could find about Eve Clay on the internet.

And with each step the little girl took, she aged a year and by the time she reached the corner of the street where she lived, she was a fully grown woman. The fully grown woman spoke.

'My name is Eve Clay,' said the woman charged with hunting

her down. 'And I too am neither one thing nor another. Part woman. Part demon.'

The mind's picture erupted and a devastating firestorm wiped everything away and the marrow in her bones changed to the marrow in their bones.

Eyes open. Look up.

Through the skylight, nuclear fires exploded on a distant star against the abominable frozen wastes of space.

30

4.30 am

Entering the empty incident room at half past four, Clay turned on the lights and thought her eyes were playing tricks on her. Her whole attention was captured by an explosion of colour on her desk where a huge bouquet of vivid red dahlias in a plastic bowl of water stood out against the bland greys and browns of the work space.

Sitting at her desk, she looked at the flowers and her mind turned to her husband Thomas. She looked at the time and decided that she wouldn't wake him, that she would thank him later in the morning when she went home to see him and their son Philip before he went to nursery.

'How can that be?' she asked herself, thinking back to her last movements in Trinity Road police station, and thinking, too, *But Thomas always gives me red roses.*

Clay picked up the bouquet and trying to drink in the aroma, found there was no discernible smell as she looked inside the flowers for a card. She dug her fingers into the stems and pulled out a small white envelope.

Evette Clay, dahlias, she read the writing on the envelope. *Sweets for the sweet.*

She tore the envelope open and pulled out a white card bearing the same disguised block-capital handwriting as on the envelope.

'Jesus...' The word rose from her like a blessing dressed up as a curse. '*Come and find me and all this will stop. Or shall I find you first?*' She read the words aloud and then silently, over and over, hearing Vindici's voice from the phone call and wishing he'd call again.

She picked up her landline receiver and connected to the custody sergeant on the front desk.

'Sergeant Penny Canter, how can I help?'

'Penny, it's Eve Clay.'

'Eve Clay as in you've either got a very attentive husband or a secret admirer?'

'When did the flowers show up?'

'Within the last half hour, I reckon. They were left at the front door.'

'Do me a favour, Penny. Have a flick through the CCTV and see if you can get a picture of the person dropping them off.'

'No problem. I'll do that right now.'

'It's the first time I've ever known flowers being left anonymously at the door of the station. Nobody saw anything?'

'Not that I know of, Eve.'

'OK. I'd be grateful if you could get on the CCTV. Thanks.'

She replaced the receiver, called up Google on her iPhone – *Dahlias facts* – and clicked on a link: *Ten things you (possibly) didn't know about dahlias.*

Next to a picture of a yellow star-like dahlia, innocent words danced from the page, gripped her scalp and made her look at the writing on the envelope and card.

Evette Clay.

She thought of her file in the cabinet in Mrs Tripp's office, her name in felt-tipped block capital letters.

Sweets for the sweet.

Long-forgotten childhood phantoms spun in the dark side of her brain.

'*Come and find me and all this will stop. Or shall I find you first?'* The menacing words, spoken to her so tenderly on the telephone, filled her with massive unease.

Why? Why dahlias?

She looked at the results of the Google search on her iPhone and replied to herself: *That's why!*

In silence she read the words: *Dahlias, the national flower of Mexico, were first discovered by Europeans when the Spanish invaders found them growing wild on the hillsides of Oaxaca.*

Clay ripped the sleeve in which the dahlias were packed and separated the flowers out, looking for anything that might have been accidentally or purposefully left within the gift. And found nothing.

Damp silence.

31

6.30 am

Eve Clay stood in the bay window of her bedroom in Mersey Road looking into the dull light of a new day and listening to the caw of seagulls circling the river at the bottom of her road.

She heard the front door of her house close and frowned when she saw her son Philip walk down the path and on to the pavement outside her home.

The noise of the seagulls was sucked into the water beneath their wings and, in the new-found silence, she heard a speck of advancing sound at the edge of her senses.

Wheels turning and the bray of a horse.

She banged on the window with the heel of her hand but there was no sound other than the wheels coming closer and the beat of a horse's heart beneath its heavy breath.

'Philip!'

Her mouth moved as she cried at the top of her voice, but all that came out was breath, and as it hit the window, her entire being was sucked into the glass, her being flattened and stretched within the thin, flat pane.

The cars parked outside her house dissolved as Philip stepped from the pavement into the middle of the road, his body and head transformed into a skeleton costume.

At the top of Mersey Road, a horse and cart turned the corner with a thin man in dark clothes and top hat holding the reins.

Philip stooped and picked up a red cat that Clay immediately recognised from her childhood. Rufus.

'Philip! Get back inside the house!'

Her voice echoed back inside the narrow expanse of glass as the horse drew the cart and driver down the road towards Philip.

In the empty cage at the driver's back, she heard the sobbing and wailing of every abducted child kept prisoner behind its black bars.

'Now! Now, Philip! Now!'

The horse stopped and the driver stepped off the cart, a bag of sweets in his hand. He offered the bag of sweets to Philip as he approached him. Philip looked up at the bedroom window and said, 'Goodbye!'

In the glass, Clay howled as Philip dipped his hand in the bag and pulled out a bolt of lightning that drenched the scene in an overwhelming haze of white light.

When the explosion of light faded away, everything had vanished except for a combination of sounds.

Wheels turning as the cart raced away. A horse whinnying beneath the crack of a savage whip. And Philip sobbing and crying, 'Mummy! Mummy! Mummy!'

Eve Clay sat up straight at her desk in the incident room in Trinity Road police station, tears in her eyes and her heart racing.

She looked at the clock, saw that she had slept for two hours and that exhaustion had hijacked her plan to go and sleep at home. She cursed the fact that she'd been beaten by fatigue.

As she looked around the empty room, relief swamped her, yet an ever-present anxiety came with it.

It had only been a dream, a bad, bad dream.

But what if?

What if?

32

6.45 am

Clay looked around the incident room and saw that everyone who'd been instructed to attend had arrived earlier than first planned. The atmosphere was tense and she tapped the bottom of her empty cup against her desk, bringing the room to silence.

'We'll begin the main meeting at seven, but I want to give you food for thought, and a major talking point amongst yourselves. I think we've got a massive internal problem.'

She made sure she made direct eye contact with every man and woman in the room before she carried on. No one was excluded from what was coming next.

'We've got a canary in our midst. It might be someone in this room. It might be someone from further afield who's working to support us in this investigation and who has access to sensitive and secret information. It might be – and I hope this is the case – it might be someone not connected to us but in the Constabulary and with that same access.'

She read the faces in the room and felt a glimmer of hope. No one looked twitchy; everyone met her eye. The glimmer died when she reminded herself that they were the most poker-faced group of detectives she had ever worked with.

'Before she died, Frances Jamieson informed the medics treating her in A & E that the killer in her home was female. *It's a woman! Just one woman!* These were her dying words.

'Last night, at the highly secret cremation of David Wilson, my iPhone went off and I received a message from the killer via the switchboard informing me that she's just killed Steven Jamieson, tortured his wife and there you go, Eve, here's the address, 699 Mather Avenue. Not only did she know where to find Jamieson, she knew the time and date of Wilson's cremation, and she timed the Jamieson murder to coincide with that cremation.'

Red-eyed and looking like a man picked on by the gods, Detective Constable Bob Rimmer half raised a hand. 'It could've been one of the undertakers,' he said.

'For now we can't rule anything out,' said Clay. 'But the pall-bearers knew nothing until the last minute. The only guy who knew they were officiating at David Wilson's cremation was the head honcho.'

'I guess a piece of me would like that to be the case,' said Rimmer.

'I don't like what I'm going to say now, but I've got to say it,' asserted Clay. 'I want you to watch each other carefully. And I want you to watch me. And I want you to watch any people ancillary to this investigation. If you see, hear or experience anything strange but with some definite substance, I want to know straight away. No information too big, no information too small. If you feel conflicted and you protect anyone who's passing out our secrets, you'll be following them out of the front door never to return. It's as simple as it's serious. Any questions?'

The room remained silent and the tension had become solemn.

'I'm sorry to get the day off to such a negative start, but I had no choice,' said Clay. 'OK, discuss amongst yourselves.'

She turned her back on the room and, against a rising babble of restrained voices, looked at the picture of Justin-Truman-in-the-sun, blond, tanned and happy at a joyous festival in a Mexican city.

Are you going to call me back, sometime, Justin? she thought. *I'd love to chat with you. Have a catch-up. Maybe you could give me a name. Like the name of your greatest fan who's carrying on your work right under my nose.*

'Who are the flowers from?' Riley came up beside Clay.

'It's either Vindici himself or she who is currently hunting in his footsteps. Take a look at this.' Clay pointed at the digits in the top left hand corner of the screen and the image beneath them.

'CCTV 24.10.19 04.05 am. The front door of Trinity Road police station and not a sign of life. Then all of a sudden...' said Clay.

On screen, the images unfolded. A young man in a grey track-suit, hood over his head, sprinted around the corner, threw the flowers at the door, turned and sprinted the way he had just come and out of the CCTV's eye.

'He's the errand boy,' said Riley.

'But who's he running the errand for?' asked Clay. 'If it's not Justin Truman then the flowers will have come from the Wilson and Jamieson killer. If we find him, we find her.'

33

6.45 am

She crossed Menlove Avenue at the lights outside the Derby Arms, clutching the plain black holdall in which she'd gathered her things and ignoring the marked police car that sailed past her in the direction of Hunts Cross.

As she walked to the lock-up garage overlooked by Dovercroft, a fourteen-storey residential tower block, she lowered her eyes to the ground, looking at the unremarkable tops of her cheap mass-produced training shoes, the bottoms of her charity-shop-sourced black jeans and the black padded anorak she'd found abandoned outside an over-full clothes bank in a supermarket car park, and smiled.

No one, she thought, *would look at you and guess. Just another badly dressed anonymous female in a world overfull of lonely women. The world sees you as this when you are another.*

She reached the double garage and, opening the lock, stooped to raise the door. The door was visible at street level from Menlove Avenue and overhead by dozens of windows on the tower block. A single-decker 76 bus sailed past. She looked and saw the only person on the bus was the driver, so she raised the door just enough to duck under it.

Inside her lock-up garage, she pulled the door down to within two centimetres of the ground and, taking a torch from the bag, lit up the darkened space.

'Hello,' she said, her voice dead against the flat walls and ceiling. The fridge in the corner whirred, greeting her back.

She took in the space as she walked to the far wall. A pair of female mannequins side by side. Two clothes rails near an open bag of fertiliser and deconstructed clocks. A bicycle propped against a wall. Unzipping her bag, she imagined the scene in the back bedroom at 699 Mather Avenue and, smiling, wished she could have hung around long enough to watch the Human Abomination being placed in a body bag by the mortuary technicians, wished she could have seen the look on the Slut Wife's lidless face when she was forced to identify the shit that was his corpse.

Placing the lantern at the feet of the mannequins, she felt that the place was transformed from an almost bare space into a shrine.

The two mannequins were life-sized. One was naked and one was dressed.

The dressed mannequin wore two items, a red duffel coat with the hood up and, beneath the hood, a blond wig. She looked them up and down, at their slender feminine legs and elegantly shaped bare feet. To her, their faces, with their inscrutable eyes and thin but perfectly sculpted red lips and delicate noses, were perfectly beautiful.

Putting down the black holdall and removing the blue woollen gloves from her hands, she placed the side of her face against the cheek of the naked mannequin and exhaled, watching the vapour rise as if *she* was breathing out, as if *she* had come to life.

She turned to the dressed mannequin and slipped her hand through the gap at the front of the duffel coat and cupped her hand around the hardness of the breasts. She slid her other hand up the coat and felt the cold closed plastic nothingness between her legs.

'I have a present for your naked sister. It is also a present for you.'

She steeled herself. There was work to do and time was finite.

She looked at the school uniforms hanging on the clothes rail, the grey cardigans, the white shirts and grey skirts. On the tray at the base of the clothes rail were neatly folded knickers and vests, white socks and polished black shoes. Beneath the shelf at the bottom of the second rail, she saw the tips of sharpened bicycle spokes against the cold grey floor.

Reaching into the holdall, she took out the present she had brought for them. She turned the mannequin in the coat to her undressed sister and opened the toggles.

Raising the present up through the first mannequin's legs and thighs, a shiver of pleasure ran through her. She lifted the straps and tied the buckle at the base of the mannequin's back. Her hand ran across the shaft of the hand-carved wooden phallus, attached to the leather harness, and she positioned the head between the legs of the other bald, naked mannequin.

The motor of the fridge revved, inviting her to the corner. She reached into the bag and took out a glass jar of pink-tinged white vinegar. In the jar floated Steven Jamieson's penis and testicles. She deposited the jar on the top shelf just as she had done with the jar in which she had preserved David Wilson's genitalia.

Returning to the mannequins, she reached down and stroked the smooth wooden phallus and, with her other hand, cupped her fingers between the legs of the female.

Tenderness consumed her and soon the space was no longer a lock-up garage, her dressing room for bloody and righteous murder. It became a palace of dreams where Vindici and she would consummate their love.

And she was no longer handling lifeless mannequins, it was he and she. She squeezed down on Vindici's manhood, felt the texture of her own body. Wood turned to flesh and plastic to the skin of her vagina; he entered her and she yielded to him.

She heard them speak in the rising passion, heard their hearts beating.

'Neither one thing,' said Vindici.

'Nor another,' she replied, yielding to him.

'Like us...' They spoke with one voice. 'Just like us.'

34

6.54 am

Clay sat at her desk flicking between two images of Justin Truman on her laptop.

She looked at the classic mugshot of Truman taken when he was arrested, an image she had seen in the newspapers and on TV in reports of his fluke arrest. Olive-skinned, handsome, his bright brown eyes shone with inner peace and happiness. Clay recalled reading a magazine article about one of the hundreds of lonely women who wrote to him in jail. She understood the deluge of mail, many proposing marriage, and devotion that would last until death and beyond. She focused on the smile that was absent from his lips but saw it stamped in his eyes.

She loaded up Google and typed in *Television news reports on the first day of Vindici/Truman's trial* and then hit Videos.

Loading up the first clip on YouTube, she saw Metropolitan Police motorcycle outriders ahead of a white prison van speeding towards the Old Bailey and throngs of people held behind a line of uniformed police officers. As the van approached, the crowd applauded and chanted, '*Vin-di-ci! Vin-di-ci! Vin-di-ci!*' When the vehicle sailed past, people cheered and threw red roses. It was like the return of a hero.

'Strange days.' Hendricks's voice came from behind her.

She closed down Videos and returned to the mugshot of Justin Truman.

'He was loved as much as the police who hunted him were hated,' said Clay. She clicked on to the picture of Justin-Truman-in-the-sun.

Truman appeared to be in a procession in Mexico. Dressed in an immaculate white suit and shirt, Truman had changed from the way he looked in the Met's mugshot, but it was still undeniably him. On either side of him were the backs of men and women dressed as skeletons following a procession heading towards a church.

'He's turned around,' said Clay. She took a moment to process the image. 'Stopped in the flow of the crowd and turned to pose for this photograph. It's the one he offered me through a third party. But why? Why, after years of nothing, does he make an appearance now?'

'And on a Liverpool-based Vindici website, when his copycat's active in the city?' added Hendricks.

Fuller in the face and tanned, it was his eyes that drew Clay's attention. He had the same smiling eyes as in the Met's mugshot and, although he looked older and his thick black hair was now short and platinum blond, there was something about him that made her uneasy, something she couldn't quite pin down.

The unease at her core sparked a sensation beneath her scalp, as if an ant was running in random patterns across the surface of her brain. She looked around the room, caught Barney Cole's eye and beckoned him with a smile. 'Over here, brainbox.'

She could hear in her voice how dry her mouth was and threw down half a cup of cold coffee as he made his way to her.

'Less of your sarcasm, Eve. What's up?'

She pointed at the picture of Justin Truman, smiling in the sun. 'Have you heard back from Sergeant Eduardo García about this?'

'He's circulated the picture locally and nationally, and he's working on identifying the manufacturer of the Weeping Child statuette. To be honest, I feel sorry for the guy. Huge swathes of Mexico has shut down for a fortnight, like it is round Christmas over here.' Cole looked at the image on Clay's laptop. 'What do you think he's up to, Eve?'

'He's making a statement,' said Clay. 'Years and years of reported sightings on every single continent but no photographs. Maybe it's a seal of approval for the copycat. Anything else, Barney?'

'I've been digging up information about the Day of the Dead. Want me to share it with the troops?'

'Absolutely.'

She looked at her laptop and then at the SmartBoard as Karl Stone called up the picture of Justin-Truman-in-the-sun. Just for a moment, she could see only one detail in his smiling face.

'Gather round, everyone!' she called across the room.

That detail was the compassion that radiated from the eyes of a multiple murderer.

And she was filled with a disturbing sense of déjà vu.

35

7.00 am

'Before I hand you over to Barney,' said Clay at the SmartBoard, 'have you all seen Hendricks's and Stone's email detailing the similarities and differences between the David Wilson murder scene and our girl's second excursion on Mather Avenue?'

She looked at every face in turn and saw no doubtful expressions.

'Any questions?' Silence. 'Want to know what our girl sounds like?'

Clay maxed the volume on her iPhone and played back the recording from the switchboard.

A television played in the background.

'Hello, police, where are you calling from?'

The sound of tears that Clay now knew came from the television set.

'I can see from my display that you're calling from landline number 496 7370.'

A door closed and the sound of the TV died.

'I'm calling from 699 Mather Avenue,' said the killer.

'What's the nature of your problem?'

'A man has been murdered and his wife has been tortured. Tell Eve Clay to get over here as fast as she can – 699 Mather Avenue.'

The dead tone.

'Male or female?' she asked the room.

'Absolutely can't tell,' replied Detective Constable Clive Winters. 'Whoever's putting that voice on has got it dead centre between the genders.'

'There's absolutely no doubt now that these crimes are the work of a woman, a Vindici copycat. Frances Jamieson's dying words were, *It was a woman, just one woman.* And judging by the cold calm with which she's dishing out these punishment killings, I'm sure we're dealing with a top-drawer psychopath who worships a mass murderer. She idolises Justin Truman, Vindici. Barney?'

'Thank you, Eve.' He pointed to the SmartBoard. 'This is Justin Truman. Anyone not receive this image?' Silence. 'He's older. He hasn't had any cosmetic surgery to his face. He's put on a little weight and he's changed the colour and cut of his hair but, yes, this is definitely Justin Truman.'

He clicked his handset and showed the zoomed-in image of Truman's eyes from the Day of the Dead picture. 'Look!' He clicked again and showed one detail, the same pair of eyes from his Metropolitan Police mugshot.

Cole returned to first picture, the whole image of Justin-Truman-in-the-sun.

'When I received that phone call, just after David Wilson was murdered, Truman asked me if I'd like him to send me a picture via a third party,' said Clay. 'I believe this is it. He's setting up a link between us and the killer and that link is him.'

'Do we know exactly where was it taken?' asked Gina Riley.

Clay looked at her, noting the small and fleeting smile at the corners of Gina's mouth, the one she wore when she saw a handsome man.

Cole replied, 'Based on the origin of the Weeping Child pottery left at both scenes, I'm going to say Puebla City in the state of Puebla at a Day of the Dead festival. You've got to hand it to the guy. He escapes from a prison convoy in the middle of nowhere between Strangeways and H.M.P. Wakefield with nothing other than the clothes he's wearing and manages to make it to another continent.'

'He didn't get to Mexico all by himself. He can't have done,' said Clay. 'We need to speak to whoever paid for his barrister and that crack legal team he had behind him at the Old Bailey. After we're done here, Karl...'

'I'll start tracking down old money bags,' said Stone.

'Here's a set of links,' said Clay. 'Whoever bankrolled Truman's legal team and helped him escape the country is either with him or is in direct contact with him. My money says Truman's pulling the strings with the copycat and is in touch with her. Whoever's running the Vindici website on which the photograph was published *is* either the killer or is *in touch* with her.'

'Any more pictures, different ones?' asked Hendricks.

Cole clicked and a picture of a skeletal bride and groom came onscreen, she in white dress and veil with a bright bouquet of dahlias in the bones of her fingers, he in tails with a top hat perched on his skull. Beneath their bare feet was a written caption: *The Day of the Dead.*

'The Day of the Dead isn't a single-day festival, it's a series of days between October and November and it's the most important festival in the calendar to most Mexicans. We're within the time window now. It happens every year. People spend quality time off with their families and celebrate the lives of their mutual loved ones who've died.' Cole indicated the skeletal bride and groom and clicked back to Justin-Truman-in-the-sun.

'What does that tell us about Justin Truman?' Clay heard herself speak her thought out loud, saw every face turn towards her. 'He's gone back to Mexico and orchestrated the publication of this specific image. He's got Mexican ancestry or some very strong connection...'

For a moment, his eyes seemed to fill the screen, obscuring all other details, and Clay wondered if she was suffering the beginning phase of a vicious sleep-disordered illness. The moment passed but she felt his eyes sear the surface of her brain like a branding iron.

'OK,' said Clay. 'I need someone who's savvy on Ancestry UK to look up Truman's family tree.'

Cole raised a hand. 'I can do that. Should be straightforward. Truman's an unusual name.'

'How can we be absolutely certain that he's not back in this country?' asked Stone. 'He managed to escape the country – maybe he's made it back here.'

'The newspaper in his hand.' On the SmartBoard, Clay returned to the image of Vindici in the carnival procession and zoomed in on the newspaper. 'He's pointing his index finger at the date, the fourteenth of October 2019. Last week, the day David Wilson was murdered. The newspaper he's holding, the *Mexico Star*, is a national newspaper, so doesn't do anything to pinpoint his location. It doesn't make it absolutely certain he's in Mexico, or that he's not here. But if I was him,' she said, 'would I take the chance and leave the safety of Mexico to come back here? Not a chance. The festival dates bookended Vindici's killing sprees. Today's Thursday the twenty-fourth of October. That gives our copycat until Sunday the third of November, ten more days to pick off more paedophiles. Is she going to do it again? Yes. She's gathered the body parts for the next excursion.'

'Should we give a shite?'

Clay's eyes tracked to Detective Constable Bob Rimmer. Father of three children under ten years and with a wife in the latter stages of terminal lung and spine cancer. She looked at him, smiled to disguise the dark uncertainty inside her.

'Sorry, Eve, my youngest had me up all night and it just kind of slipped out.' Tall, thin and normally tight-lipped, Rimmer had dropped four stone since his wife's diagnosis.

'No problem, Bob. You're probably not the only person in the room who's thinking exactly the same thing. But we *have* to give a shite.' She turned to Hendricks. 'Anything from the autopsy on Steven Jamieson?'

'Yes. When Dr Lamb opened his skull his brain was carved to shreds. He must have died in intense agony.'

Clay looked at the clock on the wall. 'Gina Riley's got a lovely job for all of you.'

Riley waved a collection of papers in the air. 'These are the names of all the registered paedophiles on Merseyside. We're going to visit the most serious offenders, warn them to be vigilant but squeeze them for any information they can come up with in relation to Wilson and Jamieson. Uniformed constables are going to be given a bunch of people to visit. If any of them come up with something interesting, bring them in for further questioning. You're going to oversee the constables and wade in if any of the paedophiles say anything useful to the uniforms. I'm the anchor on this. All informational roads lead back to me. Gather round.'

Clay headed for the door, and was compelled to glance back at the image of Justin Truman smiling in the sun.

'Time to go home, Eve,' said Hendricks.

Clay reached into her bag, took a twenty- and a ten-pound note and handed it to Hendricks.

'What's this for?'

'Can you do me another favour, Bill? Call a florist and send some flowers to Bob Rimmer's wife.'

She looked at the team, saw Rimmer waiting for his brief from Riley with a look of astonishing fatigue and sadness.

'Bob, how about you and me supervising the door-to-door on Mather Avenue?' said Riley. A look of relief passed across his face as she addressed the rest of the team. 'I've highlighted the list of heavyweight paedos. If your name's next to them, then you talk to them directly. Call me when you're done with your first batch and I'll give you more names and addresses.'

Clay hurried to the door and once she was on the corridor leading to the lift began to run, wishing she had the power to magic herself through time and space and earn just a little bit more time with her husband and son.

36

7.30 am

As Clay put the key into the front door of her house on Mersey Road, two things happened in the same moment. She heard Philip banging on the living room window but inside her head she felt Vindici's smiling eyes sinking deeper within her and forming an indelible memory that was both alien but also strangely familiar.

Go away! she thought and slammed a door shut in her brain.

She pressed her face close to the window and said, 'Whatever you do, Philip, don't poke me in the eye!'

He jabbed his index finger at the glass and she reeled back, clutching at her eye, listening to her son scream with laughter. As she carried on the drama, she heard the door open and her husband Thomas's fake anger, 'Philip! What have I told you about poking your mother in the eye?'

As Clay stepped into the house, Philip ran into the hall and straight towards her. Clay dropped to her knees and opened up her body for a hug. Dressed in Superman pyjamas and with his hair full of pillow dents, he threw his arms around her shoulders and her fatigue evaporated.

With her hands on his back, she felt the slenderness of his young body, the fragility of his growing bones, and heard Philomena's voice inside her mind, as clearly as if the nun was there in the hall next to her.

'Jesus said, "And whoever welcomes a little child like this in my name welcomes me. But if anyone causes one of these little ones who believe in me to sin, it would be better for him to have a large millstone hung around his neck and to be drowned in the depths of the sea."'

She kissed her son on the cheek and then gazed at his face: the features that came from her husband – his eyes and nose – and the accents that came from her – the way he smiled, the shape of his eyebrows – and the mystery that was his mouth, lips that had skipped a generation and, she guessed, came from either her mother or father, people she had never known.

'How can who what, Mummy?' asked Philip, looking at her as if she was the only woman in the world.

She frowned slightly and looked up at Thomas, standing over them.

'You just said, *How can they do it to them?*'

She connected with the thought that had steamrollered through her head when she first hugged Philip.

'Oh...' She thought on her feet. 'How can some people be nasty to other people? Just a thought.'

She stood up and, hooking her hands under Philip's armpits, lifted him up. 'Have you been eating rocks?' she asked. 'You are so big and strong and heavy.'

As she carried him into the morning room at the back of the house, she saw the two of them in the large mirror on the back wall of the hall. The total trust in Philip's face filled her with a tenderness that was the direct opposite to the hard-boiled grit that she had dug into on every step of her current investigation. It felt good to be normal and filled with light.

As quickly as tiredness had vanished, in the lifting and carrying of her son it returned and, carefully, she put Philip on his feet and sat in the armchair nearest the door. Then she lifted Philip again and sat him on her knee as Thomas disappeared into the kitchen.

Flattening Philip's hair down, she heard the welcoming click of a kettle being switched on and bread sinking down into the toaster, and wished she didn't have to leave so soon.

At the kitchen door, Thomas said, 'You'll never guess what Philip can do all by himself with no help from anyone?'

She pulled a puzzled face at her son and he beamed with pride as he slid from her knee.

'Go on?' said Clay.

'He can get dressed and comb his own hair all by himself in his bedroom.'

'Oh no, he can't!' said Clay to her husband.

'Oh yes I can, Mother!'

Mother, the name he gave her when he knew he was in the right.

'No you can't.' She looked at him, milking the drama.

'Mother, I can and I will and I will show you!'

A one-child stampede through the hall and up the stairs to his bedroom began.

'I wish I had one iota of that lad's energy,' said Clay, stifling a yawn.

'Sleeping regularly would help,' said Thomas, coming towards her. 'Let me have a look at you.' He crouched in front of her.

'Do I need to take my clothes off, Dr Thomas?'

He smiled. 'Stop it!' Looking into her eyes, she saw concern line his face.

'What's up, Doc?'

'You've got kinks in the blood vessels in your eyes I haven't seen before. It looks to me like your blood pressure's going through the roof. I'll go and get—'

'Don't get your bag, Thomas, please. I'm on the minutes here.'

In the kitchen, the kettle throbbed, and in his bedroom above the morning room, Philip threw himself head first into the process of getting dressed independently for nursery.

She glanced down at her clothes, the Motörhead T-shirt, jeans and Converses she had exchanged for the formal clothes she had worn at Wilson's cremation and then the scene of the murder in Mather Avenue.

'You don't look yourself, Eve. That's not a medical judgement, that's me talking to my wife.'

'I had to lift Steven Jamieson from the bed on which he was murdered into the body bag. When I went to the mortuary, I virtually boiled my hands under the hot tap. I feel terrible. A part of me wishes I'd never become a police officer.' In the kitchen the kettle clicked off and she saw the conflict in her husband's face. Stay or go? 'I'm dying for a cup of tea, Thomas.'

As he headed to the kitchen the noise from upstairs died down. 'Any more nightmares?' she asked.

'He was fine after he'd spoken to you. It was like you'd woven a magical spell over him. All the anxiety he displayed when he first woke up just disappeared.'

Philip jumped down the stairs singing and she heard the pride in his improvised song.

'Did you get my memory box down from the loft, Thomas?'

'I did. It's in the front room. I had a look through before I turned in for the night. Listen, Eve, I don't want any arguments with you. You don't make unnecessary or trivial demands and you're massively short on time. I'll take Philip to the nursery while you go through the box to find whatever it is that's bothering you.'

Into the silence, she whispered, 'Thank you.' The door burst open and Philip strode into the room, stopped in front of his mother and stood to attention.

She sat up and looked at Philip with amazement and pride. Dressed in blue jeans, a black jumper and trainers strapped at the side with Velcro, his hair was combed through, flattened and neat. He smiled at her and displayed a set of small, perfectly polished teeth.

'I told you I can, Mother!'

She stroked his face and smiled. 'You are turning into a very big boy.'

With the words came the certainty that just as one day he dressed himself, another day would come when he would leave home.

She looked at Thomas. The skills needed to self-dress had been imparted largely by her husband and she was filled with a deepening sense of loss. 'You've done very well, both of you.'

As Philip walked to his father he held out his hand and said, 'Come on, Dad, I want to go to nursery. I want to see my friends Luke and Eleanor.'

'I'll walk you to the door and wave you off,' said Clay with all the false brightness she could muster.

Thomas pulled his Nissan Micra away from the pavement and Philip turned his face to the passenger window, waved at his mother and called, 'Love you, Mummy!'

'Love you more!'

Within seconds, they were gone.

Clay closed the front door and turned into the hallway. She saw herself in the mirror again and was shocked at her reflection, as if she had seen her own ghost haunting her. She leaned back against the door for support against the lightness that filled her head and the fresh wave of emptiness that filled her core.

You've done it all wrong! The words ricocheted between the plates of her skull and echoed... *wrong... wrong... wrong... wrong...*

37

7.40 am

Clay sat on the sofa in the living room of her home in Mersey Road with her memory box at her feet and the rumble of traffic along Aigburth Road prompting her to check her watch, reminding her that the present was screaming for her attention.

She lifted the black lid of the plastic stacker box and, as she took out four large brown envelopes stuffed with photographs going back forty years, saw the edge of the thing she was looking for at the bottom of the box. Bypassing the box of letters and the collection of birthday cards, she took out the scrapbook that she'd started as a teenager and, looking at the handwriting on the cover, made a connection with the thirteen-year-old girl she had once been.

St Michael's Catholic Care Home for Children.

She opened the scrapbook, the smell of old newspapers filling her nose and throat, and looked at the first newspaper article she had carefully cut out and pasted into the book.

Smiling, she read the headline and recalled how as an adolescent she had decided to keep a record of the achievements of her all surrogate brothers and sisters in the home.

Clay scanned the words of the article but had no need to read it as she remembered the pride she'd felt when Eric Joyce, a boy three years her senior, had left the home and signed as a professional footballer for Everton.

Move on, move on, she urged herself, flicking through the book for the one piece she needed to look at.

The temperature in the room remained constant but she felt herself flush as she reached for a newspaper article with the headline:

HEROISM OF LIVERPUDLIAN TEENAGER

THREE LIVERPOOL SAILORS DEAD IN SHIPPING ACCIDENT

She put her hand over the three small black and white photographs at the centre of the article and, sitting back on the sofa, read the article to herself.

Disaster struck when three merchant seamen from the SS *Memphis Star* drowned in the English Channel just off the coast of Cornwall in the early hours of Sunday, 17 December. It is reported that an undetected hole in the vessel's hold was torn wide open as the ship battled against a gale.

Initial reports from investigators at the scene indicate that the ship's life-saving equipment was inadequate for the needs of the crew in the event of a disaster.

Clay closed her eyes and the details of the story, which had haunted her in her formative years, came sharply to life.

Captain Albert Murray, 51, fell into the water when the life raft he was in was tossed up on a huge wave. James Peace, 19, a naval rating, jumped into the water to save him. The 19-year-old swam towards Murray and away from the life raft. The teenager screamed for Captain Murray to swim towards him. Peace reached the captain in spite of colossal waves.

In her head, the scene turned from a reported memory into a series of moving pictures formed from dozens of eye-witness accounts that she had personally listened to as a young teenager attending the inquest.

The black icy-cold waters rose up like giants as the tiny ship was sucked under by the waves. The life raft was tossed about like a dying animal in the jaws of a predator. Rain lashed down from the cast-iron sky as the wind howled, whipping the sea up into a maelstrom.

The men still on board the life raft screamed for the boy to swim back to the fragile safety of the raft but instead he battled away against the waves towards the drowning man. Their fingertips connected as the boy managed to grip Murray's wrist, to turn the middle-aged man around and cup a hand under his chin. Murray suffered a massive cardiac arrest and, as he sank, Jimmy was dragged under with him. The boy's head emerged briefly but then was drawn under again by the impossible power of the sea.

Within minutes of the boy's disappearance, the storm died down. In the days that followed, the search mission recovered the corpses of Murray and another seaman called Peter Lamb, but the boy's body was lost forever.

Water. She imagined Jimmy Peace's spirit as he tried to save others and how his strength must have deserted him as the waves grew taller and the sea sucked him under. She pictured his arm reaching out from the water for something, anything to cling on to, but finding only the cruel wind.

Clay opened her eyes, the centre of her head throbbing.

She looked at the back of her hand, covering the photographs of the three dead sailors and, for a fleeting moment, saw her hand as it had looked when she was eight years old, a resident of St Michael's Care Home for Children, the hand Jimmy had held so many times.

She lifted her hand from the newspaper article and looked at the first photograph of the three. Murray in his officer's cap with a pipe in his mouth. She looked at the next picture. Peter Lamb, the ship's cook.

Then her eyes turned to the third picture and she felt as if her heart was about to explode. Her pulse quickened and the heat inside her became intense, colouring her face and throat.

It was a small grainy snapshot taken from his Merchant Navy passbook of the teenager who had been lost to the sea.

James Peace, the surrogate big brother she had briefly known, but who was now gone forever. She remembered the sunny day when he'd called to her as she watched from the window of Mrs Tripp's office, and the way he'd looked back at her through the window of the police car as they took him away for saving her on that hot day in autumn, 1986.

The picture in the paper was undeniably him but, to her complete frustration, the grainy quality of the passbook photo did nothing to help her remember what his younger face was like.

Clay remembered another name from the past. Maggie Anderson, the kindest worker in the children's home and the most consistent, who'd been there when Eve arrived as a six-year-old and still there when she left, aged eighteen, to move into the University of Liverpool's student residence, Carnatic Hall.

She closed the scrapbook and, as she placed it back in the memory box, saw the edge of her cream and red birth certificate.

It was the only time I was alone in Mrs Tripp's office, thought Clay.

She heard the hydraulics of a bus on Aigburth Road and, at the other end of Mersey Road, heard a siren from a ship heading across the River Mersey towards Garston Docks.

The day we went to Botanic Gardens. The day I took my birth certificate from my file. The day Christopher Hawkins was taken to hospital and never came back to St Michael's. The day Jimmy Peace was taken away by the police. The day I saw Jimmy for the very last time.

There was no point in looking at her birth certificate. She knew every word by heart and the disappointment she always felt never diminished when she saw the neat handwriting on it: *Mother, unknown. Father, unknown.*

Black waves crashed inside her head and, in that darkness, she saw Jimmy Peace sinking beneath the surface, gone forever.

Clay opened the Facebook app on her iPhone and typed

Maggie Anderson, Liverpool. Within a moment, three names and profile pictures appeared.

An elderly blonde with a pit bull terrier.

Definitely not you, Maggie, thought Clay. *You were allergic to dogs.*

A teenage girl with braces.

Clay looked at the time on her iPhone and headed for the front door. She slipped her coat on and looked at the third Maggie Anderson.

'Hello, Maggie!' she said. She opened Maggie's Facebook page and sent a friend request. 'You were so kind to me when I was a kid.'

38

8.00 am

In the viewing room on the ground floor of Trinity Road police station, Sergeant Carol White folded her hands in front of her closed laptop and laid her head down. She closed her eyes and the little boy's vacant face floated across the darkness of her mind's eye.

She lifted her head when she heard knocking on the door and asked, 'Who is it?'

'Alice.'

Both her and her colleague Alice's laptops were turned off.

'Come in, Alice.'

As Alice Banks came in and closed the door, Carol looked at the notice on the door for the thousandth time.

ALWAYS ENSURE THAT YOUR LAPTOP IS TURNED OFF AND THAT YOU ARE LOGGED OUT WHEN YOU ARE NOT USING IT.

IF YOU ARE THE LAST PERSON TO LEAVE THE ROOM ALWAYS ENSURE THAT THE DOOR IS LOCKED.

ALWAYS ASK FOR THE NAME OF ANYONE KNOCKING ON THE DOOR. ONLY ALLOW AUTHORISED, NAMED OFFICERS TO ENTER THE ROOM.

'You don't look well,' said Alice, sitting next to Carol at the table they had shared for months. She turned on her laptop.

'Do you mind not logging into anything for a minute?' said Carol, hearing pain in her own voice.

On the table between them Carol's iPhone sounded an incoming text and she snatched it up as she saw the number on display.

'You're tired but you're quick. What's up, hun?' Alice commented.

'I made an idiot of myself in front of Bill Hendricks. And no I didn't make a pass at the man of your dreams.'

'I'm delighted to hear it. So, do you want to talk about it?'

'No. Yes. I told him how all the porn was getting me down. I cried. I threw up. I told him about Kevin walking out. I made a right mare of myself.'

'Bill won't be fazed by that. He's our station's Sigmund Freud. Loads of people talk their problems through with him. He's the most discreet man on the planet.'

'If he comes here, I'm going out. I feel so stupid.'

Carol turned her laptop on and then walked to the kettle in the corner of the room, opening and reading her text.

'Anything interesting?' asked Alice, not looking up from the screen.

'It's from Eve Clay. There's a rat in the house.'

'Sorry?'

'There'll be an email in your inbox with the same message. Someone is dishing out contact details about local paedophiles on the sex offenders' register and on the NPC. It could be anyone, basically. Report any suspicious behaviour. Coffee?'

'Yes please.' Alice sighed. 'Here we go again. David Wilson, you little bastard.'

Carol said something, softly.

'Louder, Carol!'

'I said, *I'm glad we're nearly done.*'

'Yeah, but when we finish looking at Wilson's shit, we'll have Jamieson's to wade through.' Alice plugged her earphones in. Elbow on desk, chin in left hand, she watched the screen with a completely blank expression. 'I swear to God,' she said, 'we don't get paid nearly enough.' She glanced at Carol, who was texting as the kettle came to the boil.

'I'm texting Kevin. He'd better take Damien for a couple of days.' When the kettle snapped off, Carol gasped, shocked by a small, sudden noise.

'Jesus tonight!'

'That's a good idea,' said Alice. 'You look like you could sleep for a year.'

39

8.30 am

Outside her home on Mersey Road, Clay sat at the wheel of her car and psyched herself out of home mode and back into professional. But the trick she had trained herself to do quickly and efficiently proved difficult now.

She somersaulted from the grainy newspaper picture of the teenage Jimmy Peace and landed in Mrs Tripp's office and the last image she had had of him in the back window of the police car, his face lacking detail but his mouth moving.

Clay called Cole's landline. 'Barney, do me a favour when you get the chance. I'd like you to look on the NPC and see what you can come up with on a James Peace. Date of birth, the fifth of December 1970.'

'Is he a suspect?'

'No, he was a childhood friend of mine. If you can dig up any information about him I'd be grateful. He died in a shipping accident, aged nineteen.'

'You sound a bit down.'

In her mind, she saw the still waters of the English Channel under a leaden sky where gulls wheeled and screamed and frogmen from the Devon & Cornwall Police gathered on a stony beach.

'Are you OK, Eve?'

'I'd be grateful if you could keep this request between the two of us.'

'My lips are sealed.'

Clay closed her eyes and she tried hard but just couldn't recall Jimmy's face on that day. She picked another day. Jimmy holding both her hands and swinging her round quickly in the garden at St Michael's. She looked at his face but it was a dizzying blur.

Can I remember all the nice things you did for me, Jimmy? she asked herself. *Every day, something. Hundreds of acts of kindness, and one huge protection. But can I recall your face, what you were like to look at as a boy? No.*

Clay was hauled from the depths of the past by a gentle tapping on the passenger window. She saw the orange uniform of her regular postman and he opened the passenger door.

'Hello, Dave.'

'Hello, stranger.' He handed her a postcard.

'Thank you.'

She looked at a picture of a seagull sitting on a white, wooden fence against an impossibly blue sea. In the top left hand corner, in white writing: 'GREETINGS FROM KINSALE'.

'Anything interesting?'

She turned the postcard over to see the writing and said, 'Yes. Very interesting.'

The postman closed the passenger door and carried on up her next-door neighbour's path.

She looked at the elegant cursive writing that she'd most recently seen on the skin on Steven and Frances Jamieson's shoulders. *Dear Eve, I am Vindici. Come and find me and all this will stop. Or shall I find you first?*

Clay took a picture of the front and back of the postcard and typed a text to Barney Cole.

Pls circulate these pictures to the entire team. The postcard from Vindici arrived at my house just now. If it is from Justin Truman, he is in or has recently been in County Cork. Pls contact Garda in Kinsale and Cork and copy them in on this information.

She attached the images and sent it to Cole and, pulling away and picking up speed, a chain of thought materialised in her head: links between earth and water. *Mexico... the Atlantic Ocean... Eire... the Irish Sea... England... Liverpool...*

40

8.38 am

In a quest for insights into Vindici, Detective Sergeant Karl Stone scrolled on his laptop to the end of the fortieth newspaper article he'd come across on the internet. He looked at his spiral-bound pad and ticked off the date and headline of the article: 13/08/2009 – *VINDICI PLEADS NOT GUILTY TO MURDERING HUMAN BEINGS.*

Beneath the headline, he summarised the key point of the article: *Justin Truman/Vindici reduces packed public gallery to fits of laughter on plea/Judge threatens him with contempt of court.*

As Stone took a deep breath and prepared to look at the next article, he became aware that the usually calm Barney Cole was growing agitated at his nearby desk. He paused and took in the scene.

Cole sat, landline receiver wedged between his ear and shoulder, fingers dancing over the keyboard of his laptop. Next to him, his IT civilian assistant, Poppy Waters, was on her mobile and scrolling frantically on her laptop.

The shared printer on Stone's desk clicked into life.

Stone saw Hendricks walking towards him.

'What's happening, Karl?' he asked

'I'm not sure.'

The printer sucked a sheet of paper from the tray into the body of the machine.

Cole stood up, placed the receiver down and gave Stone and Hendricks a double thumbs-up. He pointed at the printer as a single sheet of paper shot out and floated face down on to the floor at Stone's feet.

Stone picked the paper up, turned it over and read out loud what Cole had sent to the printer. '*Mrs Annabelle Burns, 222 Springwood Avenue, Liverpool L19 6LY.* Who's she?'

'We've had a shitload of help from the very nice French people at the Réseaux IP Européens Network,' said Cole, advancing. 'They've given us a latitude 53.364478 and longitude -2.885075 and a postcode L19 6LY for one of the Liverpool Vindici sites. It seems Mrs Burns is running a Vindici fan site just off Mather Avenue within spitting distance of the Jamiesons' house.'

'Thank you, Françoise!' said Poppy Waters. She hung up, looking as though she was about to explode with happiness.

'They're going to help us with locating the other site,' said Cole to Hendricks and Stone.

Stone called Clay on speed dial and when she connected, he said, 'We've got great news, Eve. Where are you?'

'Aigburth Road. What's happening?'

'We've got a location for one of the Liverpool Vindici sites. You need to go straight over to 222 Springwood Avenue.'

Stone heard the squeal of tyres against tarmac and the sudden acceleration of Clay's car as it rose way above the speed limit.

'Let me guess, Karl. It's a woman. Springwood Avenue a stone's throw away from being next-door neighbours with the Jamiesons.'

'Correct. Who do you want with you and how much back-up?'

41

8.50 am

Parked outside Steven and Frances Jamieson's home at 699 Mather Avenue, Detective Sergeant Gina Riley and Detective Constable Bob Rimmer watched as a dozen uniformed constables knocked on doors at the Garston exit at Woolton Road. Each one returned periodically with the same repetitive and frustrating message.

No one had seen or heard a thing.

As a glum and cold-looking WPC delivered the latest piece of non-news, Riley said, 'Keep trying, constable. You're doing a good job. Here.' Riley handed her a piece of paper with a list of door numbers. 'Try these on the other side of the road.'

At the wheel of her car, Riley looked at Rimmer staring into space and saw a man profoundly disinterested in the task at hand.

'Bob?' He turned to her voice. 'Want to slip home for a couple of hours? I'll call you if I need you.'

'Are you kidding, Gina? My mother-in-law's moved in to take care of Valerie. The kids are all booked in to half-term holiday club and, chances are, Valerie'll be asleep or strung out on medication. So, thanks, but no thanks.'

Riley looked in the rear-view mirror and saw a young constable walking at speed but also directly into a strong wind that pushed him back and made him hold on to his cap.

'Eleven and a half months ago, the doctors gave her twelve months.'

'Don't you just want to sit with her, Bob? Be at her side?'

'Watch the cancer in her spine and lungs wipe her out, moment by moment?' He shook his head and Riley observed a once large and gregarious man who was all cried out, silent and thin now, as they slogged to find a killer while most of the world wished failure on them.

The constable tapped on the passenger window; Rimmer opened the door but stared straight ahead.

'Yes, constable?' asked Riley.

'Five doors down from the scene, 689 Mather Avenue. I tried them earlier but they were out. I saw them coming back just now. They've got a CCTV camera at the front of the house.'

Riley shuddered in the mean wind as she got out of the car, looked down the avenue and saw a woman standing at a gate.

'Come on, Bob.' Slowly, Rimmer got out of the car. 'Lead on, constable.'

They trudged over the grass verge on to the pavement with the wind at their backs.

'Things will get worse, Bob. But then they will get better. This won't last forever.'

'I feel like an alien inside my own skin,' said Rimmer. 'I didn't think it was humanly possible to feel so sad and carry on living.'

For once, Riley was lost for words.

'I'm sorry, Gina. I shouldn't be laying this on you. I've already said far too much.'

Riley placed a hand on Rimmer's shoulder.

The woman at the gate raised a hand in recognition and Riley noted the angle and direction of the CCTV camera above the bay window on the front elevation of the house. It was pointing directly at the gate where the woman stood and the pavement beyond that. Hope flooded Riley but she contained her enthusiasm with a modest, 'Well, this could be promising.'

As Rimmer presented his warrant card to the householder,

Riley noticed him stiffen into professional mode but he didn't look directly at the woman, only the CCTV camera.

'Good morning, madam. Detective Constable Robert Rimmer, Merseyside Constabulary.' He pointed at the CCTV camera. 'Can we have a look at what you've got, please?'

Riley's phone rang. She connected, listened and, walking away, said, 'I'm sorry, Bob, I've got to go.'

42

9.01 am

Clay stood with Riley outside 222 Springwood Avenue, a semi-detached house with a small garden of slumbering rose bushes and terracotta pots with dwarf evergreen firs, and watched a marked police car pulling up outside.

As Hendricks hurried from his car, two more of the back-up vehicles Clay had ordered as she drove from Aigburth to Allerton parked behind the marked police BMW.

'Her website's nuts,' said Hendricks as he followed Clay up the path to the front door. 'Cole filled me in on the content as I headed over here.'

Clay pressed the bell, leaving her finger on longer than was necessary.

'How can such hate come from somewhere so bland?'

'It always does,' said Clay, stepping back to look up at a bay window where a woman stood, phone against her ear. She was talking fast, pausing to listen and then pouncing back verbally on the caller, eyeing the gathering of police cars outside her house. Turning her back to the window, she marched out of Clay's vision.

'You do the talking, Bill, you know more about the website than I do.' Clay lifted the letter box, saw the same woman running down the stairs and pocketing her phone. She closed the letter box.

'All right! All right!' a waspish female voice drifted towards the front door. Annabelle Burns opened the door with a scowl, pointing her finger in the air as if pressing a doorbell. 'I'm not deaf; there's no need for that.'

She blocked the open door with her body.

Annabelle Burns's attitude and physicality sent rockets flying in Clay's mind. The woman was nearly six feet tall and had a large frame. Clay looked at her forearms and knew that she must have done a lot of manual work in her life.

'Well, who are you and what do you want?'

Clay showed Annabelle her warrant card and she scrutinised it intensely, double-checking the picture with Clay's face.

'Detective Chief Inspector Eve Clay, Merseyside Constabulary.'

'Police! What on earth do you want with me?'

'Let's talk inside, Mrs Burns. Don't want the neighbours talking, do we?' said Riley.

Annabelle opened the door wider and, as Clay and Hendricks entered, she cast a glance at the stairs, muttering something dark beneath her breath.

'Go into my living room!'

43

9.06 am

In the living room of 222 Springwood Avenue, Clay, Hendricks and Riley remained on their feet as Annabelle Burns sank on to a sofa that was wrapped in transparent plastic.

'What do you want?' she snapped.

'Where were you around about six thirty last night?' asked Hendricks.

'I was on duty, doing some overtime, in the Spire Hospital.'

'The BUPA place by Greenbank Park?' asked Hendricks.

'Do I look stupid enough to work in the NHS?'

Ballsy, thought Clay.

Annabelle reached to the side of the sofa, took a Dettol Wipe from the packet and started cleaning the plastic covering around her.

'So if I phone the Spire,' said Hendricks, 'someone will confirm that you were there?'

'I'll do that,' said Clay, taking out her iPhone. 'What's the number, Mrs Burns?'

As Annabelle reeled off the digits, Clay keyed them in and headed into the hallway to make the call.

She stopped at the door, eyeballed Annabelle. 'Who were you on the phone to, just now, up in the front bedroom?'

Clay made a mental note of the time of the call. 9.01 am.

'No one.'

Clay detected hesitation in Annabelle's voice. 'No one, Mrs Burns?'

'I was on to the council – Bulky Bob. I'm getting a new fridge and I want them to take my old one away. I was arranging a date for them to collect it.'

'Fair enough,' said Clay, leaving the room.

Hendricks held the woman's unflinching gaze and the silence between them felt toxic. He could hear Clay's voice from the hall and, in an instant, Annabelle's prickly exterior melted.

'Ah, I know what this is about. What's your name?'

'Detective Sergeant Hendricks.'

'Thank you for calling, Mr Hendricks. It's about next door's dog fouling the pavement outside. Do you want me to go get my evidence?'

'It's not about next door's dog, Mrs Burns,' said Hendricks. 'Can you stop cleaning and pay attention. Do you have an internet connection and a laptop?'

'Who doesn't these days?' The scowl returned to her face. 'Well, if it's not about that horrible brute next door, what is it about?'

'Do you run your own website, Mrs Burns?'

'I'm a single working parent. I haven't got the time or inclination to run a website. Look, is this a hidden camera prank for some cheap TV show?'

Clay returned to the room and stood in the corner. 'Your story's good, Mrs Burns. Mind if I call you Annabelle?'

She shrugged. 'If you want.'

'You had a slanging match with one of your colleagues and she had to go home in floods of tears,' she said. 'You left the Spire at eleven, after you were given a verbal warning by your manager at seven-twelve.'

'Told you so.'

'I'll still send someone round to double-check,' said Clay.

'Why?'

'Because I'm very suspicious of you, Annabelle.'

She looked offended to the roots of her being.

'Do you know a couple who live on Mather Avenue, Steven and Frances Jamieson?' asked Hendricks.

'No.' Flat and immediate. Annabelle gave the arm of the sofa a tiny rub with the Dettol Wipe.

'How would you describe your attitude towards paedophiles?'

'They're sick in the head and I wouldn't want to be around them.'

'You said you're a working parent. Is there anybody else living in the house with you?'

'Yes. My son. Lucien.'

'He'll be in school now?' asked Clay.

'No, he's at home now.'

'It's half term, Eve,' said Hendricks

'He's home-educated. No school understood him and none of them met his needs.'

'Which school did he go to?' asked Clay.

'Schools. Blue Coat, King David, Liverpool College and Calderstones.'

'Does Lucien have a laptop?'

'He's sixteen. Of course he's got a laptop. And yes, he's here right now, upstairs in his room.'

'I'd like to talk to Lucien,' said Hendricks.

'I'll get him for you,' said Annabelle, rising from the sofa.

'No, I'd like to talk to him in his room.'

'Why?'

'It'll help me get a sense of who he is. As he's a minor and you're his mother, you can be present when I talk to him.' Hendricks pointed up. 'Let's go.'

Annabelle turned as she followed Hendricks from the room and asked Clay, 'How can he possibly be in any trouble with you? He never goes out.'

'We want to talk to your son about his website,' replied Clay as they carried on up the stairs.

'Website? He doesn't have a website. He's not *allowed* to have a website.'

'Well, let's talk to Lucien about that.'

*

At the bottom of the stairs, Riley whispered to Clay, 'I'll stay here in case he tries to do a runner.'

As Clay walked up the stairs, she saw a band of bright light leaking from the gap at the bottom of a closed door.

'Cover your eyes,' said Annabelle, knocking on her son's door. 'He won't hear a thing, listening to that awful garbage – he'll have headphones on. He calls it dance music.'

44

9.18 am

Annabelle opened her son's door and Clay immediately dipped her head, shielding her eyes with the back of her hand. She looked around the brightly lit room and was surprised to see that there wasn't a bed to sleep on.

'Why's he lying on a sunbed?' asked Hendricks quietly.

The side of a body was visible between the base and the roof of his sunbed.

'Can you go and switch off your son's sunbed?'

As Annabelle walked towards the sunbed, Clay and Hendricks followed and exchanged an incredulous glance.

She turned off the sunbed at the wall and the boy shouted, 'Hey, what do you think you're doing, Mother?'

He sounded like a masculine version of Annabelle Burns.

Clay and Hendricks took the top and bottom end of the roof of the sunbed and raised it, revealing a brown-skinned muscular youth wearing round UV glasses, headphones connected to an iPhone and a baggy pair of black cotton boxer shorts.

'The rest of the house is immaculate but this room...' Annabelle turned up her nose. 'I give up.'

'Who are these people, Mother?' He took off his UV glasses as he sat up and span round on the bed, placing his feet on the floor.

Clay showed him her warrant card.

'I can't see. My eyes haven't adjusted.'

'I'm Detective Chief Inspector Eve Clay and this is my colleague Detective Sergeant William Hendricks and we're from the Merseyside Constabulary. Make yourself decent. We want to have a word with you, Lucien.'

Clay detected the onset of panic as the boy glanced across the room at the laptop in the corner.

Clay turned her back, stepped over a barbell and a pair of dumb-bells and waited as Lucien stepped into olive-green jogging bottoms. She drank in the smell of sweat and too much after shave. Eyeing the clothes on the floor, she looked for a grey tracksuit with a hooded top. There wasn't one. On the walls were pictures of half-naked women and action-movie heroes. There was a closet in the corner and a wash basket.

'Mind if we have a look in your wardrobe and wash basket?' asked Clay.

Clay flicked through the hung-up shirts and tops but couldn't see a grey tracksuit that matched the one worn by the kid caught on CCTV delivering dahlias to her.

'Boxers and a white T-shirt in the basket,' said Hendricks.

'Don't tell me you sleep on your sunbed, Lucien?' said Clay, forcing down a smile as his mother's face darkened.

'Of course not! My bed's in another room. Why do you want to speak to me?'

Clay locked eyes with Annabelle Burns as Lucien fumbled into his clothes and said, 'It's about your website, Lucien.'

'Website? I haven't got a website!'

Clay walked towards his laptop but Lucien overtook her, used his body to block her path. She looked at Annabelle.

'I think we've now got a clear sense of who he is,' said Clay, catching Hendricks's eye.

'Yes, me too. Here or downstairs, Eve?'

'Lucien,' said his mother, darkly. 'What have you been up to behind my back?'

45

9.33 am

In Annabelle Burns's living room, Hendricks sustained a deliberately uncomfortable and shrink-wrapped silence.

Clay stood at an angle to observe both Lucien Burns and his mother, out of their direct line of sight but still a presence in their range of vision. They both shifted uncomfortably on the sofa, she clutching a Dettol wipe, her son with his hands tucked under his armpits and shoulders raised. *Good,* she thought.

'Justin Truman been in touch with you, Lucien?' asked Hendricks.

'I don't know.'

Hendricks turned Lucien's laptop towards him and showed him the picture of Justin-Truman-in-the-sun.

'He sent you this picture and you posted it on your website, right?'

'If he'd sent it directly to me, I'd have been dancing with happiness. I lifted it from someone else's website, someone claiming to be in Mexico.'

'So you're denying you're in direct contact with Vindici?'

'On my life I'm not. I wish I was, but I'm not.'

'All right, we can come back to that one. Where were you yesterday, five pm until ten pm?'

'Here, on my own, doing online GCSE papers.'

'Did anyone see you between those hours?'

'I was *on my own*. As in *alone*.'

Clay studied Lucien's face. The sunbed tan, his sculpted eyebrows and pencil-thin moustache gave him the look of an embryonic silent-movie gigolo.

His head rolled on his shoulders, as if the weight of his brain was suddenly unbearably heavy.

'Lucien, stop acting as if you've got learning difficulties,' said Annabelle.

'Be quiet, Annabelle!' said Clay.

'How much do you hate paedophiles?' asked Clay.

'Loads.'

'You must do, to run a website calling for them to be strung up from the nearest lamppost,' said Hendricks. 'Running a website that venerates Justin Truman, that's real commitment.'

'I warned you about being safe on the internet, but you knew better, Lucien!' Annabelle Burns looked set to kill her son.

'Are you aware that two men have been murdered in south Liverpool on the fourteenth and twenty-fourth of October?'

'No.'

'Of course not. One was an unconvicted paedophile. The other was a time-served paedophile and he just happened to live round the corner from you.'

His eyes dithered and when he swallowed, his Adam's apple bulged in his perfectly tanned throat. Clay weighed Lucien up, and then looked at his mother's skin tone. He was a white kid from the north of England but could easily have passed for a boy from southern Italy.

'So in the light of that, Lucien, let's go!'

When Clay opened the front door of 222 Springwood Avenue, she glanced back, saw Lucien's eyes focus on the gate and then skitter up the road to the Mather Avenue exit.

With Hendricks, Annabelle and Lucien Burns behind her, Clay stopped dead in the path and said, 'Lucien, you're currently thinking, *get to the pavement and do a runner*.' She indicated the vehicles parked outside his home. 'See those three cars?

They're full of coppers. See the tall woman coming towards us with the stern face? That's Detective Constable Margaret Bruce, a national boxing champion for the Merseyside Police.'

'Are you threatening me?' asked Lucien.

'No, I'm giving you a reality check,' replied Clay. 'You might be a hero to a load of losers on the internet, which is why I reckon you've got such a high opinion of yourself, but if I was you I wouldn't mess around with any of us. Don't be a dummy. Walk nicely with DS Hendricks to his car.'

When Clay reached the pavement, Lucien snapped back, 'Are you a witch or something?'

'No, but my birth mother was.'

DC Margaret Bruce stepped towards Clay and Annabelle Burns, showing both of them the screen of her phone. 'The duty magistrate emailed the search warrant to me,' she said.

'You're going to search my house?'

'Have you got the keys, Mrs Burns?'

Bruce held out her hand and Clay was astonished by the size of her palm and fingers. Annabelle Burns didn't move.

'If you're refusing to allow us entry, we've got a ram!'

Annabelle dropped the keys into Bruce's hand. 'Would you ever?'

'Head up the search, Maggie, and report back to me. Look out for a grey hooded tracksuit.'

Lucien Burns scowled as Hendricks placed him in the child-locked back seat of his car. 'Oh fix your face, Lucien!' said Hendricks.

'Stay by my car, Annabelle.'

'I want to be with my son...'

'No, you can't travel with Lucien, you're coming with me,' said Clay.

46

10.15 am

He looked at the name on his passport, Arturo Jesús Salvador, and the picture that had been taken a few years earlier when he renewed his passport in Mexico City.

Arturo looked out of the window of the Ryanair plane he'd boarded at Cork Airport, saw a ferry crossing to England and churning the Irish Sea into countless thousands of litres of white foam.

The sight of ferry and the water was compelling. It filled him with morbid fascination at the sheer power of the sea. In his mind he reduced the image in size and imagined he was looking at a plastic boat on the surface of dark bathwater, a boat full of dot-sized people, none of who knew the moment when Death would come calling. Or whether, having called, Death would perform one of its occasional about-turns and walk away empty-handed, leaving the fortunate one to suddenly learn the value of life. And forget it just as quickly.

At his side, the air stewardess said something in English which he didn't quite hear so deep was he locked in thought.

When he looked up at the stewardess, he wasn't disappointed by her looks. She had long dark hair tied back in a ponytail and a pleasant face that belonged with her voice. He smiled at her, holding her gaze.

She indicated the food and drink. 'Would you like anything from the trolley?'

He looked at what was on offer and pointed at a small bottle of red wine. '*Vino.*' He pointed at bars of Galaxy chocolate and said, '*Tres tabletas de chocolate.*' He held up three fingers.

'No problem.' She handed him the wine and a plastic cup and three bars of chocolate and he placed them next to his hand luggage on the empty seat beside him. He took out his passport to find his wallet and handed the stewardess a fifty-pound note.

'That's too much, it's only seven pounds fifty.'

His curiosity pricked, the fat man on the aisle seat in front of him poked his head out to see what was going on.

Arturo shook his head and, smiling at her, said, '*Quédese con el cambio.*'

'I'm sorry, I can't speak Spanish.'

'It's your lucky day, darling,' said the fat man. '*Quédese con el cambio?* He's telling you to keep the change.'

'Thank you very much.'

She looked delighted and amazed. Feeling suddenly self-conscious, he packed the chocolate and his wallet away. He paused as he repacked his black passport and reflected on the image in the centre of the document. Embossed in gold, it was an elegant picture of a Mexican Golden Eagle perched proudly on a cactus and destroying a rattlesnake with one claw and its beak: Mexico's national symbol, the representation of the power of good defeating the forces of evil. The image pleased him.

He opened the passport and scanned his personal information. Arturo Jesús Salvador, age fifty, and the names of the English mother he remembered well and the Mexican father who he'd never met. Nationality, Mexican. Place of birth, Oaxaca. He closed the passport and put it away.

He reached into his bag and took out his medication, ponatinib, and popped two pills into his mouth. Pouring the red wine, he wished it was a form of good blood that combined with the medication could make him better, a holy communion of health.

Feeling the beating wings of butterflies in his stomach

– travelling over water increased his anxieties about flying – he took a good slug of wine and downed the tablets.

Arturo took an envelope from his hand luggage, and took out a picture of a middle-aged man, slightly older than himself but five stone heavier and looking fifteen years his senior. He turned the photograph over and saw the man's Liverpudlian home address. Arturo smiled as he returned the picture into the envelope and back into his bag.

Through the window, in the distance, he saw the horizon, a faint line between the sea and the sky. He felt the beginning of the plane's descent and kept his eyes firmly set in the distance. A surge of emotion passed through him, disbelief that he was so near after he had travelled so far.

The horizon grew bigger and bigger and buildings, in the form of indistinct shapes, rose up from the line. He drank more wine and felt the glow of mild intoxication as he watched the distant shapes emerging into familiar forms.

The first shape to come alive was the Anglican Cathedral. Then he saw the Metropolitan Cathedral and heard a tiny gasp emerge from deep within himself. The Radio City Tower and the Liver Buildings came into focus at the same time, shortly before the building known as the Cloud. He looked at waters around the Pier Head and saw a black dot moving across the surface. *Ferry*, he thought, *the Mersey Ferry*.

Finally, he had arrived at the city that filled his night-dreams, the land of his ancestors, a pilgrimage during the Day of the Dead to visit those of his blood who had passed before him, to welcome them back if only for a day.

47

10.15 am

'You really are engrossed.'

Poppy looked up on hearing Sergeant Carol White's voice.

'I've been standing here for two minutes and it was like I wasn't here.'

'I'm sorry to keep you waiting, Carol, but I'm starting to feel like my head's been packed with cotton wool.'

'Tell me about it,' said Carol.

I'm so glad, thought Poppy, *that I don't have to do your job.* She smiled at Carol, feeling a strong surge of sympathy for the woman.

'Two dead paedos inside days of each other,' remarked Carol, straight-faced.

Unsure of how to react, Poppy said, 'Oh!' She observed the faint but triumphal smile that crossed Carol's face.

'Not nice people,' said Carol. 'Talking of which, have you got the laptop Steven Jamieson had hidden in his pit?'

Poppy picked up a laptop in a plastic bag and Carol took it from her.

'I've cracked it open. Here's your username and password.' Poppy slipped her a piece of paper: *cwhite* V1nd!ci2.

'Let's have a look at what lurks within.' But when Carol got to the door, she turned. 'What are you working on at the moment, Poppy?'

'Amongst other things, right now, I'm monitoring the second Liverpudlian Vindici website and praying for a phone call from France.'

'So you didn't get to see what Steven Jamieson had down-loaded?'

'No.'

'If you did my job, you'd probably feel a little bit happy when these people get their comeuppance. Thanks for this, Poppy.'

Poppy watched White leave, disturbed by the sergeant's words and attitude. Did she talk like that to other civilians working in the station?

Poppy returned her attention to her own laptop and the unlocated Liverpool-based Vindici website. She opened the gallery of images and, startled, sat up on her chair. 'That's new...!'

She saw a McDonald's restaurant on a busy main road with a Farmfoods supermarket in the corner of the image and started reading the words moving across the bottom of the screen from right to left.

For a moment, she felt numb and then wondered if she'd fallen asleep and was having a wish-fulfilling dream come true.

She read the words again and, standing up, dialled Barney Cole's number.

'Hi, Poppy, what's happening?'

'Are you in the incident room?'

'Just me and Karl Stone.'

'Don't move either of you. I think we've just had a lucky break.'

48

10.15 am

'I'm sorry your colleague had to leave so suddenly,' said Mrs Hurst. 'That makes twice as much work for you.' He was utterly silent. 'Do you want me to leave you alone, Mr Rimmer?'

The cold of the day was trapped and intensified in the attic of a house five doors down Mather Avenue from a murder scene.

Clutching his coat at the neck and watching his breath condense on the air, Rimmer didn't look up at Mrs Sylvia Hurst, the woman whose CCTV footage he was watching, and who he silently cursed. *Why my wife and not you?*

'I might be here for a couple of hours, Mrs Hurst. Watching me watching this will be a little tedious for you.'

Bob Rimmer took a deep breath and was assaulted by a sudden, vivid memory of the moments after the young Asian doctor whose name he couldn't pronounce let alone remember said, *In my view and the view of other doctors who I've reviewed your case with, you have twelve months to live, Mrs Rimmer. I'm sorry.*

'Are you all right, Mr Rimmer?' asked Sylvia Hurst.

He dragged himself together and took a pen drive from his pocket.

'Can I get you anything? A coffee?'

He forced himself to look at her properly for the first time and was relieved to see there was nothing about her that reminded him of his wife.

'I'd be grateful for a coffee. Milk without sugar, please.'

'You know, you're more than welcome to be here, Mr Rimmer, and I admire the job you do greatly, but you do have a flash drive: you could record everything on it and take it back to the comfort of your office and look at it there.'

'Yes, I do understand that, Mrs Hurst.'

From downstairs came the muted but excited noise of Mrs Hurst's children playing in their rooms and on the upstairs landing.

'Bless them. How many children do you have, Mrs Hurst?'

'Three. All under ten.'

'Well, well, me too. No, Mrs Hurst, I need to watch it here, on the spot, so I can access the pavement or your driveway. In forensics it's called direct mediation,' he invented.

'Really?' She looked impressed.

'Do me a favour, I'm not used to this particular CCTV system. Can you reel it backwards or forwards to five o'clock yesterday?'

'Be my pleasure to help,' she said, crossing the caber flooring. Beneath her feet, came squealing and giggling and little voices competing against each other.

As Mrs Hurst typed in *17:00 23/10/19* Rimmer asked, 'Did you hear any news reports about what happened, Mrs Hurst?'

'No, just one of the neighbours explained why the police were all over the avenue because…I don't know their names, they kept themselves to themselves, and we were away in Wales and didn't get back until this morning, and two minutes later, the constable knocks on the door and asks about the CCTV… Then you came along, and shortly after, the lady you were with was called away. There you go, five o'clock yesterday, press play when you're ready.'

'Maybe it's just as well you didn't know your neighbour or anything about him,' said Rimmer, making direct eye contact with Mrs Hurst. 'There's a reason why *he* was killed and *not* the man next door to him.' Silence. 'It's linked to another recent murder. In Aigburth.'

Her face darkened.

Rimmer made a show of shivering. 'I'd love that coffee now if you don't mind.'

As she walked to the hatch and ladder leading down into the house, Rimmer heard her mutter, 'Oh my God!'

She climbed down the ladder but when her head was still visible, she stopped and looked back at Rimmer with an expression of horror.

Rimmer nodded, gave a little shrug. The sound of her children playing together grew louder.

'Five doors away?'

'Five doors away, Mrs Hurst.'

With her phone now in her left hand, Mrs Hurst disappeared down the creaking aluminium ladder and when she got to the ground he heard her say, 'Hi, Mary, it's Sylvia. Have you been watching the news...?'

Detective Constable Bob Rimmer, who wanted to be as far away from other people as he could for as long as he could, pressed play and watched night fall on Mather Avenue in the blessed solitude of someone else's attic.

49

10.30 am

After two calls on Rathbone Road and Wellington Road, and a visit to Grosvenor Road, Police Constables Andrew Jones and Sarah O'Neil sat in their marked car outside Edward Hawkins's home, Flat 4, 101 Arundel Avenue.

WPC O'Neil listened to the ringtone on her mobile and complained, 'Three paedos warned, seven more to go from our band of joy.'

'If he's in he's not answering. If he doesn't pick up his phone in the next minute, I say we score it as a *did not respond.*' In the passenger seat, PC Jones pulled down the visor and, looking in the mirror, straightened his cap.

WPC O'Neil closed down the unconnected call and, in her notebook, drew a line through the name Edward Hawkins.

'Smithdown Road next,' said WPC O'Neil. 'We're tripping over paedos in this neck of the woods.'

'It's not just here, Sarah.'

'Yeah, guess so. Shall we leave the car here? It's only round the corner.'

As PC Jones stepped out and on to the pavement, the door of 101 Arundel Avenue opened, and the young constable made eye contact with a fat man in a dark hallway. He closed the door twice as fast as he'd opened it.

PC Jones marched to the front door and banged it with the heel of his hand. 'Open the door, Edward, police.'

He listened and there was no sign of movement.

'Here, I'll try,' said O'Neil. 'Edward, my name's WPC Sarah O'Neil. You're not in trouble, but we do need to have a word with you. For your own safety.'

PC Jones lifted the letter box. 'He's in there. He's pretending to be a coat stand.'

'Edward, please open the door and let us in. We've got lots of people *like yourself* to talk to today and if you don't open the door really soon, we're going to have to go away and leave you...'.

Hawkins unfroze and walked slowly to the front door. He opened it wide enough to frame the width of his saddlebag jowls.

'Let us in,' said WPC O'Neil. 'We don't want to have this conversation with you in front of the neighbours or passers-by.'

Edward opened the door wide enough to allow a pair of bodies inside, one at a time.

Front door closed, PC Jones pressed the timer on the hall light and immediately wished he hadn't. Black mould lined the walls in random patterns from floor to ceiling.

'I was abused as a child. I haven't done nothing wrong for years now. I'm not one of them no more.' Edward fixed his attention entirely on WPC O'Neil and, with a huge sigh of relief, PC Jones stepped to one side and out of the frame.

'You're aware of the murders of David Wilson and Steven Jamieson?' said WPC O'Neil. 'Did you know either of these men?'

'No. Only after they'd been killed from the news on TV. No more than that.'

PC Jones noticed in spite of the cold, there was a sheen of sweat on Hawkins's bulbous neck.

'Do you have any information that you think might be helpful in finding whoever's committing these murders?' asked WPC O'Neil.

'No.'

'Please don't withhold information from us, Edward. You could hold the key to saving *your* life or the lives of others.'

'I don't know nothing. If I did, I'd tell you.'

'We've come to warn' – WPC O'Neil dropped her voice – 'everyone who's been convicted of sex crimes against children—'

'It was a once-in-a-lifetime mistake, I didn't mean it to happen, as God is my judge.' Hawkins made the sign of the cross on his heart. 'I wouldn't do it no more.'

'Be very careful, Edward, who you open your door to. And if you're out and about, especially near your home, be aware if anyone watches or follows you. If you find out or remember any information, please call the murder incident room on this number.' WPC O'Neil handed a card to him.

He looked at it and a bolt of terror shot through his face.

'Is something wrong, Edward?'

He offered the card back.

'No, Edward, you're supposed to keep the card in case you think you can help DCI Eve Clay who's...'

Edward turned away a full half-circle, showing his back to WPC O'Neil and his face to PC Jones who continued the scripted conversation. '...DCI Eve Clay who's leading the inquiry and the detectives working with her.' He went off script. 'What's wrong with you, Edward? I said *Eve Clay* and an expression with the words *seen* and *ghost* comes to mind.'

Edward bit his right thumbnail. 'I don't know what you mean no more.' He looked down at his shoes and PC Jones threw a prompting glance at WPC O'Neil.

'Do you know DCI Eve Clay?' she asked.

'No, never heard of her.'

'She's one of the most prominent police officers in the country. She's known all over the world. You've never heard of her?'

'Never heard of her no more.'

The hall plunged into darkness. Jones hit the timer rapidly and the light seemed to hurt Edward's eyes. He turned a quarter-circle, facing neither WPC O'Neil or PC Jones, but looking as though he'd been torn straight down the middle.

'If...?' he said quietly.

'If what, Edward?'

'If I did find out something. If I did ring this number. Would I speak to Eve Clay?'

'How do you know Eve Clay, Edward?' asked WPC O'Neil.

He turned at her. 'I don't know Eve Clay. You can't prove anything no more.'

'You most probably *wouldn't* speak to DCI Eve Clay, but you would speak to someone. Are you sure you don't know anything?'

From behind the door of one of the ground-floor flats, someone started playing rap music at top volume.

'I... I was wondering if you could take me to the police station and let me stay in a cell. For my own safety.'

'You're not the first to ask that and I'm sure you won't be the last,' said PC Jones. 'And I'll say what I've said to everyone. If you can prove that you're in direct danger from the killer, then we can organise protective custody for you.'

Hawkins thought about it.

'How on earth could I do such a thing?'

Without another word, he turned and starting walking back upstairs.

'He knows Eve Clay,' said WPC O'Neil. 'Do you think it's worth flagging him up?'

'Definitely.' A thought prompted a dark expression in the young police constable's eyes. 'He looks a good deal older than DCI Clay. Are you thinking what I'm thinking?'

'Jesus,' said WPC O'Neil. 'I'll call DS Riley.'

50

10.35 am

'Have you seen this?' Poppy Waters sounded astonished as she blew into the incident room.

Stone looked up from his laptop and the umpteenth newspaper article on the internet that morning.

'What's this lucky break?' asked Cole.

'Pull up the Liverpool Vindici website we're still trying to locate.'

Stone and Cole stopped what they were doing and went straight on to the website.

'Got it?' she asked.

'Yes,' said Cole.

'What is it, Poppy?' asked Stone.

'Have you managed to work out where the other Liverpool-based site's operating from?' pressed Cole

'No,' she replied. 'Not yet. I need you to help me. Go to gallery: they've put on a brand-new picture.'

'I'm looking at a picture of a McDonald's...?' Stone didn't quite finish asking his question, and read silently as words moved across the bottom of the screen from right to left.

Poppy read, '*A warning to all paedophile scum. Children and teenagers go into this restaurant. I can see this restaurant from my house. My front windows face the McDonald's...*'

'Eve said this would happen,' said Cole. 'I didn't believe her.

But she was right. The sites are linked. The people running them know each other. Lucien Burns gets pulled and the person running this site comes cartwheeling out of the closet. They've got each other's backs.'

Stone had his iPhone out; he went straight to Google.

'...and I know who you are. If I see you in or around this McDonald's, I will catch you and take you down to the rail track, castrate you and throw you under a train. I know who you are. Scum. Make a child's day. Kill a paedo.'

'I don't get it, said Cole. 'I've been looking at this site until I'm blue in the face, looking for locational clues, waiting for whoever's running it to trip themselves up. But they've been tighter than the Sphinx's arsehole about who they are and where they're based. And now this?'

'I couldn't give a shit about the why or wherefore,' said Stone.

Stone typed *McDonald's restaurants Liverpool* into the Google search engine and, two clicks later, counted the different branches.

'Twenty. There are twenty McDonald's restaurants in Liverpool,' said Poppy as Stone counted the branches.

'I'll look up six because I'm slower than you whiz kids. First seven, Poppy. Next seven, you Barney. Fifteen to twenty me. Are we all looking at the same screen?' asked Stone.

'Big colour map of Liverpool on the right and slightly over the middle. McDonald's restaurants highlighted with red plates and white cutlery,' said Poppy.

'That's it.'

'The addresses of the different restaurants on the left,' added Cole. 'Top of the list Dunning's Bridge Road, Bootle, second Walton, third East Lancs Road.'

Stone felt his pulse racing. 'Poppy, can you print off multiple copies of the picture of the McDonald's restaurant that you found on the Vindici site. OK? We're looking for domestic dwellings directly facing a McDonald's restaurant across a busy main road, with a nearby railway track and a Farmfoods restaurant to the left.'

The shared printer on Stone's desk came alive as it pushed out colour pictures of the restaurant.

Cole scrolled with his right hand and spoke into the iPhone held in his left. 'Sergeant Harris, can you come to the incident room, please? We've got some information we need circulating urgently.'

Stone took three pages from the printer and looked closely at the image. 'The road the Vindici nut lives on is a busy main road. Looks like the north end of the city to me,' he said, handing the images of the McDonald's restaurant to Poppy and Cole.

Stone called Clay on speed dial, heard the squeal of her brakes as she connected on speakerphone on her dashboard.

'Eve, can you talk?'

'Give me a minute. I'm with the suspect's mother in my car.'

She pulled over to the side of Heath Road and took her phone off the dashboard and speakerphone. She got out and shut the door.

'We're minutes away from establishing where the other Liverpool-based Vindici site is.'

'Are the French are coming up with the goods?'

'Not yet. Whoever's running the website has left a huge visual clue as to where they are. It's a matter of elimination through twenty potential sites. Why they just didn't turn themselves in to the nearest police station, I don't know.'

Clay considered the emergence of the second website in the light of bitter experience.

'Don't get your hopes too high, Karl,' said Clay. 'This could all be a time-wasting piss take. Keep me posted. I've got to go.'

51

10.48 am

'OK, Lucien,' said Sergeant Harris. 'WPC Thomas is going to take your picture now. Don't smile, don't frown, don't pull a face. We just need a natural portrait. Imagine you're in a booth posing for a passport photo.'

Lucien looked at the back of his hands; he appeared to be admiring his fingernails. 'I've done nothing wrong. What are you going to do with all this information, the DNA swab and all that, when you realise I've done *nothing* wrong?'

'Lucien, you're at the stage in the process that I like to call the cleaning-the-toilet-with-a-toothbrush moment. There's no point in questioning what's happening to you, it just makes life harder for *you*,' explained Sergeant Harris. 'Just get on with it, do it and get over it.'

'Come on, Lucien, we're not looking for a *Vogue* cover here,' said WPC Jones.

Lucien turned his attention to WPC Thomas. 'You only look a few years older than me.' He linked his hands and the muscles in his forearms knotted. 'I bet I'd look great in your uniform.'

'Lucien, if you don't cut it out, I'm going to involve your mother in the process. Do you want that?' asked Sergeant Harris.

'Just violate my human rights a little bit further and take your bloody picture of me.'

WPC Thomas raised the camera and Lucien's face emptied

of all expression. He tilted his head minutely to the left and a strange light rose up in him and registered as a pseudo Christ-like glow in his eyes.

Sergeant Harris and WPC Thomas exchanged a baffled glance, and then Harris laughed knowingly.

'Lucien, you know when you try to copy the expression on Justin Truman's face in his famous mugshot, we'll think it's your way of telling us that you've copied him in other departments – like, say, murder?'

Lucien looked as though he'd been slapped by an invisible hand and WPC Thomas took a set of rapid portraits.

'Now that's what I call the I-know-I'm-in-the-shit look. Perfect! Thank you.'

52

11.01 am

In his room on the top floor of the Holiday Inn Express near John Lennon Airport, Arturo Jesús Salvador lay on one side of the double bed, his possessions spread out across the other side.

Since landing on English soil, he had worked hard and quickly and achieved everything he set out to do within his first hour in Liverpool. In his mind he did an inventory of the different individual tasks and the one overriding objective.

He had collected his case from the baggage-handling area.

Then he had made his way to Hertz Car Rental and picked up the black Ford Focus with child-locked back doors he had pre-booked before leaving Mexico. There had only been two specifications: an ordinary car, with back doors that could not be opened from within.

He drove the Mégane to the top level of the airport's multi-storey car park and parked it in a corner.

After booking in at the Hilton, he unpacked his hand luggage on to the bed and hung up in the wardrobe the two sets of clothes he needed for his visit.

Two identical black suits, two white shirts, underwear, shoes, socks and white gloves.

He checked his possessions on the bed.

A Mexican passport in the name of Arturo Jesús Salvador. Medication. A set of screwdrivers. A wallet full of money and credit cards, all in the name of Arturo Jesús Salvador. Chocolate he had purchased on the plane from Cork. The photograph of the fat man and his address. A copy of the *Liverpool Echo* with a front-page story detailing the murder of David Wilson and DCI Eve Clay's initial investigation into the case. The paperwork and contact details for the estate agent handling his properties on Merseyside, and the keys to those properties. A large box labelled 'El Día de Los Muertos'.

Everything was there and all was well.

And although he was tired from the flight and was getting over a string of bad days with his health, he raised himself from the bed and made his way to the window.

On the horizon he made out some of the miniaturised details of the Liverpool skyline – the cathedrals and the Radio City Tower. But the thing that interested him most and drew him away from resting was much closer to hand.

On the border between the Speke and Garston districts he identified a large building with a green roof and a car park at the back. In the car park he saw eight yellow police vans, some white Scientific Support vehicles, marked and unmarked police cars.

Two tiny uniformed police officers emerged from the back of the building, made their way to a marked car, and he was seized by a reckless desire to go there and wait outside, watch the people come and go, see if anyone would strike up a conversation with him at Trinity Road police station.

But no. It would completely undermine his overriding objective in coming to Liverpool: to go completely unnoticed until his work was done.

He dismissed the desire and spent a few more moments at the window, wallowing in the deep affection he nurtured for the building – even if it was the first time he had seen it – because of its association with an individual belonging to the place.

Arturo stared at the green roof of Trinity Road police station and deeply buried warmth blossomed inside him. He tracked his eyes across the city and, towards the town centre, made out the white hulk of the Littlewoods Building, the empty, disused art deco leviathan.

Trinity Road police station. The Littlewoods Building.

Arturo experienced a lightness that was stronger than his fatigue and spiralling illness.

He felt his life was somehow suspended between two places in time and, watching from such a great height, he was utterly empowered, as if anything was possible and the lengthy waiting game was now in its closing phases. The strength inside him intensified.

And for a moment, he knew what it was to be like God. A God filled with perfect love and in the same instant with profound rage.

53

11.48 am

'Where are you, Karl?' asked Cole.

'Heading up to the roundabout under the flyover at the top of Queens Drive and Rice Lane. What have you got for me?'

Cole looked out of the incident room window and saw geese in a flying-V heading towards the Mersey Estuary. 'I'm going to email you a list of who lives where on that block of seven terraced houses on Rice Lane, but there's one person in particular who I'm sure's going to be worth calling on. 636 Rice Lane, Christine Green, thirty-two years of age. She's been in trouble with us in the past, for racially abusing a complete stranger in the street.'

Stone turned on to Rice Lane and said, 'I do hope Green's at home.'

'If the electoral register's anything to go by,' said Cole, 'she lives on her own.'

'I'm looking forward to meeting her,' said Stone.

'Maybe you could take a bunch of flowers. Red roses perhaps?' laughed Cole.

'Fuck off, wanker!' shouted Stone.

'Thanks, Karl.'

'Not you, Barney, some taxi driver's just cut me up and then starts giving me the verbals.'

'I'm going to start looking for Vindici's financier soon. Anything I need to know?'

'Yes. Truman's solicitors, Graham, Alexander and Davidson, have got more than one thing in common with his barrister Reginald Everett QC, and the wall of admin around him. They're all pretending they don't know who bankrolled his legal costs. They're all pretending that they'll call me back when they find out, after they've been through their records. Right now, they're all talking to each other on the phone, taking the piss out of me. I can see the McDonald's. It looks like the one.'

'Make mine a Big Mac, Karl. OK, let's crack on!'

Cole closed the call down and logged into the National Police Computer. He looked at the note on his desk with the name of Clay's childhood friend that she had asked him to investigate, screwed up the paper and dropped it in the bin.

Cole typed in the name *James Peace* and waited.

54

12.00 noon

In Interview Suite 1 on the ground floor of Trinity Road police station, Lucien Burns was flanked by a young social worker with hair in a black bob, and a blonde female duty solicitor, thickset and middle-aged. On the other side of the table, Clay and Hendricks faced the trio and on the table between were three items recovered from Lucien's house.

Clay took a bottle of mineral water from her bag and handed it to Lucien. 'You're sixteen years of age, right?' She double-checked.

He nodded. 'Yeah, sixteen.'

'I've formally opened the interview and I'm reminding you, Lucien, that the following exchange is being recorded both on audio and on video,' said Clay.

'For the purposes of clarity could you please state why Lucien is being interviewed in a *murder* inquiry?' asked the solicitor.

'Certainly,' replied Hendricks. 'Two paedophiles, one suspected but with no criminal conviction, and one a time-served convicted child abuser, have been murdered within a few miles of Lucien's house. Lucien runs a Vindici fan site on which he advocates the hunting down, torturing and killing of paedophiles. Seeing as this is exactly what's happened here in south Liverpool not once but twice, we feel...' Hendricks looked at Clay, who nodded, and back at Lucien. '…we need to have a little chat with Lucien.'

Hendricks pointed at the equipment on the table. 'Is this your laptop, Lucien?'

'No comment.'

'I personally removed this laptop from your room, and you were present when I did so. Does this laptop belong to someone else?'

'No comment.'

'Is this your iPhone?'

'No comment.'

'Is this your iPad?'

'No comment.'

'OK, you did us one favour, albeit unintentionally. You left your laptop on, so we don't have to unlock it. We can unlock your iPhone and iPad later but let's have a little look at your computer.' Hendricks flipped open the laptop and brought up the desktop.

'Please don't touch my stuff!' said Lucien.

'Your stuff? So it does belong to you. Thanks for that, Lucien.' Hendricks pointed at an icon on the desktop. 'What's this, Lucien?' Silence. 'It's Dreamweaver. Dreamweaver's a programme that allows you to set up and manage your own website. Let's see what your Dreamweaver leads us to.'

He clicked the Dreamweaver icon and a long list of available pages became available.

'It looks like you've put a lot of time and effort into this. I'm opening the home page…' Hendricks looked at Lucien, the social worker and the solicitor. 'Care to take a look?'

Hendricks turned the laptop around, keeping it close to his body and his hands on either side.

'The man on screen is none other than Justin Truman. The words on the computer screen read: *Avenging Angel. Vindici. Death to paedophiles. Protect a child. Kill a paedo. Gouge out their eyes. Cut their bollock off.* You forgot to pluralise that,

Lucien, but you can't do everything, can you? These words just keep skimming across the bottom of the screen. Did you make this page, Lucien?'

'Listen to me, Lucien,' said the solicitor.

'Where's my mother?'

'Do you want your mother present now?' asked Clay.

'No.'

'Lucien, is this your laptop?' The solicitor jabbed an index finger at it. 'You unintentionally admitted that when you told Mr Hendricks, *Don't touch my stuff.* I suggest you cooperate and tell the truth because, believe me, you could be in big, big trouble here! If you're not involved in these murders, cooperate and eliminate yourself from this inquiry.'

In the ensuing silence, Clay watched Lucien's face as a look of sickness and horror crossed his features and settled in his eyes.

'I want another solicitor.'

'It's not a solicitor you need, Lucien,' Clay cranked up the pressure. His head swivelled towards her. 'It's a guardian angel. Don't start messing us round, lad, over your legal support. I've got twenty-four hours to either charge you or let you go. The clock's ticking, so if you start playing the no-comment, get-me-another-solicitor card, I'm going to charge you here and now with Incitement to Murder.'

His voice stuck inside him, Lucien mouthed the words *fucking hell* and with a sob threw his head back to look at the ceiling.

She looked at her watch. 'I'm going to give you a little heads-up. Your house is being searched right now by DC Margaret Bruce and a team of officers. That means we will look into every last nook and cranny of your home. Are we going to find any other interesting things that belong to you? Any other things that you may find difficult to explain away?'

After a long silence, he said, 'No.'

'You know what, Lucien,' said Clay. 'When DS Hendricks marched you in here, I saw you and I could tell what was going on in your head. You thought you were in a real-life version of a Quentin Tarantino movie, a biopic of Justin Truman's life and you were the main part.

'So you're too old to say you didn't understand what you were doing when you were telling people to hunt down, torture and kill paedophiles. It's called Incitement to Murder, Lucien. You've systematically and repeatedly broken a very serious law. We can charge you now and keep you here ad infinitum. You will get a long custodial sentence, guaranteed.'

She watched as the information percolated into his mind.

'Do you know anyone else in Liverpool running a Vindici website?'

'No.'

'Just for the sake of clarity do you have any learning difficulties or mental health issues?'

'No!'

Suddenly Lucien shoved his chair back, grating the feet against the floor. He bent forward and projectile vomited on to the floor, filling the room with sour milk and half-digested food. A second wave followed and then a third.

Clay turned to Hendricks. 'Ask Sergeant Harris to organise a cleaner. I'll call in the custody medic and book Interview Suite Two.'

Lucien sat bolt upright, wiping his mouth with the back of his hand. 'I don't need to see any doctor. I'm not sick. I'm just scared. I won't see a doctor. I won't.'

'Lucien,' said his solicitor. 'You don't have to see a doctor. Calm yourself.'

Slowly, Lucien slumped down and looked at Clay. His eyes were red raw and tears streamed down his face. Clay formally suspended the interview and called Sergeant Harris on her iPhone.

As the call to the front desk rang, Clay said, 'Do you know the real names of female visitors to your site?'

'Yeah, yeah, I do...'

'Well, I want those names from you, Lucien. Not user names.

Real names. The most violent females you know, the ones who make the most excessive claims to kill and torture paedophiles.'

'Women?'

'Yes, Lucien, women. Sergeant Harris, I need you to take Lucien Burns down to the cells. He's going to have a little think about what's what...' Clay eyeballed him. 'Aren't you, Lucien?'

55

12.03 pm

When Detective Sergeant Karl Stone parked his car in Sefton Road, around the corner from Christine Green's house on Rice Lane, he felt the buzz of an incoming text on his phone. On the display screen: 'Sammy – 1 minute ago'. *Dear Karl, I am sorry about last night. I hope we can still be friends.*

So am I, he thought, *sorry that I couldn't take you up on your offer.*

He typed: *After all this is sorted Sammy I'm going to take you out to dinner, shower you with affection and do everything in my power to make you fall in love with me and stay there.*

In silence, he read the message back to himself and his finger hovered over send. He paused and, flooded with hopelessness, deleted the whole message.

He typed: *No need to be sorry Sammy. Of course we are still friends.* Send.

When he saw Detective Sergeant Gina Riley park and get out of her car, Stone joined her on the pavement.

'You're very quiet,' said Riley as they walked to the corner of Sefton Road and Rice Lane. 'Come on, Karl, spit it out!'

'Last night, Sammy Wilson came on to me, heavy duty, in her flat. Got me up there because she was afraid of the dark. Then she hit me with sweet talk and tried to kiss me.'

Riley stopped. 'And?'

'And I turned her down. She got a bit upset to say the least.'

'You did the right thing. You were strong, professional. Have you told Eve yet?'

'No.'

'Want me to mention it to her?'

'If you wouldn't mind.'

'I know how much you like Sammy Wilson.'

'Do I make it that obvious?'

Riley laughed. 'I can tell; others wouldn't. You know something, Karl? Even before you told me that, I could tell she's really holding a torch for you. Come on, let's go and ruin Greenie's day.'

They turned on to Rice Lane. Each of the seven two-up, two-down terraced houses on the block facing McDonald's had a small, walled garden area separating the front door from the pavement.

'What do we know about her?' asked Riley as they reached number 636.

'She's a racist and she hates paedophiles with a vengeance,' replied Stone, looking into the space between the front wall and the stone wall that met the pavement. 'And she more or less invited us over.'

In Christine Green's area were three terracotta pots in which all the plants were long dead, their remains dangling over the side into the space where the wind had blown fast-food packaging from the restaurant over the road.

Stone rang the bell but there was no sound so he knocked hard, five times, on the door. 'I hope the inside of the house is a bit better.' The front room was shielded from the pavement by net curtains that seemed oddly old-fashioned for a woman in her early thirties. 'Got the search warrant ready?' he asked.

Riley showed him the warrant on her phone, sent to her in a hurry by the duty magistrate as she travelled from Mather Avenue to Walton.

Footsteps came close to the front door.

'Who is it?' A female voice, without emotion or accent.

'Police,' said Stone

Silence.

'We're in a hurry, Christine. We need to talk to you and you need to open the door now,' said Riley.

The door opened a couple of centimetres but was secured by a chain. Christine Green peered out, a thin-faced woman with dyed blond hair and the first signs of stubborn greyness. She balanced a pair of reading glasses on her narrow nose and squinted at the warrant cards.

'What's this to do with?

The door to 638 Rice Lane opened and an elderly woman with an empty milk bottle in her hand stepped out of her house. Stone indicated the neighbour.

'I suggest we talk inside, Christine.'

Christine looked at the old woman, who stood still, watching the scene with confidence and no embarrassment.

'Turn your bloody nasty music down or as God is my judge I'll get the noise pollution people round to you, *Miss Green*!' The old woman's voice was clear and assertive and defied the fragility of her body.

The two women stood in silent deadlock, staring each other down.

'Christine,' said Riley. 'We haven't got time to waste. Inside. Now!'

'What's your name, madam?' Stone asked the old woman, sensing a potentially great witness, a feisty old lady who was openly hostile to the suspect.

'Mary Behan. You are?'

He showed her his warrant card. 'Detective Sergeant Karl Stone.'

'Oohhh.' She sounded satisfied. 'She's a bloody lunatic that one.'

Stone handed her two contact cards. 'Do me a favour, Mrs Behan.' He looked around. They were alone on the pavement. 'Write your phone number down on that and keep this one.

If you want to talk to me about anything, you can call me on either of those numbers.'

'No problem. Good luck, son. You'll need it.' She drew a circle in the air at her temple. 'Her bars are down.'

Stone smiled, watched Mary Behan close her front door and, as he made to enter Christine Green's house, heard Riley's voice.

'Jeez... what in the world's all this?'

56

12.07 pm

Jesus, thought Stone, echoing Riley's reaction as he walked though Christine's Green narrow hallway, past the red, white and black flag that covered most of the wall.

He found a light switch on the wall, turned it on but there was no bulb in the fitting that hung from the ceiling.

Stone stepped into the living room and saw Christine Green watching Riley's back as she looked at the wall over the fireplace. Riley was shaking her head as she put on her reading glasses.

One wall was covered floor to ceiling with shelving rammed with books. Stone glanced at some of the titles and authors on the spines. *The Third Reich: A New History*, Michael Burleigh; *Christian Theology*, Michael Wilcockson; *The Second World War*, Antony Beevor.

He turned away from the books and saw that Christine was now watching him. He looked past her and at the massive oil painting above the fireplace.

'An oil painting of Adolf Hitler? Where did you buy that?' asked Stone.

'The internet.'

On the wall next to the painting was an intricately hand-carved skull sitting on two femurs.

'And did you buy the wooden SS Death's Head on the 'net?'

'No, I carved it myself. Whittling wood is my hobby.'

Green gave Riley a death glare as she picked up an object from the mantelpiece and shook it. Riley showed it to Stone.

'Look at this, Karl, SS storm troopers on skis in a snow dome.'

'Put that down,' said Christine. 'It was manufactured in Dresden in 1941 as a limited edition and it's very, very expensive.'

Stone wondered if he was in the home of a suspect or would soon wake up in his favourite armchair at home, laughing at the oddness of his dream.

'Sorry,' said Riley, putting the snow dome back. 'Much as we'd love to talk about your extensive collection of Nazi memorabilia, we haven't got time...'

'Just because I collect Nazi memorabilia, that doesn't make me a Nazi.'

Riley turned to Stone. 'Did I say she was a Nazi?'

'No, you did not. Christine, we've come to talk to you about your Vindici website.'

'Loads of people hate paedophiles. Why are you picking on me?'

'Because you, Christine, on your website,' said Riley, 'and thank you for not denying that you've got a website, you go a bit further than just, say, calling them names or saying you hate them. You tell people to go and kill them. And—'

'And you think I topped those two paedos in the south end of the city. Right, I want a solicitor. I'll get my coat. I'm not saying another fucking word. Let's go!'

There was a knocking on the window. Stone went to the front door and opened it to Detective Constable Clive Winters and three officers he didn't know.

'These are our colleagues from the Walton Lane nick,' said Winters.

Winters and the three officers entered.

'Thanks for your help, lads,' said Stone as the four gathered at Christine Green's living-room door.

'Who the fuck are you?' asked Christine, indignant.

Detective Constable Clive Winters, a six-foot-five Liverpool-born and -bred powerhouse of a man, stopped at the red and white flag with the black swastika at its centre, looked at Stone and said, 'What the fuck?'

'Maybe when you've done searching the house, Clive, you could take her to your mum's house off Lodge Lane and treat her to some home-cooked Caribbean food? We've had some great nights round your mother's...'

'She's not going anywhere near my ma!'

'What's going on?' asked Christine.

'These officers are going to search your house.'

'Where's your search warrant?' Christine held her hand out. Riley placed the screen of her phone in front of her face.

Christine Green sat down and, picking up an open copy of *Mein Kampf* from the arm of the sofa beside her, said, 'I'm going nowhere. I'm not allowing you cunts to go rummaging through my things. I'm fucking staying put.' She looked Winters up and down, and shook her head in pure dismay.

'I'm leading this search,' said Winters from the doorway. 'Have you got a problem with that?'

'No, Christine,' said Riley. 'When I say it's time to leave you leave. We're going to Trinity Road. When I say so.'

Stone addressed Winters and the officers from Walton Lane. 'We're looking for a laptop, bicycle wheels with spokes missing...'

As he closed the living room door, Christine called, 'You're wasting your fucking time, you won't find nothing incriminating here, you shower of gobshites!'

'Clive.' Stone handed over to Winters.

Winters showed the back-up officers a picture on his phone of the statuette of a Weeping Child.

'Find one of these and I'll take you all out on the piss. On me. One of you upstairs with me, two downstairs.'

'Christine,' said Riley. 'We're leaving for Trinity Road police station as soon as my colleagues find your laptop.'

'Won't be going anywhere then.'

'Have you dumped it somewhere?'

She straightened the glasses on her nose and returned her attention to *Mein Kampf*.

57

12.15 pm

Clay stood at the window with the smell of vomit in her nostrils and looked around the incident room for Barney Cole, hoping he'd managed to dig up some information on James Peace, but he wasn't there.

Hendricks approached with two mugs of coffee and handed her one.

'How did you get on?' asked Clay.

'I've been on to Alder Hey in the Park and they're going to dig out Lucien's medical records. I've spoken to the schools he used to go to, and no one, *no one*, was surprised to receive a call from us about Lucien Burns. He got kicked out of the Blue Coat School aged eleven for setting up a bomb scare in the Clock Tower. He left King David after a fire broke out in the science block. Still aged eleven. He was in and out of Liverpool College aged twelve to thirteen where he acted the elective mute. Last chance: Calderstones Community School. Shown the door aged fourteen, after stalking Mary Blake, a forty-something art teacher.'

'And he doesn't figure on our records?'

'Not a mention. There's the shit that goes on out there that we know about, and there's the shit that just passes us by.'

'Anything else from his laptop?'

'One bombshell so far and Poppy's only been on it for a few

minutes. Lucien's building a new page that he hasn't published yet: "Name and Shame". He's got the names, photographs and addresses of eight convicted paedophiles on Merseyside. Our leak just turned into a stream!'

'We'll wire into him on that one,' said Clay. 'Is he accurate in his information?'

'Yes and no. Yes, the pictures and names are right but the addresses are all historical. They do tend to move house a lot.'

Walking back to her desk, Clay looked at the screen of her phone, saw one notification on Facebook and one on Messenger. She opened Facebook and saw a picture of Maggie Anderson. *Friend request accepted.*

Clay felt a huge smile spread across her face.

'You look happy,' observed Hendricks.

'I've just hooked up with a woman called Maggie Anderson who I knew when I was a child. She worked at St Michael's Catholic Care Home for Children, and she was good to me.

Clay sat at her desk, opened Messenger and saw the words Maggie Anderson wrote: *Eve, what a lovely surprise to hear from you.*

She opened the message, and carried on reading, white words on a blue background.

I know you are a working mother and are very busy but if you would like to we could meet up for coffee or tea. I am retired now and can do most times on most days. My number is 07790 143576. I will leave it for you to call me and arrange this if you would care to but in the meantime I wish you all the luck in the world. God bless, lots of love, Maggie x PS I live in a care home run by nuns up in Crosby – Nazareth House. Isn't it funny how things turn round in life?

A wave of emotion flooded Clay, happiness for the good times and sorrow for people and places that had been and gone.

She dialled the mobile phone number and within two rings,

heard Maggie's voice for the first time in many years, in a recorded message.

'Hi, you've reached Maggie. If you'd like to leave a message for me speak after the tone and I will get back to you as soon as I can. Thank you for calling.'

As the beep sounded, Clay's mind was full of Jimmy Peace being dragged into the back of a police car as they took him away from her forever. And although she still couldn't remember what his face was like in the back window, she remembered clearly that when they made eye contact, his mouth had moved as he tried to give her a final message.

'Hi, Maggie, it's Eve Clay. How lovely to hear from you. I'm going to text you three phone numbers. My home number, my work landline number and my mobile. You can get me on any of these numbers. I'd be absolutely delighted to meet up with you for tea or coffee – I seem to remember you were a big tea drinker way back when. So come back to me on any of those numbers when you get the chance. And God bless you too. Lots of love and bye for now. Eve.'

Clay looked up and saw that Cole was standing over her.

'I've got some news for you on your old friend James Peace,' he said quietly. 'Talk about weird coincidences.'

Clay felt a compression in her core and lightness in her head. *Please*, she wished, *don't tell me anything terrible*, and a large part of her was sorry she'd asked Cole to go digging.

'He was known to Merseyside Police and the Met. When he was a teenager he was brought in for questioning about beating up a worker in the children's home he lived in but the CPS refused to take it to court. Guess what? It was St Michael's, the home you were brought up in. Is that how you know him?'

'Yes.'

'Early 1989 he was working as a chef in London and was arrested for GBH. The case against him fell apart on a technicality. 1990, he was back in Liverpool and out on bail. This time round he was in really big trouble, was facing a custodial and a criminal record. He nearly killed the guy. While he was awaiting trial, he died in a shipwreck. Go on, Eve, what's the weird coincidence?'

'His targets were paedophiles. Anything else?'

'That's it. I'm still digging for you. Paedos, how did you know?'

'Educated guess. I'm grateful to you, Barney.'

The phone on Clay's desk rang and, when she picked up the receiver, she heard DS Terry Mason's voice, unusually excited.

'Eve, get down to my room, please. We've just pulled some items of interest from Steven Jamieson's filing cabinets.'

'I'll be right there,' said Clay. 'Come on, Barney. Let's go and see what the lads have found.'

58

12.23 pm

On the ground floor of Trinity Road police station, DS Bill Hendricks paused to read the laminated sign on the door of the viewing room.

PLEASE KNOCK BEFORE ENTERING.
DO NOT ENTER THE ROOM UNTIL YOU HAVE
ESTABLISHED YOUR CREDENTIALS AND HAVE BEEN
GIVEN DIRECT PERMISSION TO ENTER.

Hendricks looked up above the door and imagined another much more disturbing sign: 'Abandon hope all ye who enter here'.

He knocked on the door.

'Who is it?'

'Bill Hendricks.'

When the door opened, Sergeant Carol White, bag on her shoulder and all set to leave, gave him a weak smile. 'Hello, Bill.' He looked at White's partner, Sergeant Alice Banks, who gazed almost vacantly at the laptop screen in front of her.

'Hey, Bill,' said Banks. 'How's it out there in the real world?'

'It has its moments.'

'Excuse me, Bill,' said Carol White. 'I'm going outside. I'm desperate for a cigarette.'

Hendricks noticed that the gold wedding ring that she turned around and around on her finger continuously through their conversations was not there. 'It's you I've come to see, Carol.'

'I'm all right. I'm fine. Honestly. I just need a cigarette.'

'OK. I just found a window of time and I thought I'd see how you are. Later maybe.'

He watched as she left, and when she reached the doors leading to the stairs, she turned and asked, 'Did you look at that photograph I gave you?'

'I did,' he lied.

It was now in an unopened envelope in his desk drawer.

'And?'

'I see exactly what you mean.'

She nodded, pushed through the doors and was gone.

'Come in, Bill!' said Banks, pausing the imagery on her laptop and bringing up her screen saver.

He closed the door and smiled at Alice Banks as he sat in White's chair. In her early thirties, single, with long jet-black hair, Alice was way above average pretty and had a smile that could stop traffic.

Carol White's screen was black and Hendricks projected vivid horrors into that darkness. He took a deep breath, catching the edge of White's perfume even though she was not there.

'It's Daisy by Marc Jacobs,' said Banks. 'She splashes it on like it's holy water and it's somehow going to make things easier.'

Hendricks looked at the surface of Carol White's desk: the pens standing neatly in a mug bearing Johnny Depp's face as Captain Jack Sparrow, her closed spiral-bound notebook, Gold Spot breath freshener, a Costa Coffee takeaway coffee container, a depleted box of king-size tissues, the everyday trappings of an ordinary human being whose daily work was full of impossible demands.

'If you're feeling affected by your work, the door's still open if you ever want to talk to me.'

'No thanks, Bill, but thanks for offering.' She smiled. 'The door's still open for you, Bill. Likewise.'

He remembered last year's Christmas party, how he'd declined an invitation back to Alice's flat in Gateacre and, spiralling to the present, recalled the ten men that the Trinity Road rumour mill, six married, four not, who hadn't declined an invite to Alice's home.

'It just doesn't get to me any more, Bill. Pure and simple. Carol, on the other hand, who used to hold me together when I was going to pieces, it's like we've gone through a role reversal. She's coming up with the goods in reporting back but she's all over the place in every other department of her life.'

'Has she said anything that's made you sit up and take note?'

Alice Banks smiled. 'Are you here about that round robin email about the leak?'

'No, I'm genuinely concerned for Carol.'

'She told me about last night. She's really embarrassed about it. She's been expecting you all day and dreading you coming. Every time there's been a knock on the door, she picks up her bag so that she can claim she's off for a smoke outside.'

'She told me about her husband leaving.'

Banks sighed. 'Well, she told me for the last few months she's had two means of communicating with him. Crying and screaming.' She held Hendricks's gaze. 'I feel sorry for him. He's a lovely guy. Actually, I feel sorry for both of them. Go on, Bill, ask me. Do you think Carol is our leak?'

'Well, do you?'

'I haven't overheard anything, and I haven't seen her put the phone down suddenly or switch screens at the bat of an eyelid when I've walked in on her...'

'But?'

'She's been very erratic. She was a rock. Now, she's like a bowl of dust blown on the wind. I'm not going to accuse her. I have no evidence. But I'm watching her closely, and I didn't need a memo to prompt me to do so. Frankly, and personally, it doesn't worry me if she is the leak. What I'm worried about's her mental health. She's just not up to it.'

She looked away into the distance and Hendricks felt suddenly sad that such a good and truthful woman was wasting herself on men of little worth.

'How do you cope, Alice, with all this?'

'I've fireproofed myself with ideas that are as profound as my feeble mind can cope with.'

Hendricks smiled. 'Go on...?'

'This kind of horror and abuse has been going on since the dawn of human time, all the way through history but never acknowledged; never, ever documented. But it's a brand-new issue because in recent times, it is acknowledged and, oh boy, is it recorded! I say to myself, if it wasn't me trawling through this filth, it'd have to be some other person. I'm doing someone else a favour – maybe someone I know, maybe a stranger. My role in this won't last forever. But what will last forever is this. Some adults will abuse children. Some children will be abused by adults. I don't particularly like my job at the moment, but what I do like is when me and Carol give you the ammunition to blow these characters sky high.'

'Keep an eye on her for me, Alice.'

'Absolutely.'

Hendricks opened the door and, stepping out of the viewing room, paused when Alice Banks said, 'Keep that door open!'

He looked back at her with a quizzical smile and pointed at the door in his hand.

'No, not that one, Bill!'

59

12.23 pm

For the third time, Christine Green pressed play on her CD and moments later Adolf Hitler's voice filled the living room.

'Could you turn it down just a little bit?' said Stone, standing in the doorway to the hall and losing the will to live.

'Could you tell your bastard mates who are ransacking my house to make less noise?'

Stone looked out of the window at Riley on the pavement taking another call, and felt Christine Green advancing. He turned his attention to her, saw the red veins in the whites of her eyes and smelt coffee on her breath.

'You intrigue me, Christine,' said Stone, his voice rising above Hitler's threadbare rhetoric. He stepped away from her, walked up to the CD player and turned it off.

'Hey, you! How dare you! This is my house...'

Stone took the CD from the player and dropped it in an evidence bag.

'What are you doing?'

'Removing evidence from a crime scene.'

Christine's outrage spiralled into a momentary dumb confusion.

'If you had to describe yourself in two words, say, for the purposes of internet dating, would you say *Hitler lover* or *paedophile hater*?'

'What are you talking about?'

'I want to get a picture of how you see yourself.'

'I see myself getting victimised because I stand up for inno-cent children by the likes of you who should be victimising paedophiles.'

'Karl?'

'Excuse me, Christine.'

Stone walked over to DC Clive Winters at the bottom of the stairs.

'There's no sign of a laptop. The four of us have had the place apart and there's nothing doing.'

'Fucking told you so!' snarled Christine from the door to her front room and Stone, who thought his morale had hit rock bottom, felt his heart tumble just a little further.

'Keep this for me please,' said Stone to Winters, handing him the evidence bag with the Hitler CD. Then he turned to Christine and weighed her up. 'You're a contradiction in terms.'

'Have you been reading about psychoanalysis in *Reader's Digest*?'

'All these books. Your immense skill in fashioning wood. You're a highly intelligent woman but you present like a dumb lout.'

She put *Mein Kampf* back on the shelf, folded her arms and stared at him.

'Got any mates, Christine?'

'What do you mean?'

'Do you have any friends?'

'No. Who needs them?'

'So you've been let down in the past? How about virtual friends, on the internet?'

'No.'

'You must get people communicating with you through your website?'

'That doesn't make them my friends.'

'Do you know someone called Lucien Burns?'

'Lucien Burns?' She looked and sounded blank. 'Is he a TV chef?'

'Can I pay you a compliment, Christine?'

'What are you after?'

'Information. So listen to this and think about it. We're talking to you as part of a murder investigation, as in very serious shit and very, very seriously long custodial sentences. When we find your laptop, Christine, we'll be able to see everything that's come in to you and everything you've sent out. If you know who's topped the paedos, do yourself a favour and give me a name or names. Otherwise – here's the key.' Stone mimed throwing the key away and, for a moment, the woman was quiet and reflective.

'But you're not going to find a laptop, so do one.'

'Who do you know who's capable of killing, not just saying they'd do it, but actually killing a couple of paedophiles?'

'Loads of people.'

'Including yourself?'

'All I've done is protect children...'

'Here we go, blah, blah, blah.'

'I want to go to the police station. I want a lawyer. I'm not saying another fucking word until I've got a lawyer with me. Sly arse, trying to interrogate me like you're having a casual conversation when I've got no legal representation!'

She turned, walked into the front room and slammed the door shut.

Riley walked by the open front door, talking on her iPhone.

Desperate for a change of scene, Stone stepped past the massive swastika on the hall wall and on to the busy main road as Riley closed down another call.

'More calls from the uniforms on paedo watch?' asked Stone.

'Thirty-eight paedophiles and counting. No one knows anything. Half of them are begging to be taken into protective custody, the other half are denying they're paedophiles. One guy called Edward Hawkins, Flat Four, 101 Arundel Avenue, started speaking and acting really strangely when he saw Eve's name on the card the officers gave him – looked like he'd been sledgehammered when he heard her name. Denied knowing her.

They think he's bullshitting and does know her. Anything here, Karl?'

'There's no sign of her laptop. She's demanding a solicitor. Heads or tails, who'll take her in to Trinity Road?'

'No need. You look like you want to strangle her. I'll take her,' said Riley. 'What's your hunch?'

'She's ditched her laptop but she's an accomplice to murder. She *knows* the woman who phoned from 699 Mather Avenue and she's up to her neck in it but she *thinks* she's going to walk away in twenty-four hours.'

The door to the front room opened.

'Are you talking about me?' asked Christine.

'Get your coat, Christine. You're going to Trinity Road with me. Right now.'

'Why?'

'Because, for now, we can't find your laptop here and because I say so,' said Riley.

60

12.23 pm

The contents of Steven Jamieson's filing cabinets were set out on three tables in DS Terry Mason's office in the basement of Trinity Road police station.

'Talk me through it,' said Clay, picking up a brown paper file from the first table.

'Here we've got papers and documents related to his property business. It all seems legitimate and appears to have nothing to do with his secret self. So we'll call this the public face of Steven Jamieson even though his name didn't appear on anything public, post arrest and conviction.'

The table was piled high. Clay glanced through the top documents, saw a standard tenancy agreement, an eviction notice and an inventory of furniture fixtures and fittings for a fully furnished house. Then she turned to the second table, which was less weighed down.

'This lot is to do with purchases made for his former home in South Yorkshire and his house on Mather Avenue, receipts for things Frances Jamieson, mainly, bought for their homes,' said Mason.

At random Clay picked up a file and took out the contents; she made a mental note of the document at the top of the pile, a full structural survey of 699 Mather Avenue.

Mason continued, 'You've got contracts with estate agents,

land registry documents and so on, so this is his private self, if you like.'

Clay opened another file in the middle and saw a receipt for £8,500 for carpets from John Lewis. She pictured Steven Jamieson's dead body and Frances Jamieson bound, gagged and with her eyelids hacked off, and then imagined them alive in the carpet department of the store in Liverpool One, Mr and Mrs Ordinary needing carpets just like everyone else.

She pointed to the third table. 'And what's all this, Terry?'

'This is his secret self.'

Clay felt her skin pucker into goosebumps, a quickening of her pulse and her mouth growing slightly dryer.

'I'm not saying a word on this one, Eve. I want to know what you think,' said Mason.

She picked up the first file and took out a sheaf of Barclays bank statements; she checked the branch address, 10–12 Pinstone Street, Sheffield S1 2HN, and the name and address of the account holder.

'Daniel Campbell, 183 Queen Street, Sheffield, South Yorkshire S1 2DW,' read Clay.

'I've already spoken to Campbell. He's Steven Jamieson's solicitor. Or was. Sounds like a slimy little shit,' said Cole.

Clay heard Mason and Parker laughing as she cast her eyes down the columns, paid in and withdrawn.

Paid in 09/08/2004, £50,000.

She went to the next sheet and saw: *09/09/2004, £50,000.*

'Fifty thousand a month, every month?' Clay asked Mason.

He nodded. 'With additional amounts of money paid in as and when.'

She picked out a standing order: *03/08/2004.*

'APL Ltd. Three thousand pounds. Each month?'

'Every month,' confirmed Mason.

'APL Ltd is the only constant. Started in 2001 and still being paid up to the present.'

'Is there a pattern?' asked Clay.

'These bogus companies crop up, receive an income for so long and then close down.'

'It's a slush fund managed by his solicitor to put distance between this account and Jamieson himself,' said Clay.

'It took us a bit longer than that to work it out, but – yeah,' said Parker.

'I want you to analyse these bank statements, Barney. Get in touch with Barclays in Sheffield and get them to disclose more information. As soon as we've made copies...' She checked her iPhone contacts, saw the name Lesley Reid, the SIO who'd brought Jamieson to a form of justice. '...these can go to South Yorkshire Professional Standards Department. Every penny I've got says that he used this account to pay off bent coppers in and around South Yorkshire. And a lot more besides.'

She put the statements into the file and handed them to Cole.

Clay picked up the second file and took out a handful of letters on 'Daniel Campbell Solicitors' headed notepaper. She flicked through the letters and saw that they were all to the same medical doctor in Sheffield: Dr Damien Warner. And with each letter came a receipt for £5,000. She compared the first and second letter and saw that the only variation was in the date.

She started to count the correspondence.

Clay flicked through twelve identically worded receipts from the same doctor

'Twelve lots of cosmetic surgery?' observed Clay, wondering if Steven Jamieson or his wife had some sort of surgical addiction on top of their other issues.

She picked up the third file and took out a collection of confidentiality documents drafted by Jamieson's solicitor and on notepaper headed 'Donald Campbell Solicitors.'

'There are twelve confidentiality documents, twelve deals for silence. And there are twelve receipts from Doctor Warner,' said Mason.

Clay looked at the first confidentiality document and saw Campbell's signature and another signature in child-like writing that turned Clay's skin to ice. Next to the child's signature was another box. Beneath the dotted lines were two words: *Parent/ Guardian*. Above the dotted line was an adult signature.

'They all signed for different amounts,' said Mason. 'The lowest signed for five hundred pounds. The biggest pay off was twenty five thousand pounds. Clay checked the terms and conditions on the first page more closely, and saw there was no clear indication of the nature of the activity that demanded silence for money, but saw menace, ruination and the power of the law in case the silence was broken.

'Dr Warner didn't perform cosmetic surgery on these children,' said Clay, a dismal probability forming in her mind. 'Thank you, Terry, Paul, you've done a great job weeding these out.'

She handed the third file of confidentiality agreements to Cole.

Clay dialled Lesley Reid's number and, as the phone rang, she said to Cole, 'Block book an interview suite from three hours hence until whenever. I want Daniel Campbell's arse in it as soon as our colleagues in South Yorkshire can get him over here.'

'Lesley Reid speaking.'

'Hi, Lesley, it's Eve Clay. I think I've got something red hot for you.'

61

1.08 pm

Stone looked up from his desk, saw Clay enter the incident room and called, 'Eve, I've just taken a call from a journalist who covered Justin Truman's trial.'

As Clay arrived at Stone's desk, she said, 'Go on?'

'His legal team was bankrolled by Justine Weir,' said Stone. 'She was baptised Katharine Weir but she changed her name by deed poll to Justine, as a homage to Truman.'

'Do we know her current whereabouts?'

'She died in an RTA in Mexico City four years ago, which places Truman in or around that part of the world. Weir was his Old Faithful, would have followed him into the top of an erupting volcano. Prior to that, the last details I have of her were from around the time Justin Truman escaped from custody. She walked into her lawyer's office and instructed him to put every last penny of her considerable fortune into a range of offshore accounts. She offloaded all her assets in the Weir family building business in a fire sale and shifted that money into the same accounts and altered her last will and testament.'

'Who was named in the will?'

'Guess?'

'Justin Truman,' said Clay.

'She phoned her lawyer two weeks after her appearance in his office, said she was in Algiers and didn't know where Truman was.

You've got to understand, she had the money and connections to move mountains. Getting Truman out of the country and fitting him up with a new identity overseas – for the likes of you and me that'd be virtually impossible but for her it was nothing.'

'Any information on why he was fixated on Mexico and the Day of the Dead?' asked Clay.

'He had no family connections or friends that I'm aware of. At the time of his arrest, he hadn't even visited the country. I dug up his family tree on Ancestry UK. His family were from the Black Country and various places around the Midlands. I stopped when I got back to the end of the eighteenth century.'

Oh, Karl Stone, thought Clay, *you've just given me a great idea.*

'Does Truman have any surviving relatives?' asked Clay, mentally crossing her fingers.

'His mother's dead. When she was alive she was almost blind and crippled with arthritis. No surviving relatives. His mother was a product of the care system so there was no extensive family network. Father upped and left before Truman was born. There were huge patches of Truman's life of which there are no records; he travelled around a lot chasing work, labouring, waiting on tables, picking fruit – real grey areas, missing years.'

'Thank you, Karl.'

'I saw your eyes light up, Eve, when I mentioned digging up Truman's family tree.' Stone lifted the top piece of paper and turned the blank side to Clay.

'Hey, stop teasing me, Barney.'

He turned his writing towards her.

> Justine Weir
> Justin Truman
> Escape from custody
> Massive transfer of assets to JT
> JT named in will
> Algiers

No connection to Mexico
No surviving relatives
Ancestry UK
Justin Truman – James Peace

'If I can trace back Justin Truman on Ancestry UK, wouldn't it be the same with your old friend James Peace?'

In the silence that followed, Clay was seized by a long-buried memory of her first day at St Michael's Catholic Care Home for Children.

Jimmy had stopped her in the hall. *'First day here, kid?'*

'What of it?' she had blustered.

'I know what happened from Sister Philomena, and that it's really rough for you now. If you want to talk about it or if there's anything I can do to help you, just let me know, OK?'

'OK!'

'You're going to be all right, kid, you've got to know that.'

He carried on towards the kitchen and she asked. *'What's your name, lad?'*

He stopped, turned and smiled at her.

'Jimmy Peace. Yeah, I know who you are, Eve.'

'Who am I?'

'You're my mate, kid.'

Stone's voice brought her back. 'I'm very sorry, Eve. I didn't mean to upset you.'

'You haven't upset me. I was thinking the same as you.'

'Want me to go ahead and dig up Jimmy Peace's ancestry?'

'That's a great idea.'

'I've got to get on with sorting out Jamieson's murky finances, dodgy doctor and gagging orders first.'

'Of course you have. Stick a photocopy of your notes on my desk, please, Karl. Thank you. Thank you so much.'

62

2.15 pm

Clay formally opened the interview with Lucien Burns.

'Feeling better, Lucien?' she asked across the table in Interview Suite 2.

'This is a list of names and email addresses of the biggest psycho bitches from Liverpool who've contacted me over the website.'

He slid the paper to Hendricks who looked it up and down.

'I don't know any of them, Eve. Do you?'

She looked. 'No.'

'I've ranked them one to twelve, one being the biggest basket case, twelve being not as frigging crazy as the other bints. I can give you loads of examples and I can go way beyond twelve names.'

'How do you *know* their names, Lucien?' asked Clay.

'I've met up with them. They've all made financial donations to the website from their bank accounts.'

'Are you sure you're not just throwing us these *ladies* to put us off your scent?' asked Clay.

'You asked for names, I've given them to you.'

'We've got some really big questions to ask you, Lucien.'

'Oh, by the way, I'm really sorry for messing up your other room. It all kind of hit me at once.'

'This is a very serious business, Lucien. You're not the first person to throw up when I'm talking to them and you won't be the last. Sadly. For me.'

'Have your IT wizards got my laptop?'

'Yes.' Clay watched the mental cogs turn in his face.

'Then there's no point in lying about what is and isn't on my laptop.'

Hendricks nodded approvingly. 'You're talking sense, Lucien.'

'Where's my mother?'

'Lucien! You're here to answer not ask questions,' advised his solicitor.

'It's all right,' said Clay. 'See that piece of glass behind me? She's behind the glass. She can see you, and she can hear you.'

Lucien became very quiet and looked even more upset. He turned on his chair and faced the glass. 'Mother, get out of that room now and go away. I'm going to talk to these coppers and I don't want you hanging around and sticking your oar in.'

Silence.

'It's soundproofed, Lucien.'

Lucien looked at Clay. 'I'm not saying another word till she's gone.'

Clay stood up, picked up the list of twelve names supplied by Lucien Burns and said, 'I'll deal with your mother.'

As Clay got to the door of the interview suite, from the other side Lucien's mother shouted, 'Goodbye, Lucien, thanks so very much for humiliating me in front of the police. I'm off now, so please feel free to talk to complete strangers about the real you while you ignore your poor mother who's fed you and cleaned up after you for years. Maybe, Lucien, I just won't come back at all and leave you hanging in the dark. You're worse than your father!'

Clay opened the door. 'All right, Annabelle. That's enough. Go to Garston Village, get yourself a coffee and I'll talk to you when you come back. When you're nice and calm.'

Annabelle Burns flounced through a pair of swing doors

leading to the front entrance of Trinity Road police station, followed by the worn-looking WPC who'd been assigned to mind her.

'Jenny,' said Clay to the WPC. 'When she's off the premises, take this list of women's names supplied by Lucien up to the incident suite. Fill them in on the context and they can get the elimination machine rolling.'

Clay checked her iPhone, saw she had three missed calls, all from Riley. She closed the door of incident suite 2 and called Riley back. 'What's happening, Gina?'

'I'm driving Christine Green to Trinity Road. The traffic on Queens Drive is horrific.'

'Yes, you're driving me to the police station while all your little bastard friends are pulling my home to pieces,' shrieked Christine.

'OK,' said Clay. 'I get the picture. I'll talk to you when you get back.'

Clay met Lucien's eye as she sat across from him at the table.

Hendricks showed Lucien a list of names, addresses and photographs of the paedophiles who he looked set to name and shame.

'Where on earth did you get this information about these paedophiles?' asked Hendricks. 'You realise how highly secret and sensitive this all is?'

Lucien looked sick.

'Yeah, yeah, course I do.'

'Your mother's not here now,' said Clay. 'Talk to us.'

'OK, I can see you're conflicted, Lucien,' said Hendricks. 'And I'll tell you now, loyalty is a wonderful quality in any human being. But misguided loyalty's a terrible thing and can lead you up all manner of dangerous blind alleys. I'm pretty sure that you got this information from someone who works for Merseyside Constabulary as either a police officer or civilian support.'

'I didn't. Your IT people are going to work it out pretty quickly so I'm going to tell you the truth. I got it from the deep web. There, I've said it now.'

'Don't you mean the dark web?' clarified Clay, noticing the solicitor's bottom lip jutting out as she made notes.

'The dark web and the deep web get mixed up in people's minds.'

'How do you get on it?'

'The deep web's got sites not indexed by search engines. You need specific software and configurations to get on it. That's where I got the names, addresses and pictures of the paedophiles. Off a whistleblower site.'

Good God, lad, thought Clay, *please be telling us the truth.*

'Lucien, what's the most important thing, the most special thing that you love beyond anything and everything else? Be truthful and don't be embarrassed to tell the truth.'

He was quiet and Clay watched his face closely. She saw conflict playing out in the twitching of a muscle in his cheeks and the tension in his eyes.

'I love my body and I love my future. I want to be a dad sometime.'

'Then, Lucien, on your body and on your future and your hopes to be a father, did you or did you not receive information from a person or persons in our organisation, Merseyside Constabulary?'

'How am I, a sixteen-year-old kid, going to hook up with a bent copper and pay him or her for information that's readily available on the deep web? I'm not being funny but that's just not going to happen in a month of Sundays. Your IT person will tell you how I got it.'

'Thank you for that, Lucien,' said Clay, allowing a little bit of hope into her heavy heart. 'Can you explain why you haven't yet published the names, addresses and photographs of these paedophiles you so despise?'

'Well, two reasons. On my website, most of the verbals, the threats and ranting about destroying paedophiles, it's all a bit vague because there are no specific targets. When I went on the deep web looking for these scumbags I was certain I was going to ratchet up the website by naming and shaming them. I got the page ready but when the moment came for it to go live, I had this massive... misgiving. I do understand the whole incitement to murder thing and I thought, wait a minute, if something happens to one of these bastards, I'm going to be for the high jump.'

'Good. Good thinking, Lucien. You said there were two reasons why you didn't name or shame. What was the second one?' asked Clay.

'I went and did a bit more research. I went round to their houses, pretending to be looking for directions. The information's not accurate. Other people were living there. So I put out that information on the website, innocent people get targeted. Not good.'

'Why do you hate paedophiles so much, Lucien?'

'Because they're disgusting and selfish and they don't care whose lives they wreck, just so long as they can satisfy their twisted desires.'

'That kind of adds up, Lucien, but it's a bit vague given the time and effort you've put into this campaign of yours?'

Lucien became very quiet. He watched Clay drinking him in.

'Are you asking if I've been done by a paedo?'

'Do you want to talk around this area, Lucien?'

A dark silence lengthened. 'I haven't, but my mum says she was when she was a teenager. I don't know the details. Can we move on please?'

'Did you ever come across any on the deep web?'

'I didn't go anywhere near *their* sites. You can hire a hit man on the deep web, buy and sell drugs, you can even buy gender reassignment from well dodgy doctors. I'd have gone on *those* sites rather than rub shoulders with the paedos and the filth they peddle between their horrible selves.'

'Interesting, Lucien,' said Hendricks. 'I'm going to ask you some specific questions.'

'No problem.'

'Lucien, did you take part in the murder of David Wilson?'

'No.'

'Were you aware of the existence of David Wilson?'

'After his murder was on the news, yes.'

'With an accomplice, did you take part in the murder of Steven Jamieson?'

'No.'

'Did you take part in the torture of Steven Jamieson's wife, Frances?'

'No.'

'Were you aware of the existence of Steven and Frances Jamieson?'

'After his murder and her death was reported on the news, yes.'

'Were you in or around the Garston end of Mather Avenue yesterday?'

'Yes. I live there. But I didn't leave the house yesterday. It was cold and windy. I hate the cold and I hate the wind.'

'Do you know who killed and maimed these people?'

'No.'

'Has anybody been on your site boasting about killing and maiming these people?'

'No. You know you were talking about loyalty and misplaced loyalty? I've got no loyalty to the people who come on my website. If I knew names, I'd be, like, there you go, these are the names of the people who are bragging they've been killing paedos, so can I have my laptop back and can I go home now? I'm not going to sit here and take the punishment for other people.'

'What were you doing yesterday?' asked Hendricks.

'I got up. I worked out. I had a shower. I went online to do my work. I'm doing my GCSEs next summer. When your computer expert digs into my laptop, they'll find that yesterday, I did mock GCSE papers for Biology, Physics, Chemistry, Maths, English

Literature, English Language. Your IT expert will find it in my history.'

'Was your mum cracking the whip hard?'

'She was at work. She was on a six am to two pm shift and then she stayed behind to work an extra shift. I don't need my mother to teach me anything. To be honest she's a shit teacher but all the teachers I've ever had have been crap. She's got the patience of an angry goat. I want to do well in life, like Justin Truman. He succeeded at what he chose to do and how.'

'What do you want to do in life, Lucien?' asked Hendricks.

'I'm not sure, but I haven't got the balls to murder people even if they deserve it. But I do know you have to be physically fit and well educated to make good choices in life.'

'You're quite a different person, aren't you?' asked Clay.

'How do you mean, Detective Clay?'

'When your mother's not around.'

'I'm happy to say she works long hours. Being near her, physically, it brings out the worst in me.'

He picked up the glass of water in front of him.

'I'm thirsty,' Lucien announced. He raised the glass to his mouth and drank the water in one go, his Adam's apple bulging each time he swallowed. He put the empty glass down on the table and looked directly at Clay.

In a single second, he looked her up and down, his eyes slowing on a micro-beat as they settled on her breasts, and then he looked her directly in the eye, the tip of his tongue appearing lizard-like between his lips and disappearing back inside his mouth.

Clay looked at the social worker and Lucien's solicitor and read the same question pasted on both their faces.

When are you going to release him from custody?

'Lucien,' said Clay. 'We're going to keep you here a little longer. We've got more questions to ask you, mainly after I've had solid feedback about your laptop from our IT expert. But there are some questions I need to ask right now before I suspend the interview.'

He nodded. 'Sure.'

'You were physically, literally, round the corner from a murder scene. What were you doing last night between half past six and eight o'clock?'

He considered it, frowned and then his face fell into neutral.

'I was doing an online GCSE English Literature paper. It'll be on my history.'

'Were you with anybody who could back up the evidence on your laptop?'

'No...' Lucien held his hand to his mouth and coughed. 'I was alone. I spend most of my time alone. I like it that way. Can I ask you a question?' he said, looking at directly at Clay.

'Go ahead.'

'What do you think of the name *Lucien*?'

'It's a nice name,' she replied.

'I think it sounds too feminine. I think I'll change my name to Justin Truman when I turn eighteen. I could never, ever be as great a man as Vindici; that would be impossible. He's as close as a human being can be to God. He has the power, the wisdom and authority that give him the right to take away the cancerous lives of disgusting paedophiles and I love him with all my heart.'

'Don't do it when you're eighteen, Lucien. Leave it a few more years,' advised Clay. 'You might have a change of heart.'

Clay formally closed the interview and called for Sergeant Harris to take Lucien back to his cell.

As Lucien walked to the door, Clay said, 'Thank you for dropping off the dahlias.'

'What dahlias?' He stopped, didn't turn.

'The ones Vindici asked you to bring to me.'

'I don't know what you mean.'

Clay and Hendricks sat beside each other and waited in silence until they were alone in Interview Suite 2.

'Clever little bastard,' observed Hendricks, looking directly ahead.

'Yeah,' agreed Clay.

'Did you see the way he was looking at you?'

'Yeah.'

'Seems he's got the raging red hots for you.'

'Yeah.'

They fell back into silence.

And then burst into fits of unrestrained laughter.

63

2.43 pm

Riley pulled up at the lights at the junction of Muirhead Avenue and Queens Drive, looked in the rear-view mirror at Christine Green sitting on the back seat and handcuffed to one of the plainclothes detectives drafted in from Walton Lane police station to search her house.

'What the fuck are you looking at?' asked Christine.

Riley said nothing as she looked in the wing mirror and saw a black Hackney cab pull up behind her.

She looked back in the rear-view mirror and saw that Christine was now staring at her with contempt and anger.

'Did you find jack shit? asked Christine. 'No, you didn't, but you're still hauling me over the entire length of the city to answer a bunch of poxy questions about some crock-of-shit, trumped-up nothing.' Her eyes flashed and she said, 'Are you deaf or what?'

'Or what,' said Riley.

'I'm a smart arse, I'm a copper,' goaded Green.

Riley smiled.

'What are you smirking at?'

Riley ignored her and remembered how Barney Cole had filled her in on the details of Christine Green's past from the NPC when they were still in her house on Rice Lane.

Six years earlier, in her mid-twenties and not under the

influence of alcohol or drugs, Christine had been arrested at a bus stop on Lodge Lane in Liverpool 8 after calling an eighty-year-old Chinese man *a fucking perv and a fucking Chink* in front of a large group of black and white youths who detained her until the police arrived.

The red and amber traffic lights turned to green and Riley pulled across the junction and headed southbound on Queens Drive.

'I said, *What are you fucking smirking at?*'

'Book smart, street stupid!' replied Riley.

The black taxi behind Riley's car eased into the left-hand lane and slowly nudged forward. She glanced at the taxi driver and saw it was a tough-looking woman, a blonde whose attention was dead set on the road ahead and whose jaw pounded down hard on a wad of gum.

Riley looked at the road ahead as the rear end of the taxi pulled alongside the passenger door of her car. Her instincts started to twitch.

'These fucking handcuffs are fucking pinching me. Oww! Owwwww!'

Put a bloody big rock in it, thought Riley.

The taxi edged ahead of Riley's car in the left-hand lane and, uneasy now, she had a clear sense that she was being watched.

She glanced left at the passenger on the back seat and recognised her immediately. Samantha Wilson.

It's got to be a coincidence, thought Riley. *I see dozens of people I know in different places every single week.*

Samantha Wilson raised a hand, waved, and Riley nodded back.

Samantha turned her attention away from Riley and towards the taxi driver. She spoke to the driver, gesticulating with her hands.

Issuing instructions, thought Riley, imagining the terminally lonely Karl Stone being hit on by a good-looking but flakey woman and the conflict he must have endured.

The taxi driver slowed right down and took a sharp right turn to tuck into the space behind Riley's car.

Cathedral bells rang inside Riley's head, as the black taxi remained directly behind her in the right-hand wing mirror.

As Riley approached the junction with Derby Lane, the taxi pulled into the right-hand lane, to the turn-off leading into Old Swan. She looked at the taxi but Samantha Wilson appeared to be oblivious, looking ahead, talking either to the taxi driver or herself.

I'm not happy, thought Riley, *not one little bit.*

64

3.01 pm

Annabelle Burns sat in the window of the Full O'Beans Cafe on St Mary's Road, with an empty cup in front of her, rereading the front-page article on the diner's early copy of the *Liverpool Echo* again.

MATHER AVENUE MURDER

SECOND PAEDOPHILE TARGETED

BY VIGILANTE COPYCAT

Her eyes skittered over the photograph beneath the headline and the print seemed to swirl from the page as the enormity of her son being questioned by the police in relation to such a serious crime sent her anxiety levels sky high.

The thought of Lucien sparked a memory of Caroline, the daughter she had lost many years ago, and the memory of that little girl filled her with a sadness that time had never diminished.

She pulled herself together, reminded herself of the trouble Lucien was in, here and now, and, ordering herself to be practical, called the Spire on speed dial. Connecting with the switch-board, she commanded, 'Put me through to Sister Bishop on the nurses' station.'

As the phone rang, a teenage girl in stained overalls came to collect her cup. Annabelle folded the *Liverpool Echo* over so that the football news on the back page was visible.

The teenager reached towards the empty cup.

'I've not finished with it yet,' snapped Annabelle.

'Ooh, sorry.'

Annabelle looked at the teenager. *Go away! Keep away!*

'Sister Jenny Bishop spe—'

'It's me, Annabelle. I can't come to work this evening. Lucien's not well. I'll try and get in tomorrow. If I can't I'll let you know.

'Well, I hope he gets b—'

Annabelle hung up. She looked around. She was the only customer in the cafe and the staff were all in the kitchen behind the counter. Annabelle headed for the door and blustery road outside and flagged down a black taxi.

'Springwood Avenue. Quick as you can!'

65

3.01 pm

'Any sign of the carpets upstairs being lifted recently?' asked Stone.

'No,' said Winters. 'They're all well tacked down. We've been round every centimetre of the skirting boards in the bedrooms and upstairs landing and I'm telling you, Karl, she hasn't been messing with them. Unless she's a fully qualified carpet fitter as well as a skilled woodworker. She's converted her spare bedroom into a joinery workshop. She's got all the gear.'

'What's she carved?'

'Mostly crazy Nazi stuff. No Vindici. No Weeping Children. No Day of the Dead shite.'

Stone wondered what Clay and Hendricks would make of that, and then focused on the task at hand. 'Upstairs, we need to get the boards up, pretty please, Mr Winters. I've found the entrance to the crawl space beneath the ground floor.' He had pulled the hall carpet away from the skirting board, folded it back and weighed it down with a wooden chair from the kitchen.

'She's going to love you,' said Winters, nodding at the carpet.

'She mightn't be coming back.'

'There's nothing at all to incriminate her so far. She might be a Nazi bitch with a big mouth but, hey, if there's no evidence, there's no evidence.' Winters looked around. 'Have you noticed?'

'Noticed what?' asked Stone.

'She hasn't got much in the way of things but what she has got is all top drawer. That carpet you've just pulled back, it's a Brinton.'

'Is that good?'

'Brinton, good? It costs sixty quid a square metre in John Lewis. We've got a drawer full of paid-up utilities bills, council tax, TV licence but we've got no records of DSS payments or wage slips. Lots of money going out but none coming in.'

'Definitely no sign at all of a source of income?'

'Not that we can find. No bank account either.'

'Send Eve a text and copy everyone in on that information.' Stone clicked his torch on and off and fought down the uncomfortable sensation that was building inside him. With a claustrophobic streak that ran right through the middle of him, the prospect of going on his hands and knees under the floorboards of the ground floor of Christine Green's house filled him with dismay.

'You and the lads, take the carpets up in the bedrooms and landing. Get the boards up. I'll look in the crawl space down here.'

Stone waited until Winters was upstairs, took a deep breath and lowered himself down through the open hatch in the floorboards at the front door. He ducked, got down on to his hands and knees and drank in the dampness of earth. Turning on his torch, he scanned the darkness and saw columns of brick supporting the weight of the house.

Against one of the columns was a plastic bag and, at first glance, Stone thought it was a bag of compost. He crawled closer, shone his torch on the bag and saw it was an open bag of fertiliser. He dragged it close to the hatch and made his way deeper into the crawl space.

His left hand touched a saw that looked a hundred years old, which was next to a china doll dressed in Victorian clothes, the body broken in the middle, the lower and upper parts at odd angles to each other, the upper part clothed, the lower half naked and sexless.

He crawled for several paces, found himself dead centre of the house and saw the foundations of the left-hand corner of the back wall. He began a systematic, torchlight-wide investigation of each square foot of the earth beneath Christine Green's home.

When he reached the right-hand corner of the back of the small space, he returned in a diagonal to the dead centre and, turning a full circle, lit up every piece of the crawl space but there was no sign of a laptop.

His iPhone rang and, with his scalp touching the underside of the floorboards, his nerves jangled as he looked at the display and saw Samantha Wilson's name.

When he connected, Stone imagined he could feel the entire weight of the house balanced on his head.

'Hello, Sammy.'

'Karl, I'm sorry about last night.'

'There's no need to apologise.'

'What can I say? I overreacted. Maybe when all this is sorted out, we could go out for a drink?'

'Absolutely...'

'I was a bit fragile, after the service.'

Stone felt a door opening deep inside himself and, with it, light and ice-cold air poured through him. 'Just as a matter of interest, Sammy, did you tell anyone about your father's cremation? When and where it was happening?'

'No. You told me it was a secret. I wouldn't betray one of our secrets.' She sounded puzzled. 'Besides, I'm quite alone in this world, Karl. I can go for whole weeks without talking to another human being.'

She paused and in the silence, Stone thought, *that doesn't stop you from talking about it on the internet...*

'Since you told me about the arrangements for the cremation, the only people I spoke with were you and my mother, *briefly,* on the telephone… Karl, can you speak?' Her voice dropped to a whisper.

Stone inspected the dark empty space with his torch and said, 'Yes?'

'I don't want to scare you away, Karl, but I'm developing feelings for you. I was awake all last night – I couldn't stop thinking about your kindness. It has touched me so deeply. I want to be honest with you and I want to give you the chance to go away because I don't think I could cope with being hurt.'

Stone turned the torch off, sat in the dark, damp space and listened to the distant muffled noise of his colleagues in the space upstairs.

'Say something, Karl.'

'We'll sit down and sort it all out when this is over, Sammy.'

He felt as though his head was in a vice, and the darkness and her neediness combined to tighten the grip on his skull.

'We're friends, aren't we, Karl?'

'Of course we're friends.'

'As a friend, can I ask your advice on something, Karl?'

'Sure.'

'I've decided I need to try and build a bridge with my mother. Now, I know you told me to put her behind me but last night, while I was thinking about you, I thought about her as well and I realised she was a victim of my father too. Maybe not as much as me, no, but she was on the receiving end of his deceit and duplicity. He's gone now. So as far as I can see, it's just me and her. She was negligent, of course she was, and of course she buried her head in the sand, but she was a very good mother in other ways and I don't know if I've allowed the negatives to completely blind me to the positives.'

Stone heard water dripping somewhere and a sigh pour from his core.

'Say something, Karl.'

'I think you ought to think it through some more, Sammy.

You're in a delicate place at the moment, and so is your mother. I wouldn't go rushing in to any big reunion right now. Give it a week, a fortnight. Give your mother a call maybe, tell her what you've told me. Give her some food for thought but leave any direct one-on-one contact for now.'

'You're a wise man, Karl. A good, wise and kind man.'

'Thank you, Christine!'

'Christine?'

'I'm sorry, Sammy, I'm currently in the house of a woman called Christine Green, who we've taken into custody in relation to your father's murder. Sorry, Sammy, silly me.'

'Christine Green?' She made her name sound like quiet but profound curse.

Stone flicked on the torch and picked out the china doll, the absence of genitals like an echo of a detail from both Wilson's and Jamieson's murder.

'Christine Green,' said Stone. 'Does that name ring a bell?'

'Why should it? I don't know anyone called Christine Green. Why do you ask?'

'Because most murder victims know the person who murdered them. I'm leaving here to go back to Trinity Road in a few minutes to talk to Christine Green. It's just a thought, but if you knew her you could give me information about her that may prove helpful in the investigation into your father's murder.'

'But I don't know anyone called... Christine Green. Why should I?'

'Don't get upset, Sammy. You know me. I'm a policeman and it's my job to ask questions, even dumb, crazy questions like: *Do you know Christine Green?* I feel such a fool,' he lied, 'getting your name and her name mixed up like that.'

'Are you talking to yourself down there, Karl?' Winters's voice slipped though the open hatch.

'I've got to go, Sammy. My colleague's calling me. I'm coming now, Clive!'

'I'm sorry, Karl, I didn't mean to get upset. But the idea of you being in another woman's house, even if it is for work, it upsets me.'

'Promise me you'll hang fire with your mother, Sammy.'

'I swear on all I hold dear. You.'

'I'll be in touch shortly.'

Stone reflected. For the first time in his life he had refused a sexual come-on and in a matter of hours he had shifted from feeling utterly regretful to being completely relieved.

As he crawled back to the hatch, butt of the torch in his mouth, he felt the eyes of the china doll on him and was glad to see Clive Winters's face poking into the space.

'Anything?' asked Winters.

Stone hauled the bag of fertiliser from the crawl space and Winters said, 'But she hasn't got a garden back or front.'

'Maybe she's planning to build a bomb to blow up the Houses of Parliament and kick start the Fourth Reich...'

'That wouldn't surprise me,' laughed Winters. 'She's crazy enough I guess.'

66

3.40 pm

Clay opened the door to the incident room and saw DC Margaret Bruce, fresh from the search of Lucien Burns's house, scrolling through photographs on her iPad.

Anticipating a disappointing response based on the lack of an excited phone call from the scene of the search, Clay said, 'Hi, Maggie, no news is not good news I guess.'

'Well… we didn't find anything that relates directly to the investigation…'

'I sense there's a little *but* in your voice.'

'Look at this. Profile-wise, it's kind of interesting.' Slowly, Bruce turned her phone towards Clay, and she imagined her big right paw sheathed in a boxing glove and flying at her face at speed.

'Four rooms and a bathroom upstairs. This is Lucien's den from several angles. Sunbed, weights, sexy chicks and ice-cold killer action heroes on the wall, clearly doesn't know how to fold his clothes, a rather vain but pretty typical teenage lad.'

Bruce scrolled. 'Mum's room. OCD. Bed made as neatly as in a five-star hotel, the hooks on the hangers in the wardrobe all point out in the same direction, the shoes are evenly spaced on the wardrobe floor.'

'OK,' laughed Clay. 'I kind of got the picture when she cleaned the protective covering on the sofa in her living room.'

'There wasn't even one hair in the teeth of her brush on the dressing table. You could make a wig from the clumps in my hairbrush.' Bruce scrolled. 'This is Lucien's bedroom.' She fanned her nose. 'Oh, the smell of musk and hormones. Again, though, dead tidy.'

Clay looked at the numerous women on the walls in different states of undress and the box of Kleenex by his bed head.

'I'd say he was your average six-wanks-a-day teenage lad,' said Bruce.

'I think you're underestimating him, Maggie. He doesn't attend school so he's got a lot more time and opportunity than most. Anything in the bathroom?' asked Clay.

'No, but look at this. This is the fourth bedroom.'

Clay looked at an overview shot of the room, a baby girl's nursery, pink walls and white ceiling, a white wooden cot with a mobile of aquatic life overhead. Large stuffed toys from *Winnie the Pooh* sat on the floor alongside a tactile mat with bells, mirrors and different textured materials within the broad blue rectangle.

Bruce paused on a picture she had taken of a framed photograph above the cot.

In the picture was a younger, much happier Annabelle Burns with a baby girl, about eighteen months of age.

'What's in the evidence bag?' asked Clay.

'The picture itself.'

Clay took the framed picture from the bag and, turning it over, saw a padlock key sellotaped to the back.

'When we went through the little girl's room, we found this.'

Bruce showed Clay a picture of a birth certificate. She took in the details. Caroline Burns. 'She was born in 2001. Mother, Annabelle Burns. Father? No named father. Lucien had an older sister.'

Bruce handed Clay a second evidence bag. She took out a photo album and flicked through pictures of Caroline as she grew from a newborn in Annabelle's arms towards her sixth birthday. Clay stopped at a death notice from the *Liverpool Echo*.

CAROLINE BURNS
2001–2007
Taken suddenly by the angels 13th August 2007
You will always be remembered by your
grieving mother and little brother Lucien

Clay handed the album back to Bruce. 'Thank you, Margaret. This is...' Tragic, awful, desperate. 'Potentially very useful and interesting. Send a selection of pictures from each room to my iPhone, please.'

Clay sat at her desk and shuddered at the deepest point inside herself, imagining her own son dying suddenly.

'Thank you, Maggie. Maybe it explains the OCD and the snappy temper.'

'I'm going back to help search the garage and the rooms downstairs. I wanted you to see, give you an insight into the mother for sure and the son maybe.'

'Keep me posted and thanks for that, Maggie.'

When Bruce left the incident room, Clay called her husband Thomas.

'Hi, Eve, I was just about to leave the surgery.'

'Thomas, it's a quick one.'

'Go on, love.'

'When you go home, can you go through every room in the house and see if there's anything we can do to stop Philip hurting himself or having an accident?'

'But...OK. When he's safely tucked in bed, I'll do that. You can tell me why when I see you next! Believe me, when I'm with him I don't take my eyes off him.'

'I know that, Thomas, but...'

'I know. It's easier said than done but *try* not to worry, Eve.'

His words laid a veil of calm over her but inside, her ever-present anxiety over her son was made freshly jagged by what she had just seen and heard.

'I love you and I love Philip and I don't want anything bad to happen to either of you.'

'The same here.'

She could sense her husband holding back. 'Please, Thomas, what's on your mind?'

'It's nothing new. But every time you go to work, I wonder, *Will she come home again?* And every time you do, it's like I receive the best present ever.'

She looked around the incident room and dropped her voice. 'Oh, don't you worry one little bit. When I come home and we have time, you really are going to get the best present ever.'

She replaced the receiver and for a moment did nothing other than remember the last time he kissed her and, imagining the next time, felt a smile form on her face.

67

3.42 pm

In the front reception of Trinity Road police station, Clay waited at a discreet distance and observed Riley's exasperation as she stood behind a short, mousey woman with grey-blonde hair who looked like a natural-born victim but who peddled vitriolic hate on the internet. Clay realised that her face may well have looked pleasant at some point in her life but she had been soured by experience and whatever lay inside her.

'That's right, Christine,' said a young WPC behind the desk, looking at a computer screen.

Riley drifted towards Clay.

'I see we already have your fingerprints and DNA so we don't need to do them again but we will have to take a fresh mugshot,' the WPC continued.

Christine Green turned on the detective who had accompanied her on the back seat of Riley's car from Walton to Garston. 'I'm gonna sue the lot of you for telephone numbers,' she shrieked, rubbing her thumb and fingers together. The mouse, Clay observed, roared like a lion.

'Christine,' said the WPC. 'Would you like to see the duty psychiatrist?'

'I'm not mad, you cheeky bitch!'

'She's not denying anything about the website,' said Riley. 'She's massively into Third Reich memorabilia. Look, she's acting thick and aggressive with it. Which makes the racial-abuse charge add up. But there's definitely another layer going on underneath. She's got a massive artistic streak and is really good at carving wood. She's got loads of heavy-duty history books about World War Two and the Nazis and theology.'

'But is she *our girl*? What's your hunch?'

'She doesn't sound a bit like the woman who phoned from 699 Mather Avenue but my gut says she's involved.'

'Have you got her laptop?' asked Clay.

'I think she's pitched it. She put that post on threatening paedophiles not to eat in McDonald's and she tossed her laptop. If we find it and confront her about the McDonald's post, she's going to say, *Would I have put that on if I'd been involved in a real-life murder? Would I have given my identity and location away with that post?*'

Green looked across at Riley and Clay. 'What are you fucking looking at?'

Clay ignored her and glanced at Riley.

'I've got a couple of things to tell you, Eve. This is a bit delicate. Karl told me something that happened last night after Wilson's cremation. Karl's happy for me to speak to you about this. Samantha Wilson.'

'I think I know what's coming next,' said Clay.

'She hit on him heavily for sex, lured him into her flat on the pretext she was scared of the dark or some such shit, and then laid it on him.'

'He's a lonely lad when he's not at work, our Karl. Please tell me... He didn't, did he?'

'He kept it in his pants.'

'Thank Christ for that.'

'The journey down Queens Drive was a bloody nightmare. I had that harpy in the back seat and she wouldn't shut up. But guess who I had behind me in a black cab? Samantha Wilson.'

'I think I'll have a quiet word with Ms Wilson. You said *things*?'

'I got a call from WPC O'Neil. She's working the Wavertree end of Operation Warn-a-Paedo with PC Jones.'

'Top-of-class WPC O'Neil and PC Jones? This could be interesting.'

'They called on one guy who became a little bit agitated, to say the least, when your name came into the mix. He denied knowing you but O'Neil and Jones are convinced he does.'

'What's his name?'

'Edward Hawkins.'

'Hawkins?' Time disintegrated and, in the blink of an eye, she felt physically small with the hot sun melting an ice-cream cone in her hand and Beethoven's 'Für Elise' playing from a passing ice-cream van. 'He may have Edward in his name or just uses it as a thin disguise, but it's entirely likely his name's Christopher. If so, he worked briefly, mercifully briefly, in St Michael's, the care home in Edge Hill where I did most of my growing up. And it comes as absolutely no surprise to me that our trawl has thrown him up.'

Riley looked at Clay with intense sympathy and Eve read her friend and colleague's mind.

'No, Gina, it's OK. I had a guardian angel who wouldn't let anyone harm me. A fifteen-year-old boy called Jimmy Peace.'

'Are you still in touch with Jimmy?'

'I wish I was. He died when he was nineteen in a shipping disaster, died being guardian angel, trying to save someone else's life and losing his own.' A sense of utter dismay gripped Clay. Jimmy died and Hawkins lived? What a messed-up universe.

'You want me to go digging on this Hawkins character?'

'No thanks, Gina. If there's any digging needs doing on that nonentity I'll do it.' Clay indicated Christine Green. 'Miss Congeniality?'

'As soon as she's been booked in, I want to interview her – I have a couple of questions,' said Riley. 'I can't imagine I'll have much luck, but I'd like to give her something to think about when she's chilling out in the cells.'

As she listened to Riley, Clay nursed Jimmy Peace in her heart and wiped Christopher Hawkins from her mind.

68

3.43 pm

'Detective Stone!' Mary Behan's voice came loudly from behind Christine Green's front door and he was surprised by the force with which she banged against the woodwork.

Stone opened the front door and smiled at Christine's elderly next-door neighbour.

'You look like you've been down a coal mine, son.'

'I've been under the floorboards, Mrs Behan,' replied Stone.

'Now don't disappoint me, lad. Did you find Adolf Hitler's missing bollock down there?'

Stone laughed, felt the weight of Samantha Wilson's oppression lift.

'Look, I know you're busy so here are my contact details,' she said, handing him his card. He checked the spidery writing on the back.

'I'm about to leave. I was going to knock on your door and ask. Thanks for this, Mrs Behan.

'I saw the neighbour from hell getting carted away by that woman you were with. Hopefully she won't came back.'

'Sometimes wishes do come true, Mrs Behan.'

'Now that *she's* not here, would you and your friends like a nice cup of tea?'

'I'm sure they'd be very grateful, thank you.'

'Before I sort that out, we need to have a chat, son.' She had a piece of paper in her hand. 'I've been thinking.'

He opened the door and said, 'Come on in.'

She stopped in front of the huge swastika flag in the hallway and Stone was taken aback by the lack of reaction.

'You've been in here before, right, Mrs Behan?'

'No. Never in a million years. But this doesn't surprise me, this Nazi banner. She plays her gramophone very loud. German military bands. Hitler's speeches. I don't suppose she can even speak or understand German, the daft cow.'

'Come in the front room and have a seat.'

Stone followed Mrs Behan into the front room.

'Good God,' she laughed, looking at the walls. 'I told you she was nuts. But I don't think you're here on account of all this garbage.' She indicated the oil painting of Hitler. 'I reckon you're here about that paedophile who got murdered last night in his big posh house.'

'Yes, we are.'

'Don't sound so surprised. Just because I'm an old woman living in a small house doesn't mean I'm not intelligent.'

'Mrs Behan, I acknowledge and respect your intelligence. Would you like to sit down?'

'I wouldn't want to contaminate my backside. I'll stay on my feet and shake the dust from them as I leave this house.'

'You're absolutely on the money about why we're here but I have to ask you, how did you come to that conclusion?'

She handed him the paper and, as he unfolded it, the old woman explained, 'The daft cow stands outside Farmfoods handing these out and posting them through people's letter boxes. She didn't put one through my letter box because she knew I'd shove it right back through hers.'

'Oh, this is very interesting, Mrs Behan.'

Stone read the leaflet silently to himself.

PAEDOPHILE ALERT

Please be aware there are PAEDOPHILES living in YOUR area. The police will not inform you of their names or addresses because the law protects them. It is YOUR duty to protect YOURSELF, YOUR CHILDREN and your COMMUNITY. If you know the name and address of a PAEDOPHILE or are just plain suspicious about one of your neighbours please phone this number: 07701 345976. All calls will be treated in strict confidence. And may lead to a cash reward.

Stone looked at Mrs Behan, her face beaming *told you so*.

'How did you come to get this?'

'A lot of people refused to take them from her. The ones who did mostly dropped them in the nearest bin. It literally blew on to my step, which is where I found it. I was going to put it right in the bin but something stopped me. I thought if anyone ever doubts me about how strange she is, you'll have something to show.'

'This is great, Mrs Behan. Thank you so much.'

'Another thing was, there's a lot of you rolled up here, so I knew it was very serious. That murder last night, it hasn't been off the local radio and TV broadcasts.'

'Can I take this with me, Mrs Behan? It could prove to be quite a useful piece of evidence.'

'Certainly, son.'

'You wouldn't happen to know if she was here last night?'

'As a matter of fact I would. She left her house at half past four and came back at half past nine. And no!' She tapped her nose. 'I'm not a nosy neighbour. She can't close a door without slamming it. Makes my teacups rattle. Half past four, slam, she walks past my front window. Half past nine, slam. Starts talking to herself all loud and laughing like she's not right.'

Half past four to half past nine. Five hours, thought Stone. *Easily enough time to travel there and back and commit a murder in between.*

Winters, sleeves rolled up and dripping in sweat, came to the doorway of the living room and said, 'Excuse me. Karl, it's not a big house. We've lifted the carpets upstairs and double-checked under the boards. Pure and simple, there's no laptop.'

'Let me think about that one, mate. Wait a second, please. Mrs Behan, do you know what was she wearing?'

'I saw her leave the house in that red duffel coat she always wears. I went to give her a piece of my mind about slamming doors, but by the time I got to the pavement she was getting on to the bus heading to the south side of the city.'

'Which bus did she get on, Mrs Behan?'

'It was the 68, son. Have I just said something that's pleased you no end?'

'Oh, Mrs Behan, you certainly have. If you remember anything else, please get on the phone to me.'

'I'll keep my thinking head on, son. Oh and, by the way, make sure you wash and change before you get back to work.'

'Thank you, Mrs Behan, I will do.'

As Stone walked down Rice Lane to the corner of Sefton Road, he heard Mary Behan's voice rise above the traffic.

'Who wants a nice cup of tea?'

69

4.01 pm

'Mrs Hurst!'

Detective Constable Bob Rimmer climbed down the aluminium ladder from the attic of 689 Mather Avenue. Within moments, Mrs Hurst joined him.

'Would you like another cup of coffee?' She looked and sounded as though she'd been hit with a sledgehammer.

He shook his head. 'Where are your children?'

The former noise of play was now silent.

'Downstairs, watching the Disney Channel. I've told them to be quiet. I've developed a migraine.'

'It'll be stress-related. I take it you've been looking up the kind of man who lived so close to you and your children, and what he did in Yorkshire when he lived there.'

She nodded. 'It's just awful. That poor, poor child.'

'I've seen something on your CCTV, someone going past your house. There's a possibility that this is the person we're currently looking for to talk to about the events of last night five doors down from you and your three children. It's a very clear image. Your CCTV system is top of the range?'

'We were burgled three years ago. I was traumatised. I wanted as much security as we could afford.'

'And who can blame you, Mrs Hurst? Do you mind if I call you Sylvia?' Rimmer shivered and felt like his over-full bladder was about to explode. 'Let me guess, we didn't catch the burglars, did we?'

She shook her head. 'No, you didn't. That's why we put the monitors in the loft. So that if anyone did get in, they wouldn't be able to sabotage the system.'

'It's a terrible world we live in, right? Your CCTV system, what kind of special features does it have?'

'It operates on a seven-day cycle, it can save and back up images, it has a facility to wipe footage automatically on a twelve- or twenty-four hour cycle...'

'Twelve- and twenty-four hour cycle?'

'It can zoom in and zoom out...'

'Brilliant. I've left it on up there. Maybe you'd like to have a look at the footage, make sure everything's OK. Can I use your bathroom please, Sylvia?'

He opened the bathroom door near the ladder leading into the attic, looked back and met Sylvia's gaze. 'Technology's great but sometimes, for whatever reason, it can malfunction, even CCTV systems from the top end of the scale.'

'Yes, that's true. It's Bob, isn't it?'

'Yes. Sylvia, I don't suppose you've ever seen images of what these so-called people do?'

'Never.'

'As part of my work, I've had to. And I can tell you, it haunts me. They have no mercy. They have no concern for their victims. I had to go and see my doctor. I couldn't sleep after the things I saw. Just a thought, Sylvia. He'd have done it to your children if he'd had the chance. But he didn't get that chance, did he?'

As he closed the bathroom door, he held eye contact with her until the door shut, watching the seed he'd planted in her head germinate darkly.

He listened as her feet ascended the aluminium ladder into the attic, pulled down his trousers and pants and, sitting on the toilet, aimed for the middle of the pan. Relief flooded him and, above his head, he heard Sylvia Hurst walk across the length of her attic.

He closed his eyes and reran the footage he had watched over and over again.

One moment there was an empty path, a closed gate, a section of pavement and, on the road, a car flying past at forty miles per hour or more. In the next moment, the edge of a human being walked into shot.

He had paused it, slowed it right down and pressed play.

She walked deeper into the shot, wearing a red duffel coat, white socks and black shoes, looking at first sight like a little girl but moving like a woman. Directly in line, as if on cue, she turned her head towards the CCTV camera.

He paused the image, zoomed in on the hood and saw a human face, painted in black and white paint to give the impression of a face of a skull.

'The Day of the Dead, eh?' His words had drifted like ether into the rafters.

He pressed play and, still in super slow motion, she carried on walking towards the house five doors down the avenue.

Pausing the footage again, he zoomed in on the bag she wore on her back.

He laughed. The same My Little Pony that a girl in his youngest son's class wore to school every day.

Rimmer went through everything he'd been told about the scene and guessed the innocuous-looking backpack was full of ropes to bind, gags to silence, and an aerosol to blind.

He noticed that, as she walked along Mather Avenue, she had one hand in her pocket. *Feeling for your Stanley knife?* he wondered. Her other hand fumbled inside the lining of the duffel coat – *where your sharpened spoke was hidden, in the lining?*

Little Red Riding Hood out for bloody revenge, he thought.

When she left the shot he moved to fast forward and confirmed that she didn't come back the way she had arrived, which meant only one thing. Once she had left the Jamieson house, she had travelled, on foot no doubt, but maybe with an accomplice in a vehicle, into Garston and the direction of the Liverpool South Parkway railway station and bus terminus, a place milling with travellers even after the rush hour.

If any of the images on Sylvia Hursts' CCTV footage were circulated in Liverpool South Parkway it was almost certain to generate eye-witness sightings of the woman disguised as a small girl. The evidence was crucial.

Hearing Sylvia Hurst's feet on the aluminium ladder, he stood up, pulled his trousers up and pushed the handle.

He opened the bathroom door as Sylvia arrived from the final step, and they stood as if frozen in time.

'I'm sorry,' said Sylvia Hurst. 'It appears that the CCTV has automatically wiped the footage you were looking for.'

'I'm sorry, it appears that the chemotherapy is having no effect on your wife's secondary tumours.'

'Well, that's a shame,' said Rimmer. 'But these things happen all the time.'

Detective Sergeant Bob Rimmer walked down the stairs, to the hall, to the front door and closed it without turning to look at Sylvia Hurst who lay down on her bed and felt her throbbing temples with the tips of her shaking fingers.

On the pavement outside Sylvia Hurst's house on Mather Avenue, Detective Constable Bob Rimmer sent a text message to DCI Eve Clay and DS Gina Riley.

Eve and Gina, sorry, bad news. The Hursts' CCTV system has a self-wiping facility and the footage for our crucial time is gone. I've been hunting everywhere on the system but Mrs Hurst says the system was due for repair.

He felt the ghost of his former self haunt his heart and it wasn't a mansion. It was a prison where once the doors were locked, they could never, ever be opened again.

70

4.05 pm

Annabelle Burns's knuckles were white and her face as hot as her hands were cold on the steering wheel. As she drove under the concrete mass of the Rice Lane flyover, she looked at her mobile phone on the passenger seat and for the hundredth time since making the journey up Queens Drive to the north end of the city, willed it to ring.

Silence.

Then a mighty blast of a car's horn. She looked up at a car swerving away from her and saw that she had half strayed into the wrong lane. She jerked her steering wheel to put herself in the right lane.

She felt her heart beating in double time and fought back the urge to cry as she pictured Lucien sitting in his cell and staring at the wall, each painful second an eternity. What an idiot he had been to construct such a terrible website. And now he was in such trouble! Why did he have to be so disobedient?

As she travelled down Rice Lane, Lucien's life flashed through her. How simple their life had once been, compared to the unravelling mess that it had become through his disastrous time in secondary school. The change in him aroused a physical pain in her chest. It was like a red-hot needle piercing her to the core.

When she saw the railway station she wondered what it would

be like just to step on the next train, the first leg of a journey to the end of the earth.

Up ahead, the glaring red and yellow of the McDonald's logo made her look left at the row of houses on the other side of the road. She smiled and felt tearful again at the memory of the time they'd lived there. 'Oh my God!' A police car and a white van were parked outside the houses on the pavement, and two men, a tall black man and a smaller man with a beard and a bald head, were loading stacker boxes on to the back of the van.

There was a sudden disconnection in her brain, and her understanding was plunged into darkness, then light, darkness, then light, darkness, then light, a switch turning on and off.

The sight of the police car and the plainclothes officers made her want to make a U-turn and drive away at top speed. Darkness. Light. She looked at the black officer and thought their eyes had connected, that he was looking at her with pure accusation. Darkness. Light.

When he looked away and turned to walk back inside the house she wondered if it was the house they'd lived in in the good days. Darkness. Light. And she wondered if the police presence in Rice Lane was related to Lucien being in custody, and wondered if she was spiralling off into hypermania. Darkness.

Light. She saw the sign for Aintree Racecourse and tried to calm herself with the memory of Lucien aged six visiting there when it was almost empty and how a kind steward had allowed him through the turnstile and on to the track to stroke the horses. Darkness.

Light. Annabelle pulled left and pulled up in a side road. Darkness.

Why wouldn't the phone ring?

Light.

She had to get her head straight and return to the south end of the city, to Trinity Road police station and find out how Lucien was getting on.

The only thing she could hear as she sat stone still was her own breathing and, as she listened to herself, the parts of her brain reconnected and the darkness gave way to the pure light of understanding.

The police?

She looked at the silent phone on the passenger seat.

That was the reason why her phone was not ringing and her call had not been returned.

The police were involved.

And she was locked in the absolute silence that falls in the moment before the bitter end.

71

5.25 pm

'Get the kettle on, Eve, you've got visitors coming from Sheffield.'

'Hello, Lesley, you've picked up Daniel Campbell?'

Clay attracted the attention of Cole and Hendricks and hit speakerphone.

'We most certainly have. I've officially come out of retirement to offer you the benefit of my experience during the interview that you're about to conduct with Steven Jamieson's solicitor, Daniel Campbell.'

Hendricks held his arms in the air. Result.

'Where are you, Lesley?'

'Currently on the M1, heading a little bit north to travel west and about two hours away from Liverpool.'

'How is Campbell?'

'I can see the back of his head in the car in front. The technical term in these parts is *absolutely shitting himself*. But he's acting aloof and arrogant like he just doesn't care.'

'We've got rooms booked for him. A cell and an interview suite. Is he representing himself?'

'No, he's meeting a friend, at your nick. Milk and two sugars, please, Eve, and I'm not averse to a digestive biscuit or three.'

'The kettle will be boiling when you get here, Lesley, and the biscuit barrel's open and it's all yours. Call me when you're close at hand.'

Clay replaced the receiver and optimistically asked, 'How are you getting on with Jamieson's paperwork?'

'Two hours until Daniel Campbell rolls up here, right?' checked Cole.

'Right.'

'I'll tell you what we know, but there's more to learn, so I'll keep it brief and then get a move on.' Cole stood up, took a set of A4 papers from his desk and went over to Clay. 'The bank statements go back to the early 1990s. Standing orders and direct debits to different companies that come and go. DWR Limited for instance. I checked with the Companies House website. DWR registered in March 2013, dissolved in April 2015. Month of first payment to DWR March 2013, last payment April 2015. I've got twenty-eight such bogus companies so far, and counting.'

He handed the top sheet to Cole.

'DWR Accountants Limited,' she read. 'Dissolved. One officer. Daniel Campbell?'

'He must have a large extended family. Daniel Campbell's the officer for five companies on the Jamieson payroll. Of the other twenty-three, they're all registered to a place called Conway House on Ackhurst Business Park in Chorley. They've all got one officer, either James Campbell, Thomas Campbell, Richard Campbell – the list of Campbells goes on. They're all accountancy firms. They come and they go and they all have two or three initials in their title. They all submit crock-of-shit tax returns to the Inland Revenue and they all pay approximately five grand, funded via Campbell. It's all as bent as a hairpin. There's one firm that stands out because it's been the only constant going back to the first statement and featuring in the latest. LAB.'

Cole handed Clay the Companies House details for LAB Accountants Limited.

'You'll probably have a better idea in a few hours, when you've had a chance to talk to the delightful Daniel Campbell,' said Cole.

'Where are we up to with Dr Warner and the confidentiality agreements?' asked Clay.

'I've faxed Jamieson and Campbell's confidentiality documents over to Mark Benson at the CPS,' said Hendricks. 'I'm waiting for a callback. Yeah, if it doesn't come in the next five minutes, I'm going to harass him. Dr Daniel Warner I tracked down through Google. He won't be able to help us himself.'

'Why not?' asked Clay.

'He's dead. He wasn't a cosmetic surgeon.'

Cold, hard suspicion gripped Clay, made her wish she could click her fingers and magic Daniel Campbell into the room and make him start answering questions right there and then.

'Dr Warner was a gynaecologist. Or he was officially until he was booted out by the BMA for molesting a thirteen-year-old girl who he was supposed to be treating.'

As quickly as Clay's spirits had risen in the phone call with Lesley Reid, so they plummeted.

'Bill, when Campbell gets here, you come into the interview with me. We'll hit him with the bank statements and ask him about the services they were buying from the struck-off gynae-cologist. Great work, both of you, thank you.'

As Clay walked to the door, Hendricks answered the ringing landline on his desk.

'Yes, it is Detective Sergeant Bill Hendricks. OK! Eve, hang on a minute, please.'

Hendricks listened and as he did so, his face became clouded with disappointment. 'Could you have another look, or advise me on how I can go about searching for the missing records?' He sat on the edge of his desk and sighed. 'OK, thank you for trying again.'

Hendricks replaced the receiver. 'That was Alder Hey in the Park. They either haven't got or can't find Lucien Burns's medical records.'

Clay nodded. 'I'll speak to him.'

Her iPhone received an incoming text. It was Poppy. *Can we talk?*

72

5.33 pm

Clay passed the door of the viewing room where Carol White and Alice Banks spent their gruelling days. She tried the door handle and it was locked. She knocked but there was no reply.

She moved to the next door, a small office, knocked and heard Poppy Waters call, 'Come in!'

Clay smiled as she entered the room and closed the door. 'You want to talk with me, Poppy?'

Poppy indicated Lucien Burns's Apple Mac. 'Five-fifty through to nine last night, with some short breaks, it seems he was doing online GCSE papers according to his Apple Mac. But as an alibi goes it's not a good one. He's very close to the scene of Jamieson's murder and he's got Pages for Apple. Conceivably he could have done the work on his iPhone on the way there and back and sent it to his Mac.'

'That's very interesting. Are we getting any insights into his secret self?'

'He's a bit of a megastar on the internet and he knows it,' explained Poppy. 'He gets lots of fan mail and he's got thousands of people posting on his website, and some of it's pretty damning stuff. There's loads of people who claim to hate paedophiles enough to murder them.'

'Have you tracked down any names on Lucien's list of twelve most violent females?' asked Clay.

'One,' said Poppy. 'I've mainly been trying to track Lucien's activity. Althea Henry. Claims to be from Warrington, but that may just be a claim.

'She says: *Hang the paedo by metal hooks through their feet, smear food all over them and dangle them from a crane so birds come and peck their eyes out. Let the crows eat him alive. What that bastard did... Althea. This is the best Vindici site ever.*

'Lucien replies: *Thanks, Althea. What you say's too good for them.*

'She replies: *Why don't we get together? We could be like the Bonnie and Clyde of paedo killers? Take Vindici's work to a new level?*

'He replies: *How do you know I'm a male?*

'She replies: *Wishful thinking. Seriously, would love to get together with you. How about it?*

'He didn't reply to that one.

'She continued with a new post: *What the fuck's wrong with you, ARSEHOLE? Are you a fucking pussy or a queer bastard?*

'He blocked her after that.'

'Most lads of his age would have been salivating, taking her to one side in cyberspace and fixing up a time and place for a little ooh-la-la,' said Clay. 'Unless... he's very body conscious...'

'He's definitely not gay,' Poppy laughed, anticipating one of the next possibilities.

'I've already come to that conclusion myself,' said Clay.

Poppy went red in the face. 'He's downloaded so much porn it's untrue. There isn't *one* male homosexual image. He's a very red-blooded heterosexual male. I can tell you what his type of woman is.'

'Go on,' said Clay.

'He likes mature women, brunettes, women in their thirties and forties in all shapes and sizes.'

'A bit like me maybe?' asked Clay.

Poppy thought about it. 'Actually yes, definitely like you.'

'Have you found anything that we should be concerned about?'

'I found another list of names and addresses of paedophiles living in Liverpool.' Poppy handed the list to Clay. As Clay scanned the list her eyes paused on one name: *Steven Jamieson, Mather Avenue, Liverpool 18. No number.*

'Is Steven Jamieson on the electoral register?' she asked.

'He isn't but his wife Frances is, and there's only one Jamieson resident on the entire length of Mather Avenue,' replied Cole. 'I reckon the lad knew where Steven Jamieson lived and it was only round the corner from his house in Springwood Avenue. He made a good job of hiding the document you've got in your hand on his Apple Mac. But not *that* good a job.'

'I'm going to confront Lucien with this. Do you have your own copy, Poppy?' As she spoke, Clay called Hendricks on speed dial.

'Yes, I do, Eve.'

'Bill, we're going to have to haul Lucien back into the interview room. His alibi is full of holes and he's been lying to us through his pearly-whitened teeth.'

73

5.36 pm

The duty solicitor, John Robson, held out a hand to Christine
Green but withdrew it when she made no effort to reciprocate.

'Are you sure this bloke's a solicitor?' Christine jabbed a
thumb in his direction. 'He looks like an overgrown schoolboy
in his dad's best suit.'

Robson sat next to Christine and smiled at Riley and Stone.

'I've been in countless interviews with Mr Robson representing
all manner of people in all manner of trouble,' said Riley.

From the corner of the room, the custody sergeant, Harris
said, 'He's an excellent solicitor and, if I was you, I wouldn't
alienate him. You're going to need him, Christine.'

Stone took his ringing iPhone out and, for two rings, didn't
recognise the number, but the but the digits 0151 525 gave away
the location.

'Is that your mother telling you to get home for your tea?'
said Christine.

'Better than that,' replied Stone. He showed the display to
Riley, who in turn smiled at Christine.

As he left the room, Stone connected, shutting the door after
himself.

Riley pressed record and formally opened the interview.

'I've only got two questions, Christine. One thing's puzzling
me; the other's absolutely bamboozling me. The puzzling thing.
Where's your laptop?'

'What laptop?'

'The one you run your Vindici-worshipping, paedophile hate-mongering website from?'

'What laptop?' She addressed Mr Robson.

'OK, Christine. We will find your laptop sooner or later. The bamboozler. You've done a good job for a long time in keeping your head down. Until today. We found you because you posted a picture of the McDonald's over the road from your house. You gave yourself away so cheaply. Why?'

'Because I've got nothing to hide. Unlike all the paedos out there and the pigs like you who protect them!'

'That's nice, Christine. My boss predicted this would happen. You're not the only Vindici site in Liverpool. But you know that. Who's the other person, Christine?'

'I don't fucking know anyone.'

'You posted that picture of McDonald's to get us running after you.'

'Like I want to be here? Like I want some nigger—'

'Moderate your language!' Mr Robson looked as though he'd been stung by a wasp.

'—and his bum boys ransacking my house.'

The door opened and, still on the phone, Stone blocked the space, looking directly at Christine. 'Thank you. I'll be there directly.' He smiled and closed down the call.

'What?' She spat the word at him.

'We've got your laptop, Christine. Amongst other things…'

74

5.43 pm

Clay looked through the observation slot at Lucien Burns as he did press-ups on the floor of the cell. As he pushed his weight up from the floor, he raised his hands mid-air, clapped and counted, 'Ninety-seven.' Clap. 'Ninety-eight.' Clap. 'Ninety-nine.' Clap. 'One hundred.' Clap.

As his hands came to the floor he clenched his fists and supported the weight on his body on the tips of his toes, his elbows and forearms, all the time staring at the CCTV camera in the corner of the ceiling.

'He's going to be a monster when he's older,' Hendricks whispered to Clay. 'Do you think he's on steroids?'

'Maggie Bruce didn't say she'd found any illegal drugs at 222 Springwood Avenue.' Clay observed that his body was already that of a fully grown man, not a sixteen-year-old boy.

Sergeant Harris opened the door and told Lucien, 'You've got a visitor!'

Lucien stayed in position and turned his face towards Clay as she stepped into the cell.

'I want to talk to you, Lucien,' said Clay.

'Are you taking me to the interview suite?'

'Soon.'

'Don't I need my solicitor and social worker present?'

'You can have them present if you want them but what I'd like to talk to you about doesn't relate to this murder investigation or your website.'

In a swift and graceful motion, Lucien was on his feet. 'What do you want to talk about?' he asked, taking deep breaths and walking from one side of the confined space to the other and back.

'You're a complex young man and I want to get a better sense of who you are, Lucien, the whole person, before I interview you again. Do me a favour, eh? Stop moving around and stay still. This is important.'

He stopped pacing and sat down on the bed.

'DC Bruce led the search of your house and brought something to my attention.'

Clay turned her phone towards Lucien and showed him the picture of baby Caroline's room. His face was set but his eyes looked suddenly older and the light in them seemed duller.

She flicked forward, showed the portrait of Annabelle with Caroline at eighteen months.

'It's a big deal, losing a sibling, particularly when you're at an age where you can understand some if not all of what's happened,' said Clay.

'Let me look at her,' he said, as if speaking to himself.

'Take your time, Lucien,' said Clay, even though time was one thing she couldn't spare.

The look in his eyes spread out across the surface of his face and he looked away from the picture and at the wall behind Clay.

'No one remembers Caroline. And the one person who does...' He fell into reflective silence.

'Your mother?'

'Doesn't want to talk about her. It makes me very sad.'

'I don't remember her because I didn't know her, but I'm happy to talk about her, if you are,' said Clay.

A mixture of relief and unleashed sadness swept through his features. 'Did you ever lose anyone when you were a kid?' he asked.

'I was a little older than you but yes. I was six,' said Clay. She sat next to him on the bed and turned to face him. 'Want me to tell you what happened to me?'

He looked at her. 'Yeah.'

'The woman who brought me up from a newborn baby died when I was six years old. She had a brief but unbeatable cancer and my surrogate mother was gone. She was a Roman Catholic nun called Sister Philomena…'

'Your mother was a Roman Catholic nun?'

'No, Sister Philomena wasn't my biological mother. She was effectively my stepmum.'

'Who was your biological mother?'

'I don't know. I was abandoned at birth. Philomena found me and took me in. She was in charge of a children's home called St Claire's so she was in a great position to give me shelter. I was six and understood that she was gone but it took me an awfully long time to work out what *forever* meant.' Clay fell silent and then said, 'Caroline?'

'I was four when she died. She was six. She had meningitis. It was a few weeks before I started school.'

'It must've been absolutely horrible for you, Lucien.'

'I adored her. One minute she was here, the next she was gone.'

He fell into a deep reflective silence and then, slowly, turned his full attention on Clay.

'It was a really hot day in August and we were upstairs in our bedrooms. Mum was out in the back garden mowing the lawn. I can remember the smell of cut grass and how it drifted into the bedrooms because the windows were wide open. I was playing with my action figures in my bedroom and I couldn't hear Caroline singing. She was always singing. I couldn't hear her singing and I remember thinking, *I can't hear because all the sound's being drowned by the lawnmower.* But it wasn't just one lawnmower, it was as if everyone in the neighbourhood had the same idea: *I will mow my lawn today.* Mum stopped mowing our lawn but the others were still roaring in the background.

I heard Caroline in the moments that Mum turned her lawnmower off but she wasn't singing, she was throwing up. I went to her bedroom and saw her on her hands and knees, being really violently sick. And I remember saying, *Caroline, you should've done it in the toilet. You know Mum doesn't like mess. She'll go mad.* She looked at me but it was as if she couldn't see me. *My head,* that's what she said, but it was like she couldn't see me and wasn't talking to me, like she was talking to someone else, someone she could see but I couldn't see and it scared the life out of me because I thought she was seeing a ghost or a monster.

'She tried to get up from the floor but she rolled over on to her back and started making strange noises. I thought, *I'll clean up the sick and then I'll tell Mum Caroline's poorly.* So that's what I did. And when I did it, Caroline – she was so close to the place I was cleaning – she went asleep. In the end there was a big damp patch on the carpet but I got all the sick up because I didn't want Caroline getting yelled at.

'She was very still. I poked her on the shoulder and said, *Wake up, Caroline, it's all right now, the sick's all gone.* But she didn't move. And even though there was this big smell of grass, I could still smell the sick. So I didn't tell Mum that she'd started coming out in red spots.

'I waited for ages and Caroline was sweating.

'I heard Mum putting the lawnmower away in the garden shed and that's when I went downstairs and told her Caroline wasn't well.

'She hurried upstairs and, when she went into Caroline's bedroom, she started screaming and ran into the bathroom and came back with a glass and she pressed the glass against Caroline's skin and then she became hysterical.

'It didn't take long for the ambulance to get to us but as we waited she ordered me to tell her everything that had happened. So I told her everything. Every single thing that I've told you.

'The paramedics carried Caroline into the back of the

ambulance with Mum and the man closed the doors and off they went to the old Alder Hey Hospital.

'When she came back, Mum, empty-handed, she was never the same again. She used to be lovely and all that changed in an instant. I lost two people that day. Caroline *and* my mother.

'That's what happened that day. That's what happened. And that's that.'

Lucien got up, walked to the open door and drove his fist hard into the wall. He turned, his eyes shifting left to right, left to right, as though his brain was exploring the space with a view to departing from his skull.

'I'm very sorry, Lucien,' said Clay.

'So am I. And I'm sorry for your loss.'

'We're going to interview you shortly,' said Clay.

'Do you know what I'm sorry for?' asked Lucien. 'I'm sorry that my wish could never come true. I wish I could have been my baby sister. I wish I could have traded my body for hers. I wish I could have exchanged my life for her death. Did you say you were going to interview me soon?'

'I did. Is there anything else you'd like to say?'

'I started school a few weeks later in September. Springwood Primary, reception class. My mother didn't speak to me until the October half-term.'

'What did your mother say to you?' asked Clay.

'Go to your room and stay there.'

75

Standing at her mother's front door in Dundonald Road, Samantha Wilson felt the first blast of the predicted storm and the gush of heavy rain against her head. She felt herself shivering as she pressed the doorbell and, remembering how her mother disliked prolonged loud noise, took her finger off after two seconds.

The 'FOR SALE' sign rattled in the wind, and on the edge of the door frame she noticed a small rag of blue and white plastic, one of the last remnants of a crime scene.

She looked through the frosted oval of glass and saw her mother moving slowly towards the door, like a woman carrying an invisible but colossal burden.

'Who is it?' asked Sandra Wilson, her voice frail and fearful.

'It's me, Sammy.' She heard the cold in her voice. 'It's freezing out here, Mum. Will you let me in? Please...'

'So you can start screaming at me? Is that it?'

'No. I won't raise my voice to you. Please open the door. I have something for you and I have something to ask you. And I need to do it face to face.'

'You promise?'

'I promise...'

Behind the front door, chains rattled and bolts were drawn back. Sandra opened the door wide enough to stick her face out.

She looked at her daughter and said, 'You weren't fibbing about the cold.'

Samantha bit down hard on the reflex to tell her mother that she didn't tell lies and instead smiled. 'Can I come in please?'

'If you start, Samantha, I'm going to tell you to leave.'

'I haven't come here to start any trouble, honestly.'

Sandra opened the door wide enough to allow her daughter over the threshold.

As she stepped into the hallway of her childhood home, Samantha's senses were bombarded with the shape of the space and staircase, and the house's unique aroma: aniseed and furniture polish.

In the centre of the hall, arms folded across her middle, Sandra faced her daughter and asked, 'What do you want?'

'To give you these.' Samantha offered her mother a bunch of pink carnations.

'I... I didn't even notice...'

'They're your favourites, Mum. Favourite flower. Favourite colour. This is what I wanted to give you. I couldn't give you flowers over the phone.'

Sandra raised the flowers close to her face. 'Thank you, Samantha.' She stared at the carnations as if they were the only bunch of flowers in the world and said, 'I remember when you had your paper round and you used to buy me carnations every week when you got paid.'

Sandra raised her eyes from the flowers and looked at her daughter's face. 'Are you crying?'

'No.' Samantha smiled. 'Rain landed on my eyelashes. It's rain. That's all.'

Sandra took a balled-up tissue from the sleeve of her cardigan and dabbed her daughter's face. 'What did you want to ask me?'

Samantha looked at the reflection of herself with her mother in the mirror on the wall and felt a surge of unbridled agony.

'I want to ask you for a fresh start, Mum. I want to ask you if we can start again.'

'You do?'

'There's only so much pain we can endure in one lifetime. He's gone now,' said Samantha. 'It's all over for him. You loved him in spite of everything, and so did I in my own way. But we're still here. You and me. There's nothing to stop us having a good relationship. I can't blame him and you can't defend him because he's dead. I love you, Mum. And I can see it now. We've both been his victims. But I'm not going to be his victim any more. And I don't want you to be his victim any more. But I need you to help me do that and you need me to help you. Please, Mum. Let's start again. Day one. The new us.'

The carnations fell from Sandra's hands. Her hands flew to her face and she dropped to her knees, sobbing.

'Come on, Mum.' Samantha knelt in front of her mother and wrapped her arms around her heaving body. 'We can do this. Can't we?'

'Yes. Yes,' she breathed into her daughter's shoulder.

Samantha waited.

'I'm so sorry, Samantha.'

'No more sorry, no more regret, no more confusion, no more guilt.'

'This is... it's like the old days, the relationship we used to have.'

'This is how it's going to be. No need to cry any more, Mum.'

Samantha tightened her hold on her mother and, little by little, her sobbing subsided. After time, and in the quiet of the hall, they fell into a still and perfect silence.

'Samantha?' Sandra struggled to speak. Samantha looked deeply into her mother's eyes. 'Is there anything I can do for you, love?'

'Well, there is.'

'Anything at all, just ask.'

'I'd like my old house keys back. The ones you took off me when Dad threw me out. As a gesture of trust. To our brand-new start, to the new us.'

'I'll go and get them right now.'

Sandra Wilson got to her feet and headed towards the kitchen at the back of the house.

Samantha stood up and looked at herself in the large hall mirror.

'It's going to be just fine, Samantha,' Sandra called from the kitchen.

'It's going to be perfect, Mum.'

'I've been hoping and praying for this day for years, Samantha.'

'Yes, me too, Mum.'

She heard her mother rummaging in a drawer.

'I don't know if you noticed – I've put the house on the market.'

Her mother's footsteps, lighter than they'd been for decades, drifted towards the hall as Samantha walked towards her own reflection.

In the hall, Samantha took the keys from her mother.

'Yes, I saw the 'For Sale' sign,' said Samantha.

'So, I'm not going to be here for much longer.'

Samantha smiled, squeezed her mother's hand and nodded.

76

6.15 pm

'Where's my mother?' asked Lucien, across the desk.

'She isn't behind that observation screen if that's what you're worried about,' said Clay.

'Yeah, but *where* is she?'

'She went out for a coffee this morning and, according to my colleagues who've been searching your house, she showed up outside, got in her car and drove off. Have *you* any idea where she might be?'

He shook his head. Throughout the day, Clay had thought it strange Annabelle had not returned to the police station to find out how her son was faring. Now, after hearing Lucien's account of his sister's death, her absence added up.

'As soon as I know her whereabouts, I'll inform you. Do you want to speak to her?'

Lucien shook his head.

'Is there anything I can do to help matters between the two of you?'

Lucien ignored Clay and turned to the social worker. 'When I get out of here, I want to go into care. Can you find foster parents for me?'

'I'll need to talk to you and your mother in some detail before I can do anything concrete about that. Would you like me to try mediation talks between you and your mother?'

'You're not listening, are you?' said Lucien, without emotion. 'None of you listen to me.' He looked at Clay and Hendricks in turn.

'I disagree entirely,' said Clay. 'We've been listening like hawks to you, Lucien, and we've been pushing and pulling apart all those things you said last time we were together in this room.'

She leaned forward slightly, eyeballed Lucien. 'And we've been talking to our IT person who's been delving into your Apple Mac.'

'It's been very interesting, Lucien,' said Hendricks. 'Very interesting.'

Clay touched the list containing Steven Jamieson's name and partial address, which lay face down on the table in front of her.

'You haven't been truthful with us, Lucien,' said Clay. 'In spite of the fact that you said there was no point in lying because our IT people would find everything on your Apple Mac. What were you *thinking*?'

'I didn't think I was going to wind up in here because of my website. How sorry am I that I ever bothered. I'll take the site down as soon as I get out.'

'That might not be as soon as you think, or like, Lucien.'

'What do you mean?' There was a quiet note of horror in his voice.

'We'll start with your alibi. It's got holes in it, Lucien.'

'How come?' The note grew louder, sharper.

'Our IT specialist says that you could have easily left the house and transferred your work from, say, your iPhone or iPad on to your Mac. Making it look like you were all tucked up at home and being a model student. You could have even done your homework on your Mac in the victims' house with one corpse and one captive for company. Or, click of a button while you're actually in 699 Mather Avenue on your phone or iPad, it transfers to your Mac. We'll know for sure when we delve deeper into your devices.'

'Good luck to them. I was at home working on my Mac. In the house – 222 Springwood Avenue.'

'Lucien, you've told us lies.'

'I haven't!' He glanced at his solicitor, distressed.

'You said you'd never heard of Steven Jamieson. Remember?'

'Yes, I was telling the truth.'

'Well, look what we found, very cleverly hidden, on the hard drive of your Apple Mac?'

Clay turned the paper over, pushed it towards Lucien and pointed at Steven Jamieson's name. 'Between eleven o'clock and half past eleven last night, this list of names and addresses was wiped from your Mac's history. You used all kinds of obstacles to hide it on your hard drive. Why did you do that?'

'Tell the truth, Lucien,' advised his solicitor.

'He lived around the corner from you, didn't he?' asked Clay.

'Mather Avenue's, like, a very long road with hundreds of houses on it. He could have lived at the Tesco end or could've lived next to the synagogue or backing on to Garston or anywhere in between.'

'OK,' said Clay. 'You're a young man with a profound hatred of paedophiles. So far, you're coming over as well organised, self-disciplined and above all committed to, at the very least, scaring paedophiles out of their wits or even facilitating physical harm to them through others. You're not going to leave that gap in the list when all you have to do is go to Allerton Library and pull the electoral register.'

'I didn't do that.'

'Why not?'

'Because.' He sucked in the air and breathed out hard. 'Because I was scared of that piece of information.'

'I'll be honest, Lucien,' said Clay, locking eyes with him. 'I really one hundred per cent don't believe you. Convince me otherwise.'

'The other names and addresses didn't seem real. But that address is in my neighbourhood. I would have wanted to kill him with my bare hands but I knew I didn't have the nerve and that would have made me like such a – a coward. I was too scared of *doing*. Young Offenders Institution? Do you know what happens to the likes of me in places like that?'

'What do you mean *the likes of me*?'

In the silence that followed, confusion and sadness warred in his eyes.

'I mean, I'm an attractive young man. Please don't send me there.'

'Where did you get this information?' asked Hendricks. 'Did you hack the Merseyside Constabulary computer?'

'No, I did not.'

'Our IT person will be able to tell if you have been hacking us. Maybe you'd like to demonstrate a bit of goodwill and just tell us where you got this highly confidential information?'

'People send me all kinds of information and tip-offs. Look, I feel sick.' Lucien looked at his solicitor and social worker. 'I feel really sick actually.'

'Do you want to see the duty medic?'

'No, when I say I'm sick, I'm sick at heart. Look at me. Physically, I'm as fit as a fiddle.' He picked up the list of names and addresses, slammed it on the table and said, 'I got it from a whistle-blowing site on the deep web. I'm telling the truth.'

'You knew Steven Jamieson. You knew where he lived. Your outspoken views on pacdophilia have made you and your website a global smash with other like-minded people. All we need now are results from the forensic lab placing you set-in-stone at 699 Mather Avenue. As soon as that evidence comes back, we'll charge you with murder.'

Tears welled up in his eyes. 'Loads of other people say loads of shit about paedos on the internet!'

'We know. You said it before. But who's in here with us right now? You or loads of other people?' said Hendricks.

'You're sixteen, Lucien,' said Clay. 'We know you didn't commit this crime on your own. I'm starting to get a picture in my head. There are gaps but things are coming through loud and clear. You were working alongside an older woman, a blonde.'

'A blonde?'

'We found a blond hair at the Jamieson murder scene. Frances Jamieson was dark. So, yeah, an older blonde. Does she sound familiar? You found the target. She did the hard work, the torture, the murder. Were you there egging her on? I think so.'

'I don't know what you're on about.'

'What's her name, Lucien?'

He spoke very quietly.

'Pardon? I didn't get that,' said Clay.

'No comment.'

Clay glanced at Lucien's solicitor. 'Before Sergeant Harris takes him back to his cell, can you explain to Lucien the need to cooperate. He's sixteen. If he cooperates now and behaves well in jail, he could be out by the time he's thirty-two. Paedophiles or no paedophiles: the judge won't be bothered about the perversity of the victims' human nature. What will bother the judge is the extremely pre-meditated nature of these murders, and the need to deter other like-minded people from following his reckless example. I'm saying he *could* be out at thirty-two. He could be a hell of a lot older. Anything, Lucien?'

He looked directly at Clay. 'Yeah. Paedos fall into two categories. Did you know that?'

'Go on?'

'There are the physical ones who abuse young people's bodies and then there's the next type, the emotional paedos. They sidle up to young people, lull them into a false sense of confidence and then steal from their hearts. All that shit in the cell, Clay, about Caroline...' His face was racked with rage and, for a moment, his voice deserted him. 'You're an emotional paedophile, Clay. You're the worst kind of paedophile.'

77

6.15 pm

'When are you coming home, Bob?'

His wife's voice sounded hollow, as though the cancer in her body and the phone line had ganged up to rob her of her essence.

'Bob, are you there?'

'I'll be home as soon as I can, Valerie.'

'I got a nice surprise just now.'

'Oh yes?'

'I got a lovely bouquet of flowers from Eve Clay.'

'That's nice.'

Her breathing became laboured and in the background he heard his mother-in-law say, 'Don't tire yourself out, Val. Here, let me take that from you.'

Rimmer looked out at the rising storm, saw dead leaves bullied by the wind into a haphazard downward spiral and saw an image of what it felt like to be him.

'Robert, if you're coming home, then come home...' He heard her walking out of the bedroom he'd shared with his wife for over a decade, and her voice dropped. '...but don't be getting her hopes up with phone calls. Why don't you just apply for compassionate leave? Every good spouse under the sun would do...'

He placed the receiver down, wished he could swap places with his wife and said, 'Go to hell!'

A phone rang. He followed the sound to Eve Clay's desk and picked up the receiver. 'Hello?' he said.

'Is that Barney Cole?' A foreign accent, a man, far, far away.

'Who am I speaking with?'

'Sergeant Eduardo García, Puebla City police.'

'Yes, it's Barney Cole speaking.'

'I have good news for you, Barney. The statue of the Weeping Child found at the scenes of the murders in Liverpool... I have a manufacturer, Sanchez Ceramics, a factory owner here in Puebla City.'

'Let me get my pen,' said Rimmer, remaining motionless and counting down seconds. 'Go on, Eduardo.'

'I got the manufacturer boss Sanchez to pull his sales manager from holiday. He wasn't happy.'

García laughed and Rimmer echoed the noise, falsely.

'They opened the office and the computer showed... this isn't exactly usual... an export of a dozen statues of Weeping Children to an Englishwoman's address in Liverpool.'

García's voice blurred into background noise of people talking and moving around the office from which he was calling. Rimmer heard a name and an address in Liverpool but it sank in to the darkness inside him.

From the neck down, he was perfectly still, lost somewhere between the phone call and another wave of chaotic despair.

'Are you still there?' García raised his voice.

'Yes, thank you for that.'

'No problem. Keep me informed and good luck, Barney.'

'Thanks.'

Silently the incident room door opened and Barney Cole entered without a sound. 'Your help is much appreciated, Eduardo,' said Rimmer, and hung up.

'Hello, Bob.'

As he replaced the receiver, Rimmer looked towards the sound of Barney Cole's voice. He had the sensation he'd just fallen from a cliff, and even though the voice was familiar and friendly, it sounded like a bomb going off.

'Hello, Barney. Who's been on to Eve?'

'Sorry?'

'Who called Eve's number just now?' Cole smiled, but felt the first wave of a chilling sickness. 'You just took a call on Eve's phone. I do it all the time. You haven't filled in the missed-caller pad on her desk.'

'I was about to do that.'

'I find it easier to do so when the call's in progress, myself,' said Cole.

Rimmer smiled and shook his head. 'I've got a good memory for detail.'

Cole went to Clay's phone and pressed recent calls. '0052 222 441 4327,' he said. 'Sergeant Eduardo García, Puebla City Police.' Cole wrote the number quickly on Clay's missed call pad. 'What did he say?'

'He called to tell Eve and you that he was still working on looking for the manufacturer of the Weeping Child statuettes found at the Wilson and Jamieson scenes.'

Cole sensed Rimmer moving away, heard him putting on his overcoat.

'It was a holding call. He hasn't forgotten about the request for help, but so far he just hasn't got very far. That's all.'

'Thanks, Bob.'

Cole recognised the sickness that now gripped him. He had felt it before, years earlier, when he'd been a young police constable at Admiral Street police station and learned the unpalatable news that a popular and respected detective constable was in the pocket of a major drug dealer in Toxteth.

From the door, Rimmer said, 'I'm going home to see my wife.'

'I hope it goes well, Bob. We're all rooting for you and Valerie and the kids...' Cole looked at Rimmer and smiled.

Rimmer's face collapsed. 'What are you looking at me like that for?'

'I'm not looking at you like anything.'

Rimmer turned and left and, as soon as the door closed after him, Cole picked up Clay's receiver and dialled Eduardo García's number.

Engaged.

He pressed redial and the ring tone sounded.

'Eduardo García.'

'Eduardo, it's Barney Cole.'

'But…we've just spoken. You have a question?'

There was a pause and Cole heard the steady beating of a ceiling fan, imagined the heat and fierce sunshine.

'Can you run the information past me again?'

'Surely. I've located a name and address for the exports of the Weeping Children statuettes from here to Liverpool in United Kingdom. Mrs J. Truman, 636 Rice Lane, Liverpool, L4 5AF.'

Cole wrote down Christine Green's address. 'That's terrific news… Thank you, Eduardo. This is definitely the address the statuettes went to?'

'I saw the details on Sanchez Ceramics's computer.'

'Can you dig again for me, Eduardo? I'd love some information like dates and method of payment.'

'Sure. But don't forget to invite me to your Christmas party in a couple of months.' García laughed.

'You'll be the guest of honour. Eduardo, I've got to go. Thank you so much.'

78

6.15 pm

When he arrived at McDonald's on Rice Lane, Stone took in the whole scene. A marked police car was parked on the pavement and a group of teenage boys and girls was gathered close to the two officers guarding the scene-of-crime tape that sectioned off the bins at the back of the restaurant.

A man in his forties stood by the tape looking as if he was in a living nightmare. Next to him, a teenage girl in a McDonald's uniform chewed her right thumbnail.

'Eh, mate,' piped up a girl's voice. 'Is there a dead paedo in the bins or wha'?'

'Back off!' replied the older of the two constables.

Stone advanced on the group of teenagers and raised his voice: 'Hey!' He thrust his warrant card at them. 'This is a crime scene. Scram or I'll do you for Obstructing the Course of Justice. Who wants to be first?'

They moved back as one, turned and, as they ambled away, someone said, 'Fucking police harassment.'

Stone eyeballed the retreating group and, taking a step forward, said, 'Right!' They ran, and Stone turned to look across Rice Lane at the cracked darkness of Christine Green's door. Behind him a white Scientific Support vehicle mounted the pavement, Terry Mason at the wheel.

'Thank you for getting here so quickly,' said Stone to the

constables, before approaching the man whose badge identified him as the restaurant manager. 'Detective Sergeant Stone.' He showed his warrant card to the man and the girl. 'Adele?' She nodded. 'You did well not to touch the box, Adele.'

'That was super smart,' said Mason.

'Well, there was blood on the coat,' replied Adele.

'Can you show us where you found it?'

They dipped under the scene-of-crime tape and walked around the back of the restaurant; Stone's senses were overwhelmed with sour fat, dead meat and far too much refined sugar.

As Stone snapped on a pair of latex gloves, Adele pointed to an open cardboard box.

'I came out back for a ciggie and when I saw it I was, like, dead curious. I saw blood on the coat and a laptop and a kid's backpack and alarm bells started ringing in my head.'

Mason weighed up the box, the three layers of colour.

Red. Black. Sky blue.

A woollen coat. A laptop computer. A child's backpack.

'That's the coat...' Stone fell silent. 'Adele, thank you so much. Can you go back across the scene-of-crime tape?'

'Did I do good?'

'Tell your manager you need five stars on your badge not just one.'

They watched her go.

'It's the coat Mary Behan saw Christine Green wearing all the time. Careless bitch, leaving it here.'

'Clever cow,' said Mason. 'Not careless bitch. This neighbourhood's packed full of kids, juniors, teenagers. This is McDonald's, for God's sake, a kid magnet. She was banking on one of them finding the box, taking the laptop and bag and ditching the coat for her. We'd never have found this if that had happened.'

'That makes sense on one level,' said Stone. 'She's got a very twitchy intelligence going on underneath that thick-as-shit exterior. What are you going to do, Terry?'

'Get it into a stacker box from the back of the van and unpack it all back at the farm.'

As Mason went to collect the box, Stone looked at the locked teeth of the backpack's zip. He imagined what might lie inside and, in spite of the cold wind that streamed through the space, smiled at the prospect of Christine Green being charged with two counts of murder and one of manslaughter before midnight.

79

7.15 pm

Cole knocked on the door of Interview Suite 2, heard Clay say, 'Come in!' and felt torn about whether to follow the simple instruction. Entering, he sensed Clay and Riley been locked deep in conversation.

'I thought you were Sergeant Harris delivering Christine Green to us,' said Clay.

Cole wished he could be Sergeant Harris if only for an hour.

'Strategic chat?' asked Cole.

'You look like a man who's won the lottery on the same day as he was diagnosed with a terminal illness,' observed Riley.

'Do you want the good news or the bad news?' asked Cole, sitting across the table from them.

'Good first,' said Clay.

'You're not really going to need a strategy with Christine Green. You're just going to hit her with this. Christine Green posing as a Mrs J. Truman purchased a dozen Weeping Child statuettes from a firm called Sanchez Ceramics in Puebla City, Mexico. They were posted to her home 636 Rice Lane, Liverpool 4. I've just spoken with Eduardo García from Puebla City Police.'

A smile crossed Clay's face. 'We'll get her in here when Karl and Terry come back with her stash, confront her with García's information and charge her with two counts of murder.'

Her smile faded at the bleak expression on Cole's face and Clay wanted to know the bad news short and simple. 'What's up, Barney?'

'Bob Rimmer's our leak.'

'Do you know if he's in the building?' asked Clay, the momentary lightness blasted clear out of her senses and replaced with the prospect of grim dealings ahead. 'The no show from the CCTV from 689 Mather Avenue.'

'His text said the Hursts' system had a self-wiping facility,' said Riley.

The room was filled with a painful silence.

'All down the years, he's been such a good lad,' said Cole. 'I don't want this to be true.'

'Just tell us,' said Clay.

'I went out of the incident room for a couple of minutes, leaving him on his own in there. When I came back in, he was wrapped up in a phone call on the landline on your desk, Eve. I could have been a ghost. He claimed Ed García had called to let you know he was still tracking down the information about the Weeping Children statuettes. Then he left, said he was going home to his wife. I called García. He told me a completely different story, fingering Christine Green as Mrs J. Truman, purchaser of a dozen Weeping Children statuettes.'

'Barney, will you call Professional Standards and ask them to… God! I can scarcely believe I'm saying this… go to Bob's house and bring him in…'

Clay felt as if her head was about to split into two pieces and fall from her neck.

'Only he won't be going home,' said Riley. 'Home's the last place he wants to be at the moment.'

'Do we know where he does go? Who his civilian friends are?' asked Clay.

Cole considered the man. 'Before his wife got ill, he was always really friendly and outgoing but, at the same time, rather secretive about what his off-duty life was like. Most of us are.'

In the same moment, there was a knock on the door and Clay felt the buzz of an incoming text on her iPhone.

As Cole went to the door, Clay opened the text.

Eve, we're back at Trinity Road with the haul from the back of McDonald's Rice Lane. Karl.

Cole opened the door to Sergeant Harris and Christine Green.

'Sorry about this, Sergeant Harris, but DS Stone's just arrived back from Walton...' Clay stood up and looked at Christine. '...with a very interesting box of goods. We're going to have a look at what he's brought back and then we're going to have our interview with you.'

Christine shook her head. 'You with your mind games and your lack of respect.'

'Mind games? Lack of respect? Where's your husband?'

'What husband?' She held out her left hand, showing a row of ringless fingers.

'Where is he? I'd love to know.'

'Are you simple?'

'No. Sergeant Harris, would you take *Mrs J. Truman* back to her cell, please.'

80

7.53 pm

Mason smiled at Clay across the treasure trove of evidence on his table in his workshop in the basement of Trinity Road police station, and it felt like a lottery win.

Flanked by Stone and Riley, Clay looked at the find from the cardboard box at the back of McDonald's, Rice Lane, laid out on three clear plastic sheets.

'What's the back story on the find?' asked Clay.

'A kid working at McDonald's finds the box at the back of the restaurant. The manager phones Walton Lane police station. Walton Lane phone us.'

There was a knock on the door. It opened quickly and, without invitation, Poppy Waters entered at speed.

'Is that the laptop?'

'Poppy, slow down,' said Clay.

'Talk us through it, Terry, so that we're all singing from the same hymn sheet. And when we're done here, feed the info back to Bill Hendricks when he gets back and Barney up in the incident room. Fire away on this great find.'

'I'll begin with the laptop.'

Wearing latex gloves, he lifted the laptop lid. The dead screen was covered with a network of what looked like spiders' webs. Mason took a close look and counted.

'She's hit the screen three times with a blunt instrument in the hope of knackering the laptop. She did the same with the mobile phone.'

'It's not a problem,' said Poppy. 'It's like hitting the roof of a house with a hammer to bludgeon to death someone in the basement. I'll transfer the hard drive and SIM card into a like device. No problem.'

'When you've dusted the laptop and lifted any finger or palm-prints, Terry, pass it straight on to Poppy,' said Clay. 'Dig the dirt and fast, please, Poppy!'

Clay looked at the coat, front side up.

At the bottom of the red duffel coat, in another transparent bag, was a sharpened bicycle spoke.

'The spoke was concealed inside the coat, left-hand side, in the vertical hem where the toggles are sitting,' said Mason. 'I felt it through the fabric as I took it from the box. I had to use a folded handkerchief to get it out. It's bloody lethal. Wilson and Jamieson were awake, right? It must have been like having a fencing foil inside their skulls.'

Clay thought back to the autopsies. 'The spokes she used to pierce their stems and impale their brains.'

'The coat is covered in fresh and older bloodstains. The fresh ones are splatter from when she whipped his legs. The older blood stains are from direct contact with her victim.'

Clay indicated a dry discolouration, 'That blood will have come from David Wilson.' She looked at the fresh splatter in the middle of the coat, pointed it out. 'She must have knelt over Steven Jamieson as she whipped his legs. Humiliate the rich and powerful, and how!'

'But can you see Frances Jamieson's blood anywhere?' asked Mason.

Clay looked hard up the left sleeve from the wrist to the shoulder and saw stale stains from David Wilson and the con-tinuation of a line of splatter from Steven Jamieson. Slowly, her eyes zigzagged across each square centimetre on the front of the coat, but there was nothing that jumped out as being definitively from the female victim.

Then Clay started at the shoulder of the right sleeve and her eyes tracked across small markings of blood until she reached the cuff.

A fresh rim of blood had soaked into and dried around the cuff.

She's right-handed, thought Clay, *but what did she do with her right hand to Frances Jamieson to pick up that staining?* Something up close and personal but the mark wasn't consistent with the damage caused to the woman's eyes.

Clay looked away, cast herself back to that living room at the moment the lights came on and Frances Jamieson's bound and gagged form became clearly visible. Her back surfaced in Clay's mind, the signature 'Vindici' on the woman's shoulder.

'As the killer carved her bogus autograph in her flesh,' said Clay, 'the blood soaked into her sleeve and the rim of the cuff. That's Frances Jamieson's blood.'

Clay stepped back, looked at the fourth section of the table.

'This is a child's backpack,' said Mason.

'My Little Pony.' Clay smiled at the grim irony. The contents of the backpack were laid out and looked to Clay's eyes like a map of murder.

'We've got the thin blue ropes,' said Mason, 'identical to the ropes used to bind Frances Jamieson. A sharpened spoke, the one she used to attack Steven's brain...'

'Hang on, Terry.' Clay crouched so that the contents of the table were at eye level. 'Get the coat to the lab right now, please. Press them. Tell them to drop everything, we need the different DNA results back right now and we need to squeeze Christine Green's head just as quickly.'

Clay made a mental note of the remaining contents of the backpack: the bloodstained orange-handled Stanley knife, the incense concs and the Lynx aerosol canister.

'Have you printed off photographs of all this?' asked Clay.

There was a knock on the door and Hendricks entered the room just as Mason handed Clay a brown A4 envelope and said,

'Pictures taken *in situ* at the rear of McDonald's on Rice Lane, and individual shots of each piece of evidence taken close up as you see them on the table here.'

Clay looked at Hendricks.

'Well done, Bill! You were spot on about the wounds on Jamieson's legs. That's what he got for being rich, powerful and a complete bastard. What's happening?'

'Lesley Reid and her colleagues are here with Jamieson's solicitor Daniel Campbell.'

'Is his solicitor here yet?'

'No.'

'Bill, you come with me and we'll talk to Campbell, make him aware of just how deeply in the shit he is. We'll formally interview him when his solicitor shows up.'

'Mark Benson from the CPS has been back to me. The detail on Jamieson and Campbell's confidentiality agreements are so vague as to make the documents not worth the paper they're printed on. Campbell must've known it.'

'What do you want us to do?' asked Riley.

'I want you to come with me to Christine Green's cell. I think we need to arrange a little social event before we formally interview her.'

81

8.03 pm

Christine Green stood at the centre of her cell, staring straight ahead at the wall, her back turned to the door and the observation panel. As Sergeant Harris unlocked the door, she didn't move, turn or appear to hear.

'Christine,' said Clay. 'You've got a visitor.'

She remained silent and still. Clay walked into the cell, met her face to face.

'More of your mind games, Clay?'

'I want to introduce you to someone of a similar mindset.' Clay drilled in on Christine's face, reading some confusion beneath the tough sheen. 'He's coming down the corridor now. Can you hear his footsteps? He's three cells away from you.'

The footsteps stopped at the open door of the cell.

'Come in,' said Clay.

'Hello,' said Lucien to Christine's back.

Slowly, she turned, looked him up and down.

Neither Lucien nor Christine spoke.

Clay waited, counted slow seconds to ten and asked, 'Do you know each other?'

Silence. Seconds mounted up.

'Have you met before?'

'Who're you?' asked Lucien.

Christine turned on Clay. 'What the fuck are you playing at?'

'This is Lucien Burns, Christine, unless you didn't already know. Do you know him?'

'No I don't. I've never seen him before in my life.'

'Lucien, this lady in front of you is Christine Green, unless you didn't already know. Do you know her?' asked Clay.

'No.'

'The reason why I'm introducing you, unless you've already met before, is because you've got such a lot in common.'

'Don't insult me!' said Christine. 'What's he got in common with me? How old are you, lad?'

'Sixteen.'

Oh, I get it now.' Christine looked at Clay. 'You absolutely evil-minded bitch. You're trying to make out that my website's a smoke screen. That I've been having a sexual relationship with a minor while calling for the blood of paedophiles. That's a very clever strategy, Clay, but it's not original. It's positively medieval. I'm orchestrating a witch-hunt because I'm the biggest witch of all. Right? Wrong, you philistinic cunt. You're using this child, and you are a child in the eyes of the law, lad, to try and smear my name. What's she offered you?'

Lucien shrugged.

'*Tell me she's been having sex with you since you were fourteen and I'll get you off the burglary charge*. Is that what she said?'

'No!' said Lucien, a look of profound disgust imprinted on his face. 'No!'

'You know what, Christine, DS Riley and DS Stone were right about you. You are bright, incredibly bright.'

'Well, you aren't, Clay. None of this theatre would have been admissible in a court of law.'

'I had no intention of trying to smear your name, Christine. You're smart but you're wrong there. And I certainly wasn't intending to try and use this in the court case against the pair of you. But my goodness, you'd do well as a barrister, that was quite a piece of oration.'

'Then why have you brought us together?'

'Not because of some conspiracy theorist crap about bent policing techniques, certainly, but because, as I said, you have so much in common. You both live in the same city. You run the only like-minded websites located in Liverpool. You both hate paedophiles with a biblical vengeance. And you both venerate paedophile serial killer Justin Truman. You're both being interviewed during the same time window in the same police station in relation to the same murder inquiry. David Wilson. Steven Jamieson. I want both of you to know in the same breath what we now have as evidence. Christine, we've got your bloodstained red duffel coat. We've got your laptop. It's being pulled apart right now. We've got your backpack. We've got your phone. We've got your murder weapon. We're going to analyse every single word that you both say in the light of each other's separate interviews. I'm pretty certain you're both going to be charged in connection to the these murders before your twenty-four hours in custody is up. That's a lot to have in common. So I just wanted you both to know it in the interests of neither of you being in the dark.'

'I don't know why you're really here, lad,' said Christine. 'But she's using the serious shit I'm in here for to try and destabilise you. Get your solicitor and tell him or her what's been going on here. She's right out of line.'

'I've already had a talk with my solicitor,' said Lucien. 'She's told me to cooperate. Clay just wants to establish the fact that we either do or don't know each other. Who are you?'

'Who are you?' echoed Christine.

'Like DCI Clay said, I run a Vindici website. That's why I'm here talking to you now. Because they think I killed some paedos. Because I live...' He stopped and looked like he didn't know whether to weep or scream as the concept became concrete in his mind. 'Fucking hell. Because I live round the corner from one of the dead paedos. She' – he pointed at Clay – 'thinks that you and me are a team. Well, I didn't fucking kill no one. Don't even try and fucking well drag me down into your shit! Tell her...'

'Likewise, dickhead, with big brass bells on it. This is your shit, not mine. Wilson and Jamieson were murdered in your end of the city, not mine, not the north end. I'm not in a team with you. Who are you, Lucien? Some over- privileged snot-nosed bastard from the south end trying to blame me for what you did? Oh, but in the interests of fairness, congratulations on a good job killing paedos. Well done.' Christine turned on Clay. 'The evidence you claim you've got, if you're bluffing and playing mind games, belongs to *him*, not *me*.'

Lucien flew at Christine, his right arm raised and fist bunched to punch her. She stood still and, as Hendricks grabbed and turned him, Lucien's fist punched the air. In the same moment, Christine threw out her foot and kicked him in the knee.

Riley got hold of one arm and, with Hendricks to the left, dragged Lucien backwards out of Christine's cell.

Christine looked directly at Clay with a smile behind her eyes. 'You can see what a volatile young man he is. What a violent, violent person. Murderous rage. We've seen it with our own eyes, haven't we, Clay?'

82

8.18 pm

'Is this the first time you've been fingerprinted, Daniel?' asked Clay.

Daniel Campbell replied with a silent, contemptuous look. Beneath a neatly manicured head of grey hair, his face was lined and would have been handsome except for his fish-like eyes.

Clay drifted away from him and over to Lesley Reid and her two male colleagues from South Yorkshire Police.

'Did Campbell have anything to say on the way over here?'

'He's going to litigate against you, Merseyside Constabulary, us three and South Yorkshire Police.'

Clay looked at Daniel Campbell's possessions in a plastic bag on the desk, and saw top-of-the-range designer everything. An Yves Saint Laurent wallet crammed with credit cards next to a gold fountain pen. A bunch of keys to what she imagined was a very large house in a prestigious gated community. A notebook in a leather casing and the latest iPhone.

She looked at the cut of his black silk suit, the handmade white shirt and the damson silk tie and span back in time to Sister Philomena explaining something Jesus had said about money and the soul.

'*You can have everything in the world, Eve, but it won't do you any good if you lose your soul.*'

Clay tried to imagine the state of Daniel Campbell's soul as he stared straight ahead, and decided that if she was the Devil she would have offered two pence as an opening bid for it but would have gone no further than five.

'I'm going to take your picture next, Daniel,' said Sergeant Harris behind the front desk.

'It's Mr Campbell to you, do you understand?'

'Of course I understand, Mr Campbell,' said Sergeant Harris. 'So as you know, after I've taken your photograph, I'm going to swab your mouth for a DNA sample and then you'll be going into the holding cell until your legal representative arrives.'

In the plastic bag on the front desk, Daniel Campbell's iPhone rang.

As it rang out, Campbell said to Clay, 'I need to take that call. It's probably going to be Aaron Brierley, my solicitor.'

'By all means, take your call, *Mr* Campbell, you are allowed *one*.'

Clay watched closely as Campbell fished the iPhone from the plastic bag and connect the call.

'Yes, I'm in Trinity Road police station right now. Yes, it is hard to talk. Where are you, Barry?' Silence. 'Half an hour?' Anger. 'Can't you make it quicker than that?' Disbelief. 'I'll suppose I'll see you when I see you then.'

Daniel Campbell returned the iPhone to the plastic bag and frowned when Sergeant Harris produced another empty plastic bag.

'What's that for?'

'This bag, Mr Campbell, is for your shoes and shoelaces when you're in the holding cell waiting for your solicitor to arrive.'

'So, the picture,' said Sergeant Harris. 'Don't smile or pull a funny face, Mr Campbell. Pull a passport face for your mugshot.'

Campbell looked at Clay. 'My client gets murdered when I'm hundreds of miles away in another city, and you arrest me on suspicion of bribing police officers? You've got no evidence.'

'Yes I have, Mr Campbell. If I was you, I wouldn't talk about why we've brought you here in such a public place.' Clay indicated the space behind him.

Campbell looked over his shoulder and through Annabelle

Burns, who froze to the spot. Clay watched her reaction as Campbell blithely turned his head and faced away from Annabelle. Annabelle opened her mouth but stayed silent, the words on her mind obviously lost inside her. Then she frowned, staring at the back of his head as if she was looking at something obscene and completely out of place.

'Annabelle, come over here please,' said Clay, walking to the doors leading to the interview suites.

Once they were behind the swing doors, Clay looked out into the reception area where Campbell remained mute and furious. Clay pointed at him and said, 'You were shocked when that man turned and looked at you. Do you know him?'

'No. Just for a split second I thought it was the American actor Steve Martin. I guess it was the white hair. He's probably nothing like him. I'm stressed to the hilt. Wouldn't you be if your son was being questioned in a murder investigation?'

'If you want to be personal, Annabelle, if my son was being questioned in a murder investigation, I wouldn't have been away from the police station as long as you have. Where have you been, Annabelle?'

In the reception area, Campbell turned and faced Clay as Sergeant Harris took a profile picture of Campbell.

Clay watched Annabelle closely as she stared in the solicitor's direction but this time her face was blank.

'Everybody, including Lucien, *especially* Lucien, made it perfectly obvious that my presence was not welcome. I'm not some little dog to come running back and forth and looking desperate to be told *Beat it, Fido!*'

'Just as a matter of interest, where did you go in your car?'

'How do you know I went out in my car?'

'Detective Constable Maggie Bruce was in your bedroom window when you turned up and drove off in it.'

'I was stressed so I went to Otterspool Promenade... Look, I want to know what's happening with Lucien?'

'He'll be here for at least the full twenty-four hours.'

Clay watched Annabelle's face, imagined her juggling the word hours and turning it into years.

'And then you'll release him?' asked Annabelle.

'It depends what happens between now and then.'

Clay pictured the bay window of Annabelle Burns's bedroom. 'Who were you talking to on your mobile phone when we showed up at your house? At one minute past nine this morning?'

'I've told you. Bulky Bob. I was arranging with the council to collect an old fridge. Can I see Lucien?'

'No.'

'You're looking at me as if I'm the world's biggest, most barefaced liar,' said Annabelle.

Clay glanced at Daniel Campbell and said, 'He looks nothing like Steve Martin, white hair or no white hair. Steve Martin's got a pleasant face. Daniel Campbell hasn't. He looks dead cold from the inside out...'

'If you think I've done something wrong, arrest me and bring me in for questioning.'

'Be careful what you wish for, Annabelle.'

'I don't *wish* to be arrested.'

As Sergeant Harris escorted Daniel Campbell to the holding cell and out of their sight, Clay said, 'You can wait in reception if you like but Lucien won't be coming out in the early hours, that simply isn't happening. You can't sleep in your own house, we're still searching it. Where do you intend to go, Annabelle?'

'The Travelodge on Aigburth Road.'

'Give me your mobile number. I'll be in touch as and when I need to.'

Clay stored Annabelle's mobile number – 07704 193119 – in her contacts and typed in her name.

'Has he asked for me?' said Annabelle as they walked through reception to the main door.

'He's mentioned you...' replied Clay. 'But I'm not at liberty to tell you what he said.'

83

8.25 pm

As Clay waited alone in Interview Suite 1, she heard the buzz of an incoming call on her iPhone and saw 'Rimmer' on the display. She felt a fist forming inside her core, let it ring out a couple of times and steeled herself.

'Hello, Bob!'

In the background, she could hear the throb of his car engine and knew from the pitch that he was driving far too fast. He was silent and she wondered which of his demons was singing loudest inside his head.

Eventually, he spoke. 'Eve.'

'Yes, Bob?'

The tyres of his car squealed.

'Bob, I want you to listen to me. First thing, slow down and pull over to the side of the road, so we can speak and you can put all your attention into our conversation.'

'Are you on your own?'

'Yes, I'm on my own.'

'No, you're not.'

'Bob, you're not listening to me. If you don't slow down, you could cause an accident. You could hurt yourself or someone else.'

He laughed and Clay's skin turned to ice.

'I'm an advanced skills driver, Eve, remember? I can drive at any speed I like and be perfectly safe.'

'But even extremely experienced advanced skills drivers have accidents. We lost Roger Phoenix last year in a high-speed chase.'

'Roger was always a lucky bastard. Over and out in the bat of an eye in Sheil Road.'

'Do you want your children to lose both their parents?'

'Leave my kids out of this!'

'Bob, it sounds to me like you've been drinking.' He said nothing. 'Bob, please, pull over.'

'You're with him right now, aren't you?'

'With who?'

'Barney Cole.'

'No, as far as I'm aware he's up in the incident room. I'm sitting in the interview suite waiting to talk to Christine Green, our prime suspect.'

'So if I ring his landline number in the incident room, he'll pick up, right?'

'Bob, will you please slow down?'

'You can't make me do anything, Eve.'

'I don't want to make you do anything, I just want you to be safe.'

'Cole, he's told you, of course he has.'

'Told me what, Bob? Tell me what's on your mind?'

'You think I'm the leak, don't you?'

'I don't *know* who the leak is. It could be *anyone*.'

'I just want you to know, Eve. I'm not the fucking rat you think I am.'

'Bob, go home, try and calm down. Pull over and call a taxi. Whatever has or hasn't happened, we can sort it out one way or another. Please, go home, Bob! Go and see Val and the kids.' She felt a sudden surge of emotion and fought down the beginning of tears. 'Go and be with the people who you love and who love you the most!'

'I'm not the leak. OK?'

The line went dead.

The door of the interview suite opened and Riley entered.

'We need to send out an urgent request for all patrol cars to look out for Bob Rimmer's black Renault Mégane. I've just had him on the phone, pissed, driving at too many miles per hour and denying he's the leak. We'll send out a round robin, nothing detailed,' said Clay. 'He's having a nervous breakdown. If he calls you, keep him talking and try and find out where he is.'

'Professional Standards got back to me,' said Riley. 'They're going to dispatch a pair of officers to go to his home, and wait for him outside.'

'Well, they're going to have a long wait,' replied Clay. 'This stays between me, you and Barney Cole for now.'

84

8.30 pm

Christine Green looked between Clay and Riley and seemed to be watching something invisible to both of them.

'You know, Christine, if you don't come up with a miracle, I'm going to be charging you with two counts of murder very, very soon.'

Clay held up the envelope, took out the photographs and placed them in a carefully ordered fashion face down on the table. She turned the first towards Christine. 'Do you recognise the red duffel coat in this picture?'

Quickly, Christine Green glanced at the photograph. 'No.'

'Look closely at the picture, Christine. Can you see discolouration on the coat?'

'Yes.'

Clay watched Christine's eyes dither, sensed the pressure building up inside her skull.

'Do you know what those discolourations are?'

'No.'

'Blood. Right now, as we speak, this coat is being fast-track tested for the DNA on it. Do you know whose blood is on that coat?'

'No.'

'Then I'm going to put it to you, Christine, that the blood on the coat came from Steven Jamieson and his wife Frances. What's your view of that statement?'

'I don't know. I don't know what you're talking about.' She turned to her solicitor. 'Can you say something here? Can you stick your oar in and help me because right now you're sitting there like a silent sack of shit!'

'DCI Clay hasn't asked one inappropriate question. Cooperate, Christine.'

Clay placed two more photographs in front of Christine. On one photograph was a trio of grey-blonde hairs in the hood of the coat. In the next picture, the hairs were blown up and laid out against the blank canvas of a white card. 'Are these hairs from your head, Christine?'

'No.'

Clay eyed Christine's hair. 'It looks like your hair and it's currently being examined in our forensic lab. We have your DNA on the database. We're having comparative DNA tests done on you, Lucien and the victims. Look at the enlarged picture of the hairs removed from the hood of your coat. Can you see the flecks of blood on those hairs?'

'No.'

Clay placed another photograph in front of Christine, so she could see it head on. 'Do you know what's in this photograph, Christine?'

'No.'

'It's a sharpened, two millimetre spoke.'

'So?'

'So, Christine? So it's a murder weapon. Do you know who was murdered using this lethal home-made device?'

'No.'

'David Wilson and Steven Jamieson.'

'Oh...'

'Do you know how they were murdered?'

'No.'

'Do you know what the consistency of the human brain is like?'

'No.'

'The human brain has the same consistency as a boiled egg, Christine.'

Clay leaned forward a little and watched Christine's eyes dither in the silence.

'The sharpened spoke was inserted in the base of the skull and was used like a windscreen wiper inside their brains. Did you do that to them, Christine?'

'No.'

'Did you know that the pathologist concluded in both cases that the men were alive and probably conscious when the steel first entered their brains?'

'No.'

'Do you know where we found the sharpened steel?'

'No.'

Clay placed the picture of the sharpened steel next to the photograph of the red duffel coat. She pointed at the pictures as she spoke. 'We found the sharpened spoke concealed inside the lining of the duffel coat, right here in the vertical hem.'

'Did you?'

Clay took the next photograph, looked at it, kept it concealed from Christine. 'Do you know where we found the red duffel coat?'

'No.'

Clay turned the photograph around and showed a clear picture of the coat in a box behind McDonald's. 'We found the coat, the sharpened spoke and some other of your possessions over the road from your house on Rice Lane, in the bins behind McDonald's.'

'Bully for you.'

'Christine, did you conceal them there?'

'No.'

'We have a hugely reliable witness who said you always wore a red duffel coat like this.'

'Who?' A note of dark emotion sounded beneath the surface.

'Your next-door neighbour, Mary Behan.'

Silence.

'That's all right then,' said Christine, flatly.

'Is it?'

'Yes.'

'Why, Christine?'

'Because it's my word against hers and she's as blind as a bat but a bat makes more sense than she does.'

'I disagree. I've heard it from a reliable witness, she may be old but she's lucid, intelligent and observant. Did you act alone in these two murders?'

'I didn't.'

'Act alone?'

'Murder anyone.'

'We know you were involved, Christine. The other party was Lucien Burns.'

'He acted alone. I've got nothing at all to do with him.'

Clay took out her iPhone, went to Voice Memos and turned the volume to its highest setting.

'This a recording of a call made to switchboard from the Jamieson murder scene by your accomplice. Listen.'

As the recording flooded the room, Christine tilted her head and turned her face to the ceiling.

'I'm calling from 699 Mather Avenue.'

Clay pressed stop. 'That's not you, is it?'

'No.'

'Who is it then if it's not you?'

'I don't know.'

She tilted her head back, placed her hand close to her mouth and whispered to her solicitor. He shook his head, looking like a man with an invisible anvil on top of his skull.

Christine sat back and looked at Clay.

'No, Christine,' said Mr Robson. 'Please don't proceed any further into this interview assuming that DCI Clay has manufactured this recording or that she is merely playing mind games with you. Please proceed in this interview taking everything at face value. It is in your best short- and long-term interests.'

Clay pressed play.

'What's the nature of your problem?' asked the operator.

Clay paused the recording. 'Who's speaking now, Christine?' Clay unpaused it.

'A man has been murdered and his wife has been tortured. Tell Eve Clay to get over here as fast as she can – 699 Mather Avenue.'

Pause.

'Who spoke those words, Christine?'

'I... don't... know...'

'Who asked for me?'

'I don't know!'

'Who tipped me off from the crime scene?'

'I don't... know.'

'Please continue, Detective Sergeant Riley,' said Clay.

Riley turned over the next photograph, the contents of the My Little Pony backpack, and placed it in front of Christine.

'Is this your Stanley knife?' asked Riley.

'It speaks.'

'Answer the question,' said the solicitor.

'No.'

'Did you use this Stanley knife to carve the signature "Vindici" on the flesh on David Wilson's back?' asked Riley.

'No.'

'Steven Jamieson's back?'

'No.'

'Frances Jamieson's back?'

'No.'

'Did you use this Stanley knife to remove Frances Jamieson's eyelids?'

'No.'

'Why did you use the sharpened spoke to whip the backs of Steven Jamieson's legs before you used it to invade his brain?'

'I didn't.'

'Why didn't you whip David Wilson's legs?'

'I didn't.'

Riley turned over a photograph of the My Little Pony backpack. 'Recognise this?'

'No.'

'We found all those items inside the My Little Pony backpack, the one we found with your coat and laptop behind McDonald's.'

Riley placed a picture of the thin blue ropes in front of Christine. 'This isn't the same rope that was used to bind Frances Jamieson. Those particular ropes are currently undergoing forensic testing, but they were found in the bag which I can only assume was used to carry the tools you needed to do the job of murder. Not once but twice. Do you recognise the ropes?'

'No.'

Riley presented her with another photograph. 'The aerosol used to disable them when they opened the front door to you?'

'No.'

Next photograph. 'Incense cones and matches. Recognise them, Christine?'

'No.'

'We had a phone call from a Sergeant Eduardo García of the Puebla City police department in Mexico. He confirmed that twelve Weeping Children statuettes...' Riley showed Christine two images of the statuettes, one from David Wilson's home and the other from Steven Jamieson's. '...just like these were purchased by and dispatched to a Mrs J. Truman at 686 Rice Lane from Sanchez Ceramics in Puebla City. Who lives at 686 Rice Lane?'

'Mrs J. Truman.'

'That's your home address, Christine. When you purchased the Weeping Children, you were flattering yourself that you had a deep connection to your hero Justin Truman, that you were somehow married to him. You purchased those statuettes of the Weeping Children, didn't you, Christine?'

'I've never seen them in my life.'

'You ordered twelve, Christine. Were you planning to murder a further ten men?'

'No, I had no plans to murder anyone. I have no plans to murder anyone. How can anyone think they could match up to Justin Truman, a hero of the people, a defender of children everywhere, the light at the end of the tunnel, the one who gives hope to the hopeless?'

'Tell me more about Justin Truman,' said Clay. 'Did he start orchestrating these murders from Mexico?'

Christine took the middle finger of her right hand and drew it from left to right across her tightly sealed lips.

'Is he in direct touch with you, calling the shots?'

Silence.

'Because if he is, one of the things I don't understand yet is why he didn't tell you to leave food at the murder scenes. Sugar skulls, candy skeletons, dainty cakes.'

'In your eyes he is a criminal. In my eyes he is the saviour.'

'I'm calling a break here,' said Clay. 'When I recommence the interview, Christine, I want to know how you got the names and addresses of David Wilson on Dundonald Road, Aigburth, and the Jamiesons on Mather Avenue in Allerton. That's what we'll be talking about next, amongst other things. You wouldn't happen to be able to tell me anything about how you got that information now, would you?'

Christine looked at her solicitor. 'Do you know what the fuck she's talking about, Mr Robson?'

'Christine,' said Clay. She made eye contact with Clay. 'There's one other thing. Think about this one. Lucien Burns. The two of you gave a good show back then of not knowing each other and falling out to the point of a fist fight. But how do you know him?'

'I don't know him.'

'Of course you don't know him, Christine. In the same way as he doesn't know you.' They stared at each other across the table. 'You're very artistic, Christine, I've got to hand it to you. I couldn't whittle such a detailed SS Death's Head in wood relief if I tried for a thousand years. I couldn't produce calligraphy to such a high standard, forging someone's signature on the skin of another human being with a Stanley knife. You're artistic, for sure, but you're brutal with it. And you're lying through your teeth to me.'

85

8.35 pm

Arturo Salvador stood on the step of 101 Arundel Avenue and, picking out the bell for Flat 4, assessed the nameless blank space next to it and saw an admission of guilt in the resident's need and desire for anonymity.

Keeping his finger on the bell to the count of seven, he waited in the ensuing silence and no voice came from the intercom. Finger on the bell, he counted to twenty, imagined the abrasive noise and how it jangled the nerves of the man who was refusing to speak with him.

He banged on the front door fast and hard with the heel of his hand, enough to rattle the bones of the big old house, and was rewarded with a barely audible, 'Who is this?' through the dilapidated intercom.

'Merseyside Police. Open the door, please.'

'How do I know you're who you're saying you are?' The man sounded afraid to the point of terror.

'You don't. Open the door.'

Ragged breathing grew thicker and faster through the intercom.

'Look, you're in danger, Edward. I've come to help you.'

'What do you mean?'

'We've had a tip-off, an anonymous call.'

He left Edward dangling.

'What? What was said?'

'I'm not discussing this with you from the step. You let me in and I'll tell you what was said. You refuse to open the door, I'll have no choice other than to walk away and leave you in the lap of the gods...'

'I – I'll open the door. You'd better be who you say you are.'

'Or else?'

'I've got a knife and I'm not afraid to use it.'

'Open the door, let me in, or I'm going to get into my car and you can take your chances on your own. Three life-and-death seconds, Edward. One.'

'Don't do this to me...'

'Two. You're in deep shit, my friend.'

'What do you mean?'

The intercom buzzed and he pushed the front door open. Rap music and an unnecessarily loud television set blasted from Flats 1 and 2 on the ground floor.

He closed the door after himself, smelt damp, fried food and despair.

Ascending the stairs to Flat 4 on the first floor, he stretched his fingers inside his white leather gloves, and imagined sunshine and a mariachi band, following a procession of human skeletons marching together to celebrate the Day of the Dead.

He knocked at Flat 4 and heard someone moving behind the door. Through the wood, he drew in the stale odour of a body cooped up for too long in a confined space, a slow death by premature burial.

'You're wasting my time, Edward.'

On the other side of the front door, Edward fumbled with a bolt and a chain. 'But I haven't done anything wrong.'

'You haven't been caught for a few years, that's for sure.'

The door opened and he watched as Edward walked backwards into the darkness of the flat, the carving knife in his hand shaking.

He walked into a windowless corridor with closed doors either side.

Opening the door to the left, he shut it in the same moment against the stench of a bathroom that couldn't have been cleaned in years. The door to the right revealed a kitchen piled up with layers of junk that made access to the cooker and sink like an assault course.

'This isn't safe, Edward. You really need a big spring clean.'

'What do you want?' His voice came from the bedroom at the end of the corridor, where the brightest light in the flat shone.

He braced himself.

Edward stood by his unmade bed, across a sea of clothes tossed on to the floor, the knife still in his hand. On the table next to the bed, an electric arc light picked out a framed photograph, the picture obscured by a black sock draped over the top of the frame.

'Put the knife down,' he said, advancing, holding his hands in the air. 'I come in peace.'

The knife fell from Edward's trembling hands.

He weighed Edward up.

Bald, body like an over-full sack of potatoes, unshaved, eyes watering and looking much older than his fifty-six years.

'Was it *you* or *time* that was so unkind to you?'

He picked up the photograph frame and, discarding the sock, examined the small snapshot of Edward when he was younger, with a head full of blond curly hair that could have put him in a young Roger Daltrey lookalike contest and a smile as bright as the sunshine.

A mouse skittered past his shoe, pissing as it moved.

Hunched inside a set of greasy clothes, Edward's face had the stamp of someone persecuted on the inside and out.

Not an easy life, thought Arturo, *being a paedophile*.

'What are you smiling at?' asked Edward.

'There's a coat at the bottom of your bed. Put it on. You're coming with me to Wavertree Road police station.'

'But I haven't done anything wrong.'

'It's for your own protection, Edward.'

Edward shuffled to the bottom of the bed and picked up the grey coat. 'What's happened?'

'We had a tip-off. We were given three names, yours was one of them. The caller said the Vindici copycat was going to target the three of you. We can't be sure how true this was but we can't take any chances either. We have a duty to protect you so I'm taking you into protective custody. Make your way to your front door and no more talking until we get into my car. We need to leave as quickly and discreetly as we can. We can't be sure who's watching or listening, can we, Edward?'

Edward's eyes filled up with tears. 'I just want to say…'

'Stop! Walk!'

Edward walked out of the bedroom.

He picked up the framed photograph and, with his iPhone, took three snaps of the young Edward, a man not as yet broken by life and his own deepest weaknesses. He slipped the frame inside his coat's inner pocket.

He walked in silence and found Edward sobbing with relief at the front door of the flat.

'Thank you!'

'Shut up, Edward Hawkins!'

86

8.50 pm

If she hadn't been on the brink of exhaustion, the expression 'the Devil is in the detail' would have made DCI Eve Clay laugh her head off.

She caught Aaron Brierley's eye as he arranged his damp Armani coat over the back of his chair in Interview Suite 1.

Catching the buzz of an incoming text on her iPhone, she hung on to Brierley's stare, and thought, *You think you're going to intimidate me after the places I've been to and the people I've faced? Pussy!*

'Yes?' he challenged.

'Sit down, please,' Clay retorted.

As Brierley sat next to his client, Daniel Campbell, and looked away, Clay looked at her phone, saw the text was from Poppy Waters.

Eve, I've cracked Christine Green's hard drive. So far nothing to write home about. I'll wait for you in the incident room. I've just unlocked Lucien Burns's phone.

She formally opened the interview and made a little hay with the silence that followed it, smiling at Lesley Reid and DS Bill Hendricks flanking her.

'To begin with, Daniel,' said Clay. 'I'm sorry for the loss of your close friend Steven Jamieson.'

'He was not a close friend. He was not a friend. He was a client.'

'It was purely business then, your relationship?'

'I don't understand the relevance of your initial questioning,' said Brierley.

'Oh, you will do!' said Clay. 'Just sit back, make yourself comfortable and let's let matters unfold. Steven Jamieson trusted you, didn't he?'

'I was his legal representative for many years so, yes, he must have trusted me,' replied Daniel Campbell.

'How did you meet him?'

'Through a mutual friend, at a charity event hosted by Sheffield Wednesday FC. We knew of each other before we met.'

'So did you know he was a predatory paedophile when you had your first meeting?' asked Clay.

'No.'

'When did you first find this out?'

'When he was first charged by South Yorkshire Police.'

'You had no idea at all, whatsoever, about his sexual prefer-ences for children until he was charged?'

'Correct.'

Clay tilted her head towards Lesley Reid, met her eye and then looked directly at Daniel Campbell.

'That's not right,' said Reid.

'This isn't right,' said Brierley. 'You bring in a retired police officer from a different constabulary to act as a chorus on an interview with my client?'

Clay ignored him. 'Daniel, this interview is only going to go one way.'

'Yes, my way, right back to Sheffield while you waste time during the crucial earliest hours of a murder investigation on ephemera. You've got nothing on me.'

Clay looked at Hendricks and Reid. 'The gloves are off then? OK!'

Hendricks stood up, walked to the corner of the room and returned with a Tupperware stacker box.

'How much money a month was paid into a bank account that you managed on behalf of Steven Jamieson?'

'How is that relevant to your murder inquiry?' asked Brierley.

'Mr Campbell, I'm trying to establish how your client's dubious lifestyle may have contributed to his unlawful death. How much money per month was paid into an account managed by you?'

He looked at the box on the table. 'There was no such account.'

Hendricks lifted the lid of the box and took out a file fat with bank statements. 'Our Scientific Support officers found this in a filing cabinet in Steven Jamieson's house as they searched it following his murder,' he said. 'Would you like to have a look at the bank statements?'

Campbell looked at the statements with barely concealed horror. 'No comment.'

Hendricks took out the top statement, a single sheet, and placed it in front of Campbell and Brierley, and then flicked through the thick wad. 'Every single one of these tells the same story as the one sheet in front of you.'

Brierley picked up the bank statement.

'How much each month was paid into this account in your name?' pressed Clay.

'These bank statements have nothing to do with me. No comment.'

'All right,' said Clay. 'Bill...'

'There are three areas we want to explore with you, *Mr* Campbell.' Hendricks placed the bank statements on the table. 'We're thinking, amongst other criminal activities, police corruption in this heap of bank statements.'

He looked at Lesley Reid.

'The missing link and Holy Grail all in one bundle,' she said. 'We're pretty much 99.9 per cent sure of who the bent police officers Jamieson had in his pocket are but this is just magic.'

Hendricks took out the paperwork relating to surgical procedures. 'Dr Warner?'

'No comment.'

'Since when do gynaecologists, even those who've been struck off the medical register for sexual molestation of a minor, perform cosmetic surgery?'

'No comment.'

Hendricks produced the third set of documents. 'Do you want to tell us what these are, Mr Campbell, or do you want to tell us what's going on with these confidentiality payoffs?'

'No comment.'

'Why did Steven Jamieson employ you to buy such vague silence from so many children?'

'No comment.'

'The CPS view of these confidentiality contracts is that they are laughable in their lack of detail. Did you set out to intimidate Steven Jamieson's victims while disguising the nature of his wrongdoing?'

'No comment.'

'Are you a paedophile, Mr Campbell?'

'No comment. No! No, no, I am not a paedophile.'

Clay looked at Aaron Brierley.

'I'd like to request a suspension. I need to talk with Mr Campbell.'

'That's fine,' said Clay.

She watched Campbell looking at the three sets of paper as if he was staring into a void.

'I'm going to give you a chance here, a way forward. Is there anything you want to say in your own defence before I formally suspend this interview, Mr Campbell?'

Clay looked into his eyes and imagined him laid out on ice on the fish counter in a supermarket. Within the deadness of his eyes, she detected a deep internal struggle between an impulse to speak and the desire to keep silent.

'I...' Campbell pointed at the bank statements. 'I know nothing about this. Nothing. He's stolen my identity. He's used me as a human shield without my consent.'

Clay said nothing, sensed more, pulled a benign face, *OK…*

Campbell slammed the flat of his hand down on the bank statements. 'This'll have been Frances's doing, the duplicitous bitch.'

'Why do you say that?' asked Clay.

'You could never describe Steven as a saint…'

'That's enough, Daniel,' said Brierley.

'She was ten times worse than him on every level.'

'Enough!'

Clay took out a clear plastic carrier from her bag. There was an object inside it.

'Give me back my phone!' said Campbell.

'Given the evidence against you on the table, I'm seizing your phone, Mr Campbell, and handing it to our IT specialists,' said Clay. She called Poppy Waters on speed dial. 'I've got another iPhone for you to look at. I'll bring it to you directly.'

Campbell looked at his solicitor.

'Daniel, I think we need to talk,' said Brierley.

When he woke up, for a split second Detective Constable Bob Rimmer thought he was at home in bed and wondered why it was so cold. He guessed Valerie had left the window open because she always needed fresh air even during the depths of winter. He patted the surface of the bed and felt something spongy and damp, the texture of grass.

He opened his eyes and the room was a blur, only it wasn't a room and he wasn't at home. As his vision came into focus, the hiss of wind and water made him realise where he was: lying diagonally on a sloping bank of grass overlooking the River Mersey.

Rain pounded Rimmer's head and body as the wind blew from the water.

Across the river, he saw hundreds of specks of yellow lights illuminating the Wirral Peninsula where life carried on irrespective of his escalating despair, and he knew that he was less than invisible.

His heart was no longer his heart but instead was a landline telephone on Eve Clay's desk. It rang and, when it stopped ringing, he heard his own voice inside his head, echoing, 'Hello?' And another voice from the River Mersey crashing against the promenade wall.

'Is that Barney Cole?'

He wasn't sure what the answer was but he said, 'Who am I speaking with?'

'Sergeant Eduardo García, Puebla City police,' replied the water.

In the distance the rotating blades of the police helicopter sliced the cold night air and Rimmer turned on to his side away from the noise, seeing the world now with one eye, a fox looking left and right before scrambling up the bank and away from the Mexican cop whose voice lived in the water.

'I have good news for you, Barney!' he spoke again from the swell.

He felt the imprint of his wife's fading body, so thin now she was just a bag of bones, saw death in her face and knew he could never bear to look at her or feel her again.

Murder.

He reached into the darkness, towards the stars and heard his own voice, 'Let me get my pen.'

Rimmer rolled over, heard the sound of three children crying, recognised the unique sadness of his own sons and, looking up at the top of the bank, saw three statuettes of Weeping Children, each with a finger pointing down at him while their other fist knocked on the door of night.

The sound of their tears echoed back from the river and Rimmer cursed the power in the universe that allowed paedophiles to remain alive and healthy while his wife died a slow and agonising death.

The statuettes melted from ceramic into flesh, singlets rippling around their bare knees in the chill wind that blew in from the River Mersey.

Slowly they descended the bank, their dark hair fluttering as they came closer to Rimmer, closer to him but not seeming to be aware of his existence as they wept their way towards the water. As they passed on either side of him, he smelt a cocktail of sugar and incense. The perfume spiked his drunken senses and made him sit up on the bank and watch them walk from the grass and on to the concrete pavement that led to the railings.

They stopped at the railings, turned as one and mourned, 'Daddy? Daddy. Daddy...'

In one acrobatic and unified motion, the three Weeping Children climbed on to the top of the railings and the water enquired, 'Are you still there?'

'Yes, thank you for that.' He spoke to the backs of the children, saw them shiver as they waited on the rails and stared down into the darkness of the water.

Standing up, he heard the voice in the water soar to the sky and sing from the stars, 'No problem. Keep me informed and good luck, Barney.'

He took a step towards the Weeping Children and the first child jumped into the water. With the next step, the second child followed and, with a third step, the last of the children descended.

Rimmer watched as the three children sank beneath the cold black water, without struggle, their weeping fell into a silence that made him think the world had almost ended.

He removed his shoes and, climbing on to the rail, felt the cold metal of the bar beneath his feet. Raising his arms into the air, he gave himself up to the sky and stars and tumbled head first into the water, eyes and ears wide open as he broke the surface and fell like a boulder past his lifeless, silent children.

Opening his mouth wide, his lungs filled with water and the bitterness of salt and oil and fish took over his senses.

He stared into the water, saw the shifting ceiling of the river, sank and became one with the thing that filled and surrounded him.

Darkness.

88

9.01 pm

As Arturo Salvador turned his hire car from the top of Smithdown Road on to Tunnel Road, the storm picked up force. He glanced in the rear-view mirror and caught Hawkins looking at him as the rain pounded the roof of his hire car.

'Will you pull the window up? It's very cold here in the back,' said Hawkins.

'I can't do that *no more*,' he mocked.

'Why?'

'Because you stink of sweat and cheap fried food.'

'What's your name?' asked Hawkins.

'Why? Are you going to put in a complaint about me because I was truthful about your lousy personal hygiene? Shut up, Hawkins.'

'But I—'

As he crossed the junction with Wavertree Road and on to Durning Road, he looked over his shoulder as Hawkins fiddled with the lock in the door. 'It's child-proofed. It can only be opened from outside. There's no way you can open that door from inside.'

'I wasn't trying to get out no more.' Hawkins looked sideways and back. 'Isn't the police station on Wavertree Road that way?' Fear and dread crept into his voice.

'I can't take you that way for security reasons. I have to take you a long route. Seeing as you couldn't be bothered asking, let me ask you a question, *Edward*. Do you know it round here, *Edward*?'

He turned onto Edge Lane and pressed his foot down on the accelerator. The wind howled across the body of the car and the windscreen wipers flew back and forth at speed, throwing rain from the glass.

'Maybe you're not responding no more because somehow or other you're a bit offended because I've got your name all wrong.'

On the back seat, Hawkins bowed his head and covered his face with his hands.

'I said, do you know it round here, Christopher?'

'I'm not called Christopher no more. I like to be called by my middle name, Edward.'

'I can understand that. Look to your right, Botanic Gardens.'

'I – I don't know.'

'And the Littlewoods Building. Isn't it wonderful, all that investment from abroad, all that money pumped in by a Mexican entrepreneur to bring it back to life? I completely understand that you don't want to be addressed by the name you were charged with. Twelve years for raping an eight-year-old autistic girl. You got off lightly, don't you think?'

'I don't want to talk about it.'

'Making friends with the single mother downstairs, the woman with learning difficulties, and her kid who had no verbal language or way of communicating with the world outside her head.'

'Shush. No more.'

'You must have thought, *She's not going to be much use as a witness*. Hey? Are you not talking to me no more?'

Silence.

'If it's silence you want, silence is what you'll get.'

A seagull, fooled into thinking night was day by the bright street lights along the length of Edge Lane, flew ahead of them, crying.

He pulled up at the lights, at the entrance to the Hollywood Bowl Park. 'Get your fingers off the lock. I've told you. You can't open it from the inside.'

When the lights turned to green, he performed a U-turn and drove back the way he had come onto the city-centre-bound carriageway of Edge Lane.

'Calm down, Christopher. Look, I'm driving back in the general direction of the police station where you expect to be given protective custody. You never were the brightest, were you, Christopher?'

'You're not... a policeman, are you?'

'I am. I policed the likes of you in 2007 and 2008.'

'Who are you?'

'You're going to listen carefully. It's been a long time since I've been in Liverpool and I've spent a lot of money bringing the Littlewoods Building back to life and do you know why I did that? I did it for you, Christopher.'

He turned up a lane at the right hand side of the Littlewoods Building. 'Fancy having a little sneak preview of what's inside the sleeping giant?'

'Let me out!'

'That was a rhetorical question!'

He pulled up beside a padlocked gate, three feet wide, and showed Hawkins a key.

Hawkins pointed at a sign on the fence. 'Look, it's got twenty-four-hour round-the-clock security!'

'Yes. But not tonight. I gave all the security guards twenty-four hours off. I'm a nice guy, see. Not like some I could mention, Christopher Hawkins.'

'Do I know you?'

'I'm like an onion, I have many layers. Do you know what I mean? I mean, I am different things to different people. Not altogether one thing or another.'

'Let me go. I haven't hurt anyone for a long, long time. Please have mercy on me.'

'Look at the storm. It's growing stronger.'

'Let me go. I promise you I won't go to the police. I won't tell anyone.'

After a well-timed pause, he said, 'You're so persuasive, Christopher.' The wind howled like a massed chorus of hysterical mournful voices. 'All right, I'll let you go.'

'Thank you, thank you so much, thank you, thank you…'

'So long, Christopher.'

On Edge Lane, cars zipped towards the city centre, their head-lights like the eyes of mythical beasts.

Hawkins turned his back on him, took the first few speculative steps from the shadows and towards Edge Lane.

'Christopher? You want to know who I am?'

Hawkins stopped and turned.

'My name is Justin Truman. People know me as Vindici. This is what's going to happen to you.'

Hawkins started to walk backwards, fell over on to his backside.

Truman grabbed his collar, pulled him back to his feet, held on to his collar and pressed his face close to Hawkins. 'You're going to die tonight, Christopher, but as you've inflicted suffering on others, you're not going to die without suffering yourself – and I mean *suffering*.'

Truman threw three swift, hard punches just above Hawkins's nose, and turning him round, ordered, 'Walk this way, Hawkins!'

89

9.01 pm

'There's a real IT naivety about Christine Green,' said Poppy Waters to Clay and Hendricks. 'I put the hard drive from her smashed laptop into a comparable model and opened it from there. I entered System-Out-of-Box Experience and once Sysprep started running it took thirty seconds for Christine's hard drive to move house and be up and running on the new laptop. Her website's nowhere near as sophisticated as Lucien Burns's but, so far, and it is early days, it looks like she's never even heard of the deep web or the dark web. She uses Google to search for everything. Her history's endless, as in it appears she hasn't ever bothered to wipe it. She hasn't even got the new Justin Truman picture on her computer, unlike hundreds of thousands of others who've already shared it and liked it.'

'I've got another iPhone for you to look at,' said Clay as the door opened and Cole entered. She handed the phone to Poppy and explained, 'It belongs to Steven Jamieson's solicitor Daniel Campbell.'

'Who came in here threatening us with the full force of the law and now looks like a lump of desiccated shit,' observed Hendricks.

'Christine Green's laptop?' said Poppy. 'Apart from a pretty creaky website, there's nothing I've seen on here so far to directly implicate her.'

'You say she's technically naive,' said Clay. 'Which goes a long way to explaining why she thought she could destroy evidence on the hard drive by smashing the laptop. All the physical evidence points to her. It's like a mirror image of Lucien's position. Nothing from him rubs off from the physical evidence but his computer says he's up to his eyes in this. Lucien Burns and Christine Green? My money says you can't have one without the other.'

'What do you want me to do next?'

'At some point as soon as you can, have a look at Christine Green's phone. See if she made or received calls between eight fifty-five and nine ten this morning. If she did, let me know what the number or numbers are, please. Campbell's got enough to worry about as it is before we find whatever's lurking on his device. Tell me what you found on Lucien's iPhone, please.'

'Lucien's thought of pretty much everything to keep his phone secure,' said Poppy. He didn't save any passwords to his phone, he's used screenlock and encryption to keep his data secure. Public Wi-Fi he's kept well away from and he's used Hideninja VPN to encrypt his outgoing data. But the really clever thing he's done that makes me think he's got something worth hiding is that he's used 3CX Mobile Device Manager.'

'What does that do?' asked Clay.

'It allows him to wipe his data remotely.'

Poppy Waters connected Lucien Burns's iPhone to her laptop. She enabled USB debugging and asked Clay, 'What do you want me to trawl up first? You could choose texts, Facebook messages...?'

'Call History please, Poppy. I want to know who he's been talking to.'

Standing behind Poppy and looking over her shoulder, Cole asked, 'Isn't it hard to retrieve data that's been deleted from mobiles?' Clay saw he had the rapt intensity of a onlooker at a shamanic ritual.

'If he's been super smart, he'll have cut the SIM card into as many small pieces as he can and scattered them into the Mersey from the side of the ferry.'

'But he's been a cocky little get and kept the SIM card in the device, right?' said Cole.

Poppy previewed Recovered Files from Lucien's phone's internal memory and the lost contents of his deleted calls appeared on Poppy's laptop screen.

'Oh, Lucien, you lying little toad,' said Cole.

'Is this good news?' asked Clay.

'I think you're going to be rather happy, Eve,' said Cole.

She looked at Poppy's laptop screen and felt her open palms come together.

'He *was* a cocky little get when it came to the SIM card,' said Clay, drinking in the information on Poppy's laptop. 'How long will it take you to open up his deleted texts, Facebook messages, the works?'

'Not that long,' replied Poppy.

'Print this off for me. We'll leave him sweating in the interview suite until we've got an overview of who he's been communicating with and when he's been doing it.'

The printer on Stone's desk came to life.

Clay walked to it. She wanted to drag the paper from the machine but watched, with rising impatience, as the missing data from Lucien Burns's phone came back from the shadows in plain black and white print.

The top line read: *CALL HISTORY (8) / CONTENT / DATE / TYPE / DURATION OF CALL.* Tiredness deserted Clay as she retrieved the sheet and studied it hard to double-check that she was not lost in a futile daydream. It was all real and she felt refreshed and ready to continue the battle for truth.

The landline phone on her desk rang.

She picked up the receiver and heard voices riding over each other.

'Eve?'

'Is there a problem with Lucien, Sergeant Harris?'

'No. I've got Aaron Brierley with me right now. I was about to go and get Lucien from his cell when Daniel Campbell's solicitor asked me if his client could be called for interview. He wants to make a statement, answer questions and contextualise the evidence that was presented to him earlier. He wants to cooperate.'

She thought about it for almost a second and said, 'Yes, I bet he does. He can have a second interview. When I'm ready to call him. He's not the only fish in the pond at the moment and he certainly isn't the biggest. Let him swim after his own tail and get dizzy in the process. I want Lucien Burns in interview suite one, please.'

She paused as she went to put the receiver down, and heard Harris telling Brierly, 'DCI Clay will call your client at her convenience.'

'Barney, do me a favour. Give Lesley Reid and her colleagues a call. We're going to need them at some point soon. Gina Riley can lead the interview.'

She looked to Poppy and asked, 'Anything else?'

'Come and have a look at this,' said Poppy with a smile that filled her whole face. 'Text messages. Deleted by him. Retrieved by me.'

90

9.11 pm

DCI Eve Clay held eye contact with Lucien Burns and said, 'Last time we were sitting in this room together, you asked me if I knew how many types of paedophiles there are?'

'Yeah, and you're the worst kind, Clay. I said that. And it's true.'

'As in *Lucien Burns* speaks the *truth*?' Clay placed her hands down on two pieces of paper, face down on the table. Her iPhone sat dead centre between Lucien Burns and herself. 'Hours ago, you acknowledged that there was no point in lying to us, that our IT people would find everything on your computer. How did you think it was going to be any different with your phone?'

'I didn't think it was going to be any different with my phone. When I used the word computer, I was using it as a blanket term to cover all my communication devices – phone, iPad...'

'You were bluffing when you bigged up our IT experts. The truth is you're arrogant. You thought you were better than us. You thought you'd buried some things so deeply we'd never find them. I'm going to ask you again. Have you been in direct touch with Justin Truman?'

'No.'

'Are you sure about that, Lucien?'

'I'm certain.'

She turned over one of the pieces of paper. 'We've retrieved a log of the phone calls you deleted from your phone.' She turned the paper round so that Lucien could see it head on, pushed it towards him. He made no effort to look at the page.

His solicitor tapped the page. 'Lucien, you should look at this,' she advised.

The young social worker on his other side looked and gave an involuntary gasp.

'Lucien, look at the page!' said Clay. 'You know, our IT specialist said if you'd been smart, you'd have cut your SIM card up and ditched it in the Mersey, swiped in a new one. And I thought, *No, he's sixteen, he knows it all, he's an internet star, he thinks he's never going to get caught.* He didn't think this morning, *What if this is the day when the police come calling?* He woke up this morning and thought, *I've just got away with murder, not* once *but* twice. Look what our IT specialist managed to call up on her laptop from your phone: Deleted Calls.'

Clay leaned forward. 'I think you couldn't bear to get rid of that SIM card because it was a direct link to your contact with Justin Truman. Getting rid of it would have been like getting rid of the one photograph you had of a lost loved one.'

Lucien looked away at the wall behind her back.

'I can't force you to look, Lucien. But I can read upside down. Calls History Eight. First call in this cluster, duration eight minutes. Type, incoming. That must have been really exciting for you, Lucien. Date, seventh of September 2019. So, it's been going on for over a whole month. Two calls a week. Content, who's been calling you? Vindici. That's what it says on your Calls History.'

'Do you know—' he began.

'—how many people contact me and claim to be Justin Truman?' Clay finished his thought. 'You see, Lucien, I've got your number. I know what you're going to say next even though I've only known you for a few hours.'

'You know nothing about what I'm really like.'

'Would you like to explain what you mean by that?' asked Clay.

'I'm nothing like what you think I am.'

'Meaning?'

'Nothing is as it seems on the surface.'

'Are you hiding something? Do you want to share something with me? No? Let's talk about your transatlantic telephone conversations with Justin Truman. Of the eight, there are two conversations on two dates I'm particularly interested in. The fourteenth of October 2019, last Monday week. The day David Wilson was murdered. You had a call from Justin Truman that afternoon that went on for an hour and three minutes. Pretty big pep talk that?'

'No comment.'

'I hate to steal your thunder but I had a call from him myself the following day at just after three in the morning.'

'As if.'

She picked up her iPhone, pressed play and watched his face.

'*Hello, Eve.*'

'*Who is this?*'

'*Who am I? I know who you are, Eve, and it's good to know you.*'

'*I'll tell you what I am. I'm dead tired and I haven't got time to play games or untangle meaningless riddles when I've got so many real problems to solve. So, please tell me who you are or I'll have to hang up.*'

'*I don't mean to vex you or waste your time, Eve. I'll send you a picture via a third party. It should iron out one idea that's running around your brain as we speak. Would you like that?*'

'*Yes I would. But who are you?*'

'*I'll tell you who I am. Are you ready? I am Vindici.*'

Without taking her eyes away from Lucien, she pressed stop.

'Vindici,' said Clay. 'I am Vindici.'

'You've been had,' said Lucien. 'That's not Vindici. And before you ask, I saw a documentary and there was footage of the police interviewing him, that's how I know.'

'So the voice on my device isn't the Vindici you've been speaking to?'

'Your Vindici's a fake. Mine's the real deal.'

'In which case, Lucien, you've been had. We analysed the voice on my phone against the Metropolitan Police's tapes of their interviews with Justin Truman and the voices were identical.'

Clay moved the page a little closer to Lucien and pointed to a specific place. 'You made a phone call to him that same day, the fourteenth of October at nine fifty-nine pm. Outgoing. Duration of call? One minute fifty-three seconds. That was when you informed him that you'd done the hit on David Wilson and that I was Senior Investigating Officer on the case. That's when you gave him my landline number here at Trinity Road police station. That's how he knew how and when to call me.'

'No comment.'

Clay turned over the second sheet of paper. 'This is a different set of communications to and from another individual.' She pushed the page towards him.

'No comment.'

'Who has a mobile phone number, 07701 788654? The information related to this number was a text correspondence. Whose number, Lucien?'

'No comment.'

'This person texted you at nine forty-nine on the evening of Monday the fourteenth of October when I was in David Wilson's house in Dundonald Road. This person knew at this time that I was SIO on the case and they told you it was me and they gave you my direct landline number at this police station.'

'No comment.'

'You telephoned Justin Truman ten minutes later and in a brief call passed that information on to him.'

'No comment.'

'Do you know the time difference between Puebla City, Mexico and Liverpool?'

'No comment.'

'Puebla City is six hours behind Liverpool, so he phoned me at three minutes past nine on what was still Monday the fourteenth of October where he was.'

'No comment.'

'Guess what, Lucien? When I went to store this second number into my phone, I already had it.' She showed him her phone. 'Shall we call this person?'

'No comment.'

Clay waited in the silence that followed and looked at Lucien's Adam's apple as he stared up at the ceiling, and was reminded of a large rodent stuck in a snake's belly.

'I'm going to ring this person right now, Lucien, but I'm going to warn you not to make any attempt to let them know where I am or that you're present or that I know what they've been doing. As we speak, I know that this person is at home. As we speak, there are two unmarked police cars and four plainclothes officers outside this person's house. So, if this person suddenly leaves their house, this person will be running straight into a trap.'

'No comment.'

'I'm going to call them right now.'

91

9.20 pm

Inside the Littlewoods Building, the night traffic on Edge Lane just outside sounded like the waves on a distant shore as Christopher Hawkins came round with phenomenal pain in his head and the sense that he had experienced the worst dream of his life.

Naked and tied securely to a hard-backed chair somewhere in the cavernous space, Christopher Hawkins struggled to turn his hands and feet to loosen the tightness of the knots. As he did so, shockwaves of pain ran up and down his spine and he stilled.

With stinging eyes and blurred vision, he made out an army of points of light across the floor and worked out that these were candles. As things became clearer to him, he was aware of a huge source of light in the distance behind him.

He tried to turn his head to the sound of a pair of feet but the simple action turned the invisible vice on his neck and everything from before his blackout came streaming back into his memory.

Hawkins went to whisper, 'Jesus!' but his voice was buried in a gag tied round his mouth.

As the footsteps behind him came closer, he realised who was in the same space as him, and with that came the understanding that this was the night he was going to suffer and die.

As Vindici walked around his left-hand side, Hawkins looked down at his bloated belly that obscured his withered penis and drooping testicles and he remembered that Vindici castrated each of his victims, the detail that had terrified him the most. The gag on his mouth stifled the scream that erupted inside him.

Vindici kept walking and, three metres away from Hawkins, set down a table. He laid a white cloth on it and, as he made his way back behind Hawkins, the bound man realised he was setting up an altar.

He walked back to the table carrying two large straw baskets and, placing them down on the ground, started taking items out.

The air was filled with the sweetness of fresh fruit, chocolate and sugar. He placed a statue of the Virgin Mary with the infant Jesus to the side of the table and Hawkins wished he hadn't watched the documentaries on television after Justin Truman had been convicted and sent to jail.

How smug he had been during Vindici's reign of terror hundreds of miles away from Liverpool in the south of England, and how deeply relieved he had felt when Justin Truman was given a long custodial sentence. But how rattled he'd been when Vindici escaped and remained uncaptured.

Truman paused and looked directly at Hawkins.

Then he took silk dahlias from a basket and draped them over the altar and Hawkins heard himself whimper. His eyes welled up with tears as terror mounted inside him. Truman placed tea lights around the empty space at the centre of the altar and a ceramic statuette of a small child in a singlet with dark hair and outsized eyelashes on his or her face.

'In case you were wondering, this is a Weeping Child, Christopher. It's indicating you with its clenched fist and pointing down with its finger in the direction you'll be travelling when you die, which won't be for some time, I'm pleased to tell you.'

Slowly, Truman pulled a single bicycle spoke from the basket, kissed it and placed it on the left-hand side of the altar.

'Shall we put some sweets out for the children? I think so,' he said, scattering chocolate, fruit, a skull made of sugar and candy skeletons.

He produced a photograph frame and, keeping the image close to his chest, walked behind Hawkins, who felt Truman's fingers pull at the knot that bound the gag. As Truman pulled the gag away, Hawkins begged, 'Please let me go, please don't hurt me, I've reformed, I'm a different man to the one you think I am.'

'Shut up!'

Truman walked in front of Hawkins and said, 'Now for the centrepiece of the altar to the death of innocence.' He indicated the empty space at the centre of the altar and placed the photograph frame in it. 'Look at her.'

Hawkins turned his face away, looked down at the ground, felt his stomach turn to water and the blood rush to the centre of his body.

Truman walked behind Hawkins and forced his head up, so that his face was directly in line with the image in the frame. 'Look at her. Look at your victim. Did it make you feel important when you lured her into the shed? Did you feel excited? You like dark, claustrophobic spaces, don't you? All the assaults you've either committed or have tried to commit have been in small dark spaces. What is it with you and the dark, Christopher?'

He pointed at the sombre-looking girl in the photo frame. 'You managed to attack her. This is the one you were convicted for. There were others, surely?'

'No, it was a once-in-a-lifetime mistake. On my mother's grave. I don't know what got into me that day.'

'Is that the truth now?'

'I swear to God it's the truth.'

Truman took a CD from his coat pocket. 'If you're lying to me I'm going to make this go on for hours. Last chance. Are you lying to me?'

'I'm telling the truth, please, Justin...'

'Last chance,' said Truman, reaching into the basket and picking out an old Polaroid picture. He smiled and looked at the image. Looking back over his shoulder at Hawkins, he placed the CD into a player, pressed play and propped the Polaroid up against the larger framed picture.

'What is it?' asked Hawkins. 'I can't see through you.'

Truman moved aside and watched Hawkins's reaction to the crudely coloured Polaroid image on the altar, the questioning, the slow realisation and the horror.

Truman pointed at the Polaroid photograph. 'You've just lied to me!'

He picked up the sharpened bicycle spoke from the altar and pulled a Stanley knife from his pocket as he approached Hawkins.

Hawkins screamed at the top of his voice but the screams were lost, sucked in to the shadows and vastness of the Littlewoods Building, and drowned out by the echoing strains of Beethoven's 'Für Elise'.

92

9.21 pm

Clay turned on the speakerphone and the incident room was filled with the ring tone from her iPhone. She eyeballed Lucien Burns and said, 'You didn't get your information from whistleblower sites on the deep web, did you, Lucien?'

'No comment.'

The person picked up and Clay pressed her right index finger to her sealed lips.

'Hello, Eve.'

Clay waited, watched Lucien Burns's face.

'Hello, Eve, are you there?'

'Yes I am. I'm sorry to call you so late but there's been something of a development regarding Lucien Burns.'

'Is that the boy you pulled in today?'

'Yes, the boy who's running the Vindici fan site from Springwood Avenue. We've found something on his computer and we think you need to come in and look at it.'

'Now? Right now?'

'Yes, right now!'

'OK. I've had a couple of glasses of red wine, so I won't be able to drive over. I'll book a taxi and get there as soon as possible.'

'I don't want to inconvenience you more than I need to so I've sent a car over to give you a lift to Trinity Road.'

Beyond the silence close to the receiver, Clay heard a television playing in another room in the house and the bland sound of the outside world reminded her that Bob Rimmer was out there and no one had heard from or seen him since he'd disappeared.

'OK, I'll get my coat...'

'Thank you. See you soon,' said Clay with grim breeziness. She closed down the call. 'You don't have to give me a name, Lucien. That's the leak who's been feeding you information, isn't it?'

'No comment.'

93

9.28 pm

Justin Truman came up from the letter 'c' and drew the tip of the Stanley knife blade into a cursive 'i'.

'Don't move, Christopher, or I'll rearrange the running order and cut your slimy little balls off right now!'

Hawkins's body stiffened.

Truman removed the tip of the blade from Hawkins's skin and then jabbed it sharply back in to dot the 'i'.

'You'll get caught, Justin, if you kill me. If you let me go, I won't say a word no more.'

'You're like a stuck record, do you know that? Accept the fact that I'm as good as my word and you're going to die tonight.'

'Why don't you just put me out of my misery?' sobbed Hawkins.

'A speedy death's too good for the likes of you, Hawkins. Look at the altar. Look at the statuette of the Weeping Child. Who made the children weep?'

'Me.'

'You killed her innocence. I put that statuette there in the hope that she'll come back from the place you sent her to, and be reborn happy. The food's for her. If she returns, I want to care for her and comfort her, give her something nice to eat. That's what you're supposed to do to children, care for them. That's what's so great about the Day of the Dead festival. The unthinkable becomes an a real possibility. The dead return and all you have to do is prepare for them and believe.'

He picked up the carving knife and sharpened spoke from the altar. 'I'm going to stick this into your brain and, as you die, I'm going to castrate you with that.'

'Why?'

'Why? I'll tell you why. When you did what you did to that little girl, you didn't just violate her body. You placed yourself right in the centre of her brain. So, before you die, I'm going to stick something destructive into your brain and it's going to kill you.'

Justin Truman dropped the bloodstained Stanley knife on to the floor, stepped in front of Hawkins and watched as the first drop of Hawkins's blood splashed on to the floor between the back legs of the chair on which he was tied.

'How about this?' suggested Truman. 'How about you die with dignity? How about you stop begging? Making ridiculous promises? Ignoring reality? How about that?'

Wind leaked in through the cracks in the building.

'Well?'

Some of the candles stuttered, went out and faint smoke leaked into the cold air.

From the basket, Truman took a box of matches and seven incense cones. He placed three cones on Hawkins's left thigh, four on the right and, striking a match, lit the tips of the incense. The final thread of composure in Hawkins's being snapped and he tried to rock on the chair, in an effort to shake the incense cones from his legs, but the knots that tied his ankles to the chair were rigorously tight.

'Seven cones, always seven, Christopher. Because that's how old I was when I was abused. If I was you, I wouldn't even try and make them fall off your knees. I've got dozens and dozens of cones and I can always make you an exception and place them anywhere I like on your body. I can even push the chair over so that you're on your back and put them all over your torso. Do you want that?'

'No,' he cried.

'Then make like a statue. The smoke will cleanse the air around you, mask the stench that emanates from you, bring sweetness where there is none. I'm going to film you. Get ready to smile and read whatever you see from the page I'm about to show you.'

94

9.30 pm

You look like you've aged a dozen years in a matter of hours, thought DS Gina Riley as she observed Daniel Campbell across the table in Interview Suite 2. She looked at his grim-faced solicitor Aaron Brierley at his side and then at Lesley Reid next to her. She checked the corners of the room behind her and nodded at retired DCI Reid's colleagues from South Yorkshire Police.

'Are you still planning on litigating against us?' asked Riley.

'No,' replied Campbell.

She indicated the wad of bank statements on the table in front of her. 'This is your bank account, right?'

'No.'

'It's got your name and business address on it but it's not your bank account?' Riley stared at Campbell.

'I didn't open this account.'

'If you didn't open and manage this bank account that's in your name, who did?'

'It was set up and managed by Steven and Frances Jamieson.'

'Two dead people who can have no way of communicating their perspective on this matter. That's convenient, Mr Campbell. Why would they set up an account in your name and use your business address?'

'Because they were operating a slush fund.'

'How do you know that?'

'I know that because when the first bank statement arrived in my office, my secretary at the time brought it to my attention. I looked at the first statement and alarm bells rang out. Fifty thousand pounds a month is a lot of money to pay into an account.'

'Did you challenge Steven Jamieson about it?'

'Yes. He told me it was his wife's idea, that they needed distance from the account. He described me as their Trojan Horse.'

'Assuming you're telling the truth, how did you feel about them fraudulently opening a bank account in your name?'

'I was angry, of course I was.'

'Did he explain the purpose of the account?'

'The words he used were *to take care of people who help us and silence those who don't.*'

Lesley Reid picked up three bank statements from the top of the pile and started reading them. 'I'm assuming these PLCs that you're dropping thousands of pounds a month to are individual police officers,' she said.

Campbell looked sideways at his solicitor. 'I told him to close the account and open one in his own name. Five minutes later, the telephone rang and it was Frances Jamieson screaming on top note that she was going to sever all legal and business ties with me.'

'Why didn't you report them to the South Yorkshire Police?' asked Riley.

'Because they were responsible for over fifty per cent of my practice's income. I struck a compromise of sorts, that I'd oversee their account in my name as long as they destroyed the evidence. Which they clearly didn't. I told my secretary it was all a huge mistake on the bank's part. I went to the branch and arranged for the statements to not be posted to my office but collected personally by me and me alone. I, in turn, hand-delivered the statements to the Jamiesons. That's what you can see on the table.'

'That was a mistake,' said Riley.

'Yes I know it was a fucking mistake,' shouted Campbell.

'Calm down,' said his solicitor.

'I knew all about his sexual deviancy and I facilitated the damage limitation. We shared a toxic secret. I thought I could trust him. He swore blind that as soon as they'd seen the statements that they shredded them. Clearly not. It's the same story with the receipts from Dr Warner and the confidentiality agreements. They kept their copies because it gave them power over me.'

'Wouldn't it have been easier to hand over used banknotes in bags to the officers he was paying off?'

'You think I didn't try to suggest that to them? If anyone came on their payroll it was on their terms. The way they did business always put them in the driving seat, gave them the power. Money in a bag neutralised that power, but a standing order to a PLC put a fist around the receiver's throat.'

Campbell raised a glass of water to his lips and his hand shook so much that he had to use his free hand to steady it.

'You know what, Mr Campbell,' said Reid. 'Myself and my colleagues would be very interested in names of officers on the Jamiesons' payroll but...' She glanced at Riley to double-check. '...I guess we can come to that later, DS Riley?'

'Absolutely. I don't want to unpick the fine details, I just want you to tell me about Dr Warner and the confidentiality agreements.'

With an elbow on the edge of the table, Campbell held his forehead in one hand and looked down. 'Warner was an abortionist. Whenever Steven Jamieson got a teenage girl pregnant, I had two jobs. To negotiate a payoff for her silence with the parent or guardian and to set up an abortion.' Campbell sat back. He looked at the confidentiality agreements on the table and the receipts from Dr Warner. 'That's it.'

'You had a one hundred per cent success rate in the silence and abortion stakes?' asked Riley.

'No. How could that possibly be?'

'Any names of these refusers?'

'It was a long time ago,' said Campbell.

'How about you think, and think really hard,' said Riley.

Campbell looked at his solicitor, who said, 'My client will cooperate to the best of his ability.'

Riley took a deep breath but the air felt poisonous and the whole world sick. 'That's enough for me for now,' she said. 'How about you?' she asked Reid.

'I want a list of names, ranks, amounts of money and operations undermined by your friend's corruption,' said Reid.

'He wasn't a friend. He was a client,' insisted Campbell.

Riley looked at the counter moving on the tape recorder and, looking up at Campbell and his solicitor said, 'Did you say you wanted to make a statement?'

The solicitor nodded and turned back a few pages in the book in which he'd been making notes. 'Ready?' asked Brierley.

Staring into space, Campbell nodded.

'My client, Daniel Campbell, wishes it to be known that he is not and has never engaged in unlawful sexual activity with a child. He further wishes it to be known in advance that when his phone, computers and other communication devices are taken by police for forensic investigation that the pornographic images of children engaged in unlawful sexual activity with adults were sent to him by Steven Jamieson as a means of controlling, blackmailing and exercising power over other paedophiles who were clearly visible and identifiable in the images. My client was merely acting as a custodian. End of statement.'

As Riley formally closed the interview, she looked at Daniel Campbell and saw a man aware that life as he knew it was as good as over.

95

10.00 pm

In the interview suite, Clay waited with grim anticipation for the door to open, and a huge part of her wished that it never would. When her iPhone vibrated on the surface of the table it was as if a roll of thunder had shaken the room.

'Bill, what's happening?' she asked.

'Campbell's in with Lesley Reid and her colleagues. I watched from the observation room. There's going to be a lot of retired officers getting a knock on the door.'

An idea possessed her about cause and effect and, briefly, Clay was at the dead centre of a huge lake watching ripples roll out to a shore beyond the horizon. A man is murdered, and in the questioning that follows, dozens of lives are changed beyond recognition. And, in turn, the shape of hundreds of lives bend to an altered reality.

'That's not the main reason why you called me, Bill, to tell me about Campbell.'

'I've received an electronic copy of Lucien Burns's medical notes.'

'Did Alder Hey in the Park find them?'

'No. When the trail went cold there, I contacted his GP. The GP opened up the surgery after hours and has sent them over.'

'Great work, Bill. Anything leap up at you?'

'Eve, you know when you say to people, *Don't tell me half a story, tell me the whole thing and stick to the facts?*'

She smiled at her friend's gentle mockery. He had caught the tone of her speech exactly.

'I've gone through the notes once and I'm trying to get my head round them. I don't completely understand what I've read and I don't want give you garbled info or confuse you. I need to read more – to understand something I'm aware of but am largely in the dark about.'

'Is there anything concrete and simple you can tell me?'

'Lucien's not sixteen. He's older.'

'What's going on with that lie?'

There was a knock on the door and Clay's heart flooded with liquid lead. 'Hang on, Bill. Come in!'

Carol White stepped into the interview suite and frowned at Clay.

'I've got to go.' As she disconnected the call, Clay indicated the seat next to herself.

'Is everything all right?' asked White from the doorway.

'Come and sit down, Carol.'

As White sat down, it was clear that she'd had a lot more to drink than a couple of glasses of wine and Clay wished she had some red wine swimming through her veins rather than the cold poison of suspicion.

'Who's watching your little boy, Carol?'

Her shoulders slumped. 'He's with his father. I'm not coping well at the moment so I asked him to take the little fella off my hands until I can get my head straight.' She looked around the room with perplexed tipsiness. 'What have you called me in for?'

'I'm sorry to hear you say you're not coping well,' said Clay. 'Is there anything on your mind? Anything you'd like to talk about?'

Carol looked like a woman who could see a shadow of squares falling on her but not the net itself. 'I don't know what you mean, Eve. One minute I'm watching *Annie Hall* on TCM and trying to drown my sorrows, the next you call and tell me you want to show me something.'

'I don't *want* to show you something. I *have* to show you something.'

Clay handed her the sheet of retrieved texts from Lucien Burns's phone.

'But that's my number.'

'Yes.'

She looked closely at the sheet and asked, 'So where does this come from?'

'Same place as this.' Riley handed her the other sheet.

'Vindici?' She sounded deeply surprised. 'When you say the same place as this, where do you mean?'

'We've seen the texts you've been sending to and receiving from Lucien Burns. You've been supplying him with contact details for paedophiles in Liverpool. Do you wish to confirm or deny this?' said Clay, her scalp tingling with unpleasant heat as a coldness spread through her being.

Carol White sat back in the seat. 'I'd like to say *deny* but, looking at this, I have to say *confirm*.'

'What were you thinking of, Carol?'

'I wasn't thinking of anything. I didn't send or receive texts from Lucien Burns.'

'Carol, this is going to be much easier for you if you tell the truth from the word go.'

'I'm telling you the truth. I'm not going to jeopardise my future for the sake of getting some paedophiles topped. Never mind being drummed out of the police, I would never be an accessory to murder. You know what life in jail's like for disgraced coppers. I might be off my *head* with stress but I'm not that far out of my *mind*.'

'It's your number, Carol, and much as I want to believe you, I've spoken to you tonight on that number.'

White took her mobile phone from her bag.

'Hand that to me!' said Clay.

White pointed at the video camera in the left-hand corner of the ceiling. 'Do you think I'm that stupid I'd try and tamper with or destroy evidence in an interview room, sitting next to an extremely experienced and on-the-ball detective under the watchful eye of a camera?' She checked the camera. 'A camera that is pointing at me and recording?'

Clay held her hand out.

'You're making me angry now,' said White.

'Just give me the phone, Carol,' replied Clay calmly.

'On one condition.'

'You're not in a position to start demanding conditions,' said Clay.

'I'll outline my condition. Once you've followed my instructions, I'll explain what's happened here.'

'Go on,' said Clay.

'When I give you the phone, Eve, take off the back casing. Then remove the battery and take out the SIM card. That's not going to damage any so-called evidence on my phone, is it?'

'No,' said Clay, watching White sobering up on fast forward.

'Will you do as I've instructed?'

'All right,' replied Clay.

As she slid the phone across the table to Clay, White said, 'I'm telling you right now, I'm not going to watch another second of child pornography ever again for the rest of my life.'

Clay took off the back casing of White's phone.

'I want an immediate transfer to any department within the Merseyside Constabulary.'

Clay took out the battery and laid it on the table next to the casing.

'I don't care which nick, I don't care which department.'

Clay slid out the SIM card.

'Call me, Eve,' said White.

Clay went to Recents on her phone and called White's number. She turned her phone on to speakerphone, laid it on the table and, after two seconds of silence, the ring tone sounded.

White pointed at her dead, deconstructed phone on the table.

'You can keep ringing it, over and over, until midnight. Whoever's done this is never going to answer your call, Eve.'

Clay closed the unanswered call down and felt a collision of confusion and relief. 'What's going on, Carol?'

Clay's iPhone rang. As she connected, she took it off speaker-phone.

'Eve, it's Poppy.'

'What have you got, Poppy?' asked Clay.

'A direct hit from Christine Green's phone. She received a call at one minute past nine this morning that lasted less than a minute. The caller's number is 07704 193119.'

Clay jotted the number down and said, 'Thank you, Poppy.'

'That was the only call that Christine received in the window of time you gave me. What do you want me to do next?'

'Prepare yourself. Please start working on Daniel Campbell's phone. Thank you.'

She closed down the call and dialled the number Poppy had given her. After three rings, the recipient connected.

'Yes?'

'Are you in the Travelodge on Aigburth Road, Annabelle?'

'Well, I can't go home, can I? Can I claim my hotel bills back? Hmm?'

'Yeah, sure... I'm sending an unmarked car round for you. Lucien's given me some information about his sister dying. I need you to corroborate that information, and I'd like you to come to Trinity Road to do so.'

'I'll wait outside the front entrance.'

Clay disconnected.

'Your leak's one of two people,' said White, back straight and sober. 'You want me to explain what's happened here?'

96

10.10 pm

When the heat from the crumbling incense cones first reached the tops of Hawkins's knees, he said, 'Please take it off me. I'm begging you, Justin.'

'In less than a minute, the warmth you're feeling will get much warmer, and when it turns hot, two things will happen. You will start screaming and your flesh will begin to cook. You're lucky. I've only put seven burning cones on you.

Hawkins made a noise at the base of his throat.

'What are you strapping to my leg?'

'I'm not listening to this,' said Truman. He grabbed the gag, stood behind Hawkins as he strained in the chair, and pulled the material sharply at either end, forcing it into Hawkins's mouth. 'If you make the burning cones fall off your knees, I'm going to stop being fair to you and put you, in the chair, on your back. Then I'll put dozens of cones on your chest.'

Hawkins stiffened, his cries of pain smothered by the gag.

Truman placed a chair in front of Hawkins, sat facing him at eye level and watched impassively as he wept, eyes rolling, face twitching.

Hawkins closed his eyes, his face soaked in tears.

Truman leaned forward, pressed the sharpened point of the bicycle spoke against the top of Hawkins' right nipple and, lightly, started drawing a circle around the circumference. Hawkins opened his eyes, looked down and back at Truman with horror and terror flashing in his eyes.

'You bit that little autistic girl's right nipple so hard she had to have seven stitches. And that wasn't the only place you bit her.' Truman touched Hawkins's left shoulder with the sharpened tip of the spoke. 'You bit her there.'

Hawkins shook his head.

Truman touched Hawkins's right bicep with the tip and, again, Hawkins shook his head as his eyes followed the progress of the spoke.

'And there. When the police took an impression of your teeth, it was a perfect match for the bite marks on the child's body. I think you behaved so savagely because you were planning on killing her.'

Hawkins shook his head.

'There was a large industrial-strength bin liner in the shed. Just one. And one little girl. But you didn't manage it, did you? Stop shaking your head. These are facts that stood up in a court of law. Here's another fact. When you rolled off her and on to your back, she reached out in the darkness and she found the handle of a tin of paint. She sat up and smacked you on the head with the tin of paint, knocking you out cold.'

Hawkins made two noises, one after the other. Then he made the same two stifled sounds, louder and stronger.

Truman stood behind him, untied the gag.

'Kill me! Kill me!'

Truman sat facing him.

'Kill me!'

Smoke rose from the glowing red wounds on both his knees.

'Not yet. Not for a long while. She left you in the shed and wandered out on to the street, naked, bleeding, covered in your filthy DNA and straight into a woman who was running at night when the roads were quiet. The police were there within a matter of minutes and a quarter of an hour later they followed the girl's trail of blood back to the shed in the back garden of the house you lived in. They found you knocked out and with your trousers halfway down your legs, with a gaping wound on your forehead and your blood on a tin of paint. The girl's mother was fast asleep in her bed, with a half-consumed glass of vodka and orange and full of sleeping pills that were prescribed for you. Tell me it didn't happen. You can't, can you?'

Hawkins's head dropped as Truman walked behind him.

He made his way back with a spade.

'Yes... When you die where would you like to be buried?' He held up the spade. 'I want to respect your wishes on that one.'

'Fuck you!'

'Pardon? I'm respecting your wishes and you speak to me with such disrespect?' Truman put the spade down.

'I'm sorry, it just slipped out...'

'You're not sorry; it's what you've been thinking all along. Well – a part of you might think you're sorry but you're not. You are going to be very sorry for that outburst. You know, the thing with all of you deviants is that your personalities shine through. I've never murdered two specimens who were quite alike.'

Truman shook two ponatinib tablets from the bottle on the table.

'Are you not well?' asked Hawkins.

'You could say that.' He popped the tablets in his mouth.

'Do you mind me asking what's wrong with you?'

'Are you a doctor? Stop trying to pretend that you're at all interested in my health. Stop trying to manipulate me. You're transparent. Stop insulting my intelligence.' He took a bottle of water from the altar and washed the tablets down.

'How unwell are you?'

'Enough.'

'I'm... genuinely sorry you're not well.'

'Are you?' asked Truman.

'I am.'

'I scarcely give a damn!'

'Ahhh, ahhh, it's burning...' Hawkins's eyes swam, closed and his head lolled forward.

'It's not really a case of *fuck me*. It's really a case of *fuck you*!'

He sniffed the air. 'To me, you smell like pork, Hawkins!'

Hawkins opened his eyes and peered crab-like at Truman.

'And to answer your earlier question, the thing that I've strapped to your leg is a bomb.'

97

10.49 pm

Hendricks looked at the turning blades of the fan that cooled the overheated incident room and wondered if the combination of heat in the room and cold autumnal darkness outside the window was making his mind play tricks on him after the fourth reading of Lucien Burns's medical notes and a background investigation on the internet.

As Barney Cole put down the landline receiver, Hendricks asked, 'What are you up to, Barney?'

Cole stood up, took his overcoat from the back of his chair and slipped it on.

'I've been doing a bit of background digging for Eve.' He looked at James Peace's birth certificate on screen on Ancestry UK and saw his mother's name, Amanda Peace. He looked at his father's name, Antonio Agua. On a registrar-headed letter-headed paper attached to the birth certificate was a note: *Father, Mexican national, merchant seaman.* 'Now she's asked me to go on a message with Carol White.'

'A message with Carol?'

'She's meeting me at the front in five, says she'll explain. What about you, Bill?'

'Thinking the unthinkable and fathoming the unfathomable.'

'Business as usual then?' Cole laughed. 'This bloke I'm looking up for Eve, Jimmy Peace, his father was Mexican, a sailor.

Isn't that a weird coincidence given all the links to Mexico in the Vindici case and the shit we're wading through now?'

'Barney, I don't believe in coincidence. Do you?'

'No I don't. But maybe that's another coincidence.'

'Business as usual,' replied Hendricks as he moved on to Google, clicked Images and, from the battery of squares and rectangles that filled his screen, his attention was arrested by a Roman sculpture, a white marble figure of a sleeping woman, face down on a rippled sheet, her breasts and the front of her body concealed. Her immaculate hair was curled and her face was serene and beautiful.

He started at the top of her head, followed the curve of her back to her rounded buttocks and the folds of the sheet that covered her lower calves. Hendricks could feel the love of the sculptor for his work, the expertise and fine attention to detail.

Clicking on the image, he saw it in a larger form alongside a collection of related pictures including a shot of the same sculpture from the other side, with the detail of the hair on the back of her head visible and her face largely obscured.

The landline phone on Cole's desk rang but to Hendricks's ears it sounded as though it was ringing on a different floor.

Viewing the same object from two different angles, Hendricks had the clearest sense of its ambiguity. From one point of view the statue was male but from another female.

The ringing stopped and he heard Cole introduce himself to the caller.

He came out of Google Images and, returning to Lucien Burns's medical notes, felt the breaking light of understanding and, with this, compassion. He picked up his phone to put a call through to Clay.

'Shit, oh shit, no, no,' said Cole.

Hendricks paused at the growing dismay in Cole's eyes.

'OK. OK. I'll pass it on. Thanks for letting me know,' said Cole.

Cold air from the fan sliced through the humid dark. Hendricks, his hand growing clammy on his mobile phone, felt a dark premonition and sickness spread through his centre.

Cole placed the receiver down and stared into space. 'They found his car parked on Otterspool Prom.'

Silence beneath the chopping blades of the fan.

'Bob Rimmer threw himself into the river,' said Cole.

98

11.31 pm

At 143 Primrose Road, Cole rang the bell of Carol White's mother-in-law's front door for the third time. He glanced over his shoulder at Carol as she sat staring straight ahead in the passenger seat of his car. As they'd pulled up outside the house, Carol had said, 'Can you do this on your own, Barney?'

On the way to the first of two calls they were due to make that night, Cole had listened in grim silence to White's theory about who had been leaking secret information.

Behind his car, in a black BMW, two officers from Professional Standards watched him with cold detachment, and Cole had the feeling that whoever was in the house had had a good hard look through a crack in the curtains at those gathering outside.

'Who are you, calling at this hour?' She had no accent and sounded stern and cold.

'My name's Detective Constable Barney Cole. Can you open the door please and let me in, Mrs White?'

She opened the door quickly, beckoned him in and glanced up and down the road at other spacious detached and semi-detached houses before shutting the door at speed. 'Has something happened to Carol?' she asked.

'No.' He offered his warrant card but she didn't look at it.

'Is that her out there in the car?'

'Yes.'

'What's going on?'

'Do you mind if I make a brief phone call?'

She said nothing, so he dialled the eleven digits of Carol's mobile number and waited. His ring tone sounded, but there was no accompanying sound of a mobile ringing in the house.

'What setting does your son use on his mobile phone?'

'He doesn't leave it on silent, in case he misses a call, in case it's to do with work.'

Upstairs Carol's three-year-old son started crying.

'Be brief and to the point!' she ordered.

'Is your son Kevin here?'

'He's on duty, doing some overtime.'

Cole had met Detective Sergeant Kevin White once. A tall, well-spoken man with a reputation as a two-sided coin. He handled the victims of crime with a rare sensitivity and perpetrators with black iron.

He's not going to be the leak, thought Cole, listening to the cries of Carol's child escalating in volume.

'What's this to do with, please?' Mrs White asked, ascending the stairs briskly.

'We wanted a point of view from him on our current investigation.'

'He'll be back here in the morning. I'll tell him you called. Close the door on your way out.'

She stopped at the top of the stairs and pointed in the general direction of Cole's car. 'She really shouldn't be involving other officers to mediate in the mess she made of their marriage.'

'She isn't doing any such thing, Mrs White.'

Back at the wheel of his car, Carol asked, 'How did it go?'

'He's doing overtime.' Cole pulled away and turned the corner on to Cromptons Lane.

'Oh!' She sounded quietly surprised. 'I suppose so. He usually resists but he really doesn't get on with his mother, so... it figures.'

'Next port of call then, Carol?'

Cole looked in his wing mirror. Just behind them, the officers from Professional Standards followed, silent and dead-eyed like a pair of sharks beneath the surface of a jet-black sea.

He held on tightly to the steering wheel and, shuddering, wondered if someone had walked over over his grave.

Part Three
Dance of Death

Day Three
Friday,
25th October 2019

99

'Wakey wakey!'

Justin Truman upended a bottle of water over Hawkins's head. The man rolled his neck as he lifted his slumped head and half opened his eyes.

'Open your eyes wide!'

He blinked and his eyes bulged as he came fully to life and aware of where he was and who he was with.

'Read this!' Truman showed him a piece of paper.

Hawkins's lips moved as he read the words, stopping halfway through. His fleshy face fell to stone.

'I've decided, as this is going to be my final outing, I'm going to do something I've never done before, something maybe I should have tried earlier on in my career. We're going to do things a little differently. This time, Christopher, you're going to read all the words… Lies are your weapons, the truth is mine and every single word on this piece of paper is absolutely true. I'm going to film you and this film will go viral on the internet within hours. So try your best not to look and sound like the snivelling piece of shit that you truly are.'

Hawkins didn't move or speak.

'What are you waiting for?' asked Truman.

'I can't do it.'

'You can. You must.' Truman picked up the Stanley knife and

extended the blade a couple of centimetres. 'You can either do it with or without your balls attached to your body.'

With a poke of his toe, Truman sent the chair and Hawkins on to his back.

'I'll do it! I'll do it! I'll do it!'

'I'm going to start filming. When the phone is pointing at you and I say the word *now*, you read the words on my paper. Nothing more, nothing less.'

Truman pressed record and turned a full circle, filming at head height. He tilted the phone up and turned another circle. He stopped, held the camera at arm's length and pointed it at himself.

'Hello, Eve. There's someone here I'd like you to meet.'

Truman started at Hawkins's feet, ran the phone slowly along his leg, across his body and settled on his face.

'Now!'

100

00.10 am

As Annabelle Burns entered the interview suite, Clay held her eye until she sat opposite her and said, 'You have the right to a solicitor...'

'I've done nothing wrong. You told me you wanted to speak to me about Caroline. Why would I need a solicitor for that?'

'I do want to talk to you about Caroline but I need to talk to you about other matters.'

'Then just do it. No solicitor!'

As Riley finished formally opening the interview, Annabelle asked, 'What's happening with Lucien?'

'We have a woman in custody at the moment called Christine Green. Christine is denying all knowledge of Lucien and Lucien is denying all knowledge of her. Do you know Christine Green, Annabelle?'

'No.'

'Sure?'

'Certain.'

'When are Bulky Bob coming out to collect your fridge?'

'Tuesday morning.'

'They don't collect in your area on Tuesday mornings. Your lies to cover your lies are full of holes.'

Annabelle looked around the space. 'This room could do with a really good clean.'

'We've got Christine Green's phone.'

'Good.'

'If you don't know Christine Green, why did you phone her up on your mobile at one minute past nine am this morning?'

'This is a mistake on your part!'

'Shall I remind you of what was happening at that time this morning? We were gathering outside your house. I was in your front garden and you were in the bay window of your bedroom. I saw you. You were on the phone and you looked very agitated. In fact you were pacing. I've asked you twice today who you were calling and twice you told me Bulky Bob. That was a lie.'

'I received a missed call. I didn't recognise the number. I didn't know if it was important or not. I didn't know if it was anything to do with Lucien. I worry about Lucien. I called back the number. The woman I spoke to didn't tell me her name. I told her my name and the woman said, *I'm sorry, I don't know anyone of that name. I must've dialled a wrong number. Sorry.* Then she hung up and I didn't give it another moment's thought. It's a coincidence.'

'A coincidence?' echoed Clay. 'It's got to be the world's biggest set of coincidences ever. Do you know what Christine has in common with Lucien?'

'How could I know?'

'They're the only two people in Liverpool running Vindici fan websites.'

'It would only take an hour to get this room spotless.'

'This room is cleaned twice a day and there's nothing wrong with it. Stop changing the subject. It's extremely probable that I'm going to be charging Lucien and Christine with murder. It's that serious, Annabelle. If you know anything, you need to stop playing games and tell me.'

In silence, Clay watched Annabelle freefalling inside herself.

'Lucien…' Her normally strident voice was soft and she sounded twenty years younger. 'On one level, Lucien is a rather straightforward young man.'

Clay and Riley looked at each other with mutual disbelief.

'You only have to look at the walls of his room to know that. Action heroes, sexy young women. He's body conscious and a little bit too vain for his own good but he'll grow out of that in time.' Annabelle looked hard at Clay. 'But a killer? Never.'

'Annabelle, we've got Lucien's medical records.'

Annabelle looked at Clay as if she was either telling the most profound lie or had achieved something impossible.

'Ever worked at Alder Hey, Annabelle?'

'Once, briefly. I think I need a solicitor.' She looked around as though a solicitor was going to magically appear out of thin air. 'I want a solicitor.'

'That's not a problem,' said Riley.

'You took his notes from Medical Records when you were at Alder Hey, didn't you? But you couldn't take the records that his GP was holding, could you?'

Clay felt the arrival of an incoming text on her iPhone.

'Why have you lied about Lucien's age, Annabelle?'

She said nothing but dabbed at the back of her left hand with a tissue.

'Lucien's not sixteen, is he?'

'Like I said, I want a solicitor.'

Clay looked at her phone, clicked on the text icon and showed the screen to Riley as she formally closed the interview.

'I'll take Annabelle to Sergeant Harris.'

As Riley walked Annabelle to the door, she said, 'We're putting you in a cell.'

The door closed and Clay double-checked the screen of her iPhone.

A black screen peppered with points of light. A triangle within a circle, a clip of film to be played, and a single word in white above this.

Vindici.

101

00.25 am

As Clay pressed play she was filled with a sense of dread and awe.

A slow-turning panorama in a dark space full of what appeared to be candles, an imitation of a clear night sky but her instinct told her this was indoors. She listened and heard ragged breathing from nearby, but not from the person turning in a circle and making the film. In the background, she heard the outside world in the rumble of traffic, the clanking of a heavy vehicle going over a large bump in the road and traffic moving in both directions.

A much brighter light in the distance showed a cavernous space.

The angle of the camera changed. It was pointed upwards and again the person holding it turned a slow circle. The quality of the darkness changed and the night came into the view through tall panels of glass high up on the walls of the building. She absorbed the darkness and wondered, *Where? Where are you, Justin?*

The door opened and Riley slipped into the room, next to Clay.

'Justin Truman's sent me a film clip. It feels like *now*.'

The circle stopped and the angle dipped to reveal an altar dressed with red silk dahlias. The camera focused on a statue of the Virgin and the Infant Jesus, a framed picture of an eight-year-old girl, a statuette of a Weeping Child and a selection of sweet food, sugar skulls and candy skeletons.

'It's the real Vindici,' said Clay as a sensation like pins and needles overtook her scalp.

The phone rose up and Justin Truman's face appeared in half-light.

'Hello, Eve. There's someone here I'd like you to meet.'

He smiled and she felt as if her spirit was rising through her head.

'Eve,' said Riley. 'Are you OK? You look—'

'I'm all right,' said Clay, drinking in the silent smile on the screen of her iPhone.

She saw a bare foot and above this a black metal square with a glass facade. The person was male and tied to a chair. The thighs were like rubber and his genitals were buried in body fat from the base of his belly. Fat hung in inelegant triangles from his sagging pectorals and when the camera settled on his face, Clay had no idea who the naked man was.

Another text came through to her phone.

Just watch this, she said to herself.

'Now!' said Vindici.

'I am a convicted paedophile,' said the fat man, *'and I am about to pay for my sins. I am alone in a building with Justin Truman, known around the world as Vindici.'* His eyes welled up and tears spilled down his face as he made a whimpering noise in his throat. *'This building is close to where you once lived as a child, Eve. The device strapped to my leg is a bomb.'*

Clay pictured the shape of the windows.

In a blur of light and action, the man was upended from the floor and sat up straight on the chair. The camera stayed on him.

'Read!' said Truman.

'Vindici is going to sit on a chair next to me. He is going to strap a bomb to his body. He is going to sit with me.'

She listened to the way the huge space hollowed out the man's voice, the echo in the dark.

'There is another text. Look at it but do so quickly because

time is of the essence. You have twenty minutes to save me and Justin Truman. Please, please, Eve...'

'*Stay on script or I'll slice the time in half!'*

'*Twenty minutes. You have to come alone, Eve. If you bring anyone else into the building, Vindici will blow up both of us and whoever else in there, you included, Eve.'*

She watched as Truman focused on the bomb on the man's leg, activating the digital clock. '*Time starts now, Eve!'*

Clay's adrenaline surged as the red digits on the clock face started counting down and the man started weeping uncontrollably. The film froze.

She left the room at speed, speaking urgently: 'Block off Edge Lane at the mouth of the M62 and the junctions to Hall Lane and Mount Vernon. We need to flood the area with officers. No sirens. Quick as lightning but quiet with it.'

'Leave it with me,' said Riley.

Then Clay opened the text and saw a photograph of a young man with a head full of blond curls, smiling and seemingly without a care in the world.

Recognising his face, she felt sick.

'Hendricks, Stone and yourself: I want you to meet me outside the Littlewoods Building. Bomb disposal and paramedics. No one's to know what's been demanded of me except the three of you.'

'Why the fuck should you, Eve? Let them blow each other sky high.'

Clay glanced at her watch, sprinted to the car park, heard a clock ticking inside her head and the wind rising in the storm outside.

Twenty minutes to drive from Garston to Edge Lane and explore a derelict building bigger than many cathedrals.

'The hostage is called Christopher Hawkins. He's in his mid-to-late fifties, and he's a paedophile. The other man's Justin Truman and I've got to get them both out alive.'

102

00.25 am

At Ryman's Court, a 1960s purpose-built three-storey apartment block nestled at the edge of Gateacre Village, Detective Constable Barney Cole checked the numbers on the square silver buzzers on the intercom, and found number seven.

'Are you sure you want to come inside this time, Carol?'

'Yes I do. I felt like a total coward sitting outside Kevin's mother's house.'

'You're not a coward. You're clearing your name beyond any doubt. You have the right to do just that.'

He pressed seven and nothing happened. Cole looked up at the windows and saw many lights on in many flats. He pressed again and heard Alice Banks's voice, husky and disturbed from sleep.

'Alice, it's Barney Cole. Can I come in please?'

The intercom buzzed and they made their way to the stone stairs leading to Flat 7 on the first floor. Cole noticed that the only footsteps he could hear were his own and wondered why Carol was being so careful not to make a sound.

'Let me hang back a bit,' she whispered. 'Come and get me if there's anything I can do.'

At Alice Banks's door, Cole knocked. He saw Carol fade into the shadows near the door to the stairwell. Within moments, Alice opened the door, dressed in a red silk dressing gown and matching slippers. Her dark hair tumbled on to her shoulders and she emitted a subtle but expensive perfume.

Not for the first time, Barney Cole doubted Bill Hendricks's sanity after he'd knocked her back at the Christmas party.

Alice turned on a lamp in the corner of her living room.

'Lovely flat, Alice.'

'You haven't come here to study interior design. What's up?'

'We've had a tip-off about the leak and so we're systematically going through everyone on the team, eliminating them from the list of suspects.'

'Dare I ask? Has Carol been eliminated?'

'Probably, but she still has some way to go.'

He looked out of the large plate-glass window and saw the sleek car in which the Professional Standards officers waited, their vehicle blending almost perfectly into the night. The double-glazed window blocked out any sound from the streets outside and he was impressed by the quiet calm of Alice's living space.

'Give me a minute and I'll get my phone, iPad and iPod together.'

He tried not to notice the swell of her buttocks and the narrow flare of her hips as she walked into the bedroom. In the half-lit kitchen he saw an opened bottle of wine on the drainer. Two glasses and two plates were stacked above the dishwasher. She had obviously had company that evening.

'This is everything,' she said, returning to the living room and placing them on the wooden chest in front of her black leather sofa.

'Mind if I make a phone call?' he asked.

She shrugged.

He dialled Carol White's mobile number and two seconds later the ring tone sounded in his ear. He withdrew the phone from his ear and listened hard.

Buzz. His eyes flew to a closed door opposite the bathroom – a spare bedroom, he assumed. Half a buzz.

Cole disconnected and Carol White slipped in through the half-open front door.

'Carol, what are you doing here?' asked Alice with an undisguised note of alarm.

'Clearing my name, Alice. Clearing your name, too, I hope. There's no ringing phone here,' said Carol. 'But I'm sure I heard a buzzing from behind that door.'

'Open that door, please, Alice,' said Cole.

'This is really most irregular...' said Alice.

'The door, open it.'

'You have a search warrant?'

'No,' said Cole.

Alice stood in front of Cole, engaged his whole attention with her eyes.

'Then go and get a search warrant, come back and you can go through everything.'

'I'm not going for a search warrant,' said Cole. 'I heard the action of a mobile phone behind the door when I dialled a suspect number.'

'And I'm not going anywhere until you open that door,' said Carol, standing directly in front of it.

'Come away from there, please, Carol. This is my home and you have no right to come barging in here and opening anything.'

Eyes closed, Carol pressed her forehead against the door, took a deep draught of air through her nostrils.

'I can smell Fendi Uomo,' she whispered, and her voice was soft and sad. She turned the handle and pushed the door open. Her husband Kevin was sitting on the bed.

He sprang up. 'It's not what you think it is.'

'Then what is it?'

'I came round here to see Alice because I was worried about you. She spends so much time every day with you and knows you like the back of her hand. I wanted to find a way back in, a way we could get together again, so I was asking Alice for her advice, pure and simple.'

'Where are your shoes and socks?'

'I got drenched in the storm...'

'Shut up, Kevin!' Carol snapped. 'Give me your mobile.'

'Which mobile?'

'The one poking out of the breast pocket of your T-shirt.'

'Why do you want my mobile phone?'

'Because I do.'

'Can you all just go!' Alice cut across the group.

'No I won't give you my mobile.' Anger flooded his face. 'You've been a bloody fucking nightmare to live with for months on end.'

'I know. And I've apologised. Over and over. And I told Alice in confidence because I thought she was my friend.' She looked at Alice. 'And it's so kind of you to give my poor husband respite from the screaming harpy he has to endure at home. I really can't thank you enough.'

She span round to face her husband. 'The phone, now.'

'No, I'm sorry, I'm going!'

Cole muscled his way into the door frame. 'You're going nowhere with that phone,' he commanded. 'You give it to me or I call Professional Standards, who are sitting right outside, right now.'

The blood drained from Kevin White's face. 'You're shitting me?'

Cole looked at Carol. 'Go and get them, Carol, while I wait here...'

She left the flat, glancing back over her shoulder in stark accusation at her husband and her friend.

Cole held his hand out. Kevin White took the phone from his T-shirt pocket and handed it to Cole.

'Are you both involved in this or were you acting alone, Kevin?'

'Barney, I swear to God, this has got nothing to do with me,' said Alice.

'Get your hands off my arm, Alice!' said Cole.

Kevin White laughed. 'Nothing to do with you?'

'Yes, that's right, Kevin, it's got nothing to do with me.'

'You were the one who cloned Carol's SIM card so you could leak information while hiding behind her identity! You said getting her kicked off the force for corruption was the best way to get her out of our way!'

'That's a malicious allegation, Kevin, and it's down to you to prove it!'

Outside, the wind howled at the windows of Ryman's Court but underneath the tempest, there were two distinct flat noises.

The sound of two car doors slamming shut, one after the other.

103

00.36 am

As Clay hurtled from Lance Lane across the junction with Childwall Road and past the Picton Tower, the answer machine on her home landline kicked in for the fourth time since she'd fled from Trinity Road for Edge Lane at speeds in excess of eighty miles per hour.

'There's me, Mum and Dad. But we're not here. When the phone beeps, leave a message. Thank you.'

Philip's voice stopped and Eve Clay was filled with unbearable sadness.

Her windscreen wipers swiped back and forth throwing sheet after sheet of cold rain from the glass.

She glanced at her iPhone on the dashboard and felt a hand was squeezing her heart tighter and tighter with every word. On three occasions, before the beep sounded, she had closed down the call and dialled Thomas's mobile to hear his voice telling her he wasn't available to take her call.

'Where are you? Where are you? Where are you?'

In the background, on Church Road she estimated, she heard the siren of another police car following her.

This time when the tone sounded, she said, 'Thomas and Philip...'

The receiver in her house was lifted.

'Hello!' It was Thomas, a little out of breath.

'Where've you been?'

In the background, the police car with its siren blaring, was making ground on her.

'Philip couldn't sleep so I thought the old tricks are the best. He's been in the back seat while we went for a spin. He's fast asleep now.'

'Where is he?'

'Flopped over my shoulder. I'm just about to put him to bed. What's going on there?' Anxiety crept into his voice. 'It sounds like you're in a high-speed chase.'

'Give me a moment, Thomas, please.'

She could see the advancing lights of the car behind her in the wing mirror. The siren was coming closer to her and they were both getting nearer to Edge Lane. Clay slowed down a little, wound her window down. She stuck out her right arm, warrant card in hand, and urged the pursuing vehicle to come to her.

As it pulled alongside her, she pointed with her warrant card at the siren. 'Off! Off! Off!' she shouted.

She looked at the clock on her dashboard. Nine minutes had passed since Truman had started the countdown.

The constable killed the siren as they both crawled through the red light at the junction with Edge Lane, Clay heading in the direction of the Littlewoods Building and the constables towards the assembly point for the M62 end of Edge Lane.

'Where are you going, Eve?' She heard the deepest anxiety in her husband's voice.

'Reported crime scene. We're going in mob-handed as you can no doubt tell.'

'You're calling me when you're on your way to a crime scene. That's something you've never done before.'

'I don't think the crime scene's going to be that big a deal. I'm calling because I was worried because I couldn't get hold of you.'

'You're in danger, Eve. That's why you're calling.'

'No, I'm not. I just wanted to know you were both safe and I know that now so I'm getting off the line and back to work.'

He was silent for a moment, and she knew he didn't believe her.

'He's starting to stir,' Thomas said.

Clay crossed the junction with Rathbone Road and on to the descending path of Edge Lane. The outer edges of the rectangular tower of the Littlewoods Building loomed in the partial distance and she wondered how on earth she was going to get inside.

'Be careful, Eve.'

'There's nothing to be careful about. My back's well covered.'

She saw Hendricks's car ahead of her, slowing as he approached the Littlewoods Building, and in her head she heard the ticking of a clock.

'I love you and I love Philip and that was a great idea to take him out in the car to get him to sleep.'

'And we love you. And we need you back safely. Promise me you won't take any unnecessary risks.'

'I promise you I won't take any unnecessary risks. I never take unnecessary risks.'

She heard Philip stirring, a fragment of sleep babble escaping his lips.

'Kiss him for me, tuck him up extra tight.' She pulled up behind Hendricks's car.

'Phone me as soon as you can,' said Thomas. 'I love you and I always will.'

His words caused something to come loose deep inside her memory.

She ended the call and pocketed her iPhone. From the glove compartment she took out a large torch and hurried on to the pavement.

As Clay and Hendricks ran towards the Littlewoods Building, she asked, 'How have the troops been organised?'

'Maggie Bruce is at the M62 end of Edge Lane and Clive Winters has got the city-centre side. They're fanning out officers north and south across the length of the main road with a view to looking for Justin Truman as he looks in picture from Mexico. How are we going to get in?'

'You're not, Bill. I am. If you go in, he's told me he'll blow the whole building. Listen.'

Beneath the wind and rain, she heard piano music from inside the building.

'That's how I'm going to get in. Follow the music. Wait here.'

At the side of the building, beneath the row of tall rectangular windows, she saw a closed door. The closer she came to the door the louder the music came at her.

Justin Truman has used music to show me the way in, she thought as she opened the door and Beethoven's 'Für Elise' flooded out of the Littlewoods Building.

104

00.40 am

As Stone arrived at the Littlewoods Building, he saw Hendricks inspecting the ground with his torch. Pulling up outside Clay's car, Stone opened his door and stepped out. 'Bill, what's happening?'

'Eve's gone in there. We're to wait out here,' replied Hendricks.

Stone's phone rang and, as he connected the call, he sensed through the tense silence that he was on the line to Samantha Wilson.

'Is that you, Sammy?'

'Can you come to my mother's house on Dundonald Road?'

'I'm really busy right now. I'm going to have to hang up.'

'No! Wait! As soon as you can, come to my mum's. Please?'

'It could be hours.'

'I've got an important piece of information for your investigation into my father's murder.'

'I'll get there as soon as I can.'

'Well, I'm not going anywhere and nor is my mother until you do.'

Stone closed the call down and listened as 'Für Elise' drifted from the Littlewoods Building. 'I'm going round the other side of the building,' he said.

'Don't go in, whatever you do. Truman claims he's got a bomb in there. He'll detonate it if you go in.'

As Stone ran to the far side of the building, his anxiety levels spiked. He imagined 'Für Elise' being drowned by the sound of a massive explosion and his gut turned over and he felt Samantha Wilson's presence under his scalp, crawling into his brain.

How quickly things had changed. As much and as intensely as he'd once liked her, he now loathed her with a mounting passion.

105

00.41 am

Deep in the darkness of the derelict building, there was light.

Clay turned on her torch and inspected the space in front of her. She saw something running at great speed towards her. The mouse stopped, looked up at her and did an about-turn, scampering away and into the darkness to her left.

She checked her watch. Seven minutes.

'Hello!' she shouted but knew her voice was lost in the vastness of the building and the swelling piano music.

She inspected the ground, the wooden floor, saw it was full of holes and depressions and felt sweat roll down her spine.

Drawn by her torchlight, a large black moth flapped towards her face and she swiped it away as she jogged towards the large light in the distance, checking the floor so that she avoided trip hazards.

She heard what sounded like a human voice beneath the music and near the light.

Clay stopped for a moment, feeling a presence behind her, pressing in on her from the dark. She heard the clicking of a human tongue, making a steady *tick-tock, tick-tock, tick-tock...* The sound died as quickly as it had come to life and, as it vanished, the clear sense she'd had that someone was following her evaporated.

'Für Elise' stopped and, in the ensuing silence, she heard a man's voice cry, 'Help!'

She turned completely cold, as if she was walking out of an icy lake and the clothes beneath her coat were sticking to her body. Inside her own skin, she shrank from her full height to the size she had been as an eight-year-old girl.

The darkness seemed to deepen, the source of light shrinking into the distance, and the building mushroomed around her. She smelt a wisp of smoke and sulphur and felt as though she was buried alive in some massive coffin.

Turn around! She heard her own voice inside her, quietly urging her to go back and out of the abyss. She checked her watch. 00.42. Six minutes.

She heard the man crying, recognised the unique sound of his distress as her memory of a hot day in autumn 1986 came alive.

The sound of Christopher Hawkins's tears followed her as she climbed back over the wall of St Michael's Catholic Care Home for Children. Behind her, Jimmy Peace battered him in the garden, in the moments after he had rescued her from him in the shed.

Horrors ignited inside her; deeply buried childhood memories flared into life but she forced them beneath the surface of her mind.

Back in the moment, and without deciding to do so, she found herself jogging towards the light. As she did so, her sense of her own body swelled up to adult proportions once more.

The opening notes of 'Für Elise' rang out from the silence again and she almost leaped from the floor.

She kept combing the floor with the light of her torch and saw a stray piece of thin blue rope, of the same kind used to tie Frances Jamieson to a chair.

She kept moving, seeing her own breath materialise on the air like milk, as she made out the nature of the main source of light. It was a spotlight, high on a stand and pointing down at a diagonal angle.

She paused, saw a hole in the ground, the size of a large paddling pool.

Clay turned her torch back towards the way she had come

and all she could see was the dark, with no visible hint of the door through which she had entered the building or how far she had travelled.

Her feet and legs started to fill with a fast-setting glue as she used the torchlight to negotiate her way around the edge of the hole. Beneath Beethoven's music, a chorus of squealing rose up from the disconnected heating pipes in the basement as a pack of rats reacted to the influx of light and streamed in a dozen directions back into the darkness.

A drop of cold water hit her dead centre on her forehead and sent ripples through the fabric of her brain.

Keep moving! Keep moving! Keep moving! she urged herself, knowing that this was the only option, as the music of time blended with Beethoven's melody.

Tock-a-tock-a-tock-a-tock-a-tock-tock tock tock tock tock...

She made out two stationary figures seated beneath the spotlight and, as the music grew louder, she heard the blood pounding inside her ears.

Moths circled the spotlight, dots of life flirting with certain death, and she felt like one of them as she tuned in to the sound of a man crying.

Through the tall rectangular windows, a storm-blown cloud revealed the moon and, as a beam of light fell into her path, she could see the distance she had to cross. She looked at her watch as she advanced.

A little over two minutes.

Jesus, she thought, thinking about the distance she had crossed to get where she was. *Jesus, I'm going to die in here with them.*

She sprinted, using the ethereal light of the moon to guide her, and hoping with all her being that the sky threw no more clouds across its silver surface.

She stumbled, her ankle bending but not quite twisting as the sole of her left ankle was caught in a crack in the ground.

'Police!'

She walked quickly towards the figures. The fat man on the

left was howling but the thin man on the right was completely silent. 'Stay calm!' she commanded as she walked between their naked backs.

She shone torchlight up and down the fat man's back, saw the elegant knots on the blue rope that tied his legs and feet to the chair, the blood on his shoulder where Justin Truman had carved *Vindici* and the black box ticking on his leg, red digits counting down minutes and seconds. 01:54.

For a heartbeat, Clay looked deeply into his watery blue eyes and delivered a simple verdict.

'Christopher Hawkins!'

He looked away.

Clay trained the light on the thin man but there were no knots, no slender blue ropes binding him to the chair or sign of a bomb strapped to his body. She took in the whole of his unmoving form and heard herself say, 'Mannequin'.

She knelt down and carefully undid the three straps that held the ticking bomb on Hawkins' legs. Standing up, she gripped the black box and placed it down carefully on the ground as 01:41 blinked into 01:40.

Clay looked back at the distance she had covered on entering the building and knew, with sickness in her core, that there was no way back in time.

She stooped and started undoing the knots on his ankles and wrists. 'How did you get in?'

'Over there.'

'Where?' She freed his right wrist. 'Point!'

He pointed past the spotlight, into the corner ahead of them.

'Is it far?'

'Not far.'

'Für Elise' stopped and the building was filled with the ticking of a bomb. She untied his left hand and said, 'Stand up!'

He rocked on the seat and said, 'I can't move!'

'Stand up now! You're less than a minute away from death. Take me to the door you came in through!'

She sank her hands under his arms, felt the soaking hair of his armpits and was reminded of moving Steven Jamieson's dead body. Somehow handling the living was much worse than touching the dead. She lifted and he made an effort to stand.

Stabilising him, she glanced at the altar, second-glanced a small Polaroid picture propped against a bigger, more recent framed portrait of a girl on an altar decorated with statues and pictures, with food and flowers for the Day of the Dead.

'Move – towards the door!'

'Für Elise' started up again.

She saw the Polaroid on the altar as she hurried after Hawkins and was stopped in her tracks by the image. She snatched the Polaroid and as she sprinted her senses became super clear. She looked for the door in the darkness, using her torch.

'Faster!'

'My legs are dead.'

He wobbled and fell to his knees. Clay slapped his face and screamed, 'Get up and walk and if you can't walk, crawl!'

As she helped him to his feet, the blood in her ears blended into Beethoven's music.

With a beam of torchlight, she made out a long vertical line, followed it up to a corner, traced the light along the horizontal top of the door, to the corner and down to the bottom of the door.

'Is that the door?'

He sobbed as he limped forward.

'I said, *Is that the door?*'

'Yes.'

Clay ran towards it.

'Don't... leave me!'

She reached the door, pushed it dead centre with her shoulder and felt its unyielding weight. Clay used the torch to find the hinges and, moving to the opposite side of the door, kicked with the sole of her foot at hip height.

It swung open.

She turned around but he was gone.

Pointing her torch at the ground, she found him crawling on all fours.

At her back, cold air seethed as the storm was trapped down the side of the Littlewoods Building. She looked at her watch. Ten seconds to spare.

She looked at the expanse of space into which she could run away and back at him.

He held out his left arm, his hand begging.

She thrust her torch into her pocket.

Clay hurried in, grabbed his hand in both of hers and dragged him towards the open doorway. As she pulled his bulk with all her might, the moon picked up the time on her watch.

Three.

She was a metre away from the door but he became a dead weight.

Two.

She was almost at the door.

One.

At the door, she let go and threw herself out of the building.

The music stopped and the only thing polluting the silence inside the building was Hawkins curled up in a foetal ball and crying, 'I don't want to die!'

Outside, she ran into the space, felt like a leaf tossed by the storm.

She ran and ran and ran and, behind her, nothing happened.

Her iPhone rang.

The bomb, she thought. *It hasn't detonated.*

Her iPhone continued to call to her and she stopped running, turned and was amazed at the distance she'd put between herself and the building in such a short space of time.

She took out her iPhone and, without noticing the display, connected but said nothing. Clay plugged her other ear with her finger against the chaos of the storm.

A human voice wove into her ear.

'I'm sorry, I didn't hear that,' she shouted.

'Do you honestly...' Wind ploughed against her whole being and then dipped beneath her knees. '...hurt *you*?'

'Who is this?' she asked.

'Turn around, half a circle. Look, look deep and hard.'

She turned 180 degrees and looked into the darkness that covered Botanic Gardens, through the wrought-iron railings that separated the Littlewoods Building from its neighbouring green space.

A speck of light appeared and then disappeared.

The light came on again and the voice said, 'Can you see me, Eve?'

'Yes.'

The light went off.

'Can you see me?'

'No.' As she spoke, a deep and inexplicable sense of loss gripped her.

The light came on.

'Can you see me?'

'Yes. Who are you?'

'I am Vindici. Come and find me and all this will stop. Or shall I find you first?'

He disconnected the call.

After exploring the iron fence that separated the land around the Littlewoods Building and Botanic Gardens with her torch, Clay found a missing section of rusting wrought iron, a makeshift entrance into the adjoining green space. As she walked through the gap, she wondered if Justin Truman had taken the same path.

Walking deeper into the park, the wind that whipped her back and the rain that hammered her head seemed to lose power and strength, and she heard her own inner voice warning, *You're walking into a trap.*

She stood still, the wet earth beneath her and her ears and head full of the wind's chaotic music as it moved towards the river. Her iPhone vibrated with an incoming call and she felt it as a pulse under her skin that travelled deep into her body.

She connected.

'Hello, Justin,' said Clay.

He remained silent but the wind at the other end of the line was the same as the wind around her. *Same weather*, she thought, *same place.*

'Justin, is that you?'

'Yes and no. Where are you, Eve?'

'I'm in Botanic Gardens. You're still here, aren't you, Justin?'

'Nature can be cruel, don't you agree?'

'I agree with you completely.'

'Nature gives life and the forces of nature take life. Human nature is kind and human nature is vicious in the extreme. You know that, don't you, Eve?'

'Yes, I know. Justin?'

'Yes?'

Listening to his voice, Clay was filled with the sensation that she was locked in an invisible glass case. The wind and rain eased and, standing at the edge of the weather system, all she could hear was his voice and her own.

'What do you mean when you say, *Nature gives life and the force of nature takes life?* Are you talking about yourself? Are you the force of nature that takes life?'

'No. No, I'm not talking about myself. I'm talking about the storm around us. In storms, people die, there is loss, terrible loss of life, and there is nothing that any of us can do about that. We are born through nature. We die through nature. Do you know anyone who has died in a storm?'

She thought of Jimmy Peace dying at sea just off the Cornish coast.

'Why have you brought me here, Justin?'

'To refresh your memory.'

'How do you know I have memories of this place?'

'You grew up nearby. You must have memories of this place.'

'Justin, turn on your light, show me where you are, let's talk face to face.'

'What will happen if we come face to face? What will you be forced to do, Eve?'

She heard him end the call and she put her own phone away.

'I'd have to arrest you,' she said to the darkness, as the glass case around her shattered into a thousand narrow daggers that stabbed her heart in as many places.

Turning her torch to the space in front of her, Clay walked along the mud-drenched grass, felt her eyes stinging as the last of the rain slanted into her face.

Opposites piled up in her head as she walked deeper into

the dark. The darkness of night, the lightness of a sunny day in 1986. The cold around her and the heat back then. The power of the storm and the superficial calm of a hot and windless autumn day.

She sensed her mind playing tricks on her, felt the stickiness of melting ice-cream against the back of her hand, index finger and thumb and wondered if she was going out of her mind.

'Nature gives life and the force of nature takes life.' As she spoke to herself, wondering exactly what Truman had been getting at, she thought of Jimmy Peace's untimely death, imagined the levels of self-belief that made him display such courage and the horror he must have experienced when he knew that the wind and the waves had beaten him, and death was a moment away. And she wondered: had he lived, what would he have made of his life? What about the women who never knew his love and the children who were never born?

Turn around, go back to Edge Lane and do your job.

Inside her, the voice of reason was firm, a little unkind even, but certainly had Clay's best interests at heart.

But I am doing my job! she reasoned back. *I could have died doing my job just now.*

Carrying on deeper into the pitch blackness of Botanic Gardens, she closed her eyes for a moment and gave herself up to total darkness. From the depths of that tunnel, a tiny speck of light appeared in her mind's eye.

They'll be wondering where the hell you are and what the hell you're doing? the voice of reason prompted her.

I'm pursuing... The light glowed and grew.... *a murderer.*

The light exploded and overwhelmed the darkness, making a motion picture of a sun-soaked Botanic Gardens from her past inside her head as the physical storm withdrew towards the River Mersey. Clay felt her knees grow wet and realised she was kneeling in the mud. She hauled herself to her full height, straightened her spine and, opening her eyes wide, moved on.

Searching the darkness for a sign of life, a glimpse of the

killer, the motion picture inside her skull went backwards on fast rewind, and she saw the world once more through the eyes of her eight-year-old self. Night turned to day. Cold to hot. The present into the past. Faces blurred into the fabric of a green space, children played in erratic patterns, roads were crossed, pavements walked on, a wall was climbed, a garden crossed and she was in the dark shed at the back of St Michael's Catholic Care Home for Children, Christopher Hawkins looming over her, his heavy breath mingling with the heat of the day and the varnish and paraffin on the shelves.

'*You look like you could do with a cuddle,*' said Hawkins, twirling the ends of her hair between his thumbs and index fingers.

She jerked her head away and said, '*No I don't. Rufus isn't here at all!*' Very angry and even more scared, she walked back a couple of paces but there was nowhere to go, no way out.

Christopher Hawkins blocked the door and, as she felt ten times smaller than she really was, he suddenly seemed ten times bigger, able to pick her up like an insect and crush her to death with one hand.

She sensed him smile a horrible smile in the darkness. '*Yeah, but we are.*' And she heard the smile in the sound of his voice.

At this point in her memory, where everything always went black, the light stayed on in her mind and pictures continued unfolding.

He took two steps forward and she reached into the shadows for a hammer or a spanner or anything to smack him with but all she grasped was darkness.

'*Listen, Eve, how about we do a deal, a little deal that's secret between me and you. Do you want to know who your real mother and father are?*'

'*Yes, but...*'

Confusion overwhelmed her. He smiled down at her.

'*How do you know who my real parents are? No one does. I was abandoned when I was a newborn. Not even Sister Philomena knew and she knew almost everything.*'

'*She didn't know who your real mother and father are. But I do. I could tell you but I'd be risking my job here. So you'd have to give me something in exchange. It wouldn't hurt you and it wouldn't harm you but you'd have to swear on Sister Philomena's soul in heaven that you wouldn't tell anyone.*'

'*How do you know who my parents were?*'

'*Because I know them. And I know where they live.*'

'*Just like you knew that Rufus had come back to the garden.*'

'*I wasn't lying. I* did *hear Rufus. Anyway, I had to say that so we could have a bit of personal space. Do you know, Eve, I could even show you things from your file, the one in Mrs Tripp's office. In exchange for one teeny-tiny favour.*'

He bent his knees and his face was close to hers.

'*Stop breathing on me,*' she said. '*I don't like it.*'

He tilted his head to the left and whispered a stream of strange and vile words in her ear that made her entire being crawl.

'*You're disgusting! Get away from me now!*'

And she came to the point where the blackout ended and her regular memory kicked in.

The shed door opened, banged against the wooden wall and Jimmy Peace stepped out of the light and into the darkness of the shed. '*Get away from her, yer fucking perv!*'

Hawkins tried to push past Jimmy Peace but couldn't. In a split second, Jimmy Peace had Hawkins in a headlock and out of the shed, clearing a path along which Eve could escape. Peace threw three bolts with his fist into Hawkins's ear, his face filled with rage.

He looked at Eve and the rage subsided. He smiled and said, gently, '*Go back to Botanic Gardens. You're not going to get into any trouble. I'm going to have a little chat with Chris.*'

'*Honest to God, mate, on my mother's life, I was only trying to help her find her bloody cat. I wasn't going to hurt her no more.*'

The wind sobbed and, as an eerie calm crept into the darkness, Clay heard another sound. She felt tears rolling down her face and listened to herself crying.

'I found you first. Or did you find me? Don't be sad, Eve.' A voice came at her back. She froze. 'There's nothing to be sad about tonight.'

Justin Truman was behind her and within touching distance.

'Did you really think I was going to let you die in the Littlewoods Building with that excuse for a human being?'

Clay steeled herself, tried to knit the ever-gaping divide at the centre of her being.

'Don't turn around,' he said.

The light from his torch played out on the ground beside her and in front of her, like an irresistible offer to comply.

'Who are you?' she asked, all certainty lost in the tail of the departing storm. 'Who are you?'

'I need you to do something for me, Eve. I need you to call your colleagues and let me know who is and isn't in the building.'

'Justin Truman?'

'Make the call, Eve, and all this will stop. Make the call and let's see if we can make the world a safer place.'

108

00.57 am

At the centre of the Littlewoods Building, Detective Sergeant
Bill Hendricks made out two chairs, one empty and one with a
still human form on it. There was a table laden with things he
couldn't quite make out. As he came closer he recognised it is a
Day of the Dead altar.

'Für Elise' came to an end and he listened hard to the silence
but heard nothing.

'Eve?'

Silence.

'Hawkins?'

Silence.

Once more the opening notes of 'Für Elise' filled the cavernous
space and he saw that the figure on the chair was a mannequin.

Instinct told him he was alone.

Hendricks saw a pile of cheap, greasy clothes and guessed
wherever he was or whatever had become of him, Hawkins was
naked.

On the floor beside the empty chair he saw a black box with
a small digital clock on its body, still and dead, the red digits
locked at 00:00. Hendricks knelt next to it, sniffed it but couldn't
detect the fertiliser used in a home-made bomb.

He approached the altar, and the first thing he noticed was
the presence of food. Skulls made from sugar. Chocolate. Candy

skeletons. An altar prepared for the Weeping Child statuette near to the framed picture of a little girl with a stern but Christ-like serenity in her face and what he recognised as a physical marker of autism.

Food at the scene of the crime. So, thought Hendricks, *Justin Truman is in town. Food especially for little children.*

A door banged, close at hand and to his right, and then heaved open like an invitation to come back out into the night.

Hendricks walked to the open door and, beneath the music, heard someone crying in the dark outside. He followed the sound as he left the building.

A fat man sobbed on the ground, hands tucked around his knees, eyes shut, curled in a ball.

'I'm a police officer,' said Hendricks, approaching.

The man opened his eyes wide, screamed, raised himself on all fours and crawled away.

'Get away from me, Vindici!'

Hendricks followed, torch on, keeping a distance from the man and observing the dark bloodstain on his back.

'I'm not Vindici. My name's Bill Hendricks, Detective Sergeant Bill Hendricks. Merseyside Constabulary.'

'The bomb! The bomb!'

'There is no bomb,' said Hendricks. 'It's a hoax.'

The man kept crawling as fast as he could and sobbing in the direction of Edge Lane. 'I didn't do nothing to her no more...'

'Stop!' shouted Hendricks.

The man froze.

'Come back! The building's safe and you can't walk on to Edge Lane bollock naked.'

He held a hand up to Hendricks, squinting blindly into the light of his torch.

'Are you there?' In the distance, Gina Riley's voice drifted on the icy breeze.

'Here, Gina!' shouted Hendricks, giving her a target to move towards.

Riley came into view, hurried towards him.

Hendricks and Riley took a hand each and hauled the man to his feet.

'Get back inside there now, and don't come out until you're decent.'

As Hawkins hobbled back inside the Littlewoods Building, hands cupping his genitals, Hendricks and Riley looked at the back view of him with morbid fascination.

'Last time I saw an arse that size,' Stone's voice was behind them. 'I was in the elephant enclosure in Chester Zoo.'

Hendricks's iPhone rang out and he connected. 'Hi, Eve, where are you?'

'I'm not far.'

'Do you want me to come and meet you?'

'Not yet.'

'You safe?'

'I need you to do something for me, Bill. I need to know what's going on around the Littlewoods Building at the moment?'

'I checked the building out after the bomb didn't go off. You weren't there, nor was Hawkins. I came across a classic Vindici altar and Hawkins's clothes. I went outside and Hawkins was naked on the ground.'

'So the building's empty?' asked Clay.

'No...'

Clay could hear 'Für Elise' and knew that Hendricks was taking the call outside the Littlewoods Building.

'I sent Hawkins back inside to get dressed.'

'He's on his own in there?'

'The only people in the vicinity are me, Karl Stone and Gina Riley. We're outside. Hawkins is inside the Littlewoods Building.'

'I've got to go, Bill. I'll be back soon...'

109

01.06 am

'Turn around, Eve.'

His voice was rich with a layer of warmth that didn't come through on the telephone or the taped interviews that the Metropolitan Police had supplied to her, as though technology had eroded an essential piece of him.

'Turn around and look at me, Eve.'

She turned.

He took off his bloodstained white gloves and dropped them to the ground. She watched his face, the way he smiled in the moonlight, and noted that he looked genuinely pleased to see her.

He took his mobile phone from his pocket, looked in the direction of the Littlewoods Building. 'Anyone in there as we speak?' he asked.

'Why do you want to know?' replied Clay.

'It's a matter of life and death. I need to know.'

Clay weighed it up, pushed back at the rising suspicion inside herself and said, 'One person. Hawkins. My colleague told him to go inside and get dressed.'

'Definitely no one else in there apart from Hawkins?'

'Definitely.'

He walked a few steps away from her in the direction of the Littlewoods Building and pressed a digit on his phone's keypad.

A slice of wind whistled through the wet grass and, a moment later, there was a *boom* in the near distance followed by the sound of windows smashing out from the Littlewoods Building.

He turned, put his phone away in his coat pocket and held out a hand to Eve. 'It was under the altar, the real bomb. There was no way I was going to put you in danger. It wasn't a big bomb but it was big enough to finish a job I've been meaning to finish for years.'

'What do you mean?' asked Clay. A call came through on her iPhone and she was back to Hendricks. 'Bill, what's happening?'

She read shock in his silence.

'There's been some sort of small-scale explosion inside the building. Jesus, my ears are ringing.'

'Do not go in, any of you!'

'No way! Do you know what's going on, Eve?'

'I'm not sure...' She closed down the call, saw a ribbon of smoke drift from a broken window in the Littlewoods Building. 'What do you mean, a job you've been meaning to finish for years?'

Hendricks, Riley and Stone stood at the boundary between the land around the Littlewoods Building and Botanic Gardens. Above their heads, the air churned as the police helicopter hovered in the sky.

Hendricks raised an arm and directed the pilot's attention at the door of the Littlewoods Building through which Hawkins had entered minutes earlier.

The helicopter's powerful beam picked up the open door, the wall and the ground around it.

'What's that noise?' asked Riley.

'What?' asked Stone.

Bang and the sound of breaking glass.

'Yes,' said Stone.

In the doorway, the helicopter's light picked out something small and black moving out of the building.

'A rat?' asked Stone. 'Two rats…'

'They're not rats, Karl,' said Hendricks. 'They're hands.'

A human arm emerged supported by a hand, and then another, and then a blackened head. The smell of burning flesh accompanied Christopher Hawkins as he dragged himself out of the building and into the bright light.

Soon, on all fours, black and red from head to foot, his smoking body made it into the fresh air. He fell and rolled on to his back.

Hendricks stepped towards Hawkins's body, stooped and looked into his blackened face. Hawkins blinked, opened his eyes, his head flopped to the left and he made a noise like air rattling in a pipe.

The dim light in his eyes faded and there was silence.

'I'm calling an ambulance,' said Riley.

'No point, Gina, said Hendricks, looking down at the still, leftover meat of a human life. 'He's dead.'

111

1.07 am

'What do you mean?' asked Clay.

He smiled at her through the darkness and the light of her torch.

'You just triggered that explosion?'

'Yes.' He held up his right hand.

'With Hawkins in the building?'

'With this hand. With this finger. Do you want to hold my hand?'

Even though there was no menace in his voice and Clay read his words as a simple invitation for human contact, she summoned up every monster she had ever encountered and survived and said, 'I'm not scared of *you*, Justin.'

She dialled Hendricks on her iPhone.

'Jimmy Peace was my best friend. I don't want you to be scared of me. That's the last thing I want. He told me all about you. And he was right.'

He nodded in the direction of the Littlewoods Building.

Pick up, Bill, she thought, anxiety mounting as the ring tone burned into her ear.

'You had the power of life and death over that man. You chose to spare him. I had the power of life and death over him and I chose to destroy him. You put your life on the line tonight for a man you have every right to despise, a man who would have robbed you of your innocence and may well have warped what you became as a human being. I kidnapped and tortured him, put him through extreme mental anguish by strapping a fake bomb on him. By the way, I'm sorry I put you through that theatre. There was no way I wasn't going to damage him, kill him if possible, but if I failed in that I wanted at least to make him experience something that would give him nightmares, that would make him wake up screaming every single night for the rest of his miserable existence.'

She noticed that, in spite of the cold, he had a sheen of sweat on his face. His left hand rested on the left of his abdomen.

'Are you unwell?' asked Clay.

Hendricks connected.

'Eve?' said Hendricks.

'Is everyone safe, Bill?'

'We're all fine, Eve. Apart from Hawkins. Doctor Lamb isn't going to have much to work on with his body.'

'Keep away and stay away from the building!'

Clay closed the call down and stared hard at the man in front of her.

'Can you smell that, Eve? On the wind, burning human flesh?'

'Hawkins is dead, Justin. The others are safe.'

He glanced in the direction of the Littlewoods Building with a look of quiet satisfaction.

'I'm going to arrest you,' she said.

'Of course you are. I came to here to be arrested by you, Eve.'

In the distance, the sound of a train's horn curled in on the wind as it made its way into Lime Street Station and Clay's head was filled with the rhythm of its heartbeat and motion.

I-need-to-buy-time, I-need-to-buy-time, I-need-to-buy-time...

'You chose one path, Eve. I chose another. I finally found out how you turned out, and I'm happy. You did your best, you did your duty, but don't feel sorry for him, you can't.'

'Like yourself, I can't help the way I feel.'

'How do you feel about your husband and son?'

'I absolutely love them.'

'If Hawkins had managed to attack you, what might that have done to you as a person, a human being? He could have put you in a place where you wouldn't be the woman you are today, the mother you are to your son, the wife you are to your husband. He wanted to curse you and in cursing you, he would have cursed the people you love in the next generation and beyond. That's why I spent my life doing what I did. The only safe paedophile is a dead one. Jimmy saved you. I saved hundreds and thousands. My life was a mission and tonight my mission is accomplished. Well?'

'I agree with you.'

'You do?'

'And I disagree with you. I'm a mother. I applaud your strength of feeling about protecting children.'

'But?'

'Not a but, an and.'

'And?'

'And you put your life and liberty on the line for that principle. But...'

'But?' he echoed.

'What if everyone was remotely like you? You've got millions of admirers around the world and down the years, people who sit around in pubs saying, *If only there were few more Vindicis on this earth, what a great place this would be,* while doing absolutely nothing about it themselves. But eventually one person did do something. A deeply challenged teenager from Liverpool...'

'Oh, Eve...'

'I've listened to you; you listen to me. This kid's made two hits in a fortnight and one of them wasn't even a convicted paedophile. Suspected? Yes. Convicted? No. You know something, Justin, you were great at what you did best but just how old were you when you began your murder spree?'

'Thirty-eight.'

'Did you know Lucien Burns had not long turned eighteen?'

'He told me he was twenty-three.'

'Even with that fabrication, you could have told him to hang fire – *Wait until you're as old as me if you want to follow in my path*. He might have grown out of it.'

'It felt like the stars, fate, God – whatever you want to call it – were reaching out to me, using him as a bridge to bring me back to…'

'…to me? Me?'

I-need-to-buy-time, I-need-to-buy-time, I-need-to-buy-time…

'Yes.'

Clay looked at him, scrutinised the bone structure of his face and felt a pearl of recognition form at the centre of her brain.

'Paedophiles are nasty, sly, manipulative, horrible, despicable, but there isn't one person in their right mind who would've wished that destiny on them on the day they were born,' said Clay.

'Yes indeed. But I'm not interested in them. I'm interested in protecting the innocent, kid.'

'*Kid?*'

He held out his hand to her. 'I'm not well, kid.'

'What happened to Jimmy Peace?'

'He grew up, moved to London to work – casual labour, building sites, hotels, anything and everything he could get. He made friends with another young drifter called Justin Truman. He told Truman all about that autumn day in 1986. Jimmy wanted you to know that he never forgot about you and that he loved you very much.'

'But if he loved me…'

'He did love you, Eve. Believe me. Catholic Social Services moved him out of Liverpool. He moved around the country, usually every three months or so. Physically, he couldn't get near you.'

He stopped walking, looked at her with the rarest tenderness, and she felt the stirrings of a deeply buried and indefinable emotion. She felt the texture of his fingers, the heat of his blood in her hand.

'I'm sick of life, Eve. Do you understand?'

'How long have you got left?'

I-need-to-buy-time, I-need-to-buy-time, I-need-to-buy-time...

'A year.' He wiped his brow with the back of his hand and carried on walking. 'I want to die in peace. I'm sick of looking over my shoulder. I'm tired of hiding.'

She felt the weight of the past in her coat pocket, a frozen moment in a square of captured light.

Clay took the Polaroid photograph from her pocket. He shone his torch on the image of her, seven years of age and smiling under the Christmas tree in the dining room of St Michael's Catholic Care Home for Children.

'This was on the altar. Where did you get this?'

'Jimmy gave it to me just before he last went to sea. He asked me to take care of you. It was like he knew something terrible was going to happen, that he was going to die. One of the members of staff brought the camera in. It was her Christmas present. She let him take a picture of you. You were amazed at the speed with which the photograph came out of the camera.'

'I remember. It was Maggie Anderson's camera.'

The threads of the past came together in her head, tied themselves into neat bows.

'When the police took him away, I looked out of an upstairs window and saw his face framed in the back window of a police car.'

In the silence, she felt her heart turning inside out. In her mind's eye, she looked out of Mrs Tripp's window, and she didn't see the blur of Jimmy's face but remembered his bone structure, his eyes, his mouth.

The pearl of light in her brain swelled to the brightness of the moon, illuminating the whole of her consciousness.

She stopped in the open gateway into Botanic Gardens, looked at him and recognised him as she heard herself ask, 'What became of the real Justin Truman?'

He said nothing, smiled at her.

'Tell me…'

'How do you mean?'

She stared into his face and was filled with awe. 'Tell me the truth. What happened to Justin Truman?'

'He died of an AIDS-related illness, kid. I survived the sea. I was in big trouble with the law. When Justin died, his legacy to me was that I could take on his identity and avoid jail. I'd battered a paedophile within an inch of his life. When I survived the SS *Memphis Star* disaster, I went to live with Justin Truman's mother in Tamworth. His mother was almost blind, a cripple with dementia. She didn't know I wasn't her son. Jimmy Peace was forever lost at sea. Case against him closed. Jimmy's dead. Long live Justin.'

Clay looked at him intensely, saw the imprint of the boy's face in the man's features, after years of trying to visualise him as he was taken away, at the age of fifteen.

'Jimmy?'

'Yes, Eve. Hawkins was a detail in the margin. You're the full page. I came home to see you before I died and to let you know there wasn't a day I didn't think about you. There wasn't a moment I didn't love you. You were the best thing that ever happened to me and you made my life worth living. My name's Jimmy Peace and you're going to be all right, kid, you've got to know that.'

112

2.05 am

At the door of the holding cell in Trinity Road police station, Sergeant Harris showed Clay a bottle of tablets.

'How is he?' asked Clay.

'Very calm. Waiting for his lawyer to arrive.'

'What are his tablets?'

'Ponatinib,' replied Sergeant Harris. 'He's got chronic myeloid leukaemia.'

Clay made a massive effort to keep her face neutral even though her heart was in freefall.

'I've explained to him that he'll have to be under guard but he'll get chemo or whatever he needs medically.'

'What did he say?'

'No chemo, he's not putting off the inevitable. He wants pain relief, nothing else.'

She looked away for a moment and then nodded.

Clay knocked on the door of the holding cell and Sergeant Harris opened it.

Jimmy Peace sat on the bed, looking up at Clay.

'Is there anything I can get for you?' asked Clay.

'I'd like to see Lucien Burns. Is that all right with you, Eve?'

It's like you can read my mind, thought Clay. 'He's three doors away.'

*

Clay opened the observation slot and saw Lucien lying on the bed, arms across his chest. 'Sit up, Lucien,' she said. 'You've got a visitor.'

Lucien sat up slowly and Clay stepped back, making space for Jimmy Peace to stand in the cell's doorway. Head slumped and eyes downcast, Lucien looked beaten and terrified.

'Look at me, Lucien!' said Jimmy.

Lucien looked up and the brokenness lifted from him. He leaped to his feet, his face lighting up with shock and disbelief.

'Stay where you are, Lucien,' said Jimmy, walking into the cell. 'What did Eve Clay tell you to do?'

'Sit up!'

'So why are you standing?'

Lucien sat on the bed again, his eyes fixed on Jimmy and welling up with tears. 'I have a dream, Vindici, of you and me as man and wife.'

'Is this to do with the thing you told me of, about yourself?'

'I have two parts to my sex. They thought I was a girl when I was born.'

'I'm old enough to be your father, Lucien. How can that dream ever come true?'

'I'm a boy as well. I can be anything you want me to be.'

'You can?'

'Yes, I can.'

Lucien stood up and sidled closer to Jimmy.

'I can't believe you're here, Vindici.' Tears flooded Lucien's face. 'I'm not sixteen. I'm eighteen. When I was born, they thought I was a girl. When I was a child, I developed a urine infection. The doctor discovered I was a boy. He found a penis and testicular tissue inside my vagina. Caroline died and Lucien was born. I'm an adult hermaphrodite. I can be anything you want me to be.'

'Do you know what I want you to be?'

'Tell me.'

'I want you to be completely truthful with Eve Clay. That's

what I'm going to be. That's what I want you be. Will you be completely truthful with her?'

'If you say so.'

'Why do you think so highly of me that you've copied me and committed murder?' asked Jimmy.

'I was terrified people would find out about me, about my condition, hunt me down and lock me up in the dark so that they could use me and sell me to their friends because I was different to other children. When I learned about you, I stopped being frightened. You are my protector. You are my hope. You are my saviour. I wanted to do for others what you'd done for me. And I wanted you to love me for it.'

Lucien looked Jimmy up and down. 'What's wrong? Why are you clutching your stomach like that?'

'There's nothing wrong with me, lad.' He looked at Lucien closely and asked, 'What are you going to tell Eve Clay?'

'The truth, the complete truth.'

Walking out of the cell, Jimmy pointed at Clay and Lucien looked directly at her.

'Where are you calling from?' asked Clay, repeating the question from the switchboard during the call from 699 Mather Avenue.

Something dark shifted in Lucien's face, as though his soul was transforming into a glacial rock.

'I'm calling from 699 Mather Avenue.'

Lucien spoke with the same androgynous voice as the caller from the Jamiesons' house. He looked and sounded fifteen years older and the effect sent chills to Clay's core.

'What's the nature of your problem?' asked Clay, stepping into the cell.

'A man has been murdered and his wife has been tortured.' Lucien stared directly at Clay. 'Tell Eve Clay to get over here as fast as she can – 699 Mather Avenue.'

Lucien made a telephone receiver with his right hand and replaced it into thin air.

A pair of footsteps came down the corridor, speed and urgency in each pace forward.

Lucien's features softened and, within half a minute, he became an approximation of his own self again.

The footsteps stopped behind Clay in the doorway of the cell. She glanced back, saw Barney Cole and knew from his face that something of massive significance had emerged. She stepped towards him.

'I need to talk with you, Eve,' he whispered calmly. 'Before you take Lucien back to interview. The DNA results have come in.'

'You need to let Christine go,' said Lucien. 'I'll tell you the truth, the complete truth, the absolute truth. Oh... and tell Detective Sergeant Hendricks to bring the photograph that Sergeant Carol White gave him to the interview.'

'Has Sergeant White been feeding you information, Lucien?'

'Absolutely not. It's her colleague Alice Burns. She's been telling me everything. Alice and her boyfriend. Kevin White. Carol White's husband.'

113

2.20 am

'Where's the social worker?' Lucien's solicitor appeared perplexed.

'Do you want to tell her?' asked Clay. 'Or do you want me to?'

Lucien looked over his shoulder. 'Is Vindici in there, behind the glass?' His face was flushed, his eyes red raw with the tears he had shed.

'Yes,' replied Clay.

'Who?' asked his solicitor.

'I'm going to tell the truth,' said Lucien to the glass.

Clay addressed the solicitor. 'Lucien is over the age of eighteen. He's not sixteen and doesn't need a social worker present. In the eyes of the law he's an adult.'

Clay placed her hands on the brown envelope containing the DNA results and looked at Hendricks as he formally opened the interview.

'Have you released Christine yet?' asked Lucien.

'No. You've stated that you're going to tell the truth, Lucien.'

'I've told you some truths but I've told you lots of lies as well. That's all going to stop now.'

'Did you torture and murder David Wilson in his house in Dundonald Road on Monday the fourteenth of October 2019?'

'Yes and I did it by myself.' There was a mixture of pride and fear in his voice. On the table, Lucien's hands trembled and he knitted his fingers together to still them.

'Did you torture and murder Steven Jamieson in his house on Mather Avenue on Wednesday the twenty-third of October 2019?'

'Yes and I did it myself.'

'Did you tie up and torture Frances Jamieson in her house on Mather Avenue on Wednesday the twenty-third of October 2019?'

'Yes and I did it myself.'

'Did you order the Weeping Children statuettes?'

'Yes and had them sent to Christine's house.'

'Why twelve?'

'Because I was planning on killing twelve over a series of years, all during the Day of the Dead festivities.'

'With the exception of your laptop, iPad and iPhone, our search of your home has yielded no incriminating evidence. Where do you keep your clothing, weapons and items associated with your crimes?'

'I rent a double lock-up garage at the Woolton Village end of Menlove Avenue near to the block of flats.'

'Does Annabelle pay for that?'

'People send me donations. I've got over fifty-four thousand pounds in the bank at the moment. The bank statements and details are in the lock-up garage.'

Clay thought for a moment.

'The key to the garage is on the back of the picture of you as a baby from Caroline's room?'

'The spare key.'

'Tell me about your movements on the night Steven Jamieson was murdered?'

'I went to the garage and dressed as Caroline. Black shoes, white socks, grey skirt, white blouse, grey V-neck cardigan, school tie, red duffel coat. I packed my bag and gathered my weapons. I walked across the golf course, I walked down Wheatcroft Road on to Mather Avenue. I didn't see a soul. I turned left and walked to 699 Mather Avenue. I rang the bell. They opened the door.

I dispensed justice. I came back the way I had come. Your IT people were right. I transferred the homework on to my laptop from my iPad.'

'When you say you *dispensed justice*, what exactly did you do?'

'I disabled the Human Abomination and his Slut Wife. I murdered him and opened her eyes forever to the filth they so loved and the pain they inflicted on so many others.'

'You say *they inflicted*?'

'Have you got the photograph, DS Hendricks?'

'How do you know Carol White gave me a photograph?'

'Alice Burns told me Carol White was a paedophile masquerading as a good cop. Alice told me she'd given you a picture and was pretending to mourn for the innocents.'

'Carol White's not a paedophile, Lucien. She's a good woman.'

'Have you seen that picture yet?'

Hendricks reached inside his jacket pocket.

'No. I haven't looked yet. I didn't believe it had any direct impact on this investigation.' *And part of me couldn't face it*, he thought.

'You ought to look at it, DS Hendricks.'

Hendricks opened the envelope with a sense of mounting dread and pulled out a single sheet of photographic paper, blank side up.

'Turn it over,' said Lucien. 'Look at it.'

Hendricks turned it over on the table and looked at Clay.

'Who's the woman sexually abusing that bored little boy?' asked Clay.

'Frances Jamieson,' said Hendricks. 'Do you know who the boy is?'

Silence.

'He's one of millions. She was as bad as her husband,' said Lucien.

'So why didn't you kill her?' asked Clay.

'Death was an easy option for the Slut Wife. She got away

with it for years and hid what she was from the world. I'm genuinely sorry she died. I wanted her to live and be exposed for what she was.'

Lucien looked over his shoulder at the glass. 'Am I doing well at telling the truth?' Then he looked at Clay.

'What's Christine's role in this?' asked Clay.

'She took the evidence away from the garage, cleaned it up, replenished the ropes and anything else I needed. If I got caught, she was going to take the fall for my so-called crimes, make it look like it was all her doing.'

Clay took the DNA results from the envelope. 'I can well understand why she'd do that for you. When our forensic lab technician was looking at the DNA for subjects involved in this investigation, she came up with this.'

She spread the data out in front of Lucien. 'These numbers refer to microsatellites, markers found in a person's DNA. The pink numbers belong to your mother. The blue column is your father. Your column is in the middle, Lucien. The combination of pink and blue numbers makes you the son of these two individuals. Genetically you're XY, that casts you as a male.'

He looked at the numbers. 'They match.'

'You're a match, you and Christine, mother and son. How aware are you of your biological background?'

Lucien looked at the three columns of DNA.

'Who is Annabelle to you, Lucien?'

'She's my grandmother.'

'Who's your mother?'

'Christine Burns. She changed her name by deed poll to Green when we all moved to Liverpool when I was a newborn. She wanted a new start. I know all this.'

'Where were you born?'

'Sheffield.'

'Do you know who your father is?'

He fell into a conflicted silence.

'He's dead.' He looked over his shoulder at the glass.

'Who's your father, Lucien?'

'I killed him. Christine was fourteen when she gave birth to me. Steven Jamieson paid us off every month for years through that scumbag solicitor of his. My father's name was Steven Jamieson. And I'm the happiest I've ever been in my life because he's finally dead and I'm responsible for that.'

'Did the Jamiesons follow you to Liverpool?'

'I don't know the truth of that.' Tears welled up in his eyes. 'My life was over before it had even begun. I've spoken, and I've spoken enough.'

Lucien stood up and walked to the glass. 'Did I do well? Did I do well in speaking the truth?'

Lucien looked at his reflection in the glass, imagining Vindici watching and approving. In the empty room behind the glass nothing moved and no sound was made.

'What am I?' Lucien asked his reflection. 'Who are you, Vindici? Hmm? You are...who? You understand me, don't you? You understand I'm neither one thing nor another. But you accept me for what I am because you understand the horror that brought me into this world; you understand the horror that you tried to fix. You understand that I have done the same thing. I know you, Justin. I accept you for what you are as you accept me.'

He placed the palms of his hands against the glass and pressed his cheek between his hands, as if proffering his face for a kiss.

'And I love you for that.'

114

2.35 am

When Samantha Wilson opened the door of her mother's house in Dundonald Road, Stone was completely taken aback by her appearance. She was barefoot and dressed in a sleeveless evening gown that was as red as the lipstick she had applied, her eyelids were black and thick mascara fanned out her eyelashes. She reminded him of a vamp from a film noir.

'Do you like the way I look, Karl?'

She turned, walked back inside the house and Stone followed, closing the door and sensing trouble.

She stood in the kitchen at the back of the house with a glass of red wine in her hand. Thick lipstick was printed on to the rim of the glass and there was another glass on the table and an almost empty bottle of red wine.

'Yes, you look just sensational. Are you going out?'

She shook her head. 'Where could I go to? You took a long time.'

Stone took a handkerchief from his pocket, wiped the end of his nose and lifted the lid of the kitchen bin with the pedal to throw in his tissue. In the bin, he saw two empty wine bottles.

'I've really only got one question for you, Sammy.'

'Sit down.'

'I'll stand, thank you.'

'My mother's an alcoholic, did you know that?'

'No, I didn't know that.'

'Would you care for a glass of wine?'

'I'm on duty. What's this piece of information you have for me about the investigation into your father's murder?'

She placed her glass down on the table and, turning her back to Stone, poured herself another glass of red.

'Sammy, can I take a picture of you on my phone?'

'No problem.' She looked profoundly pleased.

He pointed the phone at her, selected camera and took snapshots of the woman in front of him.

He forced himself to smile at her.

'That's better. You looked like Mr Grumpy up until then.'

'I've seen some strange and difficult things this evening, and I'm very tired.'

'You could always have a lie down.' She pointed at the ceiling.

'So, what's this information about the investigation into your father's murder?'

'The information? Oh yes, I'll come to that later.'

'OK.' He smiled but wanted to scream at her to stop playing mind games.

'Cheers.' She raised her glass and took a large sip. 'I've got a question for you, Karl, Karly Warly. Who's this Christine Green you've been going to visit?'

'I told you earlier. She currently in our custody.'

'Cosy. Wander down to the cell to pay her a little visit? Comfort her? Tell her it's all going to be all right. Give her a little back rub, whisper sweet, smutty nothings in her ear.' The muscles in her face shifted like clouds over a glacial mountain, in varying degrees of unpredictable darkness.

'No, I most certainly do not go down to her cell and engage her in physical or emotional contact. Each cell is hooked up to CCTV that's played out live twenty-four/seven to a bank of screens on the front desk where they are constantly supervised by the custody sergeant and his assistant constables. If I did any such thing I would be immediately suspended and very quickly drummed out of the police.'

Her entire body shifted with relief.

'What did you want to tell me about your father?'

She smiled at him, reached out a hand. He stepped past her and asked, 'Can I use your bathroom?'

'What?'

Stone walked out of the kitchen and headed directly to the stairs. At the bottom of the stairs, Sammy blocked his way.

'I'll tell you about my father,' said Sammy.

'Tell me as I go upstairs.'

'He wasn't a paedophile.'

'Pardon?'

She shook her head and he pressed record on his phone.

'Say that again, Sammy.'

'My father, David Wilson, was not, repeat, was not a paedophile.'

'What about your allegations that he raped you when you were a teenager?'

'Lies. I lied. I was an attention-seeking liar back then, but I've grown up now and I don't tell lies which is why I'm coming out with the truth, see.'

'He never raped you at all, ever?'

'He never laid a finger on me. He didn't so much as slap me on the back of the hand when I was being naughty, when I was little.'

'What about all the paedophile porn we found on his laptop?'

She giggled, covering her mouth with her hand. 'He was almost a cretin when it came to IT. I downloaded it to give substance to my lies, but I'm not lying any longer.'

He thought of Sandra Wilson and a sickness spread through him.

Stone looked up the stairs and called, 'Mrs Wilson?'

'Why do you want to talk to *her* when you can be with *me*?'

He pushed her out of the way, hurried up the stairs.

'He was an ordinary decent man and I made up copious malicious lies about him...' She followed.

Stone went to the small front bedroom, turned on the light, saw that Mrs Wilson was fast asleep and breathing.

'Mrs Wilson?' he double-checked.

Her eyes fluttered open and she looked like a woman waking into a dream. 'You?' She sounded happy but very tired.

'Just checking you're OK.'

'More than OK. Sammy's come back to me. We're going to be together. We're going... to be... so...' Her eyes closed. '...happy.'

He left Mrs Wilson, turned off the light and looked at Sammy, who was standing at the top of the stairs and watching him as if he was the last man on earth. Opening the bedroom door that Sandra Wilson had once shared with her husband David, he looked inside and remembered what he had witnessed when he arrived at the murder scene.

David Wilson, castrated, face down and tied to the mattress, his brain mutilated by Lucien Burns's bicycle spoke.

'We're going to be happy, so happy.' Sammy opened a back bedroom door. 'This is my room, Karl. Do you want to have a look?'

'Why?'

'Why what, darling?'

'Why did you lie about your father to me? Why did you set him up with the porn on his laptop?'

'I know you want me and I know how badly you want me. But I know, too, what's keeping you back from me. We both do, don't we?'

'Give me a clue.'

'You think – because you believe that my father had sex with me – that I am damaged goods. So I'm coming clean and telling the truth so that we can remove that obstacle and take our relationship to the next level. Silly lies, that's all it was.'

Stone walked to the top of the stairs. 'Goodbye, Sammy. I hope your mother's right and that you'll both be very happy together.'

'Are you going?'

'Yes.'

'Are you coming back?'

'No.'

He walked down the stairs, stopped when she said, 'Karl? I could always put a complaint in about you. I could always complain about how you tried to touch me inappropriately in my mother's house as she slept.'

'Which isn't true, is it, Sammy?'

'No, it's not true. You've always been a perfect gentleman around me. But it'd be my word against yours.'

He carried on to the bottom of the stairs. 'No, it wouldn't be your word against mine. It'd be your malicious threat to me and your admission that you lied and framed your father. I've recorded the things you've said on my phone.' Stone showed her his phone. 'Still recording, Sammy.'

He opened the front door and heard her coming down the stairs.

'Karl, I don't understand. What did I do wrong?'

Stone walked to his car.

'What did I do wrong?'

He walked faster as she followed him down the pavement.

'What did I do wrong?'

He got inside his car and turned on the ignition.

She pounded the roof of his car with the heels of both hands.

'What did I do wrong?'

He pulled away, looked at Samantha Wilson's reflection in the wing mirror.

'What did I do wrong? What did I do wrong? What did I do wrong?' she screamed.

115

6.04 am

In Lucien Burns's double lock-up garage at the Woolton Village end of Menlove Avenue, DCI Eve Clay turned a full circle for the fourth time, taking in each and every detail. She stopped and focused on the female mannequins, one made masculine with a perfectly formed wooden phallus strapped to its groin.

'Is this your work?' Clay asked. She pressed record on her iPhone.

Handcuffed to Hendricks, and just beyond the scene of crime outside the garage, Christine nodded. 'I'm good with my hands. I'm good with making things out of wood.'

'Did Lucien ask you to make it, the phallus?'

'Yes. Why have you brought me here?'

'This is quite a place,' said Clay. 'Talk me through it.'

There was a softness about Christine now that was the direct opposite of the hard-nosed fishwife she'd portrayed herself as earlier.

'Correct me if I'm wrong, Christine, but is this the real *you*? This calm, quiet woman?'

'I've had to construct acts to protect myself since I was a little girl. I don't like the woman who shouts and swears and insults people at the drop of a hat. But I need her. I despise the woman who hands out hate leaflets, making people cross one of the busiest roads in Liverpool to avoid her, so that they don't have to breathe the same air as her. But I need her. The racist woman is a necessary embarrassment. It alienates people. Nobody comes near me. Nobody wants me. Nobody needs me. Nobody touches me. I need her.'

'What about Lucien?'

'He doesn't love me. Why should he? He doesn't see me. I don't see him. We've communicated through Annabelle for years. It's only been in recent months that we've been in direct contact.'

'How do you feel about him?'

'I'm his mother. I gave birth to him when I was fourteen. I love him. But he's a constant reminder of his father who I hated. My child is like a ghost of his father. Lucien blames me for giving birth to him, for making him the way he is. *Neither one thing nor another*, as he so often says. I'm torn, constantly torn.'

'He told us that you tidied up after him, that you were going to take the fall for his crimes.'

'That's how I hoped I could earn his love. By helping him to destroy his father and expose his father's wife. By working together to annihilate the Human Abomination and his Slut Wife.'

'You'd have framed yourself, Christine.'

'If I went to jail in his place, I hoped he'd come and visit me. It was a risk, a dangerous one, but I took it in the hope we'd get away with it. In playing my part in destroying the Human Abomination, I was destroying the thing that was haunting me. And there was something I wanted so badly. A new start for me and him in a world where the Human Abomination no longer existed.'

'So it was your idea to kill Steven Jamieson?' asked Clay.

'Yes, it was my idea.'

'I don't believe you, Christine. Lucien's told me it was his idea. He told me that he asked you to set up a Vindici website. He told me that he put the copycat killing plan to you and that he was going to go it alone but you came back and said you could help. Lucien said that his response was to tell you Vindici acted alone but you reminded him that Justin Truman had the help and support of Justine Weir. You would be like his Justine Weir.

Not rich and powerful like her, but you'd do what you could to assist him, like taking the blame for his crimes and providing him with everything and anything he needed.'

Christine's head dropped.

'Do you provide everything in this lock-up garage, Christine?'

'Pretty much.'

'Like I asked earlier: talk me through it.'

'It's much the opposite of every message Lucien sends out to the world. I've realised that in the months since we started communicating. The things in his rooms in Annabelle's house are a reflection of the way he wants the world to see him. A series of ordinary straight lines. The garage is what he really is. A kaleidoscope of contradictions. I asked him to allow me into that place where the contradictions lie so that I could hide pieces of me alongside him. And he did.'

She indicated the filing cabinet. 'There's a drawer full of me. Have a look, DCI Clay.'

Clay walked to the top drawer of the filing cabinet and started looking from the front. Plastic wallets containing bank statements, payments from Campbell's office to a company called APL Ltd, a confidentiality agreement but no paperwork from Dr Warner.

Clay took out the confidentiality agreement and saw that Jamieson had agreed to pay £3,000 per month for eighteen years for Christine's silence.

'Clearly, I didn't have the abortion. Do you know what he said to me when I told him I was pregnant? That he was happy. That he loved me. That of all the girls he'd ever met, I was the only one he loved. That his wife couldn't have children and he was overjoyed that I was pregnant. That we could run away and make a life together. He started making plans through Campbell. His wife found out through a spy in Campbell's camp. She threatened to have me murdered. When I gave birth to Lucien, Jamieson gave me money and told me to escape. I came to Liverpool.'

'Why Liverpool?' asked Clay.

Christine shook her head. 'Why not?'

Clay pulled a slender black photograph album from the filing cabinet and opened it at the first page. There was a large colour picture of Christine, aged fourteen, holding a sleeping Lucien in her arms. She smiled with her mouth but her eyes were filled with terror and confusion.

'I don't understand Annabelle's part in this,' said Clay.

'How do you mean?' asked Christine.

'Why didn't she intervene? Or did she know all along and turned a blind eye?'

'She didn't know all along. But when she found out, when I became pregnant, it was all too late. When she confronted Steven and Frances, Frances turned around and threatened her, said that she *had* known all along and that she'd approved of the relationship. They'd given her generous financial gifts at a time when she was down on her luck. It was her word against that of Steven and Frances. If she tried to drag Steven down, they would all go down together. Frances said, *He paid you for your daughter's services and you took the money with both hands.*'

Christine's eyes drilled into Clay and she felt the weight of twenty overburdened years pressing down on her from the muddy light in the woman's gaze.

'What are you thinking, DCI Clay?'

I think Annabelle should have taken her chances and gone to the police, she thought.

'I think this is one of the saddest things I've ever known,' she said.

116

6.45 am

Clay looked through the observation slot of Jimmy's cell and saw him lying on the bed, both hands pressed to the left of his abdomen beneath the pale blue blanket wrapped around him.

For a few moments, she thought she could hear muffled Christmas music filtering through the walls of the building, and the sight of him lying on the bed sent her back to her first Christmas Day in St Michael's Catholic Care Home for Children, the first Christmas after Sister Philomena died.

She closed her eyes and remembered the crack in the ceiling above her bed and how she felt unable to get out of bed, incapable of moving, such was the weight of her sorrow.

There was a smell of Christmas dinner outside her bedroom and a knocking on the door.

'Can I come in, Eve?'

She checked her face for tears and wiped them away with the sleeve of her pyjama top.

'Come in, Jimmy.'

As Jimmy crossed the room, she sat up in bed. She felt dizzy as he sat at the bottom of her bed.

'Seeing as you won't come down for your Christmas dinner, I've brought it up to you.'

She looked at the tray between them, saw two plates full of food, knives and forks and two crackers.

'You've been looking forward to this dinner for weeks, Eve.'

'I'm not – I just can't, Jimmy.'

'Well, if you're not eating yours, I'm not eating mine.'

She looked at him and a thousand words collided inside her head but all she could do was stare at him. He picked up a cracker and held it out to her.

'You can pull a cracker with me, surely to God, Eve.'

She felt a thin line of light weave through the darkness as her hand extended and she gripped the cracker.

'Before we pull this cracker, I want to promise you something and I want to ask you a question. Deal?'

'Deal.'

'I promise you if you have something to eat, you'll start to feel a little bit better. It's something to do with your blood and your sugars or some such stuff I did in a science lesson in school…'

'What do you want to ask me?'

He pointed at the empty space between them. 'If Sister Philomena was sitting right there, on your bed, now, what would she say to you?'

'Eat your dinner and have the best Christmas Day ever.'

'If you eat your dinner, Eve, and I eat my dinner, then guess what we can do when we've finished?'

'What?'

'All the other kids have opened their presents.'

'I can go downstairs and open my presents?'

'No, Eve. *We* can go downstairs and open *our* presents.'

'You haven't opened your presents yet, Jimmy?'

The narrow light inside her flooded.

'Let's pull the cracker.'

She felt no resistance on his side and the body of the cracker came towards her, the plastic toy, joke and hat falling on her legs.

'Eve, do you think for one second that I would open my presents without you being there? Do you think I would or could celebrate Christmas without you?'

Jimmy lifted a plate of Christmas dinner from the tray and slid the tray up the bed towards her. She picked up the knife and fork from the tray as he balanced his plate on his lap.

'I don't know what to say, Jimmy.'

'Well. If we were in France, I believe it'd be bon happy tit!'

A volley of laughter escaped through her nose. She looked at him and was filled with the sense that Sister Philomena was somehow close and looking down on her.

'Happy Christmas, Eve.'

'Happy Christmas, Jimmy.'

'Tuck in, kid. Food now. Presents next...'

Clay knocked on the cell door. Jimmy didn't move or look but he spoke softly: 'Is that you, Eve?'

'It's me.'

Slowly, he sat up, looked at the door and smiled.

'Can I come in?'

'I asked for you to come and see me.'

She looked at Sergeant Harris and he handed her the key.

Clay opened the door, and butterflies flapped inside her as Harris's footsteps retreated down the corridor.

'Come and sit beside me, Eve.'

They sat in silence for what could have been a minute, an hour, a month.

She felt the weight of his left hand between her shoulders and he stroked her spine.

'Go for the treatment. Go for the chemotherapy.'

'No. No thank you.'

'Maybe the doctors here can find a way.'

'I went to some superstar cancer experts in Florida and California, the big buck boyos. There's nothing left for me, kid.'

'There's nothing I can say or do to make you change your mind?'

Silence was his answer.

'I'm sorry I put you through that tonight in the Littlewoods Building.'

Even though the smell of the Littlewoods Building was still fresh on her skin, her visit there seemed to have happened years ago, as if time was collapsing and the order of events far and near was turning upside down.

'I know a lot of things about you, about how you turned out. But it's been thirty-three years since we've been together face to face. I knew you'd married, I knew you'd become a mother, I knew about all the cases you'd worked on and the people you'd brought to justice. But I didn't know if you were the extension of the girl I left behind at St Michael's or whether you'd been warped by experience and time into a different version of you.'

'I don't know the answer to that,' she replied. 'I'm not the best judge of me.'

'I didn't come back to judge you, love.'

'I didn't mean it like that...'

'You showed yourself to be everything I hoped you'd be, everything I'd dreamed of, the Eve I was forced to leave behind, only older and more experienced. Not many would have done what you did tonight and no one, *no one*, would have blamed you for abandoning *him*.'

His hand stilled on her back.

'What's your greatest achievement, Eve?'

'My son. Did you ever have children?'

'The world's too dangerous a place for children.'

'What's *your* greatest achievement?' asked Clay.

'Intervening that day and saving you? Who knows? But you are who you are, and I hope I'm a part of your success, that I made a difference.'

He looked at her and years slipped away from his face.

'Christopher Haw—'

'Don't even mention the bastard's name in my presence.'

Clay laughed.

'Like Sister Philomena,' said Jimmy. 'She took risks to battle evil so good would triumph. You do likewise, as a matter of course. I'm so glad I came back.'

'Even though you're going to spend the time you have left in a cell when you could be enjoying your final days in Mexico?'

'There's only so much sunshine one man can take, Eve. Only so many fancy cocktails... Yeah, you're right, get me out of here and on the next plane back.'

As he looked into space, the smile dissolved from his face but not from his eyes.

'Happiness isn't where you are or what you're doing. It's who you're with. And I simply couldn't be happier than I am at this moment. As soon as I was diagnosed, I knew I'd have to take my chances and come back to Liverpool. The thought of dying was one thing, and I could take that. The thought of dying without seeing you again or getting the chance to say goodbye, that was unbearable. I can do prison, I know that. But absence from you? That's been my real punishment for far too long.'

Outside, in the corridor, she heard Sergeant Harris's footsteps walking up a few protective paces and back again, near but far enough away.

Jimmy looked at the open doorway and then at Eve, and they both knew it was time to say goodbye for the time being.

'There wasn't a day I didn't think of you, Jimmy. There wasn't a day I didn't remember how you saved me. Or all the other everyday kindnesses.'

She looked at the door in her turn, wondering what she was going to tell people he'd said. She decided she'd be non-committal to the point of giving nothing away.

'I'll see you again, Eve.'

'You'd better be sure of that, Jimmy.'

'I remember you looking out of Mrs Tripp's window that day, when I was getting hauled away by those fat coppers. You looked so sad. Do you remember?'

'I remember.'

'Do you remember what I looked like?'

She was about to explain her mental block, when a key turned in her brain and her memory cleared.

For the millionth time she saw his face framed in the back window of the police car but, for the first time, his face came into focus like an image on the lens of a camera and she saw him, looking up and back, fifteen years old.

'I remember exactly what you looked like. You looked so handsome. You looked full of love and defiance.'

'Did you hear what I said to you?'

'I saw your lips moving, but I couldn't hear.'

She pressed down on his hand, gathered him in her heart.

'I said...' began Jimmy. He smiled at her.

'You said... *I've always loved you and I always will*. The same, Jimmy.'

'I've always loved you and I always will, Eve. Whatever happens, don't forget that, kid.'

Epilogue

At the reception desk in the corridor of Nazareth House, Clay watched her son Philip track the progress of one of the elderly residents being escorted by a nun who was not a great deal younger. She smiled at her husband Thomas, and wondered what thoughts were forming behind the intelligence in her four-year-old's eyes.

As the elderly resident and nun turned the corner and disappeared out of sight, Philip looked up at Eve. 'Mum, is this where you lived when you were a kid?'

'No, love. This is a home for old people. I lived in a kids' home, St Michael's.'

Philip looked at the statue of the Virgin Mary and placed his index finger on the snake trampled beneath her feet.

'Philip,' said his dad. 'If that statue falls over and lands on your feet, we'll end in A & E at Alder Hey.'

The little boy pressed his hands between his armpits and said, 'It's too quiet to be a kids' home here. I'm not too crazy about this place.'

Clay looked down the corridor and saw an old woman walking towards reception. Watching her come closer, she recognised the woman by the way she leaned slightly to the right and said, 'It's Maggie. Maggie Anderson.'

'Philip,' said his dad. 'The beach is just over the road. Shall we go and see what we can find washed up on the sand?'

'Yes,' he whispered. 'Can we go now, Dad?'

Clay leaned over her son, kissed him on the head and said, 'I'll come and find you on the beach.'

At the front door, Thomas looked back and mouthed, *Good luck, Eve*.

The door closed and Clay listened to Maggie's approaching footsteps.

'Eve?'

She looked at Maggie and a thousand little long-lost kindnesses circled in her memory. Clay opened her mouth to speak but the words were lost inside her. The woman was an older version and an extension of her former self, her face still stamped with compassion and patience.

'Shall we go and have one of our little chats. Remember our little chats?'

Clay nodded and sank into Maggie's fragile embrace.

'I've got some things for you. Come with me.'

Cold sunshine poured through the large bay window and flooded the day room.

'It's been too long, Maggie,' said Clay, with regret in her heart.

'You have been rather busy, Eve. And, well, we're here now.'

The sound of snoring filled the room and Maggie looked across at a man in his nineties, sleeping soundly in an armchair.

'Welcome to my world!' Maggie laughed. 'Put a sock in it, Buster!' she said to the sleeping man.

Maggie opened her handbag, took out an envelope and handed it to Clay.

Clay felt stiff squares through the paper and said, 'Photographs?'

Maggie reached into her bag and placed a 1970s Polaroid instant camera in the space on the couch between them. 'I know who you want to talk about, Eve. Jimmy Peace.'

'You always could read my mind.'

'It was tragic what happened to that lad. So, so sad.'

Clay bottled the compulsion to tell Maggie the whole truth and instead nodded.

'He came to St Michael's two years before you did and he was an absolute nightmare. Thieving, fighting, breaking things, setting off fire alarms, and that was before breakfast, effing this, jeffing that, would use an "f" where a "c" would do. Funny with it, mind you. Then, one day in October 1984, you walked in with a social worker, days after Sister Phil passed. I watched him watching you as you climbed the stairs on the way to Mrs Tripp's office and, I swear to God, it was like watching an inexplicable phenomenon, a miracle if you like. It was as though he was having the most massive growing-up spurt. The chaos in his face dissolved and when you were out of sight, he turned and looked at me. I was the only adult in the home he'd talk to. He asked me about you. I told him you were six years old, you'd been abandoned at birth, you'd been rescued by Sister Philomena and that she'd just died. He was silent for once. And he looked so sad. I told him, *She needs someone to look after her, show her the ropes round here, set a good example, someone who's not going to behave like a divvy.* The miracle played out.'

Maggie clapped her hands together. 'Instant change. In all the years I never saw a bigger scally turn into a model young adult so quickly, so completely. Do you know what it was, Eve? He had a hole in his heart and when you walked into his life that hole was filled. You know that *we* don't pick love, love picks *us.*'

Clay thought of Philip and Thomas, and Sister Philomena and how easy it was to love them. Then she considered Jimmy Peace, the sensitive boy who had saved her when she was a child, who grew up to be a cold-blooded serial killer.

'I agree, Maggie. Love picks us. Be that as easy or incredibly conflicting as it can be.'

'Well, love picked Jimmy when you arrived at St Michael's. And it was love at first sight, the love of one abandoned child for another. He was your soul mate, your big brother. He no longer had a reason to be angry but he now had a reason to be.'

As the first of her tears fell, Clay laughed at the sudden gale-force resonance of the old man snoring in the corner.

'You had a good two years together and then... what happened happened and Jimmy Peace was moved away and died a few years later trying to save other people. I cried so much over that lad, for weeks and months.'

'He saved me that day in 1986.'

'He did indeed. But *you* saved *him* in 1984. Don't forget that, Eve.'

The door opened and a smiling nun said, 'Maggie, it's time for mass. Are you coming?'

Clay read conflict in Maggie's face. 'I'll come back in an hour, after I've found my husband and son.'

'Would you bring them back with you so I can meet them?'

'Of course I will.' Clay stood and helped Maggie to her feet.

'The camera's yours, as are the pictures, Eve. There's one last picture in the camera.'

'I'll see you in an hour, Maggie.'

As Clay walked on to the beach, she took the two photographs from the envelope and, pausing on the sand, looked at them.

Christmas 1984. She, aged six, and Jimmy, just turned fourteen, in front of the Christmas tree in St Michael's.

Christmas 1985. An almost identical image, but both of them a little older and dressed differently.

Both images had one strong link in common. The love shared by two lost children.

The wind whistled around her head as she put the pictures away. She looked to the sea and saw two figures at the water's edge, a man and a boy throwing stones into the water.

She walked towards her husband and son and within a few steps was running towards them, freshly understanding how blessed she was.

Thomas picked Philip up and, spinning him around in a circle, made the little boy shriek with laughter. His laughter carried on the wind, filling Eve's ears like precious balm.

'Hey! You two!' she called.

The spinning slowed down and Thomas held Philip to his body. They turned to Eve.

'You've been crying, Mummy?'

'It's the cold and the wind, son, that's all. Say cheese!'

She held Maggie's camera to her face, framed the image of her husband and son against black water and a grey sky and her heart danced inside her. She took the picture of love with the camera but also with her mind's eye, an image she would hold on to through whatever storms she would face in the future.

Eve handed the camera to Thomas and wrapped her arms around both of them.

'What have I got to cry about, Philip? Thomas? What have I got to cry about?'

Acknowledgements

I'd like to thank Steve Le Comber, Alfie Harris, Martin McKenna, Peter, Rosie and Jessica Buckman, Laura Palmer, Maddy O'Shea, Lauren Atherton and all at Head of Zeus, Nicholas Jackson and Abby Brennan, Frank and Ben Rooney, Paul Goetzee, John Gunning, Linda and Eleanor Roberts, Conrad Williams.